For Want of a Fiend

By the Author

The Pyramid Waltz

For Want of a Fiend

For Want of a Fiend

by

Barbara Ann Wright

2013

FOR WANT OF A FIEND

ISBN 10: 1-60282-873-3
ISBN 13: 978-1-60282-873-5

This Trade Paperback Original Is Published By
Bold Strokes Books, Inc.
P.O. Box 249
Valley Falls, NY 12185

First Edition: May 2013

Credits
Editor: Cindy Cresap
Production Design: Susan Ramundo
Cover Design By Sheri (graphicartist2020@hotmail.com)

Acknowledgments

Just as before, this book would never have been possible without the love and support of so many people. First, my husband Ross and my mom Linda Dunn. You both keep me going. And thanks again to my Houston writing group, Writer's Ink: Nia George, Erin Kennemer, Janet Mallard, Trakena Prevost, and Sarah Warburton. You always rise to the occasion. New thanks to my Austin writing group with Matt Borgard, Jim Reader, and Jeb Seibel. Not only are your critiquing skills top-notch, you also saved me from quite a bit of hate mail. Special thanks to my staunch defender Pattie Lawler.

Thanks to Radclyffe and Bold Strokes for continuing on this journey with me, and thanks to Cindy Cresap and Stacia Seaman for their wonderful editing work. And thank you to CenTex writers, Abusing the Universe, Ladies-in-Writing, and the Austin Speed-Writers for welcoming me into your wonderful groups. I'm having the time of my life.

A last thank you to my wonderful pets. You've never minded that I talk to myself.

Dedication

For Pattie. Feelings at you.

Chapter One: Katya

Katya crouched in the bushes, the backs of the unsuspecting highwaymen not fifty feet in front of her. Six of them lay in wait for her decoy, the carriage that rattled toward them down the dirt road. As the jingle of the harness and the clatter of the wheels drifted forward on the wind, the highwaymen stiffened. Katya braced herself to charge. Beside her, Brother Brutal did the same, gripping his overlarge mace.

The carriage rounded the corner, a hooded Pennynail driving it; the highwaymen wouldn't see his mask under the hood. The highwaymen leapt from cover and waved their arms to drive the horses off the road. Katya waited a heartbeat, long enough for a crystal pyramid the size of a child's fist to come sailing from the other direction. It cracked between the highwaymen and the carriage in a burst of light. When Pennynail threw off the hood, revealing the rosy cheeks and long nose of his laughing Jack mask, Katya and Brutal leapt from cover. A red-fletched arrow struck the shoulder of one highwayman and spun him around but didn't drop him.

Brutal slammed his mace into the back of one man, who pitched forward onto the road and lay unmoving. Katya's opponent turned. She slashed at him, and he backpedaled into one of his fellows. Both of them toppled, so Katya turned her attention to another who aimed his sword at her ribs. He wore a fur mantle around his neck, and his creased face seemed nervous but determined. Katya blocked the thrust, and threw Fur Mantle's sword wide. When he was open, she kicked and made him stagger into the other two who were climbing to their feet.

A body slammed into Katya from the side. She went with the force, rolled along the road, and came up to face the man with the arrow in his shoulder. The other three were getting up, all glaring at her with hatred in their eyes.

A knife thudded into the back of Arrow Man's head, and he fell. An arrow skimmed by one of the standing three and clipped one on the shoulder. When he shied to the left, Katya lunged and sank her sword into his chest. Fur Mantle and his friend thrust at her with short swords; one grated along her chain shirt and drew a line of pain across her ribs.

Katya drew back, knocked the sword out of the way, and tried to keep both men at bay. Brutal slammed his mace into Fur Mantle's head with a nauseating crunch.

The other pitched forward, an arrow in his back, the last of the highwaymen to fall. Brutal rested his huge mace on the ground and straightened his red robe. Katya felt along her ribs. Torn cloth poked through the nicked rings of her chainmail, and her bruised flesh ached.

Averie dropped from a tree beside the carriage, her bow slung around her middle. She tossed her long brown braid over her shoulder where it blended with the browns and greens of her leather hunting outfit. "I'm sorry," she said to Katya. "I'm not used to shooting from trees."

Katya nodded but focused on trying to see if any of the links of her chain shirt had actually broken, if she'd been cut at all. "You did fine, Averie." But she missed her young cousin Maia. Katya had to swallow as she thought of Maia in the grip of her murderous Fiendish uncle Roland.

"What was that?" Brutal whispered in her ear.

Katya didn't look at him. Instead, she watched past his shoulder as Starbride climbed out of the tree beside Averie. As the only Allusian member of their party, Starbride's red/brown skin and black hair stood out, though she dressed in the same hardwearing leather as the rest of them. Hers was borrowed, though. Katya preferred her in silk.

She glanced at Katya's torn shirt with concern plain in her dark eyes. Katya smiled and fought not to wince. She glanced at Brutal. "I don't know what you're talking about."

"Talking about you taking on three at once instead of waiting for help." He prodded the bent chain links, making Katya hiss. "I'm talking about this."

Katya stared hard into the baby face that contrasted so much with his tall, muscled frame. "Are you going to help me patch myself up or not?"

He frowned, and his eyes slid to the side as Starbride joined them, a look that promised there would be words between them later. He lifted her chain shirt. "You'll have a nice bruise as a reminder."

Averie let out a slow breath, clearly relieved. She wasn't the crack shot Maia had been, and she knew it. *Still was*, Katya reminded herself, *the shot that Maia still was.*

"Are you all right?" Starbride asked.

"It's just a bruise. You did very well."

Starbride beamed. "The flash bomb is the only destruction pyramid I'm really good with. Sorry I didn't bring anything bigger."

"It's all right." Another loss. Crowe couldn't come with them into the field anymore, not with the wound given him by Roland; it still pained him. The king's pyradisté had to be content with waiting at home, even though he could have brought many pyramids to the fight.

"Do you need me to see into any of their minds?" Starbride asked. "I think one or two are still alive."

Katya shook her head. "They're just regular robbers, not conspirators."

Starbride nodded, but Katya could see the question in her eyes: Why was the Order of Vestra out in the woods fighting robbers? Katya didn't know how to answer, just like she didn't really know the answer to Brutal's question. She supposed that if she couldn't find Roland and Maia, thwarting robbers was the best she could hope for.

They loaded the bodies and two wounded prisoners into the empty carriage, collected their horses, and began the ride back to Marienne, mostly in silence, all lost in their own thoughts. Pennynail split from them before they came within sight of the stone walls, taking the carriage and two prisoners with him. The rest of them rode past fields and country homes and then, along the main thoroughfare into the city itself.

As it always did, the sight of the palace proper, a series of long rectangles with the occasional turret or tower rising out of the jumble, made her both anxious and relieved. Relieved to be home again with all her party safe, anxious at having to assume her role as numbskull princess again, a woman reported to love weapon-craft and hunting and not have many brains in her head. It was a good cover for the leader of the Order of Vestra, a good place from which to protect her family from traitors to the crown.

Well, that was until a member of her own family turned out to be the biggest traitor of them all. Roland knew the palace as well as she did, another reason for the place to make her anxious.

As she passed the statues of the ten spirits that lined the wide passage into the courtyard, Katya let her glance linger on Ellias and Elody, twins of love and beauty. She gave them a small salute. They'd brought Starbride into her life and let her leave behind one piece of her court persona: the rake. There was that sense of relief again, a sense of wholeness that only love could bring.

Brutal saluted Best and Berth, twins of strength and courage, the patron spirits of his brotherhood. Katya made sure to honor Matter and Marla as well, needing their sharp intellects and wisdom to stay one step ahead of her uncle.

Averie saluted Jack and Jan, twins of skill and deftness, much as Pennynail would have, but he wouldn't have sported her guilty expression. Katya held in a sigh. Averie seemed to have adopted Maia's insecurity along with their position. Everyone saluted Fah and Fay, spirits of luck, the twin statues perched precariously atop a stone egg. They'd need all the luck they could get.

When they left their horses in the royal stable, Brutal pulled Katya aside. "Well?" he asked.

"I'd really like to get back to my quarters and spend some time with Starbride."

He kept pace with her into the hallways, past the stable area where bare floors gave way to sumptuous carpets, statues, and paintings. Starbride's brow was drawn in curiosity, but she kept her distance and pulled Averie back as well.

"I know why you took three of them on," Brutal said.

"Could it be Maia?"

"I miss her, too, Katya, but what you did wasn't about her, and you know it."

"What do I know?"

"It's about you not having a Fiend."

Katya nearly faltered. "I don't want to talk about—"

"We're going to talk about it if you keep pulling stupid stunts like launching yourself at three opponents at once."

"You can't—"

"Let me finish, or you'll be hearing this from Crowe."

Katya clenched her teeth on her response. Crowe was too weak to be yelling at anyone.

"You lost your Fiend, and now you're trying to prove you're as strong as when you had it."

"Why is that bad?"

"If you'll just remember, you used your Fiend exactly twice, and that was when there was no other choice."

"And what do I do if there's no choice now?" She clipped the words when she wanted to scream them.

"You don't need to prove yourself, Fiend or no Fiend. If Roland comes again, we'll think of something."

Katya nodded, and Brutal fell silent, but her insides were in turmoil. She could've beaten three men, even without the others, but as the pain in her side proved, she wouldn't have come away unscathed. But it had been her Fiend as much as *her* that had thwarted Roland, and even then, she'd only succeeded in driving him off. If he came at them again, if he used Maia against them, how could she hope to defeat him without the strength of the Fiend?

Brutal left her before she reached the royal apartments, past the guards and the guardian pyramids that glittered in the walls. Katya felt a light touch on her shoulder and turned to Starbride's caring face. Even after a month of having the title of princess consort, she hadn't learned to keep her expressions carefully neutral. That or she didn't care what anyone else thought, another reason to love her.

"Am I coming with you or are you coming with me?" Starbride asked.

Katya grinned, happy that one or the other was a given. "Averie will want to check my bruise or she'll fret herself to death."

"I'll get changed, say hello to Dawnmother, and meet you in your room."

Katya leaned in for a kiss. "Perfect."

Alone, it wasn't as perfect as she imagined. Katya sat in her private sitting room and stared at the domed ceiling painted in the colors of rose tinted dawn. Not it, nor the comfortable settees, divans, and carpets or the fully stocked drinks cabinet could distract her for long. She couldn't keep her mind off the emptiness inside her, the place the Fiend had resided.

"I'm sorry you were wounded," Averie said. She had changed into the high-necked blue dress that was her livery. Her fingers twitched at the crest embroidered at her hip, Katya's hawk and rose, as if she were nervous she might have to pluck the emblem out.

"You've been out with us so many times, Averie, why are you so nervous?"

"I'm not as good as Maia. I can't shoot from just anywhere, and people are a lot harder to shoot than deer. When I…" She swallowed and closed her eyes for a moment. "When I went with you in the past and didn't split off to hunt, I could always count on Maia to outshoot me. I was happy watching the horses; I knew I wouldn't have to shoot anyone and that nothing bad would come of it if I missed my target."

"No one's asking you to replace Maia, but we do need an archer, and you're stupendous, Averie. I made a stupid mistake."

"Now you're just trying to make me feel better."

"Ask Brutal if you don't believe me. You're not only a first-rate archer, you're a world-class lady-in-waiting. Starbride will be here soon."

"I'll fetch you something. With refreshment, I know exactly where I am."

There was one person squared away; only scores to go. Like Maia. Was she with her father, and if so, what was he doing to her? How was he poisoning her mind? Had he found some way to bring on her Aspect, let her Fiend out, without her having to Waltz?

The Waltz, yet another thing Katya couldn't do without a Fiend.

Someone knocked softly on the wall behind Katya's mirror, and she toggled the latch that opened the secret passageway. Starbride emerged, clad in simple trousers and shirt, foregoing fancy embroidery when out of the public eye. As they embraced, Katya did notice that the simple clothing was well fitting, deftly showing off Starbride's curves.

Katya let her hands wander until Starbride stopped her. "We are waiting for Averie to return, are we not?"

"I was just admiring this fabric."

"I'll have one of my outfits sent over. Then you can admire it always."

"It wouldn't be as fun without you in it." Katya stroked the soft hair that Starbride wore loose around her shoulders now that the dangerous part of their day was done.

"Are you going to keep your conversation with Brutal a secret? You know how much I like figuring out secrets."

"He did all but call me a fool for taking on three opponents, and he was right."

"Ah, the Aspect again?" Unlike Averie, she didn't seem to feel guilty, even though she'd drained Katya of Yanchasa's extra essence. The power that had allowed Katya to defeat Roland would have killed her had she held on to it.

"It wasn't your fault," Katya said anyway.

"Yanchasa took back what was rightfully his. Love is never a reason to feel guilty."

Averie came in with lunch. Starbride and Katya sat to eat and talked of less important things. When they'd finished, they drank wine together on a settee, fingers entwined.

"Coming with me to report to my parents?" Katya asked. "Father sent a note. He wants to discuss what's to be done with Brom."

"Not a pleasant topic. And I'm definitely not coming if *they'll* be there."

"Reinholt will be too busy with his children to waste his bitter anger on you."

"Oh yes, I thought so, too, but then his children arrived, and he still has time for petty little comments, asking after Hugo and such."

"Hugo chose you over Roland. Reinholt's own wife didn't do that."

"Hugo did not *choose* me. He…he may be…infatuated, but it's a crush, that's all. He goggles at every woman he meets."

Katya didn't press the issue. The young ex-lord might have ogled the other women of court, but he followed Starbride like a puppy and talked of almost nothing but her. Down in the dungeons, Brom spoke only of her children, rarely of her husband Reinholt. "I'll have another word with Reinholt."

"If it makes you feel better."

"And I'll have another word with Lord Vincent."

"No, no, not in my hearing please. A bigot is a bigot and will probably never change."

"He's just old-fashioned."

"When we met, he ordered me to take his cloak! Even though I was wearing the damned consort bracelet and was dressed as well as the rest of you, he saw that I was Allusian and assumed I was subservient."

"He lived in Oldsport, and the Farradain families there—"

"Employ Allusian servants, I know. But we're far away from *Old*sport. I'm not the only Allusian courtier here. I wonder if he asks the others to take his cloaks, too."

Katya had to laugh at the idea. "Since you were properly introduced, the champion of Farraday has been polite and civil."

"I can *feel* him disapproving of me. Is he teaching your niece and nephew to be bigots? I bet Reinholt is helping there."

Katya sighed for the hundredth time. "My parents wouldn't allow that. Besides, Bastian and Vierdrin love you."

"They're very sweet."

"Lord Vincent protects them. He doesn't teach them."

"Thank Horsestrong for that."

Lord Vincent had shown up on their doorstep only a week or so after Roland had attacked. Despite the promises Roland had given to Brom, someone *had* come after the children, proving that Roland had even more allies than the two he'd sneaked into the palace before, Darren Sleeting and his late brother, Cassius.

"I'll scout ahead," Katya said, "and if either of them is in my parents' rooms, you can wait in the hallway until I chase them off."

Starbride agreed, and Katya led her through the halls to her parents' sitting room. Luckily, Reinholt and Lord Vincent had left the king and queen of Farraday to babysit their grandchildren.

Bastian and Vierdrin ran for Starbride and Katya at top speed, and Katya swung her niece into the air while Starbride knelt and hugged little Bastian. Like all young children, they quickly lost interest in cuddles and retreated to the toys on the carpet.

Ma had a strained smile that looked very tired around the eyes.

Katya nodded at the children. "Wishing for a little of that distance you were lamenting before, Ma?"

"I'm not as young as I used to be."

"You're twice as beautiful, Cat," Da said from where he played with the children on the rug. "Now, come sit with me, daughter-in-law." He shifted so Starbride could sit on the chair next to him.

Ma clucked slightly. She'd never liked giving out titles until they were a real and honest fact. Katya said nothing, not minding the title one bit. If Starbride kept being so perfect, Katya didn't know how she could wait out the year of consortship before marrying her.

Chapter Two: Starbride

After Lord Vincent had returned and greeted her with frosty politeness, Starbride retreated and walked alone to her spacious apartment in the royal wing. A chance to relax in her own sitting room might make her forget how much Lord Vincent angered her. It wasn't Katya's fault that the champion of Farraday was an ass, but part of Starbride wanted Katya to throw him out of the palace for being rude to her.

She told herself not to be silly. How long ago was it that Starbride forbade Katya from using her title to solve problems? Not long enough, it seemed.

When she returned to her apartment, Dawnmother was folding the laundry and putting it away. She threw her long braid over one shoulder and planted her fists on her hips. "Don't tell me you spoke with one of them again."

"You can tell just by my face?"

"It's the only thing that makes you downcast anymore. Which was it? Or did you have to endure the scathing of both?"

"Lord Vincent."

"Better a bigot than the crown prince's irrational hatred, I suppose. Easier to understand, anyway."

"Not any easier to deal with."

"The princess should send them away, or at least keep them from speaking to you."

Starbride shook her head. "She has to keep the peace. And she can't command her brother to do anything. He outranks her. Lord Vincent is polite if cold. I was naive to think all of Farraday's inner circle would be welcoming."

"Makes me long for Lady Hilda's company."

"Speaking of scheming nobles, anything interesting in the notes and letter pile today?"

"I haven't been through the basket yet. Let me see." Dawnmother dumped a stack of papers onto the sitting room table and shuffled through them. "Courtier, courtier, a letter from Countess Nadia, a—Oh, Horsestrong preserve us."

"What is it?" Starbride froze as she recognized her mother's handwriting. "Oh no."

"I told you to write her, and now here she is, writing you."

"Mother never writes."

"Not unless she has something very important to say."

Starbride took the note with trembling fingers and scanned it quickly, past the recriminations about not staying in touch, past the guilt about a mother's worries for her daughter's safety and well-being and straight to:

"So if you will not write, I must assume you are acting contrary to my wishes and spending all your time in the libraries of Farraday instead of out meeting people as you should. If I am to get any news, I see that I must come to you to get it. Expect me a month or so after this letter, as fast as the carriage can get me there. Your loving mother, Brightstriving."

"She's coming here," Starbride said.

"Oh, good. I thought she was going to command you to return to Newhope."

Starbride swallowed. "My *mother* is coming *here*."

"She'll be thrilled."

"Yes." But what would happen when the demands started pouring in for royal favors? Would Katya forgive her mother as once promised?

With thoughts of her mother lying heavy on her mind, Starbride returned to Katya's private sitting room just in time for Katya's return. A few strands of Katya's blond hair had fallen out of its loose bun. Starbride smoothed it out, lingering at the new gray strands at her temples, a relic from their last adventure with Roland. She wished she could do something to cleanse the pain from Katya's cobalt blue eyes, but that wouldn't be smoothed away so easily, nor could the slight stoop in her trim, athletic body. Her coat and trousers seemed loose on her, and Starbride wondered how much weight she'd lost in the month since Roland had shown himself. Katya had always seemed like a sparkling creature out of a dream, as strong and capable as she was beautiful, but lately Starbride began to add weary to her description.

Starbride couldn't leap into news of her mother, not wanting to add to Katya's worries. She steered Katya to a divan and sought another topic of conversation. In her haste, she jumped to something almost as painful as her mother's visit.

"What's to be done with Brom?" It almost hurt to ask. Starbride had liked Brom, had seen in her a fellow outsider among the tremendously powerful Umbriels. That wasn't exactly the truth. Brom was the daughter of a duke, nobility as well as a traitor.

"Reinholt won't make a decision."

"You can't make him responsible for executing his own wife if it comes to that."

"I think he's the only one who *can* be responsible."

Starbride kept herself from gaping. "It's too much guilt. Too many chances that his children will resent him. I'm not trying to tell you your family business, but if someone else makes the decision, it will give him someone to be angry at besides himself, a little family resentment for the sake of his own soul."

Katya was still for a moment before she pulled Starbride into an embrace. "You see so clearly, Star, even toward someone who's been less than kind to you."

"I feel sorry for him. To be so betrayed by someone you love, and yet…I feel sorry for Brom, too. Even though I'd be a Fiend for you, Katya, I can understand why she wouldn't want to."

Tears hovered in Katya's eyes. "You'd carry a Fiend for me?"

Starbride kissed her long and deep. Here was a hurt to soothe away at last. "I've thought about it, thought about *her* a lot, and yes, I'd do it. And if there was some way I could give it to you if you wanted…" But since she'd drained Katya of Yanchasa's Aspect, she had no way of knowing whether Katya could ever carry a Fiend again.

Katya laughed breathlessly. "Well, the ritual to pass the Aspect to another person requires a sexual act. That or you have to be born with it. So you'd have to lie with a member of my family while a pyradisté performs the magic, and then make love to me under the same circumstances."

Starbride ran through the roster of Katya's family in her head and sputtered a laugh. "That's just…no."

"Hugo has a Fiend, dormant because he hasn't Waltzed, but it's there. Crowe confirmed it."

Starbride gave Katya a dark look.

Katya grinned. "And he loves you."

"A crush."

When Katya laughed, Starbride stuck her tongue out, making them both laugh harder.

"Brom's father, Duke Robert, is coming to court," Katya said. "If Reinholt agrees, my father will grant them a divorce and give Brom back to her family."

"What will her father do to her?"

"Duke Robert only knows the public story, that Brom was part of a plot to take over the kingdom. Who knows if he believes it, or if he thinks Reinholt wants to throw his daughter over for someone else? As long as his grandchildren are still in line for the throne, the duke can't really protest. My father won't grant Brom permission to marry again. He'll demand she confine herself to the duke's estate in Baelyn."

Starbride shook her head slowly and weighed the possibilities. "Roland could find her there. Even though she's never Waltzed, he could find a way to release her Fiend, or capture her and use her as some kind of brood mare."

"And we can't expect the duke to protect her from a pyradisté as powerful as Roland, and yet we can't even tell him he should try."

"Put like that, it seems kinder to kill her."

"I doubt the duke will see it that way. Frankly, I'd like her to live with what she's done."

Starbride had to wonder how many mothers would make the same choice Brom had. She'd thought she was saving her children, but she was dooming everyone else. "I'm so sorry for all of you."

Katya kissed the top of her head. "Are you staying for a while?"

"I wish I could, but it's me that's dashing off this time. I have to train with Crowe."

Katya slumped in her chair. "Everyone leaves me in the end."

"It's your acting. It stinks." She jumped and yelped as Katya smacked her with a cushion. "Scoundrel!"

"You earned it. Are you taking the secret passage to Crowe's room?"

"Oh yes. Anything to avoid your brother or Lord Vincent."

"Reinholt takes the passages."

"Lord Vincent doesn't. It's a small thing, but I'll take it."

After a farewell kiss, Starbride went on her way to Crowe's study. In the dark secret passageways, she held her lantern high and recited the path in her mind while keeping an eye on the symbols that marked each intersecting hallway. It was only a few short turns, but she remembered how easily she'd gotten lost in the palace before, and that was in the hallways. At the first junction, she stopped to read the markings on all four corners and opened her lamp to turn up the wick. Before she could close it, a gust of air snuffed her light as if it had never been.

Starbride froze. Someone had just entered or left the secret passageways nearby. She fumbled in her small belt pouch for matches. A soft sound, the scuff of foot on stone, made her pause again. It wasn't the steady boot tread of Katya or her father. It could have been anyone in the royal family or the Order of Vestra. It could have been Reinholt.

Starbride's stomach shrank. Angry as he was, Reinholt wouldn't actually hurt her, would he? After all, she hadn't actually *done* anything to him.

But he was angry, and angry people were unpredictable. The dark thought led to darker thoughts as she realized *Roland* knew the secret passageways, too, and had undoubtedly described them to his henchman Darren, who was no stranger to violence of many kinds.

They'd sneaked into the palace before.

Starbride gripped the matches but didn't light one. She pressed her back against the cold stone and waited as light crept down a hallway nearby. Her fear lessened with the light, even though Fiendish eyes would still need it to see. She suddenly thought of how silly she'd look if the queen turned the corner to find her cowering in the dark. She should have brought a light pyramid with her. Maybe then she could've given a lame excuse about wanting or needing to practice in perfect darkness.

Pennynail crossed a junction several halls away from hers, his masked face unmistakable. Starbride's stomach unknotted at once. Here was one secret she had yet to deduce, who Pennynail was and where he spent his time. Her feet began to move almost before her mind caught up. She'd have to stay close behind him or risk losing her way in the dark.

She tried to tell herself to turn back. She'd gotten into trouble too many times by following Katya or the Order, but it was too late; after two or three turns, she no longer had any idea where she was. Starbride hurried to catch up. Pennynail's soft leather boots made almost no noise in the darkness, but Starbride wore slippers, even quieter.

They reached a narrow spiral staircase, somewhere she'd never been. Her heart pounded, and her palms started to sweat. Thoughts on how she would get back to familiar territory drowned in the idea of an adventure, a discovery of something even Katya didn't know.

Before she could reach the top of the stairway, she felt the *whoosh* of another door opening, and then the light was gone. She swallowed and continued to climb while feeling in the darkness for a way out. She prayed to Horsestrong that there was only one door, and that it led into the palace rather than into another dark passageway. If she lost Pennynail, well, no one knew where she was. They wouldn't find her in the endless passages. Even if she lit her lamp, she wouldn't be able to find her way; she'd wander, lost and lonely until she eventually starved in some forgotten hallway with the walls of the palace crushing her on all sides.

Thought abandoned her. She stumbled ahead, tripped, and barked her shin on a step. She smacked into a wall that gave under her pressure, and she fell with a cry as the door opened and dumped her into a circular room.

A red-haired man stared down at her. "What the hell are you doing here?" he asked in a voice that wasn't much more than a harsh rasp. His brows came down slowly, surprise turning to anger.

Starbride scrambled up and glared back at this man who spoke as if he knew her. She opened her mouth to tell him to mind his own business when she took her first good look at him, at his leather outfit and the slender knives in their sheaths. "Pennynail?" she asked, anger fading into astonishment. "You're—"

He put his fists on his hips. "Were you following me?"

There was no way to dress it up. "Yes." She looked him hard in the face, trying to see why he might want to hide it. He had a rough scar around his neck, but his face wasn't marred. Narrow and lean, he seemed handsome enough. His red hair was short; the long ponytail he sported must have been attached to the mask. He had sideburns that almost reached his jawline, and penetrating green eyes that hadn't ceased their glare. He was older than Starbride, than Katya and Brutal, maybe Reinholt's age, mid-twenties. She wondered then if it was really Reinholt that had introduced him into the Order, and hot on the heels of that thought was the realization that she was being rude.

"I'm sorry. I…can't resist a mystery."

He sat down heavily on a tattered chair. All the furniture in the room had seen better days. Perfectly round, the space was dominated by the column of stone that housed the stairway. The rest was full of odds and ends, bits of junk perched on rickety tables. One shuttered window offered the only other way out. Starbride realized they must be inside one of the towers. She hadn't known that the palace towers held rooms at all.

"I suppose you'd have found out soon enough," he said. "Crowe's grooming you to fill his shoes, and since I help Crowe with difficult jobs…" He gestured at her.

"Difficult jobs?"

"Like disposal."

"Disposal of…" She realized he meant killing people, and her stomach turned. Crowe led prisoners to the dungeons, which she supposed meant that he "dealt" with them, with Pennynail's help. "Ugh."

"I thought you might feel that way."

Starbride fought hard not to squirm. It was still difficult to believe this man knew her. Pennynail knew her. She was comfortable with him, but this person? Her mind flashed on the time Pennynail had helped her undress when he'd posed as her in order to capture Darren. He'd unlaced her dress, had seen the back of her underwear…

"So," she said, "who are you?"

He snorted. "Want all the answers right away, don't you? Feeling that noble's entitlement?"

"Just wanted to put a name with the face."

"Pennynail's just fine."

"No, I know Pennynail, at least a little. You?" She shrugged. "I can't work with you if I don't know you at all."

"All right, but don't be too afraid." He put a hand on his chest. "I'm Freddie Ballantine."

"Which part am I supposed to be afraid of?"

He frowned. "Frederick Ballantine. Freddie Ballantine." When she shook her head, his mouth dropped open. "I'm *the* Freddie Ballantine!"

"Ever been to Allusia?" she asked sweetly.

"You haven't heard of me since you've been here?"

"I'm sorry, no."

"Forget it."

Starbride shuffled her feet, embarrassed for him. "What are you famous for?"

He waved and sank lower in his chair. "Never mind. The moment's sort of deflated, don't you think?"

The sarcasm and gestures reminded her so much of his masked persona that she smiled. "People would recognize your face and your voice?" She stared hard at the pinkish scar around his neck, and realization hit her like a hammer. "Someone…hanged you?"

He looked up under his lowered brow and said nothing.

"Lawfully?"

When he nodded, she nodded, and some of the fear he'd warned her about seeped into her mind. If he'd been lawfully hanged, no matter that it hadn't worked, then he was a criminal. And since he'd warned her not to be afraid, she guessed it wasn't because he was a forger or a con man or a shady horse trader. "Were you…Did you…murder someone?"

He sighed deeply. "I have killed more people as Pennynail in service to the crown than I ever did as Freddie Ballantine. I was a thief, and I may have killed some people who deserved it, but when they hanged me, it was for someone I never laid a finger on."

"I don't have the right to ask. I'm sorry. And I'm sorry I followed you. You'd be justified in dangling me out the window until I learned to not follow anyone else."

"I think we can forgo that. Katya would never forgive me."

"Thank Horsestrong for small favors," Starbride said with a slight smile, and she tried her hardest not to shift away from him.

Chapter Three: Katya

After Starbride left, Katya couldn't get Reinholt out of her thoughts. He hadn't shown up to take his children while Katya had visited her parents. He'd left them to their nannies and to Lord Vincent. Katya didn't want to confront him though, not about his children, his behavior, or about the abysmal way he treated Starbride.

Not yet anyway.

She could sit and brood, wander the hallways listening for gossip, or find something useful to do.

Crowe still didn't trust their visitor, Roland's son Hugo. Crowe needed excuses to set his mind at ease, so Katya would give him one more reason to relax. At the same time, maybe she could dump the gossip-sorting duty that always dogged her steps.

Hugo didn't have free run of the palace. They'd given him a room in the royal wing, and he'd behaved so far. Katya thought it silly, but Crowe had tuned the pyramids to incinerate Hugo on the spot if he did anything nasty. Katya had told Hugo about them, just in case, citing the fact that Crowe liked to overreact. The one time Katya had seen Hugo in the halls, she'd noted that he walked in the middle of the carpeted hallway, and then very slowly.

Neither Starbride nor Crowe had found the telltale blocks or holes in Hugo's mind that indicated pyramid influence. When Hugo had switched sides, he'd even hurt Darren, Roland's chief henchman. Katya didn't think Darren had the sort of ego that would let him be wounded by someone as young as Hugo just for the sake of Roland's machinations.

Still, Crowe wouldn't be satisfied. Katya would keep an eye on him, too, even if Starbride and Brutal thought he could be trusted. After all, she'd never thought Maia would run away with Roland. Katya would rather have Maia by her side, but that didn't make Hugo any less her cousin. He even carried a Fiend, though Crowe guaranteed that it couldn't present until he'd Waltzed.

Her bastard cousin carried a Fiend. It made him more Umbriel than her.

Katya tried to banish the maudlin thought and focus. She had a Waltz to organize; it was time for Hugo to recognize the true worth of the Aspect. He'd volunteered to help them pacify Yanchasa during the ritual, and they had to act soon. The last Waltz had gone badly, with Katya's essence being returned to Yanchasa where he rested in his prison underneath the castle. Some of his essence had to be drained, or he might wake.

Katya fought the headache building in her temples. There was so much to do, and all the while she had to fight to keep the Fiends and the Waltz deeply buried secrets. The populace knew about Yanchasa, but they didn't know what it took to keep the great Fiend asleep.

Hugo had found out the hard way, but still he was willing to help. Even if that offer of help was a cover, if he planned to run rampant once his Fiend had been unlocked and his Aspect could present, he was in for a surprise. Katya couldn't remember the few times her Fiend had been in control of her body. Without the help of a pyradisté as powerful as Roland, Hugo would never be able to control his.

"Come in?" Hugo called when Katya knocked at his door. She smiled at the question in his tone. When she stepped inside, he stood from the settee where he'd been reading. His tousled brown hair hung almost in his light blue eyes. It gave him a boyish cast, almost as much as his smooth cheeks did. When Katya had met him, he'd had his first facial hair spotting lip and chin, but it seemed he'd started shaving since then. Who'd taught him how? Brutal? Or did men just come to that naturally? She supposed thirteen might be a good age for them to start.

Katya shook the thought away and gestured to Hugo's book, the heavy history of the Umbriel family. "Catching up?"

"There's so much my father never told me. What can I do for you, Highness?"

"I wanted to see how you're doing. You don't need to stay in here all the time, you know."

He blanched a little, and she knew he was thinking of the pyramids in the halls.

"The more you make yourself useful," Katya added, "the quicker Crowe will take those down."

"I don't blame him for not trusting me, not after…what my father did, what he'll do again if he gets the chance."

"Your father was a noble man when he was human, Hugo. He sacrificed himself for the Order, for his duty. If you need to blame someone, blame the Fiend."

"Would I…I mean, will I…will my Fiend…" He looked at her, eyes pleading.

"The Fiend you carry would gladly consume everyone you know. It would kill without thought, without reason, until someone put it down."

"You didn't."

She heard the awe in his voice, and it nearly made her chuckle. He was so young. How could that possibly be a false face? He'd needed his father's help just to suppress his thoughts, proof that he wasn't a capable actor. "Starbride suppressed my Fiend with a pyramid. Even then, I had to fight the urge to kill everyone. Your father is the only person I've ever met who could retain control of his thoughts with the Aspect on him, but the Fiend has warped his mind into something terrible, just not mindless. Your father's brilliant mind with the Fiend's sensibilities."

"Do you think we can get him back? I mean, I don't really remember him before the…Well, it was just me and Mother for a long time. And then he took her away. He said I'd see her again once everything was over." Hugo bit his lip and looked away.

Katya could only nod. Roland had used Hugo's mother Layra in some sort of experiment, animating her body after she'd died and using it as a mindless puppet. Maybe he'd even murdered her to do so, who knew? She didn't have the stomach to ask Hugo if he knew.

"He won't give us the chance to get him back, Hugo," Katya said. "When next we see him, we have to try like hell to kill him. It took me becoming a greater Fiend to beat him the first time. We won't have that luxury again."

Hugo nodded slowly, and Katya couldn't imagine what it felt like to contemplate becoming an orphan by your own hand. She gave his knee a friendly pat, much like Crowe had always given her. He looked at her with gratitude almost like worship. It reminded her so much of Maia at his age that her heart ached.

"You could do a tremendous favor for me, Hugo, if you're willing?"

"Certainly, Highness."

"I always loathed wandering the halls for gossip…"

Hugo sat so straight she thought his posture might carry him off the seat. "I can do that for you, Highness, my pleasure."

Katya gave him a gracious nod. Crowe would have to take the Hugo-specific pyramids down now.

"Is Miss Starbride coming to meet us?" Hugo said. "I mean, the princess consort." He stared at the door with a blush in his cheeks. When he finally glanced at her, the redness spread all the way to his ears. "I mean, it's fine if she doesn't."

Katya wondered if she knew him well enough to tease him. Well, maybe a little. "And what if she does?"

"No…nothing. I just wondered."

Starbride hadn't had much experience with suitors, but even if someone else could turn her head away from Katya, it damn sure wouldn't be this shy young man. Still, if Starbride ever wanted children…Katya cocked her head and considered the idea of using Hugo for stud service.

"What?" He leaned away with a suspicious, worried stare.

"Do you miss being *Lord* Hugo?"

"Well, I am actually a lord."

Katya blinked at him.

"Oh, yes. Father bought the Roanth Highlands. There's nothing there but sheep, but a lordship comes with the property. I guess my father thought that if things didn't work out, at least I'd have that."

More likely, Roland had purchased the land so Hugo's story would stand should someone check it. But Katya couldn't burst the hope that maybe his father had loved him after all, despite the Fiend. "Well, *Lord* Hugo, I'll be anxious to hear what you uncover in the halls."

"Oh! I've got something for you already. When I went to the library, I heard various rumors as to why the crown prince is keeping to his rooms. During one conversation, when someone wondered aloud about the prince's seclusion, several of the ladies and gents giggled and wouldn't tell the reasons for their mirth, no matter how pressed."

Katya frowned. Tight lips made her anxious. A courtier who wouldn't gossip usually knew a measure of truth. "Thank you, Hugo. Please come to me with anything else."

Even as he bowed, she left. She needed to outrun any rumors now and find out what Reinholt was up to that made courtiers laugh but not share.

Reinholt had taken his old apartment, just like hers, with a formal and private sitting room and a separate bedroom. But he'd had all of Brom's things removed. When Katya's knock received no answer, she tried the handle to his formal sitting room door and found it unlocked.

She poked her head inside. The place was a ruin, one of the chairs knocked over and several articles of clothing strewn about the rug. A vase had been overturned on the large dining table. Where the hell was Reinholt's valet? Or any of the servants from his retinue?

For the first time, Katya was glad the children had their own apartment and were looked after by nannies and tutors. She hoped he never let them into this pigsty.

If the formal sitting room was such a mess…

She knocked at the door to the private sitting room. Again, no answer, but when she tried the door, it wasn't locked either. Her ears ringing in the silence, Katya slid her rapier from its scabbard. A servant who had ducked out to fetch something would have locked the door to Reinholt's personal rooms. He could be in trouble.

Katya eased the door open just enough to listen and peek inside. She cursed the cold season that had caused her family to move deeper into the palace, away from the chill of windows. Everything was dimmer by candlelight.

Katya raced into the room and ducked behind a chair so she could look around from cover. Her boot squelched into something. She'd stepped on a tray of food.

This sitting room was covered with clothing, uneaten food, and the stubs of dozens of candles. Wax had dribbled onto antique tables and fine books. The centuries-old tapestry on the far wall had a chicken leg stuck to it. Katya's lips pulled back as she finally smelled the place, unwashed bodies and rot.

A noise came from the bedroom, a loud, clear moan, a man's voice. Katya sheathed her rapier. Reinholt was grieving again. Perhaps in that grief he'd fired his servants and thrown food at the walls. She crossed to his bedroom, her heart going out to him. "Rein?"

The moaning ceased, followed by quick sounds like someone shuffling around the room. The door opened slightly, and Reinholt's sweaty face appeared in the crack. "Little K?"

He was out of breath, dark blond hair disheveled, and he was naked from the waist up except for his pyramid necklace. He had two days' worth of stubble on his handsome face, and his light blue eyes were bloodshot. He held a wadded sheet around his lower half.

Katya's mouth worked for a moment before she gestured over her shoulder. "Where are your servants?"

"I sent them away. I'm busy."

"Doing what?"

He gave her the ghost of the old Reinholt leer.

Katya frowned. People had a right to deal with grief in their own ways, but… "You're still…" She'd been about to say, "married," but she couldn't bring herself to speak it.

Reinholt wasn't a fool. "Married?" he asked with a sneer, as if the word were a joke.

From behind his shoulder, a man's voice said, "Come back to bed, darling."

On the heels of that, a woman laughed. "Yes, it's cold without you."

Katya's stomach dropped. This wasn't grief; it was pure hedonism. She grimaced at the idea.

Reinholt narrowed his eyes. "Our family's in charge. We can do what we want."

Katya gawked at the words so different from what their father had taught them that they nearly knocked the wind out of her.

Reinholt let the door open a little wider so she could see that he indeed wore only a sheet. "Go away, Little K. Run and tell Ma and Da what the crown prince has been up to. I'll be too busy doing it to care." He shut the door in her face.

Katya gawped a moment longer until the sounds of pleasure resumed. She walked away, woodenly for the first few steps, and then anger quickened her. Handsome, charismatic Reinholt never got rejected; he always got what he wanted. And he'd wanted plump, girlish, good-natured Brom, a choice that had seemed out of character for anyone who didn't know him. He'd picked the one girl guaranteed to be faithful, the one most likely to love him for life. But she'd betrayed him. She was loving and loyal, but to her children before her husband, and that had all come crashing down on Reinholt's head. Instead of taking it like a prince, he'd decided to be petty and angry to his family and a complete pig with everyone else.

In the hallway, Katya nearly ran into Lord Vincent. She put an arm out as he started for Reinholt's door. "He's busy," she blurted.

Lord Vincent closed his mouth on what was probably a greeting and bowed instead. "Highness." He stared at her, and she realized with a start that he was waiting for her to leave first, a propriety almost no one stood on anymore.

Lord Vincent wasn't that old; he only had a few years on Reinholt's twenty-five. His handsome, unlined face conflicted with his silver hair, but he'd been silver-haired since birth. He seemed stuck in traditions that only made their home in the estates of the oldest nobles. After a moment passed and Katya hadn't moved, Lord Vincent stepped to the side, still looking at her quizzically, as if wondering if he was in the way.

"I'm sorry, Lord Vincent. I didn't mean to snap at you."

"Your Highness need never apologize to one such as me."

Katya wanted to roll her eyes to the sky. And Starbride wondered why Lord Vincent was classist to the point of bigoted. It was true that nobles sneered at courtiers and courtiers redirected those sneers to commoners, but anyone could be elevated out of each rank. Apparently, Lord Vincent didn't think that was proper. "What did you want of my brother?"

"Ah, it was young Prince Bastian, not me. His royal highness wished to know when the crown prince might visit him."

Katya thought of the sweaty sheet and truculent attitude. "Not anytime soon."

Lord Vincent bowed again. "I will convey this, your Highness." And still he stood there, waiting for her to leave before he took his own.

"Walk with me."

He bowed and fell into step beside her. She wondered how quickly he'd jump to it if she ordered him to stand on his head.

"How well did you get to know my brother while staying in his household?" Katya asked.

"The crown prince and I often spoke of hunting and weapon craft."

All terribly proper, Katya assumed. "Did you ever speak of personal matters?"

"Personal, Highness?"

Katya waved the question away. She'd been hoping for a confidante that could pull Reinholt out of his funk, but Lord Vincent wasn't the right person. When she glanced at him, he stared straight forward, his face mostly impassive, but years of observing people alerted Katya to his slight frown, the pinched expression around his eyes, as if her questions worried him. Maybe Reinholt had let him in on a few secrets after all, and Lord Vincent worried that if Katya demanded to know them, he would have to speak them.

Reinholt's sexual indulgences might be backlash from what had happened with Brom, or perhaps he'd been breaking his marriage vows for longer than she thought. Katya supposed it didn't matter, though it took more of the gloss from the shining image of her brother that she'd carried for years.

Chapter Four: Starbride

Starbride stared at the box of small, delicate tools: chisels and a polishing cloth, a little pouch of sand. Their case was old and weathered, the velvet lining full of holes. "I can't take this," she muttered. "You love this too much." She glanced up at where Crowe sat behind his enormous desk. Pennynail leaned on the untidy bookshelf behind him.

Crowe snorted. "You're my replacement."

Starbride wanted to argue. He was alive; he didn't need replacing, but one look at his hunched form, at his pale face, spoke volumes. He'd never been a large man, and he was sixty-some years old *before* being wounded, but now he was gaunt, cheeks and eyes sunken. His breathing was almost always labored—never mind his level of activity—and his color was sallow, his forehead lined with marks of pain.

He smiled, and his gray eyes were kind. "You *are* my replacement."

Starbride tried to smile, but his casual acceptance of death wouldn't allow it. "I don't know how to use them."

"One of the many things I'll teach you." He stood, and Starbride thought she heard a little grunt. She almost rose to help him, but she knew how angry he'd be, how he'd wave her off. When she saw he was headed to a little work table in the corner, she followed on his heels.

Halfway there, Pennynail took his elbow and forced help upon him. "I'm not a baby," Crowe protested.

"You never want help," Starbride said with a sigh. "Even from Freddie."

Crowe nearly whipped around. "What did you say?"

Starbride bit her lip. "I'm sorry. I assumed he told you before I got here."

Pennynail slipped the mask from his head, becoming Freddie once more. "I was waiting for the right time," he said in his raspy voice.

"I don't like being kept in the dark," Crowe said.

Starbride couldn't resist a laugh. "And yet you keep others there so well."

Crowe shook a finger at her, but she could see his anger wearing away. "None of your lip, miss."

"That's none of your lip, Princess Consort."

Freddie snorted a laugh much like Crowe's. "Has Lord Vincent been putting your nose out of joint again?"

"How do you know about Lord Vincent?" she asked.

"Katya told the Order about him," Crowe said, "but I'm the only one who's met him. He wouldn't willingly associate with commoners, but I suppose I get a pass because I'm the king's pyradisté. Only a slight pass, mind."

Freddie leaned against Crowe's desk and crossed his arms. "Sounds like a prick."

"You say that about every noble," Crowe said. He glared at Starbride. "How did you get him to take off his mask?"

"Get me to?" Freddie asked.

Starbride lifted her chin. "I followed him."

"Clumsy." Crowe glared over his shoulder.

"That," Starbride said, "or a skilled point in my favor."

"No, it was clumsiness on my part," Freddie said. "I didn't expect to be followed in the secret passageways. She didn't even have a lit lantern."

"Trying to learn how to see in the dark, are you?" Crowe asked.

Starbride shrugged, but she had to shake away the remembered feeling of creeping terror. "My lantern went out, and I was trying to figure out who was in the dark with me. When I saw it was him…"

"Your natural nosiness took over," Freddie said, but he had a soft smile.

Crowe ran a hand through his thin white hair, grimaced, and then touched his stomach. The wound was a month old, but they all suspected it was killing him slowly.

Starbride tried to turn the conversation back to something he enjoyed. She tapped the box of tools. "All right, show me what I can do."

"Before we get to that," he said, "I have a surprise of my own." He reached below the table. "I got this for you." He handed over a leather bag.

Starbride stared at it for a moment and wondered what she needed a leather bag for, but then it hit her. It was a pyradisté's satchel. "You…"

She didn't want to say, "bought this for me," because of course he did. She tried to fight the welling in her eyes. "Crowe..."

He waved her gratitude away, but her reaction brought a bit of color into his cheeks. "Whether you're learning here or at the academy, every pyradisté needs one of those." He cleared his throat. "Now, let's get to work."

Crowe produced a lump of unworked crystal and a completed light pyramid from a drawer in the table's side.

"Light again?" Starbride asked. "I don't need another light pyramid."

"We start with the easiest thing."

"When am I going to learn how to make fire pyramids or something more dramatic?"

He didn't grace that with an answer. Instead, he took the tools and spoke of how to knap the crystal, how to chisel and polish, of how a mind could fall into the unworked stone and see the possibilities there. "Light pyramids are good to start with because they need a certain amount of precision. Destructive pyramids can sometimes be poorly made—like the death pyramid—but that's the lazy path. A person who can construct a poor pyramid, even one strong enough to kill, cannot construct a light pyramid because they haven't learned *precision*."

Starbride shivered at the thought of making an ugly pyramid only designed to kill. It was like making a knife out of any old piece of metal, anything dirty enough to get the job done. She resigned herself to light pyramids before anything showier. Hesitantly, she laid the tools against the unworked crystal and began to shape it.

Hours later, the pyramid seemed clumsy to Starbride's eye. The sides were fairly clear, but there was the odd cloudy spot. When she held it up in front of her, the apex leaned slightly to the right. She opened her mouth to point this out to Crowe, but Freddie touched her shoulder, stopping her.

"He's asleep behind his desk."

Crowe slumped in his chair, chest rising steadily. Freddie had covered him with a blanket. Starbride gathered the tools and the pyramid as well as another lump of unworked crystal, the better to practice on. When Freddie inclined his head toward the secret passageway, Starbride gestured for him to lead the way.

After a smile and a shake of his head, Freddie did so. When they were just inside the passageway, he rested his mask atop his head, ready to pull it down at a moment's notice.

"You care about him a great deal, don't you?" she asked.

He blinked at her.

"The blanket gave you away."

"Did it ever occur to you that some things aren't your business?"

"Did it ever occur to you that secrets are easier to bear if they're shared? How do you Farradains cope without bond servants?"

Freddie leaned in close, and Starbride tried to lean away, but the cool wall of the passageway was against her back. "Sometimes, sharing a secret can get your friends killed."

Starbride felt her flush deepen. What would Katya do to take control of the situation? She put her palm in the middle of Freddie's chest and pushed slowly, forcing him to straighten. "Sometimes, *not* sharing a secret can do the same thing. Maybe you should let your friends decide if they like you enough to risk their lives for you." She pushed past him without waiting for a response.

When Starbride got back to her room, she could feel the frown on her face. Dawnmother turned from whatever she was doing, and her face fell. "What's happened now?"

Starbride rubbed her forehead and tried to iron out her expression. "They still think I'm naive."

"Well…"

"I know, your life for mine and also the truth."

"They've lived here longer than you, Star, lived their roles longer than you have."

"I don't mean all that," Starbride said. "I mean their secrets. They still feel they have to warn me about them. I've seen through all their tricks, and still they have to warn me." She tried to imitate Freddie's raspy voice, "Secrets can get people killed."

"Who was that supposed to be? Crowe? That's not funny, Star, the man is dying."

"No! It's…" She hadn't been forbidden to tell. Still, she never could keep all of a secret from Dawnmother. She still didn't understand why the Umbriels would want to keep a secret from Dawnmother. Her bond to Starbride made her the most trustworthy person they could hope for. "I know who Pennynail is."

"Who?"

"A name I didn't recognize, and I doubt you would either, but somehow, I suspect he'd be mortified if I told you. I just asked him what his relationship was to Crowe since he seemed to care about the old man, and he treated it like a kingdom secret. I know about the Fiends and the Order, but *this* is a kingdom secret."

"He told you not to be so nosy, I suppose."

"That was the gist." She shuddered. "He got very close to me to do it."

"He didn't hurt you!"

"He was just trying to intimidate me. So I did my best to intimidate him back." She pulled the newly created pyramid from her satchel and wished she'd had something a little more substantial to seem intimidating with.

"You should tell the princess." Dawnmother marched to the bed and began tidying a room that was already tidy.

Starbride stared into her ugly pyramid. Freddie Ballantine was a criminal, that much was clear, and if he was as famous as he thought, Katya would recognize his name. Katya would have to deal with the fact that an outlaw was a major part of her Order. "I can't do that."

"Why, in Horsestrong's name?"

Starbride sighed, feeling like a fool. "Because he was right. Secrets are necessary sometimes. Telling Katya would put too much pressure on her."

"You get so angry when she decides what you can and can't handle. Now you're doing it, too."

"Payback?" Starbride asked with a smile.

"It'll end in tears."

Starbride suspected she was right, but there was nothing to be done about it at the moment. She took the next few hours and tried to shape her light pyramid into something serviceable. When she tired of practicing, she researched the pyramids she wouldn't attempt for a while. If she was going to be the Order's primary pyradisté, she needed to learn all she could. She made several notes, questions to ask Crowe about the four categories of pyramids: destruction, mind, utility, and Fiend magic, everything that could help the Order and anything she could think of to ward off the knowledge that she'd probably have to use what she learned sooner than she thought.

Chapter Five: Katya

After Katya ditched Lord Vincent, she went back to her parents' rooms. Even though he'd mocked her, Reinholt was right about one thing. She couldn't leave him alone in his breakdown; she had to tell the king and queen. What the crown prince did affected them all.

She rubbed her temples as she walked and wondered how long she'd flounder from one crisis to another that day. All the striding through the royal quarters almost made her long for the languorous gossip mongering she'd foisted onto Hugo. It was already wearing on into evening, and her stomach rumbled, reminding her that business or not, she'd have to eat soon.

Once her father had returned from a meeting and her mother had ordered them tea, Katya blurted her thoughts. "I'm worried about Reinholt."

Da slumped in a chair as if the world was too heavy. "I know what you mean, my girl."

Katya bet that he didn't, not exactly, and she really didn't want to elaborate.

"He's been so sad," Ma said, "so angry. I just don't know how he'll ever be happy again."

"That's my fault," Da said. Katya and her mother protested together, but Da shook his head. "No, it is. My father kept me close, the tyrant, all lessons, all politics, and all the time." He sighed and rubbed his bearded chin. "I didn't want to be like him, so I made Reinholt constantly visit the provinces, always meeting people, always making contacts. It made him beloved, but his nannies and tutors gave him everything he wanted. And now the only girl he's ever really chosen has broken his heart."

"It's his first time," Katya said softly. "His first broken heart." She thought of her own heart, broken several times. Still, she didn't know if those experiences would help if Starbride ever left her. No, not just left, betrayed. Katya shook her head and tried to rid herself of the black pit the idea opened inside her.

"We won't let him wallow," Ma said. "Let's order dinner, a family dinner. We'll have one every night if we have to, and we'll make sure he comes. I'll go to his apartment and drag him here if I must."

Katya thought of the voices of at least two lovers and shook her head. "I'll, um, I'll get him."

"And it would be better, perhaps, if Starbride were to skip this dinner."

Anger bloomed in Katya's chest, and she missed the warning burn of her pyramid necklace that kept her Fiend inside.

Ma held up a hand, forestalling Katya's argument. "I know it's not fair, but we're trying to pull Reinholt out of a slump. And he's angry at Starbride."

"Irrationally so," Katya said.

"I know that, my girl," Da said. "We both do. He's extremely jealous."

"Yes," Ma said. "And we must make him some allowances."

Katya clenched her fists behind her and paced. "Starbride is a member of *my* family."

Before Ma had a chance to speak, Da piped in with, "Quite right. And she'll understand, my girl, I know she will."

Katya gave her father a fleeting smile and then sighed. "I'll go and tell Reinholt."

She'd drag Reinholt to the family dinner and then she would rush from it as quickly as possible and spend the rest of the evening with Starbride, apologizing until she was blue.

On the way to Reinholt's room, Katya stopped by her own and sent Averie with a note to Starbride. It was the coward's way out, but if she had to see Starbride's disappointment, Katya would be angry at Reinholt before she even reached his room. Make him some allowances; the thought made her grind her teeth.

She didn't bother to knock. Reinholt wouldn't have gotten any new servants in a few hours. Everything was as she'd left it, but the door to the bedroom was slightly ajar. Katya heard voices. If Reinholt was still occupied, she was leaving.

But the voices didn't sound passionate. They were just two men talking, and one said, "Are you certain this is the best course for you, Highness?"

Katya recognized Lord Vincent's voice. She edged closer.

"Thought you never questioned your betters, Vincent," Reinholt said.

Katya crept toward where the bedroom door was open a crack. She shifted until she could see them standing by Reinholt's bed. He swigged from a wine bottle and wore a loosely tied silk robe.

Lord Vincent clasped his hands in front of his immaculate coat, the breast embroidered with crossed swords held by the hawk of Farraday, the champion's crest. "I would never question you, Highness, but my station does permit me to worry for you."

"Have you been speaking to my family about your worries?"

"Her highness the princess expressed some concern for you as well."

"Did she?" Reinholt took another swig. "And what did you tell her, eh?" He grabbed Lord Vincent's upper arm. "Did you tell her this wasn't the first time I've been unfaithful to my wife?" He stepped close, their faces inches apart. "Did you tell her there are some needs a wife can't fulfill?"

"No, Highness," Lord Vincent said, so softly that Katya had to read his lips.

Reinholt kissed him. Lord Vincent didn't react, and Katya tensed. She couldn't let Reinholt force himself on anyone, even someone too hidebound by tradition to refuse the desires of a prince.

Before she had a chance to storm in, Lord Vincent's arms curled around Reinholt's shoulders and pulled him closer. The bottle slipped from Reinholt's grasp as the two embraced. When they broke away, they were both breathing hard.

Reinholt barked a laugh. "Spirits above, Vincent, no one kisses like you do."

Lord Vincent smiled his enigmatic little smile. "Thank you, Highness."

Katya backed up quietly until she stood just inside the sitting room door. "Reinholt?"

He opened the bedroom door wider and smiled when he saw her, but his smile hadn't lost its bitter edge. "What do you want now, Little K?"

Lord Vincent hadn't come with him. Katya had to wonder if he was hiding from her. "Our parents want us at dinner. It's just the four of us, by their order."

Reinholt lazily scratched the exposed skin of his chest. "Do tell."

"They want you there by hook or by crook, so either get dressed and come with me, or our parents will descend upon this pigsty. Do you really want them to see it?"

Reinholt's nostrils flared. She bet his pyramid necklace was burning. So, he had some pride left after all. "As my sister commands. Will you give me a moment to dress or will you step inside and make sure I get the job done properly?"

"I can fetch you a servant."

"Don't. I'll be right behind you."

Katya waited in the formal sitting room; Reinholt must have been used to being dressed by Lord Vincent. That or he had learned how to properly dress himself. How long had he and Lord Vincent been lovers? How many more might there be? Reinholt loved Brom; Katya knew that, but she was starting to learn just how selfish a man he was, how selfish a man he'd always been. Their father was right; Reinholt had been getting everything he'd wanted for far too long, and that had taught him no respect for those around him, for his family, for his wife. How much of responsibility did he know at all?

When Reinholt emerged, dressed in an immaculate black coat and trousers, hair neatly combed, Lord Vincent still didn't show himself. Katya didn't bother to ask. Instead, she just escorted Reinholt toward dinner. He stared straight ahead for the most part, eyes darting toward her occasionally, mouth smug, as if daring her to comment. Katya kept her bored court face on. She'd leave it to her mother to dispense disappointment.

To Katya's surprise, her mother didn't turn a frosty eye on him. Instead, she welcomed him with a warm smile and open arms, a move that stopped him in his tracks; his smug face fell to something like sorrow. When she embraced him, he trembled as if he might burst into tears.

He recovered quickly and broke from her embrace, but the smile he had was strained.

Da simply said, "Let's eat."

After the servants served the initial helpings, they withdrew from the private sitting room. No one seemed willing to fire the first volley. They ate and talked of unimportant things, though Reinholt's responses were monosyllabic at best.

The servants didn't reappear with dessert. Skipping sweets was an old tactic of her parents, a prelude to a "serious discussion." Katya wondered if Reinholt remembered that. He blinked around slowly as if just waking up, clearly waiting for either the dessert, so he could resume the wooden way he'd eaten dinner, or some other cue.

"The fall festival is in a few weeks," Ma said. As opening salvos went, it was a gentle one.

Reinholt frowned. "I know."

Ma continued to stare at him. Katya copied her father and watched the walls.

Reinholt pushed back from the table and crossed one ankle over his knee. "Waiting for me to say I'll dance for the populace like a good little puppet, Ma?"

"You're the crown prince of the mightiest nation in the world," Katya blurted.

Da cleared his throat and gave her a warning look, but not before Reinholt turned his scathing eyes on her. "Care to step into the breach, Little K? Want to duel me for the position?"

Katya almost said she would if she had to, but Ma said, "Enough." Her calm wasn't shattered, wasn't even chipped. "You have responsibilities, and being seen is one of them."

"You don't have to explain my position to me."

Katya resisted saying, "Could have fooled me." She pinched her own knee under the table and tried to keep the scowl from her face.

"I know you're hurt," Ma began, and before Reinholt got a chance to eat his foot once more, she hurried on, "but long, emotional sabbaticals are something we cannot afford, not if we're going to maintain control. We have to be seen, and to be seen doing well and being obeyed."

Reinholt stared at the table, face red, the picture of a sulky child. These were lessons they had learned from the cradle. Did he remember them at all?

Da nodded as if they'd worked everything out. "I'll have one of my clerks deliver you an itinerary."

Reinholt sighed long and loud. "Fine."

Katya supposed it was the best they would get. She had to put in appearances at the festival's myriad activities and plumb her contacts for any threats to the crown. The king's Guard would be out in force, and any time an Umbriel made a public appearance, he or she would be protected, but it was the job of the Order of Vestra to make sure no secret villains like Roland waited in the shadows.

Reinholt knew all that. And all he had to do was show up.

When her parents finally excused them, Katya left in a hurry, both to avoid another walk with Reinholt and to get back to her rooms fast. She wanted to have a few words with the Order, and that meant a few moments to see Starbride before they gathered. She grinned even as she thought of all the trouble that was to come.

When she came back to her room, though, Averie had a pinched look upon her face. Katya stopped in the doorway. "What is it?"

"Nothing too bad."

"That's not very encouraging."

"It's just...I heard a rumor that she's back...for the festival."

Katya's first thought was of Maia. Her heart seemed to skip in her chest. "Her?"

"Castelle Burenne."

Katya's heart beat again, and it took a moment for the name to filter through the walls she'd built around it. Castelle, she of the soft black curls and eyes like a summer sky, with her quick fingers and light laugh, the woman who'd taught Katya so much about love and life.

The woman who'd broken her heart into pieces.

"She's...here?"

"At court. That's what I've heard, and I've heard it enough..." Averie spread her arms as if to ask what else there was to say.

Katya felt her blush and hated it. Castelle was only three years her senior, but when they'd known each other, when they'd been lovers, Katya had been seventeen and Castelle twenty. She'd seemed decades older, eons even. She'd always made Katya feel like a child, even when she'd been taking Katya to passionate heights. Castelle had been the only woman besides Starbride that Katya had invited to meet her family. Ma had said no, had somehow been able to see through the spell Castelle had cast.

Castelle had made it clear that she wouldn't have gone even if she'd been approved of. She'd laughed and waved the invitation away, too much of a free spirit to be tied to one person, too much of a rascal to care about one person too long.

"It's all right, Averie. She's not come to steal my heart again, and even if she tried, it's already spoken for. I suppose I should even thank Castelle. Much of my rake persona I based on her."

"She shouldn't have hurt you."

"Jewel of my heart, you are forever loyal."

Averie's mouth twisted to the side, and she bowed. "If she gets flirty, I can shoot her."

"If she gets flirty, I have to see if I can out-flirt her. That would be quite a challenge."

"Don't. You'll wind up in bed together, neither of you wanting to admit defeat."

"If she tries to take me to bed, then shoot her."

"Are you going to introduce her to Starbride?"

Katya almost tripped on her way around the settee. "Now there's someone she'll flirt with mercilessly."

"I'll bring two arrows in case I have to shoot her twice."

Katya chuckled. "Will you ask Starbride to come here?"

"You have to tell her about this right away. She can't hear it from court gossip."

"Who are you? Elody? Could it be that I'm talking to the incarnation of the spirit of love?"

"If it helps you to think so." She hurried from the room and returned a few moments later with Starbride before she made a discreet withdrawal.

"How was dinner?" Starbride asked after Katya kissed her hello. She had a bit of starch in her voice, no doubt due to Katya's note.

"I protested leaving you out, but now I'm glad. You didn't have to see my brother acting like an ass."

"To tell the truth, I'm not really angry. Having dinner with your brother is something I'd rather skip."

"I don't ever want you to feel left out."

"Please, he can leave me out all he wants. Besides, I got to spend the time practicing with my pyramids. Are you gathering the Order?"

"I'm surrounded by spirits today. Averie is Elody, and here you are, Marla, spirit of perception."

"What advice did the spirit of love have for you?"

Katya half turned, one leg crossed over the other. She decided to deal with the news of Castelle's return the same way she dealt with all things, by blurting them out. "One of my old lovers has returned to court."

Starbride straightened. "My, my. I've never asked, but I thought you had, well…"

Katya resisted the urge to grin. "A lot of lovers?"

"And still at court."

"This one, well, we were…in love." Katya laughed softly. "I was in love."

A soft touch on her cheek brought her back to Starbride's sympathetic gaze. "She didn't love you back?"

A stab of hurt wandered through Katya, surprising her. She thought the feelings of three years ago gone and dealt with. "No."

"Well, I was going to be jealous, but I won't now that I know she's a fool."

Katya wrapped her arms around Starbride, and Starbride met her halfway, surprising her with some heat behind a long kiss. When Starbride's tongue snaked gently into her mouth, Katya moaned, shifted closer, and pulled Starbride into her lap, over her leg. Starbride caressed her, fingers brushing her cheek, her hair, her ear. Katya slid a hand up Starbride's bodice, making her moan in turn.

Starbride kissed her way to Katya's ear. "Does the Order have to meet right now?"

"No, no," Katya said, half a whisper, half a moan as she traced Starbride's ear with her tongue.

Starbride pushed Katya backward, cutting off all conversation.

Chapter Six: Starbride

In Katya's abandoned summer apartment, Starbride sat at the table with the rest of the Order of Vestra. She couldn't help but think of how her life had changed in such a short while, from law student to princess consort to member of a secret order, protecting the crown of a nation many in her homeland considered an enemy. But those Allusians who thought of Farraday as an enemy hadn't fallen in love with its princess and taken her responsibilities to heart.

Katya began with the itinerary for the fall festival. "It's mostly following my family and keeping an eye out. Standard stuff."

"The old wait-and-see-what-happens." Brutal leaned back in his chair. "My favorite."

"I'll have my own troubles just getting Reinholt to go," Katya said. "I'm tempted to have you carry him over your shoulder, Brutal."

"If the crown prince wants to start down the path to enlightenment via my chapterhouse, I will be happy to teach him."

"I'd pay to see that," Starbride said.

Brutal glanced at where Maia had sat. "Maybe…" He gave Starbride a look.

She took his cue. "Maybe we should put someone there." Her stomach hurt at the thought of replacing Maia at all, but if Brutal was ready to fill that empty chair…

"Who?" Katya asked.

"Hugo," Brutal said. "He knows our secrets, and he seems capable."

"Have you been talking about this behind my back? All of you?" Katya touched her chest, and Starbride knew she was missing the burn of her pyramid necklace.

Pennynail made a motion across his throat as if he hadn't been speaking about it. Katya barked a laugh. "You're excused."

"There's nothing to be angry about," Brutal said. "You just need time to consider it."

"We talked about it before the fight this morning," Starbride said. "Horsestrong preserve us, was that only this morning? It's been a long day."

"My bruised ribs confirm it was only this morning," Katya said. "I'll think about Hugo. He did volunteer to listen to gossip for me."

Starbride smiled a little and caught Brutal doing the same. Before Katya could catch them, they both hid the look.

All of them turned as the door to the secret passageway clicked open, and Crowe limped inside. Pennynail helped him to a chair, but everyone else tensed as if ready to give aid.

For once, Crowe didn't wave Pennynail's help away. He clutched a cane that King Einrich had given him, another thing he rarely used.

"Crowe," Starbride said. She wanted to follow with, "You should be resting," but no doubt he knew that.

Katya filled in the gap. "You should have sent a message rather than come yourself."

He sighed, too tired to argue it seemed. Starbride counted the heartbeats until he got his breath back. She shook the thought that he'd be gone soon before it could bring tears to her eyes. He was there *now*.

"A contact of mine in Dockland has sent word," Crowe said. "He's seen Maia."

The room seemed to have less oxygen as they all took a breath. "He's certain?" Katya and Brutal asked on top of one another.

"My contact is not a man who makes mistakes with identity."

"Where is she?" Starbride asked.

"The Warrens."

Katya rubbed her temples. Brutal squeezed his eyes shut.

"What is it?" Starbride looked from one pained face to another. She remembered how poor Dockland was, though plenty of money passed through it from the docks to Marienne, but that hadn't made everyone look so anxious before.

"The Warrens holds the poorest of the poor," Brutal said. "A refuge for thieves and criminals and the only sanctuary for the lame and the mad."

"I've heard that even the city Watch doesn't go there," Katya said. "I've never been."

"No," Crowe said. "The kind of criminal we usually deal with considers himself above that place."

Starbride grimaced as she remembered the opium dealers and kidnappers the Order had once had to associate with to get information. "What would Maia be doing there?"

"It's the perfect place for Roland to hide," Crowe said. "Unlucky for him, Maia showed her face, and a face like hers stands out in the Warrens."

"Maybe she was trying to escape," Brutal said. The words hung in the room like a haze.

"We go in tonight," Katya said.

Starbride opened her mouth to protest the long day again.

Before she could say anything, Crowe said, "We cannot devise disguises that will fool the people who live there. We can't pretend we belong."

"Someone who only visits, then," Brutal said.

Crowe shook his head. "Who does?"

Katya rubbed her chin. "Not even the Watch."

They were getting out of hand; no one pointed out that night had already fallen, that they should give up on their plans until the next day. But Starbride felt the thrill of adventure pull at her, something she'd only read about before the Order. The only people who would visit a rat's nest such as the Warrens were… "People looking to exploit the residents. Do prostitutes live there? They're certainly exploited. We could pretend we're looking for a good time."

Katya grinned slowly. "A good time?"

Starbride blushed. "I read that once."

"Exploited as prostitutes are," Crowe said, "they don't frequent the Warrens. The streetwalkers who don't work in brothels tend to stick together in the better areas of Dockland." At Starbride's quizzical look, he smirked. "I don't have to read. I know people."

"I'll bet," Brutal said.

While Crowe glared at him, Starbride snapped her fingers. "We could pretend we're looking to hire thieves. Do people hire thieves?"

Pennynail shook his head. Crowe echoed the gesture. "One would hire a burglar if he wanted something stolen, which is just a higher class thief. I don't think people would go to the Warrens to hire a burglar."

"What if it's something darker and more sinister?" Starbride's eyes fixed on the table as she became lost in her own manufactured adventure. "What if we're rogue scientists or pyradistés, something like that, and we're looking for poor unfortunates to experiment on?"

She glanced up to find everyone staring at her. "What?"

"I think you read too much," Brutal said.

Crowe shrugged. "It's different. It could work."

"It is good," Katya said, "but I wouldn't know how to dress for that part. And if someone did ask us what we were doing, we could hardly blurt that out. We'd get mobbed."

Pennynail shook his head again. He took a purse from his waist and shook it, making the coins jingle. "He's right," Crowe said. "More likely we'd be awash in offers as the residents tried to sell one another to us."

Starbride's bile rose. "That's awful. Maybe the way to do it is to simply not be seen."

Pennynail clapped at the idea.

Brutal snorted. "That's fine for him, but I'm not exactly unremarkable and neither is Katya."

"I can be stealthy when I need to be," Katya said.

"When hiding in the forests or sneaking through abandoned houses in the country," Brutal said. "City skulking is not your cup of tea and you know it."

"Peace," Crowe said before Katya could rebut. "You can all go to Dockland and then wait outside the Warrens while Pennynail reconnoiters."

Starbride frowned. "You'd normally go with him, Crowe, to back him up."

"And I'd do it now if I could."

"I'll look after him for you," Starbride said.

"Everyone, ready your things," Katya said. "We meet by the servants' stables in fifteen minutes." She gripped Starbride's arm and waited until the others filed out.

"Please tell me you didn't mean you were going into the Warrens with him," Katya said when they were alone. "You were just reassuring Crowe, yes?"

Starbride licked her lips, stalling as she thought of something diplomatic. "Katya—"

"No."

"You didn't let me say anything!"

"I can read your face. You're not Crowe, Star."

"I'm his replacement."

"Not yet."

Starbride stood and paced, hands landing on her hips only to swing free and then plant on her hips again. "Then when? When will I be trained to your satisfaction?"

"In a few years—"

Starbride snapped her fingers. "Wrong. The answer is never. You will never be comfortable with me taking on the dirtier parts of Crowe's job."

Katya's mouth worked for a moment "And so?"

"Then be uncomfortable with it. I have accepted a responsibility, Katya. I can't go staying home every time it gets hard."

"No one's suggesting you stay at home. You're going, just—"

"Just under your watchful eye." She tried to keep her rising temper from blowing off her head. "I will not be the only member of the team that must be protected."

Katya touched her chest as if searching for the necklace she no longer had to wear. Starbride should have made her another of the damned things. She didn't need it to keep a Fiend at bay, but maybe Starbride could make it flare from time to time and give Katya the heat she was looking for.

"We watch each other's backs," Katya said.

"You watch my back and my front and every side." Starbride pointed a steady finger in Katya's direction. "And if you leer at that statement, I will fling a chair at you."

"I'm too angry to leer." She dropped into a chair and drummed her fingers on the arms.

Starbride slid into a chair beside her and tried on her best reasonable face. "I will skulk, sneak, and stick to shadows and rooftops. I will do as Pennynail bids me."

"Can you promise me you'll be safe?"

"If you promise me the same."

Katya kissed her hard, and Starbride slid her arms around Katya's neck. When they broke apart, Katya pressed their foreheads together. "I want you in and out quickly."

"Yes."

"You don't follow him into the building. Just stay nearby and let him go in alone."

"Yes."

"If he doesn't come out, you head back for us instead of following him. I will come for you if you're overdue."

"Yes, yes, and yes again. I love you, my worrier. Now let me do the job which you recruited me for."

"I'm never going to stop damning myself for dragging you into this."

Starbride kissed the tip of her nose. "Then you'd better damn me too for going willingly."

Starbride dressed in a black leather outfit she'd had specially made, just in case skulking was ever on her agenda again. As Dawnmother braided her hair into a bun above her neck, Starbride watched herself in the mirror.

"This will do very nicely. Katya will be pleasantly surprised."

Dawnmother snorted. "Only because your outfit's tight enough to be scandalous."

When a knock came at the secret passageway, Starbride grinned. "Time to find out." After Dawnmother made a discreet withdrawal, Starbride called, "Come in."

She'd been about to sprawl seductively on the divan. When Pennynail walked through the door, Starbride stood so quickly she stumbled. "I didn't expect you."

After a quick glance around, he pushed his mask up on top of his head. "Had that made did you?" He pointed at her outfit and grinned like a loon.

Starbride fought the urge to cross her arms. The outfit wasn't tight enough to warrant the look he gave her. "I thought it apropos."

"Yeah, if the look you're going for says, 'I'm Captain Obvious of the Sneaky Squad.'"

"Look who's talking!"

"Don't tell me you had a hood made as well?"

She just stopped herself from saying, "It's detachable." She left it where it lay, dangling down her back. "Says the man in the mask."

"Mine is functional. And brown, I might add, which blends in so much better than black."

"And the buckles? How are they meant to blend in?"

He looked down at his outfit. "They're so I can get out of it quickly. What did you think they were for? Striptease?"

Starbride felt the blood rush to her cheeks. "I have to tell Dawnmother I'm going. Since almost everything else I own is for court, this will have to do."

"Don't worry. Once I have my mask on, I won't tease you at all."

Starbride ignored him and opened Dawnmother's door. "It's Pennynail. I'm going."

"Won't you let me come with you?"

Starbride shook her head. She put the satchel Crowe had given her across her body and tightened the straps until it hugged her. Crowe had supplied her with pyramids she thought she'd find useful, mostly flash bombs, but a few fire pyramids as well, and one that could detect other pyramids in use. She even brought one for sorting through someone's mind, if it came to that.

"I've been practicing climbing, Dawn. You've just been watching."

"Because it's silly."

Starbride gave her a look. "I promise, when we go out gathering information in Marienne, you can come along."

"I'll hold you to that. And if you're not back by morning, I'm coming looking for you."

"You and everyone else," Starbride mumbled, but she hugged her all the same. "I'll be fine, Dawn."

"Just keep in mind that if you're not fine, your mother will hold me responsible."

Starbride cringed. "I have to tell Katya she's coming."

"You haven't told her yet?"

"See you later." Starbride kissed Dawnmother's cheek and then nearly ran back to Freddie. "Ready when you are."

The smell of Dockland was almost a living thing, creeping through the darkened streets along with the fog and a general feeling of unease. The feeling and the smell seemed to coalesce the closer Starbride and the Order came to the Warrens.

They'd left the horses outside of Dockland. The animals would have made them too conspicuous and probably would have been stolen besides. They strode quickly through the city. By the time they reached the entrance to the poorest district, Starbride was tempted to pull her hood around and hook it over her nose and chin, just to keep out the stench.

They stopped in front of a darkened storefront. Katya's lips brushed Starbride's ear as she whispered, "We wait here. Remember what I said."

Starbride shuddered both from the contact and the ominous tone. To Katya, though, she winked, feigned confidence, and did her best to disguise her excitement. Brutal and Katya stepped to the storefront where they would stay until Pennynail and Starbride came back.

Pennynail took her arm, and then they were off through the short alleyway that separated the Warrens from the rest of Dockland. The denizens had dealt with the poorest area of their city by forgetting it existed, building apartments up to the edge of it in an effort to wall it off.

At the exit to the alley, a dark shadow detached itself from an entire nest of them near the back of an apartment building. "Toll," it said gruffly.

Pennynail slammed an open palm into the shadow's face. It collapsed, cursing. There was a scuff of feet on stone, but Pennynail drew one of his long knives. Silence enveloped them again. No other shadows came forth. Pennynail took Starbride's arm and hustled her into the small square that followed the alley, and then across into a side street.

It all happened so quickly. Starbride had just shaken off her stupor enough to slip a hand into her satchel. She let out a breath and wondered when in the exchange she'd forgotten to breathe. Pennynail looked back and forth down the alley and then pushed his mask up over his head. He folded it as small as he could and stuffed it in the back of his leather outfit.

Starbride gaped at him in the gloom from the square's only streetlamp. He moved close to her ear. "I don't often use it when they're not around," he said, inclining his head in the direction of the Order. "Or here in Dockland where no one cares."

Starbride shrugged. Whatever made them less noticeable, she supposed. They hurried through the streets and angled for the building that was supposedly holding Maia. No one else accosted them. Starbride guessed that the demand for a toll was only levied on those who weren't known in the Warrens. Or maybe Freddie's punch was some kind of code signifying that he had every right to be there.

Many shadowy figures flitted past them, going about whatever business suited them. Starbride found the place quieter than any city street she'd ever encountered. Maybe everyone in the Warrens had learned the value of silence.

Well, that was until one poor fellow careened down the street, half-dressed and raving about the Fiends who lived in his closet. When he turned a corner, his cries cut off in one harsh scream. With a shudder, Starbride hurried on. Even if she and Freddie managed to save the poor wretch from whatever had caught him, what would they do with him? The thought comforted her a little, even though she knew his cries would haunt her dreams.

Their target building was as dark as any of the others. The windows were shuttered, save for a few at the top whose shutters had broken off. Occasionally, the wink of a candle or lamp would appear through the smashed planks of wood, but they disappeared as quickly as they came.

Starbride drew a pyramid from her satchel, one that would detect other pyramids in use. She held it up for Freddie to see and then inclined her head at the building. He nodded. Any pyradistés would know she was there if she detected them, but this would tell them if Roland was using pyramids or if he had any guarding nearby.

Starbride focused and fell into the pyramid easily. Her vision lost all color, but sharpened into black and white, letting her see more clearly. She looked for the glow of an active pyramid on the outside of the building. When she saw none, she closed her eyes and reached with her pyradisté's senses. She couldn't sense the emanations of another pyramid anywhere in the vicinity. She put the pyramid back in her satchel and shook her head.

Freddie gestured to a small alcove, half hidden by a barrel, in a nearby street. After a quick look to make sure the hiding spot was unoccupied, they ducked behind it.

"I need to go in and have a look around," he whispered.

Starbride's insides curled at the idea of being alone, but she'd promised Katya she wouldn't go inside. She dug a pyramid out of her satchel. "Take this. All you need to do is smash it, and it will create a flash bomb. Break it near the windows, and I'll know you're in trouble."

"And then what? You'll run for the others, or you'll fly to my rescue?"

Starbride rolled her eyes. "I'll start weaving your shroud." She gave him a little push. He didn't run toward the obvious door at the front, but became lost in the shadows on the side of the building. No doubt he'd climb to some forgotten window.

Starbride leaned back on her heels and tried to find some way to be comfortable without actually sitting down. How long would her missions be like this? How long until Katya trusted her to care for herself? Besides making sure the building was clear of active pyramids, what good was she actually doing?

She supposed clearing the pyramids might be enough. Maybe that was all Crowe had done, most of the time. Somehow, Starbride doubted that. He would have stuck to Freddie's side.

Starbride was better at climbing and sneaking now. She had the damned leather outfit, no matter that Freddie had made fun of it. How long would she have to wait to feel like a full member of the team?

It wasn't trust, she tried to tell herself. It was worry. Katya loved her and wanted to keep her safe. Starbride's frown only deepened. She could keep herself safe. She and Freddie could watch each other's backs like the other members of the team did.

As angry as she was, Starbride knew she'd have to tread carefully with Katya. So many things had happened to disrupt Katya's life lately. Starbride was used to such disruptions, had been getting used to them ever since she'd learned she was coming to Farraday. Or, she told herself, maybe she was just better suited to dealing with hardship than Katya. Years of feasting did not teach one to suffer famine.

Starbride tried to force the smug thought away and focus on the building. She looked for any signs of trouble, any sign that Freddie needed help, or that Maia was actually within. After all, the best remedy to calm Katya's nerves would be a series of successful missions, and this one was a wonderful place to start.

Time passed, slowly approaching the deadline. Starbride shifted again and again, fighting cramps and the urge to just plant her rear in the dirt. She yawned and rubbed her arms. As warm as the leather was, it couldn't block out the chill. She switched knees for perhaps the tenth time, but the brief rest she gave each leg wasn't helping anymore. No one had come or gone from the shuttered building, and she'd seen the same brief flickers of candlelight from the top stories. She'd watched each window carefully, and then the door and the sides of the building, waiting for Freddie's return.

The idea that she might have to leave him made her stomach ache. She'd been so certain he would arrive on time. Worry made her forget about her cramping legs as she pulled them under her in a crouch. She'd have to leave Freddie to his fate while she sought help.

Or she could go in after him. No, that was pure folly. If a master of sneaking could get caught, she certainly would, and there was no telling whether a well-placed pyramid could get both of them out. She wanted to be trusted. Now she had to prove that.

Starbride scratched an arrow in the dirt, pointing back to the entrance of the Warrens. She'd retrace her steps quickly and keep a pyramid out. If she ran afoul of trouble, she'd detonate a fire pyramid. That would bring Katya running and surprise any attackers long enough to hold them off. She stood in the shadows and stretched, ready to run, when she caught a glimpse of light from an alley across the way, two figures moving around the other side of the building. The wan streetlight reflected from a long metal object in the larger one's fist.

Starbride squinted and hoped it wasn't what she thought it was: Brutal's oversized mace. She nearly called out, certain of it as her mind played it over, as the two figures disappeared around the side of the building. Katya—reckless, lovesick fool that she was—had rewritten the plan and come in after them before they were overdue.

"Darkstrong take the woman," Starbride muttered. They were going to have words over this one, Katya's inability to cope be damned. Starbride gave one more quick glance at the dark streets around her and then crept toward where Katya and Brutal had gone, doing her best to stay in the shadows.

Chapter Seven: Katya

"We should have given them more time," Brutal rumbled at Katya's back.

Katya resisted the urge to snarl at him. She'd heard him the first hundred times. The fact remained that Pennynail and Starbride were almost overdue. She'd be damned before she'd leave Starbride in danger any longer than necessary. Starbride had obviously gone into the building with Pennynail, and they'd gotten in over their heads. Fiend or no Fiend, Katya was going to get them out.

Brutal pulled on her shoulder. "At least let me go in first," he said before they reached the back door. "No sense in both of us getting our heads sliced off in a trap."

She let him take the lead, though she wanted to dart around him and run through the building. Memories of Starbride tied to a table, the threat of having her fingers cut off, loomed in Katya's mind. And Starbride had been captured twice, held as part of an elaborate trap concocted by Roland and his henchmen, Darren and Cassius. Only Roland had protected Starbride from Darren, then. Katya doubted Roland would care to keep Starbride in one piece now.

Katya tried to shake the thoughts, but they kept rising, even as she and Brutal ducked through the door into blackness. If Roland hurt Starbride, Katya would burn the building down; she'd burn the Warrens, maybe all of Dockland.

No, a voice inside her said, without the Fiend, she wouldn't be able to do anything.

Katya did snarl then, but at this nagging lack of confidence she couldn't seem to shake. Brutal lit a candle and held it high. A narrow staircase started up before them and turned sharply at a landing before continuing upward. A long, dark hallway sat beside it and continued into the building, into blackness, and another hallway struck off to the right. To their left was a door, shut and bolted as if to keep something inside rather than out.

Katya stooped. The floor was filthy and tracked by many feet. She lamented the fact that they'd left Averie just outside Dockland with their horses. Maybe she could make sense of the mess of footprints. Whoever said the building had been abandoned was much mistaken. Listening hard, Katya heard the sound of muted footsteps above them.

She pulled on Brutal's arm until he lowered his ear. "We start at the top and work our way down."

He moved toward the staircase. They stayed close to the wall and tried to avoid the creaks and groans that would plague the middle of the stairs, but they couldn't escape them all. Anyone listening from above would know they were coming.

They passed the second floor, looked down it briefly, but saw no one. Halfway to the third floor, a flash of brilliant light came from above, a flash bomb. Katya rushed past Brutal and took the stairs two at a time. When she reached the top, she ran down the hallway, headed toward a spot of candlelight coming from one of the rooms.

Inside the room, a woman leaned out a window, looking outward as if tracking something's fall. A cloak obscured her form, but the hood was down, and very pale hair cascaded down her back.

"Maia?" Katya breathed. She stepped forward.

A scuff behind her made her turn and bring her rapier up.

The sight of Darren almost made her pause. His arm moved, and she tried to leap out of the way of whatever he threw at her, but it slammed into the side of her head and brought stars to her eyes.

She staggered, swung wildly, and heard him laugh. "Funny how we never get the one we're expecting."

Behind him, the hallway exploded in fire.

Chapter Eight: Starbride

From above, Starbride heard a crash. The sound of someone crying out in pain echoed down the stairway. A rush of heat billowed downward, and a flash of light brought the dim stairway into stark relief.

Starbride resisted the urge to rush up the stairs. She pressed her sleeve to her mouth and crept through the smoke. More yelling came from above and another cry of pain. What had Katya gotten into?

Someone ran up the stairs behind her. She lifted a pyramid, but Freddie slid to a stop on the dimly lit landing below her, hands raised.

"What's happening?" they asked at the same time.

He hurried to her side. "I followed a woman through several streets. Took me forever to figure out it wasn't Maia. Why did you come in alone?"

She almost smacked him. "I'm chasing Katya."

"Katya's in here?" He pulled his mask out of his clothes and slipped it on.

"Upstairs, by the noise." More smoke drifted down the steps. "We have to hurry."

He took the lead, but she kept her pyramid out. Light flickered from the third floor, a sure sign of fire. Now there were more voices, more footsteps. Pennynail and Starbride flattened against the wall as people hurried past them, all of them dressed in filthy rags or leather ensembles not unlike Pennynail's. Starbride tried to peer into their faces.

"Katya!" she shouted. "Brutal! Maia!"

Several members of the fleeing mob took a cue from her and started screaming. She and Pennynail continued their climb.

Brutal's huge form emerged from the smoke. He kept two people at bay, both of his attackers with cloths tied around their noses and mouths. Pennynail drew a dagger and leapt to Brutal's side. Starbride slipped past them and ducked to stay near cleaner air.

The hallway was on fire; the flames nearly blocked access to one of the rooms. Starbride peered inside it to see a figure against the wall, almost on its knees. It shook its blond head and coughed. A long rapier glittered in its grasp.

Starbride fixed her hood around her mouth and nose, kept low, and dashed past the flames.

The air moved over her head, as if something just missed connecting with her skull. She tossed her flash bomb over her shoulder. It struck something and shattered in a burst of light. She skidded to a halt as someone cried out.

Darren backed away, his face recognizable even with his fists pressed to his eyes. She saw it sometimes in her nightmares, asking how many times he could cut her before she screamed. He waved his sword blindly. Starbride ducked out of the way and hurried to Katya.

When Starbride touched her shoulder, Katya tried to swing her rapier, but she seemed unsteady, staggered even. Starbride batted the blow away. "Hold on to me!"

The flames in the hallway crept up the walls. Katya draped an arm around Starbride's neck. Starbride covered Katya's nose and mouth and led her past the flames.

In the hallway, someone rammed into them. He gave way as easily as a bundle bag of sticks. "Keep hold of me," Starbride said to Katya. "I won't let you go."

But more people dashed from the rooms like rats. "Brutal!" Starbride tried to yell above the screams. "Pennynail!" Someone grabbed at her ankle, some poor soul who'd fallen in the press. Starbride jerked her leg loose, but she couldn't offer the fallen person help, not while supporting Katya. Her stomach turned over at having to leave a person under so many feet.

A cry of pain sounded from up ahead, and then Brutal moved through the mob. They parted for him like the tide, occasionally smacking against him and then rolling to one side or the other. He reached for Katya and hauled her over his shoulder.

"Hang on to my arm!" he cried.

"Wait, wait!" Starbride clung to him and looked for the fallen person who'd grabbed her, but there were so many people, too many panicked faces, too much smoke.

"Now," Brutal yelled. Starbride had to go with him or risk joining whoever was on the ground. Katya's rapier dropped. Starbride grabbed it and kept it tight to her side lest it cut someone.

Pennynail met them at the head of the stairs, two dead men at his feet. Brutal and Starbride caught him in their wake, Brutal still leading the way. Starbride held on to him and Pennynail held tight to her. When they hit the street, they kept going, all the way out of the Warrens and through Dockland. Brutal didn't put Katya down until they were outside the city and a bit into the trees where Averie waited with their horses.

Chapter Nine: Katya

Katya had to wonder how many times she'd woken up without remembering going to bed. It always took a few groggy moments for things to fall into place. "Maia," she whispered. A heavy hand on her chest kept her from sitting up.

"Lift your head and you'll regret it," Brutal rumbled.

Katya opened her eyes. "I saw Maia."

"You and everybody else. Pennynail thought he was dogging her through the streets."

"But..." Katya tried to think. "Darren hit me." She took a deep breath and coughed. "Why does my chest hurt?"

"You breathed in smoke. Someone lit the building on fire, but they didn't bank on at least one of us *not* charging in like a loon."

Katya glared at him. "You, I suppose."

"No, I was Mr. Crazy right behind you. Starbride, however, kept her head."

Katya vaguely remembered being saved by Starbride's quick thinking. "I thought it must have been the spirit of love."

"She saved you without my brawn or Pennynail's skill...or a Fiend."

"What are you—"

"A good crack to the head would have felled you just as easily if you'd had a Fiend. Maybe what you lost was your common sense."

Katya tried to keep glaring, but the truth of his words sunk in. "Perhaps."

"Hmm, maybe you didn't lose all your sense."

"And where is my beloved now?"

Brutal continued to stare at her.

Katya rubbed her forehead. "All right, all right, lesson learned. I will follow the plan from now on, or you may throw this series of events into my face at every opportunity."

His mouth twisted as if he wasn't sure. "She's outside. I wanted to have a little chat with you first." He stood and passed out of view.

A moment later, Starbride smiled down at Katya and sat on the edge of the bed. "How are you feeling?"

"Better for seeing you. I'm sorry I worried you, Star."

"I want you healthy before I yell at you about your trust issues."

"I'll stay in bed forever then." She tried to leer, but her head ached too badly.

"Well, since you have a mark against you, I can finally admit mine."

Katya lifted Starbride's hand and kissed it. "You saved me, Berth, spirit of strength. What could you have possibly done wrong?"

"I didn't tell you that my mother is coming to visit."

Katya blinked and tried to think of what that might mean. Her lovers' mothers had never seemed like a consideration. Now here came one who would one day be her mother-in-law. Still, the idea wasn't that upsetting. Even if the woman was as fierce as Starbride made her out to be, she couldn't hold a candle to Katya's mother. "I'm sure we'll get along."

"Oh, she'll love you, especially your title."

"I'll be the spirit of patience."

Starbride's cool lips pressed against her forehead. "Glad to hear it. You won't mind staying in bed for a few days, then."

Katya did summon up the energy to leer then. "If you promise to stay with me."

"Rascal." She brushed Katya's hair away from her forehead. "When I saw you in that room, and you were barely moving…"

Katya caressed her warm cheek, guilt tying her up inside. "Star—"

"I know how it hurts when someone you love is in danger. But I still trust you to watch my back."

"Understood." And she supposed it would have to be. After all, her Fiend never gave her the ability to trust someone else to do what was right, what was safe. Her Fiend never cared to protect anyone. She'd have to trust those around her to protect themselves and then help them as she could.

It would be a hard lesson to take to heart.

Katya spent a week in bed under the watchful eye of not only Starbride, but Averie and Dawnmother as well. She ached to investigate the strange Maia sighting, but her family and friends wouldn't let her shift until she could walk without her head threatening to explode. Crowe came by several times to report that he'd heard nothing else about Maia and could only conclude that Darren and Roland had decided to see if they could kill any of the Order. Whether Maia had actually helped them remained unclear.

The day that Katya was ready to be on her feet again, she decided to take care of an easier matter, one that had been in the back of her mind. Rumors about why she hadn't come out of her apartment for days abounded, according to Hugo. The leading rumor had it that she was hiding from Castelle Burenne. Katya had to nip that rumor in the bud, and there was only one way she could think of.

"Star, we better meet Castelle and get it over with," Katya said after Averie helped her dress. "We can't have people saying that I'm either scared of her or that you're physically trying to hold me back."

Starbride laughed. "You couldn't keep me away."

They dressed simply but elegantly, Katya in coat and trousers and Starbride in one of her Allusian outfits, fitted trousers and a loose shirt held tight with a bodice. In the halls, they followed the gossip until they found who they were looking for.

Katya expected her breath to catch upon first sight of Castelle; she expected to feel a pang in her heart. She paused a moment and waited for the crowd to part, for her first glimpse after two years.

Castelle's curly black locks were still lustrous, even though the top of her head was hidden by a hat with a wide, floppy brim. Rakish, as always. Her eyes were as bright as turquoise, and she'd added a small tattoo that curved around her right eye. As Katya and Starbride moved closer, Katya saw it was a thin vine of roses, thorns and all.

Castelle smiled, her teeth shining in a face only slightly darker than those around her, a nod to the barony she hailed from, a land close to Allusia. She ran her fingers along the brim of her hat before she pulled it from her head and executed a bow that managed to be teasing and elegant at the same time.

"Your Highness," Castelle said.

Katya's heart thumped, a feeling that almost surprised her enough to keep her from speaking. Castelle was beautiful, Katya told herself, but she was also the past. "Baroness, I see you've been keeping well."

Castelle smiled as she straightened and kept her hat by her side. Her trousers were fashionably tight, but her blue coat was cut far too short, just at her waist, and its sleeves ended halfway down her arms, showing her white shirt underneath. The style was several years out of date, but the way she moved, her confidence, made it seem that fashion had it wrong, not her.

Before Castelle had a chance to speak again, Katya said, "Have you met Princess Consort Starbride?"

"I have not had the pleasure." But she'd probably heard of nothing else since her arrival.

Starbride stepped forward gracefully, and Castelle's eyes narrowed, a sign that she liked what she saw. Katya nearly smirked. Castelle liked almost everyone she saw. Flirting had been one of the many lessons Katya had learned from her.

"I am honored, Princess Consort," Castelle said.

Starbride smiled warmly, maybe to try to convince Castelle that she was completely outclassed, if Castelle had any designs on taking up where she and Katya had left off. "Please call me Starbride, Baroness."

"Then I must be Castelle to you, or Cass, if you prefer."

Starbride inclined her head. Courtiers clustered around them and watched as closely as hunting birds; their heads whipped back and forth from one speaker to another. "I've heard you are an adventurer, Castelle."

"A bit of this and that. I've recently been on the coast playing thief catcher for a count."

"And how many have you caught?" Katya asked in her court drawl.

She winked. "Enough, Highness."

Still a flirt, as if they had no history at all. Katya glanced away as if bored. She beamed at Starbride then, as if she'd forgotten Castelle even existed. She could almost hear the gossip starting in the minds around her.

Starbride took the hint and bestowed a beautiful smile up at Katya. "That's very interesting I'm sure," she said, half over her shoulder, to Castelle.

"Well," Castelle said. "I'm sure you're very busy. Please, don't let me…" She glanced back and forth between them.

Katya waved, and the crowd parted for them. She waited until they were around a corner before she pulled Starbride half behind a statue. "That was perfect. You were perfect."

"No lingering feelings, then?"

"Only for you."

Chapter Ten: Starbride

After Katya left for a meeting with her parents, Starbride stayed in the hallways of the palace, being seen, as Katya called it. She didn't loathe it as much as she used to. Some of her newfound confidence had come from the consort's bracelet, but not all. She'd dreaded wearing it in the beginning, suffered the demands on her time by scheming courtiers, and hated the way nobles pretended to be her friends while waiting for more grist for their rumor mill.

Elevation in rank hadn't made her feel above everyone around her; an increase in responsibility had done that. The adventurous side of her life put her above the palace's petty schemes and torments, even as an inner voice reminded her that petty schemes and torments could be just as dangerous as Roland. That voice sounded a lot like Countess Nadia, who'd told Starbride that nobles and courtiers weren't above killing to get what they wanted.

Lady Hilda, who'd once fancied herself Starbride's competition, had stayed out of the way since Starbride had become princess consort. Starbride had no illusions that she'd given up, though. No doubt she waited and hatched some colorful scheme. As courtiers and nobles bowed in the hallways, Starbride couldn't let the idea bother her too much. After all, she had position now.

She also had pyramids in the pouch at her belt.

Lady Hilda had missed her opportunity. Starbride let herself feel immense pride that she hadn't made that mistake; she'd accepted Katya. Now she just had to accept everything that went *along* with Katya.

The Order had discussed preparations for the fall festival and keeping the royal family safe. They'd talked of the crown prince, of the king and queen, of the child princess and prince, but no one spoke of who would defend Katya. Everyone assumed she could take care of herself. But they hadn't seen her crumpled against a wall, dazed to the point where she couldn't even run from a fire.

Starbride wouldn't argue that Katya should stay indoors and hide behind guards. After years of freedom, that would drive her mad. But the other Umbriels weren't Roland's only targets; hadn't their last mission proved that?

Up ahead, Starbride caught sight of Castelle turning a corner and leading a troop of nattering courtiers. All of them, men and women, laughed and flirted with her; she did the same. When Starbride first arrived at Marienne, she would have thought they were just having a bit of fun—her fragile ego assuming it was at her expense—but now she knew that everyone was always grasping after something.

Castelle had a quick word to her followers. They glanced in Starbride's direction, lips pursed or amused, before they hustled away.

Starbride and Castelle bowed, just enough for each one's station. It warmed Starbride's belly that she outranked Katya's former lover. It wasn't jealousy, she told herself, just satisfaction.

"Princess Consort," Castelle said after she'd straightened. "Starbride. I hoped we'd run into one another again."

"And why is that, Castelle?" She couldn't bring herself to say the nickname. It sounded too much like shortening an Allusian name, an intimate practice.

"If I may say, I admire your directness. I've heard it lamented many times that you don't play court games. May I walk with you?"

Starbride shrugged and continued walking while studying Castelle out of the corner of her eye. She was lean, but not without curves. Barely taller than Katya, she was far taller than Starbride, and she had power in her frame, even under her clothing. Like Katya, she was built for adventure.

"Court games?" Starbride asked.

"The politics game, the getting-ahead game. My father used to call it the courtier shuffle."

"I would have liked your father."

Castelle glanced at her as if surprised, and her face softened into an almost affectionate look. "Many did. He…" A slow, calculating smile took over her mouth. "Do you even think about it?"

"What?"

"Your lack of guile. Are you cunning, artlessly or not?"

Starbride fought the urge to get angry, like she always did with these people. "I say what I think, that's all."

She felt a gentle touch on her shoulder and turned to find Castelle watching her with a pinched brow. It made the tattoo curving around her eye wrinkle. "I'm sorry. I didn't mean to offend you. It's just...Honesty is hard to find here, real honesty, I mean. A lot of people use the word as an excuse to say whatever they want, the meaner the better. You're rare."

Starbride barked a laugh. "In more ways than one."

"Ah. Blame your honesty on your Allusian heritage?"

"Oh no." Starbride's mother wouldn't think of herself as dishonest, not an outright liar, but she could play the courtier shuffle with her hands tied behind her back. "It's just...me."

Castelle chuckled, and Starbride almost expected her to say something silly like, "I can see why she likes you." But she must have known that any reference to Katya wouldn't be welcome. Starbride didn't let anyone pry into their lives, no matter who they were.

Before they came within sight of the royal apartments, Castelle made as if to turn aside. Starbride couldn't resist a small jab. "Not wanting to run into her?"

Castelle turned slowly, mouth turned up. "I was wondering if one of us was going to mention her."

"I couldn't resist. I'm sorry." But she wasn't, not really. She *could* be dishonest after all.

"Our history is just that."

"I know. But you didn't part on good terms."

"Are you going to thrash me for the history or just on principle?"

"No, no." She wouldn't need to thrash; she had pyramids. "I suppose I'm just curious."

"Then why aren't you having this conversation with her?"

Her crossed arms were reminiscent of Katya, and it almost made Starbride pause. "I have. But as Horsestrong said, different perspectives help make a clear portrait."

"I was young. We were young. I won't apologize for who I am or who I was. I can only say that I hope we can all be friends, or at least comrades."

Starbride tilted her head but didn't comment. Only Katya would know how to heal her old wounds; only Katya could say if she wanted to be friends or comrades. Like Dawnmother, though, Starbride would keep her eyes open.

Something of her thoughts must have showed on her face. Castelle's grin widened. "Don't worry, Princess Consort. I wouldn't leave you out in the cold. If I'm going to be friends with her, I'm perfectly aware that I'll have to be your friend, too."

Starbride shrugged again. "Well, you can try." Before Castelle had a chance to respond, Starbride walked down the hall into the royal apartments where Castelle couldn't follow.

Chapter Eleven: Katya

Robert Rochester, Duke of Baelyn, had been an imposing man in his youth. Katya could still see some of his former girth in his shrunken frame, but she couldn't remember him without the limp or the bow in his back. He was stooped and gray now; the only imposing thing about him was the deep, rich voice that sounded as if it should come from a younger, healthier man.

Katya stared at him as he stared at the floor. He couldn't have been much older than her father, but he seemed as old as time itself and just as weary. "What did she *do*?" he asked again. He glanced at Katya's father, but he didn't look Da full in the face, not yet.

"Brom informed our enemies of the crown prince's movements. He was nearly killed," Da said, the story they'd all agreed upon.

"I had heard that there was an earthquake, and that it had something to do with…what the royal family must do to pacify the great Fiend?"

Katya shifted slightly. The populace knew too much to be completely deceived and too little to really understand why pacifying Yanchasa was such an ordeal. Still, she let her father handle the explanation.

"She waited for that time so that her machinations were less likely to be discovered."

Duke Robert smoothed the gray whiskers of his goatee. "I just can't believe…"

Katya pitied the old man. He couldn't be long for the world, and he had to see his daughter dishonored before his end. At least Brom wouldn't be dead.

Da gently patted Duke Robert's shoulder. "If you like, I could have my pyradisté blank her memory. The world would know she'd been returned to your house, but she wouldn't know why, and she could live blithely on."

Katya lifted an eyebrow. Everyone would know of Brom's divorce, of her dishonor, except Brom? Wouldn't she wonder why she was shut away? Crowe—even with Starbride's help—couldn't selectively erase Reinholt from Brom's memory. They'd have to take entire years, including the memories of her children. Wouldn't she wonder what had happened to her?

Unless Da was suggesting taking her memory wholesale and letting her father invent any past he chose, a fall from her horse, perhaps, that had stolen her memories.

Duke Robert bowed his head again, considering.

Katya thought of Brom, alone in the dungeon in her chains. Not an hour ago, Katya had leaned close to her and whispered, "Speak of our secrets to anyone, and you die."

Brom had nodded, not looking up.

It wasn't good enough. "If you tell all that you know, your children could be removed from the succession. Who would guarantee their safety then?"

Brom had glared murder at her, but Katya hadn't let on that she lied. She'd hoped the mere idea might make Brom behave.

"No," Duke Robert finally said. "She will live with her shame."

He loved her too much to kill her, yet he was still angry enough to shame her. That was good. An ashamed father wouldn't lightly forgive her or seek revenge on her behalf.

Moments later, Ma accompanied Brom into the formal sitting room, leaving the guards in the hallway. Dressed in a simple shift, Brom had been bathed and shod. She was no longer bound, but her sleeves hung well over her wrists, hiding any marks left by cold steel. She'd been plump, but now her cheeks had sunk in, and her dark hair lay lifelessly across her shoulders. When she saw her father, her brown eyes flooded with tears, and she stepped forward.

Duke Robert turned away. Brom stopped, mid-stride, and tears fell down her cheeks.

"Your Majesties," Duke Robert said as he bowed. "I thank you for your mercy."

"Mercy?" Brom whispered.

Duke Robert didn't look at her. "Shut your mouth, girl." He bowed to all three royals again. "Please apologize on my behalf to his highness, the crown prince."

Da nodded, but Katya doubted he'd do it. Reinholt wasn't anywhere near the mood for apologies.

Duke Robert started for the door, still not looking at his daughter. "Come, Brom."

"Where are my children? I can't say good-bye?"

Katya glanced at her parents' faces and saw the same coldness she felt in her heart.

"Come, Brom," Duke Robert said. "Now."

Brom drew a deep breath, but before she could speak, Duke Robert was beside her, his fingers digging into her arm until his knuckles whitened. He spoke directly into her ear, though Katya could hear him from where she stood. "Do not speak. Come. Now."

Brom made a shallow sob but walked out the door. Duke Robert kept his grip upon her arm. After a nod from her father, Katya followed them through the servants' quarters and then to the servants' stables. There, Katya signaled to Brutal, already astride his charger and waiting behind the stalls. He followed the duke's carriage and guards as they left the palace.

When Katya climbed up the stairs and ducked into a secret passageway just outside the servants' quarters, Starbride was waiting. She'd been following through the walls at Katya's request, pyramid at the ready, just in case. A lantern sat near her feet. Her arms opened, and Katya leaned into them.

"Come back to my room," Starbride said, her breath warm against Katya's cheek.

"I wish I could, but I have more unpleasant business to attend to. Mother has asked me to make sure Reinholt has ordered the proper outfit for the opening of the fall festival."

"Babysitting again." Starbride put on a haughty, somewhat evil smile. "Oh, I'll be all right, I suppose. Castelle has volunteered to be my friend."

"Did she?"

"I could go see what she's doing if I'm lonely."

Katya fought down a surprising jot of jealousy as the image of the two together popped into her head, forcing out the thought of getting rid of Brom. "Castelle's not doing anything nearly as special as what I can do." She brushed Starbride's cheek with her lips.

Starbride laughed, a smoky sound. "But you have so many duties..."

Katya tilted her head back and forth, more than ready to banish darker thoughts from her head. "We have only a few moments, and I love a challenge." Before Starbride could speak again, Katya stepped close and demonstrated some of the things she had learned, both from Castelle and from others.

Starbride responded with a passion that matched Katya's, and after a short time, they were both breathing hard and leaning on the hard stone, clothes shifted or unlaced or unbuttoned. Katya grinned, surprised to find that her passion had been ignited not only by the need to put away dark thoughts, but by the danger of making love in the secret passageways where her family or the Order could find them.

Starbride grinned, and Katya knew she'd been thinking along the same lines. "Well, well." She laced her bodice and pulled her shirt straight.

Katya groped for her trousers. "That was fun."

"We have to do this more often."

"I can always spare this kind of time."

"Oh sure. Time for a conversation, absolutely not, but for this..."

"Tell me your priorities aren't the same!"

"Well," Starbride said, and even in the glow from the lantern, Katya could see her blush. "I have to admit, this is time better spent than most."

For the next few weeks, all Katya's time seemed to be spent either preparing for the festival, counting down to the festival, or enduring the awful family dinners she'd been commanded to attend. Starbride earned points in her mother's favor by volunteering to sit out. Little did Ma know that Starbride counted herself lucky to be excluded.

Without more Roland or Maia sightings, Katya could let the normal work of the Order consume her, anything that kept her from dwelling on her brother's behavior, the imminent arrival of Starbride's mother, or the presence of Castelle at court.

She kept reminding herself to take one thing at a time. Crowe's contact in Dockland had no more information about Maia or Darren, though they couldn't trust his word anymore. He'd surely been found out as snitch to the king's sneak. They'd all been used in a trap, probably to find out how vulnerable they were with Crowe out of commission. He'd have to double-check all his information from then on.

Almost before any of them realized it, the fall festival was upon them. Opening day, Katya and her family stood on a newly built dais in the square in front of the palace. The people of Marienne packed the square to capacity, ready to hear the royal opening speech.

Reinholt was being an ass, as usual. He crossed his arms and fidgeted from where he stood just beside their parents. If the cleaners had left any dirt on the wooden dais, he would have been kicking it. Katya could have slapped him.

Standing just behind her mother and father, Starbride at her side, Katya adopted a regal stance. Starbride kept trying to swallow a grin. She wore the same deep blue gown she had worn at Reinholt's welcoming ball, a large glittering creation that made her skin shine. She'd even talked Katya into a coat that was neither black nor blue. Deep green, she'd said, would remind the people that warmer times were coming. Katya couldn't argue with that.

Master Bernard and the heads of the Pyradisté Academy made the academy's capstone sparkle and shine, cycling from bright white to orange and yellow and red, all the colors of fall. It accentuated the bunting and decorations that covered the square and extended down every street in the city.

"Each year," Da said, "we gather to celebrate the harvest and the farmer, the lifeblood of Farraday. We honor your labor and the products of your work. Without you, we could not survive. May the merriment of our revels keep us warm in winter winds and remind us that spring must come again!" The crowd erupted in cheers. Reinholt rolled his eyes. Katya stopped herself just short of kicking him.

The merchants around the square and through the streets lifted the awnings from their booths. The crowd surged toward their favorites to buy up goods or flowers or souvenirs. Wandering vendors with trays slung around their necks sauntered into the open, selling pastries or roasted nuts. The smell washed over Katya and stirred up memories that made her smile. She leaned close to her mother and father.

"It's time."

With a final wave to the crowd, the royal family trooped back inside the palace, glad-handing nobles as they went. When they were halfway back to the royal apartments, Reinholt pulled up short. "We always wander through the crowd."

"Not after Roland," Katya said.

Reinholt sneered at her. "You may be head of the Order, Little K, but I outrank you."

"You don't outrank me, my boy," Da said quietly. His tone was soft and fatherly, but his posture was made of steel.

Reinholt's nostrils flared, and his eyes turned fearful for a moment, but he stood his ground. "Brom's gone, Da. I just need a little normalcy."

"Under guard," Ma said softly.

After an unblinking moment, Da nodded. "With Katya, her team, and Lord Vincent." He stepped close to Reinholt, and Katya didn't catch every word, but enough to know that he wanted Reinholt to take Katya's orders when it came to staying safe.

Katya bent close to Starbride's ear. "Gather the Order and meet me in front of the palace in five minutes."

Starbride's mouth turned down, no doubt at the idea of spending time with Reinholt and Lord Vincent both, but unlike Katya's churlish brother, Starbride didn't argue with her duty. She nodded and hurried away.

Katya nodded to Reinholt, tried to summon up some sisterly feelings, and tried on a grin. "We'll collect Lord Vincent on our way."

He smiled at her, a ghost of his former self but better than a sneer. He even offered his arm, which she pushed away with a laugh.

"Would you throw your body into the path of an assassin's knife?" he asked.

Katya blinked at him. "Of course, Rein."

He stared at her for half a second, but said nothing. Lord Vincent joined them, and when they reached the main hall, Starbride waited with Dawnmother and Averie. She tilted her head to both sides as if stretching. Katya got the message. Brutal and Pennynail were around.

Reinholt took the lead with Lord Vincent at his side. Katya followed close behind them, her arm entwined with Starbride's. Dawnmother and Averie brought up the rear, both carrying baskets should anyone decide to make a purchase. They wandered through the main market and down several side streets, following the line of booths. The festival had spread through the streets like a giant, many-armed monster. In one square, the booths sat in front of closed shops and homes. The people played games, bob for apples or splat the rat. In a corner, a troupe put on a puppet show for a gaggle of children, some of them wearing finery and others dressed in homespun smocks.

Starbride and Katya put their heads together and tried to look as if they made idle conversation as they traded information. "On our right, thirty feet, blue hat," Katya said.

Starbride looked in the indicated direction as if searching the booths. "He's waving at someone behind us."

As they wandered from the square and into another street, the booths began to thin. Katya pulled Reinholt's arm and leaned close as if to share a joke. "I think we should find another way."

"We can cut through this small street to a broader one," he said, not bothering to keep his tone low.

Katya fought a frown and laughed instead. "True enough," she said loudly. Then in a lower tone she said, "That doesn't mean we should."

He shook her off, and the look he cast her from the corner of his eye said he'd welcome trouble if it found them. Blood pounded in Katya's temples, and she ached to grab his arm and pull it behind his back until he lifted onto his toes. But she couldn't brawl with him in public. Katya glanced around the narrow street and then toward the more jovial streets they'd left behind. If they wandered farther from prying eyes, maybe she *could* beat some sense into him.

A couple of drunks staggered into the street from the side door of a tavern. Katya put a hand on her rapier. Lord Vincent stepped in front of Reinholt and mirrored Katya's posture.

"Wha's this? Who's that?" one of the drunks slurred. He peered at them in the torchlit gloom.

Katya opened her mouth to say they should turn around, but Lord Vincent spoke first. "Out of the way, good peasants," he said in what he probably thought was a complimentary manner. "Your prince needs egress."

Katya nearly groaned. She could have talked their way through without the two drunks knowing who they were. She glanced behind and saw no one else, but two fake drunks would be the perfect cover for a robbery. Starbride, Averie, and Dawnmother backed up a few steps and watched the rear.

One of the drunks burst out laughing. "He needs what? Wha's that he needs?"

"Egress? That a bird?" the other asked, stepping closer.

"Get back," Lord Vincent said.

"Vincent," Reinholt started.

"Is the prince!" the closer drunk said. "Fuckin' prince on our street!"

"Watch your tongue," Lord Vincent said.

"It's all right." Reinholt waved the words away. He dug in his pouch as if he'd pay the drunks a toll to get by.

"Just go around them," Katya said.

"Didn't your wife run off?" the drunk in the rear asked. "Ran back to her father?"

"S'right," the lead one echoed. He nodded like a bobbing apple.

Reinholt stiffened into stone. "Get the hell out of my way."

The drunk in the rear stepped up, and Katya got a better look at him. Unlike his friend, his coat had a hint of brocade. "Reinholt," she said, "go around them."

Reinholt sneered. "Move these people, Vincent."

Lord Vincent shoved the drunks away. The one in brocade pushed back, face purpling. "Who the hell do you think you are?"

The one behind him laughed. "He's the prince!" he shouted and almost fell over guffawing.

Lord Vincent hustled Brocade Coat to the side. "Give way, man!"

"Not our fault your woman couldn't stand you," Brocade Coat said. He probably thought it was a mumble, but it came to Katya's ears as clear as glass.

Katya's fingers closed over Reinholt's arm just as Reinholt called, "Kill the slanderous dog!" He drew his sword.

Katya hauled back on his arm and used the momentum to launch herself forward, but Lord Vincent moved almost as fast as a Fiend. He drew his blade and ran Brocade Coat through the heart.

Time seemed to slow. Brocade Coat toppled as Vincent whipped his sword back. The other drunk knelt and entreated his friend to rise. Reinholt had gone wide-eyed and pale.

"You killed him!" the man on the ground wailed. "You killed him." His cries grew louder, becoming full-throated sobs.

Lord Vincent looked over his shoulder, no remorse in his eyes, but a definite question. "No," Katya said, answering his silent entreaty about whether he should kill the other man. Lord Vincent's eyes shifted to her and then back to Reinholt.

Katya stepped in front of her brother and pulled him close. "Don't say a damned word, Rein! By all the spirits, you will not make this worse."

He glared at her, but he obeyed. She whirled to Lord Vincent. "Sheathe your sword." He did so, obeying royal commands immediately. Too damned immediately.

"Katya," Starbride said. She gestured over her shoulder and then pointed in front of them. A crowd began to gather at both ends of the street, drawn by the drunken man's wails. Too late to cover things up, then, even if Katya wanted to, and suddenly, she didn't want to. The days of the nobility killing whoever they liked were long gone, and more than that, she didn't believe royalty had the *right* to do whatever it liked.

"You there," Katya said, pointing into the crowd. "Fetch the city Watch."

After one last peering glance, the messenger took off. Katya stepped close to Lord Vincent. "Escort the prince back to the palace."

Lord Vincent stepped to Reinholt's side. Reinholt hadn't stopped frowning, and now his arms started to cross. "Go, Rein," Katya said. "Please, go."

He snapped around on his heel and left. At the end of the street, he passed Brutal among the crowd. Katya nodded after her brother, and Brutal stayed with him.

Katya tilted her face up and tapped her temple, signaling Pennynail to stay put, wherever he was. There wasn't a damn thing he could do for them unless the crowd decided to rush them. She only wished he'd been fast enough to stop Lord Vincent somehow, but what was done was done.

The drunk on the ground was still wailing, but no one stood close enough to know what had happened. Reinholt had been removed from the situation; that was another mark on their side. The Watch was on its way to keep order, and no high and mighty champion was shouting about peasants.

"Stand back," Katya shouted as the crowd edged forward, eager to see a dead man.

Starbride drew a pyramid. Katya nearly warned her that it wasn't time to use a flash bomb or anything deadly, but Starbride merely held the pyramid aloft. It brightened and sent light dancing off the walls. Starbride acted as if it had nothing to do with the crowd, as if she was using it to see better, but the crowd crept back all the same.

"Give way, give way!" a group of men and women called from the end of the street, and then it filled with the dark blue uniforms of the city Watch. Unlike the king's Guard, the Watch wore chainmail instead of polished breastplates. Katya was glad of that, less showy.

A woman stepped to the front, the stripes of a captain on the collar of her coat, above her chain shirt. She pushed her metal helmet back and smoothed dark blond strands of hair away from her face. "Is the man dead, Sergeant Rhys?"

One of her men knelt beside Brocade Coat and gently pushed the wailing drunk away so he could feel the corpse's neck. "Dead as a coffin nail, Cap." He rolled Brocade Coat flat and peered into the dead man's face.

"Well, now, miss, I'm Captain Ursula Laurent." She looked Katya in the face and paused. Starbride brought the light closer, the easier to see Katya's features as well as the hawk and rose on her coat. "Attention!" Captain Ursula cried and stiffened just as her men did. "Truly sorry, Highness."

Katya waved the attention away. "Do you know who this is?"

"It's Georgie!" the drunk said. He wiped his nose and sniffled. "My own brother Georgie Appleton."

Several of the people in the waiting crowd sucked in a breath, and even Captain Ursula seemed startled. Sergeant Rhys nodded from where he still knelt beside the corpse. “He’s Magistrate Anthony’s assistant all right, Cap.”

Katya’s stomach dropped. A magistrate’s assistant, and not just any magistrate, but a man whom Katya had heard called the champion of the poor. Now his assistant had been struck down by the champion of the crown.

“Highness,” Ursula said. Her eyes had gone from surprised to calculating, as if she wondered whether she dared draw steel if Katya refused whatever she was about to say. “Respectfully, you should come with me.”

The crowds murmured and shifted. News of who the dead man was spread so quickly it was almost visible in the air. They couldn’t *know* what had happened, but they’d make something up. Katya guessed someone was already flying to tell Magistrate Anthony.

“Captain,” Katya said. “I think coming with you is a wonderful idea.”

Ursula let out a breath before she snapped off a salute. Katya took a firm grip on Starbride’s arm and followed in Captain Ursula’s hurried footsteps. Averie and Dawnmother stayed close, still silent, though Katya imagined they were as tense as she was.

Some of Ursula’s squad surrounded them. Sergeant Rhys and another officer stayed with the body and with the witness. At a wave from Ursula, the rest strode toward the nearest Watch house and bellowed for the crowd to give way. In the light of the pyramid, the faces in the crowd seemed angry, grimacing like faces in a nightmare, but they obeyed Ursula’s thundering presence, though how long that would last, Katya couldn’t say.

Chapter Twelve: Starbride

Starbride clamped her lips together to keep from shouting, "Katya didn't do it!" The city Watch clearly thought she did. No doubt the crowd did, too. Katya's jaw clenched so tightly her tendons stood out. She'd take the blame for Reinholt no matter what the surviving drunk said. If he was *led* to a conclusion by the Watch, the drunk could suddenly "remember" anything.

Starbride wouldn't stand for it. She'd shout the truth to the rooftops, no matter what the Umbriels wanted. She wouldn't let them sacrifice Katya, wouldn't let Katya sacrifice herself for the sake of the spoiled brat Reinholt.

Another glance at Katya's stony face told her it wouldn't be easy. Katya was tied up in obligation, in responsibility, something Reinholt didn't understand. She would put duty first, and Starbride had agreed to be part of that duty, part of the Order. Could she turn her back on everything Katya believed in?

Yes, she told herself. She'd break her oath for Katya. Starbride swore at that moment that she'd do whatever it took—including kidnapping—to make sure Katya didn't take responsibility for this crime. She wouldn't see Katya imprisoned or, Horsestrong forbid it, hanged.

Captain Ursula led them into a cramped Watch house and through to an even smaller office, all polite bows and offers of whatever meager repast the house could provide. Averie and Dawnmother were left to wait in the hallway, right outside the office door.

Ursula smiled, but it didn't have friendliness behind it. Katya returned Ursula's stares with half-lidded looks, neither of them giving anything away, content to sit in silence until Starbride wanted to scream.

"They'll be bringing in the drunk," Ursula said.

"To tell his side of the story," Katya replied without skipping a beat.

Starbride nearly smiled. If this woman thought to intimidate Katya, she might as well try to frighten the wall.

Ursula did smile, a slow look that had seen it all. She took her helmet off, smoothed out her rumpled hair, and rested the helmet on a battered wooden desk. "Good time for you to tell me what happened, Highness."

Not, your side of the story, but *what happened*, implying that whatever Katya spoke would be the truth. Starbride crossed her arms. Flattery was another interesting tactic, but it also wouldn't work.

Katya shrugged, more of her bored princess persona. She could walk from the office whenever she wished. She was buying time for Reinholt to reach the safety of the palace walls, damn him.

"The light was very bad," Katya said.

Not so bad that they couldn't have seen Reinholt command the death of a citizen of Farraday. Captain Ursula's door opened, and Sergeant Rhys poked his head inside.

Ursula leaned toward him, and he whispered in her ear before he bowed to Katya and Starbride and ducked out of the room. Ursula smoothed her hair back so hard, it pulled her eyes wider. "Excuse me for asking, Highness, but do I have this right? The crown prince ordered the execution of a citizen?"

Katya's bored mask didn't slip. "I'm sure I can get you an answer from the palace." She stood.

Starbride stood with her, her heart slowing. If the drunk could remember that much, Katya couldn't possibly take responsibility for the death. Starbride didn't know whether to laugh or cry.

"Begging your pardon, Highness," Ursula said, "but I was hoping the palace could give me an answer right now."

Katya smiled slightly, and Starbride could tell she admired this woman. Ursula was willing to risk royal wrath if it meant getting the truth. But she couldn't detain Katya; she didn't have that power.

"You'll be hearing from me," Katya said.

Starbride bet the old Katya would have included a leer, but not even the rake Katya had been would include such a look in front of Starbride, or so she hoped. To be sure, she nudged Katya gently toward the door. Captain Ursula was forced to open it for them.

Dawnmother and Averie wore identical blank looks, perfect ladies-in-waiting ready to spring into action. Their eyes flicked toward Starbride when Ursula turned her back. Starbride nodded toward the door to the Watch house, and both ladies started that way as if to clear a path. Ursula merely bowed as she stepped aside, and the Watch officers stopped whatever they were doing and bowed as Katya passed.

Outside, the four of them hurried through the streets, Starbride barely holding her tongue as they strode through the night. Averie and Dawnmother pulled closer as if to ward off any other attacks with their very bodies, and Starbride knew Pennynail was still following them. Near the Watch house, the festival was in full swing. A mere murder couldn't stop the party of the year, no matter who was dead. The booths were open and lively. Vendors stalked the streets and called out their wares.

Every splash of color, every runaway scent seemed obscene. Starbride kept seeing the dead man on the ground and kept hearing the cries of the drunken brother. It all seemed so senseless, and the festival saddened her; it made her think the world had already forgotten Georgie Appleton.

She knew that wasn't the truth. Soon, she knew, everyone would know his name.

Katya didn't stop when they reached the safety of the palace. They hadn't noticed any crowds waiting for them in the streets, but news of Appleton's death had to be winging through Marienne. Instead of going straight to the king and queen's apartment with Katya, Starbride paused.

When Katya looked at her questioningly, Starbride said, "I'll get a report from the Order and catch up with you."

Katya frowned but nodded. "Take great care with yourself."

Starbride wanted to say, "Because death can happen instantly?" but she couldn't get those words out, couldn't mock what had happened. "And you."

Katya gave her a quick kiss before she strode away, Averie behind her.

"Stay with me, Dawn," Starbride whispered.

"Always."

Starbride felt some of the pressure in her chest lessen. When Crowe answered her knock on his study door, his voice tired and punctuated by coughs, Starbride almost turned around. But Crowe had been covering up the "unpleasant tasks" for the Order for too long; he was invaluably knowledgeable, not to mention that he would rather die than be left out, no matter his condition.

"Has Pennynail told you yet?" Starbride said before Crowe had risen from his couch.

His confused face answered her. Starbride related what had happened in the dark street as quickly as she could.

Crowe wiped his bloodless lips. "Appleton? Are you certain?"

"You've heard of him?"

"The assistant of Magistrate Anthony, the people's magistrate, if I remember correctly. Appleton was so instrumental in the rise of the self-made magistrate that people often said they held the position together. I'd say the spirits of luck have decided to curse Reinholt personally."

"The people were very angry."

"Katya is telling the king and queen?"

Starbride nodded. Dawnmother walked to the small cabinet in the corner and poured two glasses of wine. Crowe gave her a wry smile as she set his before him. "Not too proud to serve a servant?" he asked.

"You would be the one to give me lessons in pride, Crowe," Dawnmother said, though the smile she gave him was affectionate.

"I was just getting used to you calling me Mulestubborn." A fit of coughing seized him.

Dawnmother rubbed his back and cast a glance at Starbride. They couldn't stay long. "Pennynail should be along shortly," Starbride said.

"I don't need a nursemaid."

Dawnmother shook her head and tsked. "You remind me so much of my father."

"He was a paragon of stubbornness as well?"

"He was a good man." Before Crowe could smile too much from the compliment, Dawnmother added, "Who worked himself to death."

To Starbride's surprise, Crowe simply sighed and rested a hand on his belly, on top of his wound. "We have to work quickly. I'll send Pennynail to find out what the common people are saying and to see what he can do to bank the fires of anti-monarchial sentiment."

"What should I do?" Starbride asked.

"I don't know what you *can* do." He tapped his chin, lost in thought, before he snapped his fingers. "You and I are both commoners. We can use that. We can remind the rich and the noble that the common people have power. The Umbriels are going to have to hold a funeral for Appleton and make significant contributions to whatever charities he and Magistrate Anthony fancied, whatever causes they championed. Now more than ever, you'll have to be seen."

"I'll catch up with Katya, and we'll see what we can do."

❖

Starbride didn't take the secret passage to the king and queen's quarters; she went the traditional way instead. Two guards had been stationed discreetly down the hall from the royal apartment, but by their wary expressions, they'd heard some yelling. Past them, Averie stood right outside the king's door.

The guards stood to attention as Starbride approached. "I'm sorry Princess Consort," one said. "They're not to be disturbed, on order from the king."

Starbride pointed past the guard. "I'd like a word with the princess's lady-in-waiting, please."

The guard sighed, as if relieved she'd not yelled at him. Averie hurried down the hall and then walked with Starbride and Dawnmother a few steps away from the guards.

"How's it going?" Starbride whispered.

"They're all in there now, except for Lord Vincent. From what I could gather, the king isn't holding the champion responsible."

Starbride would have loved to place some blame on the champion's shoulders, but Reinholt was the one at fault. She told Averie what Crowe had said they should do.

"No doubt Katya will agree with him," Averie said.

Starbride had to admire Averie's calm. If forced to just wait in a hallway, she would have been wringing her hands; she felt like wringing them now. "I could go out again with Dawnmother and see if we can pick up the general mood."

Averie's face went very still, diplomatically so. "With respect, you should leave it to Pennynail."

"I can go where Pennynail can't."

It was true, and Averie's expression said they both knew it. Averie didn't know Pennynail's identity, but unless he was a courtier or a noble, he would be barred from places where Starbride would have easy entry, private clubs or expensive taverns.

"We shouldn't be making decisions without Katya."

"I'll go with an escort. Pennynail from the shadows when he isn't lurking in dens of ill repute and Dawnmother the entire time."

"Don't be ostentatious," Averie said, her eyes far away, and her mind obviously working. "Something fine but sensible. And you should have one more guard."

"I know just the one." Starbride strode away. It felt so good to have a course of action, no matter that the course was a little dangerous. Anything was better than waiting around the damned palace. She was getting used to adventure, but she had to be cautious lest it swallow her whole.

❖

Hugo was more than happy to join them, just as Starbride thought; he made an excellent guard. No one would question a lordly escort, and Hugo had proven himself a capable fighter.

Starbride replaced the gown she'd worn for the opening of the festival, opting instead for one of her finer Allusian outfits, deep red trousers, and shirt with a cherry-colored bodice embroidered in gold. She left the consort's cuff behind and wore rubies instead of diamonds. A wine colored cloak hid her from neck to toe.

Dawnmother walked at Starbride's side, so close they occasionally bumped into each other. She didn't see Pennynail, but she wouldn't until she needed him.

She only hoped she wouldn't.

The fall festival was still going strong, even though it was approaching midnight. Many of the families had gone, but street children flocked everywhere, and the crowds were only a bit thinner though a lot rowdier.

Close to where the murder had taken place, the streets seemed dangerously quiet. Starbride passed near the tavern the two drunks had come from, but she walked quickly to a nicer neighborhood. The sign above her destination was a bar of gold surrounded by a stack of gold coins. Starbride sighed. And the rich wondered why the poor didn't always think highly of them.

The guard on the door frowned as he looked at Starbride's features. She opened her cloak enough to show her fine clothes, and tucked a strand of hair behind her ear. That and a look at Hugo's finery convinced the guard to step aside, bowing as he went.

Starbride didn't spare him a glance. Inside, music and chatter washed over her. The floor and tables were made of dark wood, highly polished. The shutters had been thrown wide open, but they'd been covered with loosely woven material that caught some of the dust from outside. Bolts of striped silk hung from the ceiling and met in the middle of the room above a giant chandelier. The chandelier wasn't lit by common fire, oh no. Sparkling pyramids perched in its silver branches.

Starbride was almost disappointed the crowd wasn't wilder. Though men and women gathered in the aisles as well as at the tables, the conversation wasn't loud enough to drown out the lute-playing singer in the corner.

"Shall I secure us a table, Miss Starbride?" Hugo said. "Princess Consort, I mean."

"If you can't just call me Starbride, Hugo, then miss will do." She leaned close to him. "And absolutely not Princess Consort, not tonight."

He flushed but chuckled and started for a nearby table, no doubt to tell its occupants to make way for her. She grabbed his sleeve.

"Let's mingle," she said. "We're after information."

It had been mere hours, but gossip about the murder had spread like wildfire. Evidently, neither the Watch nor the drunk nor the crowds had been silent, but like all gossip, everything had been tainted. Of what they heard, the prince had killed the princess; the princess had killed an entire squad of the Watch; a magistrate was dead by the prince's order, by the princess's, by the Watch. Most disturbing of all was that whenever the Umbriels were mentioned, the crowd made a point of saying how the royals were "within their rights" to kill a member of the public. And most of the people in the crowd weren't nobles. Some were courtiers or wannabes, all wealthy, with little or nothing to do. The Umbriels were like the spirits in their eyes.

"Whoever this man was, no doubt he deserved what he got," one said before taking a sniff out of a perfumed silk handkerchief.

He'd been doing that all night, and the bar didn't even smell bad. The handkerchief must have held more than just perfume. "Surely, no one deserves to be killed in the street," Starbride said.

Silk Handkerchief blinked at her, his eyes glassy. "But you… you're…" He clearly didn't know what to say, probably torn by her obvious position and the humble background he thought implied by her race.

"Tensions will be running high." Starbride raised her voice to capture the attention of everyone within earshot. "We must coexist in Marienne, however you may view your…less fortunate neighbors." She smiled as they chuckled, some toasting what they thought was a veiled insult. Starbride let them think as they would. "The Umbriels will do what they can to smooth this matter over, and I think we must set a conciliatory example."

Sage heads around her nodded, but some of the younger dandies and bravos laughed. "What could a bunch of peasants do?" one of them asked.

Starbride gritted her teeth.

"They could shut the city down," Hugo said.

Everyone around them quieted and looked at Hugo as if he'd grown another head. "What in the spirits' names are you talking about?" Silk Handkerchief asked.

"We'd have no bakers, no farmers, no butchers; no one to drive the carts, clear the roads, or tend the livestock. They could just…stop."

Silence spread from their little bubble like a crashing wave. Even the noise from the singing lute player died down. "They…couldn't do that," someone in the crowd said.

Starbride shook her head. "You can't beat a man back to work." Hopefully, Horsestrong's wisdom would further cut through the entitled haze. Around her, eyes peered into drinks and brows furrowed. She'd given them something to think about, all she could do at the moment.

Well, that and hurry back to the palace to practice her pyramids and wait for Katya. Crowe had been showing her how to use more destruction pyramids, and she needed to alter her clothes to carry more than one when she didn't have her satchel. Flash bombs were all fine and well, but it was past time to make sure she had something dangerous.

Perhaps by preparing for the worst, she could somehow stave it off. Dawnmother and Crowe both would have scolded her for such thinking, but she couldn't put it away, couldn't put away the hope that people would prove reasonable under pressure. It didn't matter that she suspected it wasn't true.

Chapter Thirteen: Katya

After the shouting had died down, no one said anything for quite some time. Katya stared mostly at the floor, a tactic favored by her father when he wanted to avoid losing his temper. Her family's pyramid necklaces had to be working overtime. Katya wished again for the warning burn of her own necklace, but she was almost happy her Fiend had gone. She feared it would have leapt forth hours ago.

Da paced up and down the carpet and gripped his coat, surely seeking a connection with the pyramid that lay underneath. Ma had blooms of color in her cheeks and forehead. She hadn't shouted. Her voice had taken on the low, husky quality it always did when she was enraged, as if anger took her very breath away.

Reinholt stared at the wall, his shoulders pumping up and down as he seethed and refused to accept any responsibility for what he'd done. His anger over everything that had happened in the last month came out like a flood. He'd nearly screamed as he tried to be heard over their father's yelling about duty and nobility. Katya bet his necklace was about to ignite. Maybe Crowe had given him more than one.

At a lull in the shouting, in a petulant little voice, Reinholt had said, "Vincent killed him, not me."

Da had gone purple with rage. "He is the arm of the crown, you sulky little bastard!" He'd stepped so close that Katya thought he might beat some sense into Reinholt.

Katya wished he'd had.

Now the yelling was done. All that was left was what they could actually do about Appleton's murder. Reinholt should have admitted what he'd done and sought forgiveness, but here was the petulant child again, the sulky little bastard, as their father said. Katya looked to her mother. Ma's eyes darted toward the slight movement. Katya furrowed her brow, silently asking what she should do, what either of them should do.

Ma's gaze drifted toward Reinholt and then Da. The prince had to give ground to his father the king. The queen or the second-born child could offer advice, entreaties, pleas, or accusations, but this wasn't just a disagreement between father and son. Appleton's murder had to be settled between the king of Farraday and his heir.

And the heir should have seen that, but Reinholt had his arms crossed, not looking at anyone. He didn't even realize he was committing treason. In the not-too-distant past, it would have gotten him killed.

Katya's mind raced. There had to be a way to get Reinholt to see reason without her actually pointing it out. She feared that if she gave voice to her thoughts, Da would have no choice but to put Reinholt to the sword.

Katya edged close to Reinholt. Like their mother, he looked toward the movement. Katya tried to put all the anger out of her expression and let him see her fear.

He frowned, confused. Katya wanted to yell at him to stop being a fool. If he didn't bow to their father's wishes, it could mean his life. Couldn't he see that?

A knock on the door made them jump. "We're not to be disturbed!" Da bellowed.

Katya moved toward the door. Another knock sounded. She glanced at her father. His face incredulous, he nevertheless nodded.

Katya cracked the door open to reveal Crowe. "You know?" she whispered.

He nodded. Katya almost sighed in relief and thanked the spirits for Starbride.

"The nobles' council is gathering," Crowe said. "Some of them will try and use this situation to their advantage." He glanced past her, and she knew what he wanted. Her father had to be at that meeting.

Katya shut the door. "The nobles are gathering, Da."

He straightened his shoulders and smoothed the creases out of his dark blue brocade coat. He turned to Ma, an old sign that asked if his attire was acceptable.

She unclasped the thick gold chain from around his neck, the one he wore for official functions like opening the festival. It was far too happy a symbol.

Da turned at last to Reinholt, and in his eyes was the same sort of entreaty Katya had tried, a plea from the father for the son to obey the king.

In her mind, Katya pleaded for Reinholt to say he would go along or go in Da's place. Charming Reinholt could find a way to both accept responsibility and remain confident in his place as crown prince. It was a tightrope, but he could walk it, if he only *would.*

The old Reinholt flashed in those eyes, and he stood a little straighter. His leaned forward as if on the cusp of striding in their father's wake. Pride filled Katya once more.

Slowly, Reinholt's hand wandered to his chest, to where his pyramid necklace rested under his coat. His gaze went pained, far away, and Katya knew he was remembering the night of the Fiends as if she could see through his skull. Katya thought he mouthed the words, "I'm tired," but she couldn't be sure. He turned away and stared at the wall.

Ma's mouth opened softly. Without a word, Da strode toward the door. Katya gripped her rapier.

At the door, Da barked, "Katyarianna!"

She whirled around. "Yes, Father?"

"To me." He flung the door open. Katya hurried to his side. Crowe waited for them in the hall and fell into step behind them.

They passed Averie, but Katya waved her off. There was nothing she could do. Katya stayed a half-step behind her father and to the side, as was her place. She had a brief worry about the injured Crowe keeping pace, but he left them when they crossed from the royal halls into the palace.

Katya cast all other thoughts aside and put her neutral face on.

She thought Da would take her into the nobles' council with him, to stand beside his chair at the head of the room, but when they reached the door, he simply pointed for her to wait just outside.

He leaned to her ear. "Let nothing short of war disturb us."

Katya stood where he commanded and kept hold of her rapier. The guards kept the curious from even coming down the hall, but Katya still watched the hallway carefully while keeping her ear tuned to the sounds within. If someone shouted at or threatened her father, she'd be through the door in an instant.

Hours stretched out like miles. Pain started between Katya's shoulder blades and grew to engulf her neck and head. When Earl Lamont opened the door behind her, Katya nearly jumped, but she'd been practicing keeping her head for too long.

"Your father wants you, Highness."

Even as long as she'd known him and as kind as he'd always been to her family, Katya let Earl Lamont step back first so she could see her father standing unmolested at the head of the table. She walked past Earl Lamont, her face set, but her stomach shrinking before the serious faces on the men and women inside the long room. All the nobles in the kingdom couldn't be gathered on short notice, but most of those living in the palace were in attendance. As Katya looked down the table, Countess Nadia van Hale and a few others gave her a supportive nod.

Katya's guts tightened further. Supportive of what?

When she reached her father, she fought the urge to swallow. His face was like stone. "Kneel," he said.

Katya obeyed. The thought seized her that he was going to cut her head off. Maybe she had to take the blame for Reinholt after all.

But no, pride was in her father's eyes. Resolve and sadness and the stoniness of kings, but satisfaction as well; she'd pleased him.

He drew the dagger from his belt and placed the flat on her right shoulder. "Katyarianna Nar Umbriel," he said, "by the power granted me as Lord of Marienne, Foe of Yanchasa the Mighty, and King of all Farraday, I name you crown princess and task you with guarding Princess Vierdrin, future Queen of all Farraday, until the day she is old enough to accept the duties of crown princess."

Katya couldn't breathe. It felt as if the sea was rushing in to fill the room. Her ears pounded with the noise of it. "What?"

Her father smiled, but it had the fleetness of something imagined. He sheathed his knife, and she let him guide her to her feet.

"Should I die before Princess Vierdrin is of age," he said, "you shall rule as princess regent and keep Farraday safe and free of strife, serving always as Yanchasa the Mighty's greatest foe in Vierdrin's name."

The nobles applauded, though only a few wore smiles. Others seemed calculating or outright angry. Katya couldn't catch her breath.

As Da guided her from the room, Katya recalled some of her more opportunistic ancestors; if her young niece had been in their care, Vierdrin would have been dead before morning.

On the way back to their rooms, Katya whispered, "Da—"

"Wait."

Katya felt her court mask slipping. Instead of taking her back to his apartment, Da steered her down another hallway, toward Crowe's office. He rapped sharply on the door and then entered without waiting for an answer.

"Sit, Crowe." Da then told him of Katya's new elevation and how it would soon be all over the palace, then the city, then the kingdom.

Crowe's mouth snapped shut. "I see."

Katya had been listening to the tale as if it had happened to someone else.

"You can't lead the Order like you used to, my girl," Da said, "though you'll still collaborate closely with it. Crowe, you're back in the saddle."

Katya nodded woodenly before she said, "Wait—"

"This is the way it has to be."

"Don't worry," Crowe said. "We won't leave you out in the cold."

Katya felt the world continue to drop away from her feet. No more Fiend, then made crown princess, and now no longer leader of the Order? "You're not going to put Reinholt in charge of the Order are you?"

Da's brow darkened. "Absolutely not! The lazy son of a…" He barked a laugh. "Well, I guess his mother and I are to blame."

"Da…" Katya wanted to cry, shout, and throw the furniture around. It was like several people had died at once, all of them as close as family.

"I need to tell him now," Da said. "Before he gets away from his mother."

"Spirits above." How Reinholt would hate her! She turned to Crowe. "Do you know where Starbride is?"

"We couldn't wait for you. She's out in some of the more well-to-do taverns, trying to discern popular opinion about what's happened. She's got Pennynail, Hugo, and Dawnmother with her."

Katya's heart skipped a beat at the thought of Starbride out in what could become madness, but Katya supposed that if she was sticking to the affluent parts of town, she should be all right. "Hugo's first assignment."

"With a little training, he could be a good asset," Crowe said. "I heard his name mentioned as a candidate for membership in the Order."

"And he is your cousin," Da muttered. "Get some sleep, both of you. It has to be nearly dawn."

They all bade one another farewell, and without knowing what else to do, Katya went back to her room. Averie was already there.

"Highness," she said, "I'm so sorry."

Katya almost laughed. Here was one person at least who understood her. "Thank you, Averie." Katya shut her eyes for a moment, and tiredness hit her like a brick in a sack. "All I want to do is sleep."

Averie helped Katya out of her clothes and into her nightshirt. She plucked the pins that held Katya's hair. Katya barely felt any of it except the wonderful feel of sliding between her crisp sheets. She thought her head had just hit the pillow when soft arms went around her. Katya's head lifted as she tried to sort out what was going on, if it was morning already, and why she hadn't heard the door open.

"Shh," Starbride's voice whispered in her ear. "It's not yet dawn. Sleep."

Comforted, Katya sank into sleep once more.

❖

The next morning, Katya rose early despite the hour she'd gone to bed. She could almost feel the palace buzzing around her, and she couldn't wait any longer to see what everyone was saying.

And she had to find out how Reinholt had taken the news.

Starbride sat up just as Katya finished pinning her hair up at her vanity. "I didn't mean to wake you," Katya said.

"As if I'd let you start this day alone." She kissed Katya briefly before they both dressed. Katya wished they had a few moments more to stay in bed and stare up at the starry sky painted on the ceiling, but the palace wouldn't wait.

"What I learned last night was about what you'd expect," Starbride said. "The rich are on your brother's side. Though now, I guess they'll be on yours."

"The common people won't look on murder with such forgiveness."

"I think Hugo convinced some of the rich people to keep their mouths shut. He has a good heart and an even better head on his shoulders."

Katya just avoided shaking her head, remembering how easily Hugo had fallen for her stories in the past. At least he was an honorable man.

"You'll need his help running the Order with Crowe," Katya said, and it came out sulkier than she intended. As Katya finished buttoning her coat, she felt Starbride's caress on her shoulders.

"I know how much the Order means to you." Starbride turned Katya around, and her face was as earnest as Katya had ever seen it. "I will never ever shut you out. Well, no more than Crowe does."

Katya kissed her deeply with all the love she felt. Of course Starbride wouldn't hide anything. Someone who hated secrets as much as she did wouldn't keep Katya in the dark. "I need to speak with my parents, and then I suppose I'll have to be seen. Convincing Reinholt to be seen is something I doubt will happen."

"Will Reinholt or Vincent be punished further?"

Katya shrugged, but the indignant tone creeping into Starbride's voice nearly made her grimace. "Reinholt's just lost everything, Star."

"Except his freedom or his life."

"The crown will make financial restitution to Appleton's family."

"It might not be enough, Katya. According to Crowe, there are angry mutterings throughout Marienne. Reinholt wandering the town looking remorseful might help. I don't suppose your father would put him and Lord Vincent in the dungeon for a while?"

"A hundred years ago, this wouldn't even have raised a stink, but we don't live in those times anymore."

"Thank Horsestrong for that."

"And where are you off to? Not to follow me around all day, I hope. I'd love to have you, but I'd hate to see you wasting your time waiting for me to collapse."

"Well then, I'll speak with Crowe if he's awake. If he's not, I guess I'll prepare for my mother's arrival."

"Spirits above!" Katya slapped her forehead. "I completely forgot. I don't know if I—"

Starbride lifted a hand. "It would be better if you weren't there to greet her. I thought I'd just lead her to my apartment in the royal wing and let her figure it out, though it might be amusing if you popped in from nowhere and kissed me."

Katya couldn't resist stepping forward to do just that. "I love you, Star, even if you are a sneaky rascal."

Katya found her mother sipping coffee in her sitting room. She gave Katya a weary smile and looked as tired as Katya felt.

"How did it go with Reinholt last night?" Katya asked.

"Not well." Ma set her cup down with hardly a sound, something years of training had taught her. "Reinholt went white as a sheet before turning as bright a red as I've ever seen. I thought he might weep."

"Did he say anything?"

Ma shook her head and sipped her coffee again.

Katya fought down disappointment. She'd been hoping for a mea culpa at last, some sign that he knew his fate rested on his own head.

Ma turned a gaze as probing as the sun in Katya's direction. "How are you?"

"Shocked and disappointed in my brother, but I can do this, Ma." Inside, she felt that was true even as a stab of fear called her a liar.

"I know you can, darling. Your father and I are both very proud of you."

Katya didn't want to ask how her mother was, didn't want to know how Ma loved Reinholt despite what he'd done. "Is Da around?"

"He had an early meeting with the nobles' council. You'll need to address them later."

"I'll be there."

Was it her imagination, or did ghostly tears hover in her mother's eyes? Katya stood, unable to bear them. If there were tears, they were Reinholt's fault. "I'm going to take the temperature of the halls."

Ma stared at her a moment, as if she suspected something else, but she nodded slowly. "Take care of yourself."

With thoughts of her mother's tears fresh in her mind, Katya hurried toward Reinholt's apartment. He didn't outrank her anymore, she told herself, so by the spirits above, she'd finally say her piece.

Reinholt's doors were as unlocked as before. The bedroom door stood open a crack. Katya sidled close again, desperate for information no matter how it came, some clue as to whether her brother could be saved.

"Come with me," Reinholt said.

"I can't," a softer voice, Lord Vincent's.

"You too? After everything we've shared? First my family, then the nobles, and now you?"

"I'm sorry, Highness. My sworn duty is to protect your children. I can't leave Marienne while they remain here."

Katya opened the door without thinking, relieved that when it did open, everyone had his clothes on. "You're leaving Marienne?"

Reinholt's face contorted into a hideous mockery of itself. "What the fuck do you want, traitor?"

"I'm the traitor?" Katya's fists clenched in a desperate attempt not to close around her rapier's grip. "You're the traitor, you miserable, spirits bedamned child! You're an arrogant, selfish, murderous bastard!" She screamed the last word, all her pent up aggravation barreling out of her.

Reinholt stepped back as if pushed by her anger. Lord Vincent's mouth hung open, shocked beyond his usual decorum.

"Well?" Reinholt tore his gaze from Katya and settled it on Vincent.

Vincent looked from one of them to the other. "I…I cannot, Highness. Please." He glanced at Katya again. "My duty supersedes whatever my feelings might be."

Katya barked a laugh. "He doesn't understand, Vincent. He wouldn't know duty if it bit him on the ass."

Reinholt took a step toward her, his arm raised. "You little—"

Katya stepped to meet him, her own fist lifting. Lord Vincent jumped between them, his arms outstretched. Katya pulled up short.

Vincent had his back to her, facing Reinholt, guarding *Katya*. His duty was to protect the young heirs, but if they weren't present, he'd protect the highest ranking person in the room, even from a lesser ranking member of the family.

By the look of utter betrayal on Reinholt's face, he saw it, too.

"So," Reinholt said, and it was the loneliest sound Katya had ever heard. It almost made her feel sorry for him.

She stiffened her spine, though. There was no way Reinholt was leaving Marienne. Katya would dress him if she had to and pull his strings for the public.

Reinholt shoved his hands in his trouser pockets, the kind of posture Katya had come to expect. She stepped to the side, ready to begin ordering him about, but he pulled something from his pocket and hurled it at the floor.

Light stabbed into Katya's brain like a shard of ice. Blind, she stumbled against a nearby chair and heard a crash somewhere in the room. "Vincent!"

"Here, Highness." Katya heard another crash. "I'm trying to find you!"

"Forget me, find Reinholt!" Katya groped her way forward until she encountered someone's arm.

"Highness?" Vincent said.

"Yes." Katya blinked as fast as she could, but the purple and gold lights in front of her eyes wouldn't dissipate.

"There's another door. I feel a hole in the wall."

The damned secret passageway! Katya groped toward the wall and tripped on the bed. When she finally made it to the entrance, she felt only the smoothness of Reinholt's long mirror. Her vision was coming back in a gray haze. She toggled her brother's mirror and staggered into the passageway after him. "Get to the royal stables and stop him," she said over her shoulder. "Sit on him if you have to. He mustn't leave."

"Yes, Highness."

She heard him stagger away. Katya groped along the nightstand for a candle. Reinholt had taken the lantern. She charged through the passageway as fast as she could, squinting into the dimly lit tunnel and willing her vision to be better. The way before her cleared, little by little, but not fast enough. Luckily, she knew the way to the royal stable almost by touch. She came out in the barn and staggered into the daylight.

"Princess!" one of the groom's cried. "I mean, Crown Princess. I didn't mean to—"

"Where's Prince Reinholt?"

"Highness?"

She nearly grabbed his collar. "Prince. Reinholt. Where is he?"

"He…I haven't seen him."

Katya peered into the yard over his shoulder. Lord Vincent stumbled out of the palace doors. He sprinted toward where the yard emptied into the road on the side of the palace. When he came back inside, he looked to Katya.

"I don't see him, Highness."

Katya bit back a curse. "Go to the front stable," she commanded. Lord Vincent took off at a sprint. Katya ran for the back stable, the tradesmen's and servants' entrance.

The place bustled with activity, servants hustling to and fro, traders yelling at their hired servants to hurry no matter how fast they went. Nearby, Katya heard barking from the palace kennels, all of the noises adding up to one horrible din. She paused on top of the steps, and the servants parted around her as if she were a rock among the surf; they did their best to bow under their parcels and loads of linens as they passed.

Katya spied a cloaked figure on horseback at the edge of the yard. She hurried down the steps, not wanting to run or cry out in front of so many eyes. She'd reason with Reinholt if she could, and if she couldn't, she'd slam a fist into his throat or gut and tell the nearby servants that he'd swooned.

"Stop that horse!" she called. Several waiting men and women held out their arms and called for the horse and rider to stop.

The horse shied, and the rider threw back the hood, exposing hair as black as night.

Katya skidded to a stop as Castelle swung down from her saddle with flawless grace. "Highness?"

"Sorry," Katya stammered. "On your way." She turned for the doors but sensed the rush of air as Castelle hurried to keep pace.

"You're troubled."

"Nothing to concern you."

"You're looking for someone? Let me help you." Castelle laughed, a throaty chuckle that stirred Katya's insides. "I do have some experience locating people who don't want to be found."

Katya snorted a laugh. Castelle might have become a thief catcher recently, but Katya had been finding traitors to the crown for over three years. *There* was a group of people who didn't want to be found. She walked faster. "I'm all right."

"I heard what happened. The murder, your…elevation. I'm sorry I wasn't at the nobles' council, but…Your face is like a thundercloud. Are you looking for your brother?"

Katya almost stopped. She'd been practicing her court face for a long time, and Castelle had been absent for almost two years. How in the hell could Castelle still see right through her?

"Yes, I want to gloat," Katya said, putting on as much of a sneer as she could.

"Stop trying to run me off."

"What do you want?" Katya stopped, making Castelle stumble to a halt, a small victory.

Castelle's face softened into what Katya had always called her loving face, the one that signaled its complete devotion to the recipient of its beauty. No matter what Castelle did or said, how many times she loved and then left, that face could drag out every ounce of forgiveness Katya possessed.

Katya crossed her arms. She didn't have time for the loving face or any other.

"I want to help you." Castelle glanced at Katya's crossed arms, and half her mouth quirked up. "I didn't treat you as I should have years ago. I can only hope to serve you in a thousand small ways to equal one large apology."

Katya started walking again. "You and I have no quarrel." She wanted to follow that with, "You and I have no anything," but that would be too childish, no matter that it was true.

"I'm guessing Prince Reinholt didn't take your promotion well?"

"The royal family has no public statement at this time."

"Ah, I see. I'm the public now."

"At your request."

"I deserve that, but you have many friends among the nobles, surely we can—"

"No, I *don't* have many friends among the nobles, or did you forget that? Did you forget that you're one of the few people who really knows that?"

"I'm sorry, I just…"

Katya shook her head, not knowing what Castelle couldn't say and not caring. Lord Vincent trotted toward them. As a baroness, Castelle outranked him, so he bowed low for both of them, but then his eyes flicked toward her, signaling that he would get rid of her at Katya's order.

A chill went up Katya's spine. Vincent would *kill* Castelle at her order. No doubt Castelle would try and stop him. She was an excellent fighter, but Vincent was a striking serpent, and an obedient one at that.

Katya motioned Vincent closer. "No sign?" He shook his head. "See to Bastian and Vierdrin. Make sure Reinholt doesn't try to take them."

Vincent took off at a sprint.

"Something's going on." Castelle's fingers drummed the pommel of her rapier. "I can fight, if you need me. Or I can fetch the Guard."

Katya's heart softened at the concern in Castelle's gaze. No matter what she was in private, Castelle was loyal to the crown. "I'll let you know if there's anything you can do." She gestured back the way they'd come.

Castelle bowed and then walked away; she cast small glances over her shoulder as she went. Katya had a moment to wonder what she'd been up to at the servants' stable. She shook the thought away before taking off for her parents' apartment again.

Chapter Fourteen: Starbride

Brightstriving arrived in a carriage, a contraption few in Newhope, if not Allusia, could afford. As lavish as it was back home, the plain vehicle paled in comparison to the riches of Marienne. Starbride shook her head; what a knock her mother's pride was about to take.

Starbride stepped forward with a smile. She never could think of her mother as "Mama," no matter how often the childish name slipped from her mouth. In Starbride's thoughts, Brightstriving was only "Mother."

Her mother gave her Allusian-style outfit a glance, disappointed no doubt that Starbride wasn't dressed as a Farradain but surely impressed by the silk and jewelry. Her eyes rested briefly on the consort's cuff, but she couldn't know what it meant. She embraced Starbride, a cautious smile on her lips while her servant Rainhopeful hovered behind her.

"New clothes?" Her mother held out the sides of her own petal-like gown. "I've come to prefer these."

"I've started quite a trend."

"From the library?"

"Not exactly."

"Where are we going? I thought the courtiers were housed near the front of the palace."

"I don't live with the courtiers."

"You let them stick you away in some hole, didn't you? Didn't even kick up a fuss? Please tell me you're not in the servants' quarters."

Starbride kept walking, forcing her mother to follow. Her chatter ceased when they entered the royal halls with their pyramids glittering in the walls. Members of the king's Guard stood at attention, resplendent in shining breastplates. Her mother's face went carefully blank when they entered Starbride's apartment. She waited until Dawnmother and

Rainhopeful had served them refreshment and retreated to a corner of the room before she turned her expressionless gaze on Starbride once more.

"We can't afford this."

"No."

"If you are the king's mistress..."

Starbride almost choked on her wine. "No."

Her mother shook her head, and then a smile slowly took over her face. "Since the prince does not live in Marienne...The princess?"

Starbride grinned. "I'm the princess consort, Mama."

With a squeal, she threw her arms around Starbride's neck. Starbride resisted the urge to laugh. As misguided as it was, her mother's pride still felt good.

When her mother sat back, Starbride took a deep breath. "I've so much to tell you. I didn't write because, well..."

"You knew I'd be happy."

"Yes, but not for the right reasons. I love Katya, Mama, Katyarianna Nar Umbriel, and she loves me. She's not...an opportunity."

"But, darling, she can give you everything you've ever wanted, everything *we've* ever wanted. Position, validity, help for our people."

"I know, I know. She has helped, as much as I'll let her. I'll tell you everything, including why she shouldn't help as much as she might."

Starbride laid out the tale of how she'd met Katya, of some of their trials together. She left out the Fiends and the Order of Vestra, making the tale hard to tell, but she'd had a long time to plan what she was going to say. Being part of the Order had taught Starbride the value of some secrets; it had been harder keeping them from Dawnmother than from her mother.

She slowed at the news that Brom had been involved in a traitorous plot, and that she'd been returned to her father, her marriage to Reinholt dissolved.

Starbride didn't miss the calculating look on her mother's face. "No, Mother. I will not consider moving up from the princess to the prince. I love Katya, remember?"

Her mother shrugged as if she couldn't be blamed for trying.

"There's a little more. Prince Reinholt's disgraced himself, and he's not the crown prince anymore."

Her mother blinked, but then her forehead tightened as if she was trying to keep her skull inside her skin. "Then, the princess is now..."

"Yes."

"And that makes you..."

"Yes."

Starbride had never heard her mother crow before. She had to cover her ears.

Starbride left her mother alone in her apartment while she went to see Katya, wanting a moment alone before they were all scheduled to have tea with the queen. She arrived to find Katya shoving several letters into Averie's hands.

"Those are the last," Katya said. Averie rushed from the room.

"What's going on?" Starbride asked.

"Have you seen Reinholt?" Katya asked, almost on top of her words.

"No, I've been with—"

"How could he have gotten past everyone?"

"What's happened?"

"Reinholt…" Katya's face was flushed and tears stood in her eyes. "I don't know whether to shout or cry."

"Suicide?" Starbride whispered.

Katya paused before she choked out a laugh. "Star, you have more honor in a lock of your hair than Reinholt does in his entire body. No, he ran away."

"Ran away?" Starbride said the words, but she couldn't believe them. No, she reminded herself, she couldn't believe a *prince* would run away; she absolutely believed Reinholt would.

"He got away from me and Vincent, and now no one can find him. I'm having the stables watched, and I've sent letters to everyone I know in the countryside, asking them to write if they see the prince on his 'sabbatical.' Spirits above, Star, I've never seen my parents so sad."

Starbride wrapped her arms around Katya from behind. She rested her cheek against Katya's nape, Katya's fingers linked with hers.

"What am I going to do, Star? Everything is falling apart."

Starbride nodded against her back. Katya's life had been changing yet unchangeable for so long. Reinholt's disgrace, his leaving must have been like stars falling from the sky. "We'll weather it together. You, me, your family…and my mother."

Katya turned and wrapped Starbride in an embrace. "I think we'll have to postpone your mother's welcoming tea."

"She'll get over it. Though her caressing the *objet d'art* and not-so-subtly asking how expensive they were might cheer you up a bit."

When Katya leaned back, Starbride wiped her tear-stained cheeks. Uncertainty danced in Katya's eyes, so Starbride leaned forward and kissed her deeply. "I will never leave you."

Katya held her for a long time. "I'll tell my parents your mother is here, and they'll think of some suitable way to welcome her."

"The dungeons spring to mind."

Katya smiled softly. "I'll have one cleared out for her."

Starbride took her mother to meet the royal family in a muted luncheon the day after she arrived. If she'd heard rumors about the murder or Reinholt's disappearance, she wisely didn't mention them.

To Starbride's surprise, her mother also secured a room in the courtiers' quarters. "You and the princess need your *space*," she said with a knowing smile. Starbride blushed to her roots. "Don't worry. I'll be around during the day so you won't miss me."

Dawnmother said that Starbride's mother mixed easily with the courtiers and nobles. They couldn't afford to ignore her; she was the crown princess consort's mother. Every opportunity Starbride passed up, her mother pounced upon like a hungry hawk. She appeared at every party and met every person of even remote importance. With Dawnmother as her guide, she explored every path to power in the palace and used Rainhopeful to gather information about the maids and valets of the powerful. She was a fish that had finally found its way home to the sea. Starbride was more than relieved that she only had to hear about her mother's adventures.

Starbride had expected thousands of suggestions on how to get ahead, but her mother waved those expectations away one afternoon. "Whatever you're doing for the princess seems to be working."

"Mother!" Starbride said, feeling her face go hot. "Don't speak like that."

"I'm making connections so you can go on doing what I'm evidently not allowed to speak about."

Starbride wadded the bottom of her blouse, a nervous gesture she thought she'd kicked in childhood. "As long as someone doesn't come to me looking for the things you promised them."

"I promise them nothing but empty air." Her mother sat at Starbride's desk and bent over several sheets of paper; a pencil bounced in her fingers as she read, ready to make notes.

"What are you doing?"

"Oh ho, nosy, do you care all of a sudden? Well, you may have won the princess over with honesty, but that won't work on the rest of them."

"What do I care what the rest of them think?"

"You're so naive. The more the court loves you, the harder it will be for the princess to cast you aside."

"Katya would never 'cast me aside.'" When her mother only snorted, Starbride stood. "I'm serious, Mother. And being liked by the court wouldn't help. Look at Baroness Castelle."

"I have. She's a good-looking woman. If she puts her mind to having the princess back…"

"She could put her mind to it all day long and still wouldn't have her way." Starbride stalked over to the table and poured herself a glass of wine.

"You should call Dawnmother to do that."

Starbride only frowned. Arguing with her mother was like fighting with bricks. Still, she couldn't keep a small jibe inside. "Putting oneself above others begins the surest path to evil deeds."

"Horsestrong wasn't royalty. If these Farradains think I can't play their games, they're wrong. They think their royalty is above them, so as royalty, we shall be above them."

"We?"

Her mother didn't comment. "Countess Nadia seems fond of you."

"You've spoken to her?"

Her mother gave her a look, as if to say she'd spoken to everyone. "A countess is good, but you've been neglecting these duchesses and dukes and earls and so on." Before Starbride could object, her mother said, "Don't worry, you can't hurry after them now. That would seem too eager. I'm splitting them into groups for you, those you should make casual contact with and those whose parties and such you should make an appearance at." She tapped her pencil against her lips. "Maybe you should host a party yourself, invite the princess…or not. Then all the focus would be on you."

Starbride gripped her wine glass and wondered if she could squeeze it hard enough to break it. "I've got my own life, Mother."

"How? You spend all your time with the princess or the royal family or their aides. Your little law project is all sorted out since your friends are coming to the Halls of Law in a few weeks."

"Little law project," Starbride said, nearly a growl.

"You've already got the princess's affection, so why are you wasting so much time—"

Starbride slammed her glass on the table. A shard of it streaked along the varnished surface. She couldn't tell her mother about the Order, but maybe she could let something else slip.

"Well," her mother said, "if you're going to be childish—"

"I'm an *adsnazi*. A pyradisté."

She didn't hear so much as feel her mother rise and cross the floor to stand behind her. "You're…How?" As if Starbride could unravel why she had the gift when her parents did not. "This is your father's fault!"

"In Farraday, pyradistés don't have to leave town and congregate in the hills. Katya's fixed it so I can be trained by the king's pyradisté, but still, not many at court know, and even if they did, it's an honor here."

Her mother's eyes resumed their calculated gleam. "Oh. We could announce it at the party, maybe. Then they'd see you as powerful both politically and in your own right."

"Mother," Starbride said with a sigh.

"I don't know much about pyramids, but I've heard they can be used to convince—"

"That's not only unethical, it's illegal."

Her mother dropped it, though Starbride didn't think it was the ethical part of the quandary that convinced her.

"Plan your party," Starbride said with a sigh. She thought of everything the Order had yet to do. Now she knew why Katya resented parties so much. They took up so much time and did so very little.

Her mother's knowing smile dropped. "My Star," she said softly, "why so sad?"

"There're some family issues I'm not looking forward to."

"I've heard the prince has become a bit of a churl after all that's happened. Don't let him upset you too much. Just smile, nod, and inside curse him as a diseased pig."

Starbride burst out laughing, remembering her mother's indulgent smile when talking to some of the courtiers. She wondered how many might wake tomorrow as diseased pigs. Still, her mother had the right road but the wrong end, as Horsestrong said. Starbride didn't correct her, couldn't let her find out that the prince was not only a churl, but a coward as well. "I'll try."

"And I'll be busy with the servants planning your party. Maybe I'll throw a brunch." She cupped Starbride's cheeks. "Don't worry, my Star, it'll be an affair to be proud of."

Starbride smiled indulgently, but inside, she hoped the entire endeavor would fall apart.

❖

Starbride listened to the prattle at her mother's brunch and wished she could strangle someone, maybe all of them.

Someone made a joke, and Starbride made herself smile. "Would you like a scone, Princess Consort?" Baroness Jacintha Veronda asked.

"No, thank you, Baroness." Starbride smiled, but it was more for the remembrance of a similar tea party where everyone had hung on Baroness Jacintha's words instead of Starbride's. Then she'd found it tedious but amusing. Now she barely avoided pacing, understanding the pressure Katya felt. She needed to be up doing things, helping Katya. She could have been out searching the countryside for Reinholt. It didn't seem fair that both she and Katya were caught in the palace putting on brave faces and pretending that the Umbriels had everything under control.

She was truly royalty now, she supposed, or near enough; she only had to look around to confirm it. Some watched her with open simplicity, just hoping she'd notice them. These were the ones who couldn't play the game. Better players gave her shrewd glances or amused smiles as if making fun of the game with her.

Someone settled next to Starbride and displaced Baroness Jacintha. Starbride smiled at the newly arrived Countess Nadia.

"Careful," Countess Nadia said. "Your face is almost screaming, 'I'd rather be anywhere but here.'"

"I thought I was hiding it rather well."

"As the consort to the crown princess, you can be as bored as you want. At least, that was how things used to be. As they are, it might be wise to cultivate as many friends as you can."

Starbride wanted to ask why, but too many people in the room were paying too much attention; they leaned toward her and Countess Nadia as if trying to puzzle them out. When Starbride met their eyes, they smiled and offered slight bows. A cold feeling bloomed in Starbride's gut. If the nobles didn't like how the Umbriels dealt with the death of Appleton, they could cause problems, including stirring up their connections in town.

Starbride tried to drink her tea, but it felt like drinking lead. Would someone stir up the people enough to cause a civil war—where people would die by the thousands—just to roust the current monarch?

Countess Nadia's soft touch on her arm reminded her to school her face better. She couldn't afford to be naive. Of course these people would start a war. They wouldn't be the ones dying, and they could win a kingdom. "Who should I meet?"

"That's the crown princess consort I've come to know." Countess Nadia stood. Starbride followed her lead. "Let's start with the duchess holding court in the corner."

After an hour of half-promises and guarantees that the Umbriels knew what they were doing, the brunch ended. After all, it was still fall festival time, and the nobles had one commitment after another. Dawnmother hung behind Starbride and made note of different parties and gatherings, no doubt to help sort through them later with Starbride's mother.

After the last guest had left, Starbride's mother hugged her from the side. "You did beautifully. I was worried that you were going to spend the entire party on that settee."

"Thank Countess Nadia. I need to go see Katya, Mother."

"Something else has happened, hasn't it? Something besides the murder."

"I don't know what you mean."

"You and the princess are as busy as bees. The prince hasn't been seen in days. Everyone is in a tizzy."

Starbride sighed. Her mother could keep a secret as well as anyone, especially in the nest of intrigue that was the palace. "The prince has left." She dropped her voice even though they were nearly alone. "I don't know what the family is going to say publicly. They may say he's gone into seclusion or on a sabbatical."

"I expected more from the prince. No wonder the king took his position away." She leaned forward and kissed Starbride's forehead. "Go. See what you can do to help. I'll take care of the thank-you notes."

Starbride threw her arms around her mother, suddenly taking back every mean thought, though she knew she'd think them again later. "Thank you, Mama."

"Go on. I'll start with the countess. I think she and I will get along very well."

With their elder child gone, Starbride found the king and queen's apartment open to her again. Queen Catirin stood up from a settee and greeted Starbride with a smile and a nod. Starbride bowed in return.

"Katya is in her father's office," Queen Catirin said. "They should be back soon." She had the same frosty elegance as before, the same grace, but dark circles under her eyes spoke of too many late nights. If she were anyone else, Starbride would have asked that she unburden herself. But she'd come to know that Queen Catirin loved all things to be in their proper places, people included.

Starbride sat and kept herself from fidgeting. If Queen Catirin were any other noblewoman, small talk would be the expected route, but the queen was privy to the same secrets as Starbride; she knew the depth of every situation. Starbride had to offer her something real.

"I'm not sure about the…etiquette of what I'm about to say. I wanted you to know that I've seen many bad mothers in my lifetime, and you aren't one of them."

Queen Catirin smiled softly but lifted a hand toward the corner of her mouth as if to tuck the expression back where it belonged. "It may help you to know that the 'etiquette' for such a statement does not exist, but thank you."

Starbride nodded. "Any advice you have for me would be welcome."

"As far as your duties in the Order go, you'd be better advised by Katya or Crowe. As for being a consort, your life will change now that Katya is the acting crown princess. The court has a way of being both long- and short-termed in their thinking. They know Vierdrin will eventually replace Katya, but they also acknowledge that anything can happen. Some of them will want to groom you to be a queen at Katya's side."

Starbride's stomach went cold, as much from that possible scenario as from Queen Catirin's matter-of-fact tone. How could she speak so calmly of the elevation of her second child above her first and of the possibility of her grandchildren dying? Starbride tried to banish such uncharitable thoughts. Queen Catirin was only letting her words reflect the attitudes of the court.

"Well." Starbride fought not to stammer. "My mother is already helping me decide who to spend time with."

"Your mother works quickly."

Katya emerged from the office a few moments later, paler than Starbride liked to see, but resolved. When her eyes hit Starbride, her shoulders relaxed a little, as if the mere sight of Starbride took some of her tension away. She took a chair and held Starbride's hand as if it were an anchor.

"We've got most of the duties sorted," King Einrich said. "Katya will open the hunt tomorrow morning, and then she'll go straight to the redberry tasting and meet us." He touched Queen Catirin's knee as if to forestall the argument. "Everything will be tasted before we eat it, just like always. If we don't eat the redberries, it'll support the notion that we don't care about the populace."

Queen Catirin turned her face away, a sure sign that she disapproved. "Mother," Katya said, "that's not the bad news."

"We're going to hold Appleton's funeral before anything else," King Einrich said. "I met with Magistrate Anthony today. The man's a ruin. He and this Appleton fellow were closer than kin, from what I gather. Hopefully, our offer to give him a state funeral will help smooth things over."

Queen Catirin frowned, but Starbride didn't think she would argue. If keeping the peace meant that the Umbriels had to share some of their perks, so be it. "What else?"

"We're coming to the end of our grace period with Yanchasa," King Einrich said. "After Yanchasa reabsorbed Katya's Aspect at the last Waltz, we need to do it again."

Katya's grip tightened.

"We had planned to use the two of us, Reinholt and young Hugo," King Einrich said. "But now, well, I don't want to use Vierdrin or Bastian. If neither of them is mature enough to open the hunt, they're not mature enough to have the Aspect."

"Oh spirits," Queen Catirin said. "A child whose Fiend can present?"

"Children can get very angry," King Einrich said.

"Or they could just forget and take their necklaces off," Starbride added.

"Or take them off on purpose." Katya shrugged as they all stared at her. "I don't think of my niece or nephew as malicious, but I'm sure we can all remember a time in childhood when we wanted revenge. It's easy to not think of consequences when you're four."

"There is Brom," Starbride said.

"Right after we sent her away?" Queen Catirin asked.

"She'd do it if the only other option was her children," Katya said. "She betrayed Reinholt for them, after all."

"So she claimed." Queen Catirin sniffed. "I think she refused out of fear for herself, which means she'd never agree to help."

"There is one other option," King Einrich said. "My mother."

Starbride blinked several times. She almost blurted, "Your mother is alive?" but kept that contained.

"Your mother is nearly seventy, Einrich," Queen Catirin said. "The transformation is a strain."

"Those are the choices before us, dearest. I shall send for both of them. I'll have to offer Duke Robert something to get him to bring his daughter back, probably my permission for her to marry again, but if he won't allow her to come, or if once here, she fights us, it'll have to be Mother."

"Poor Grandmother," Katya said. "I'll bet she thought her Waltzing days were long behind her."

Chapter Fifteen: Katya

They held the funeral for Georgie Appleton the next morning, before any more festival events. Four white horses pulled the black cart through the streets, Appleton's coffin barely showing from the sea of flowers inside. The festive decorations in the square in front of the palace had been replaced with black bunting, and many sleeves sported black armbands.

Katya thought it'd be written in the history books as the most lavish funeral ever held for a magistrate's assistant. Even so, from her position on the dais, she noted angry faces in the crowd. In Magistrate Anthony's district, she'd heard that people wept as the coffin rolled by.

How many were wondering where Prince Reinholt was? Everyone in Marienne had heard about his demotion; the people had to be waiting for a show of public remorse. Da hadn't issued a statement about Reinholt's whereabouts; Katya had heard no end of rumors, the foremost being that the king had killed his own son for being an embarrassment.

Magistrate Anthony stood on the dais, too, a few steps down from the royals. His face had gone stark white under his mop of dark hair. His light gray eyes were red-rimmed and glassy. He had tear tracks on his cheeks that he wiped away. When Da offered his condolences, Magistrate Anthony said, "Thank you," in a soft voice, but he had a hardness in his eyes that said he wouldn't lightly forgive.

Magistrate Anthony turned and caught Katya staring. She offered a nod. He didn't return it, didn't even bow. When the coffin rolled to a stop in front of the dais, he clomped down the steps to join it.

Da started his speech. Katya barely heard it. The crowd shifted and fidgeted, but Katya focused on anyone who seemed intent on getting to the front.

Several men and women slipped through the crowd like serpents. They weren't looking at Da or anyone on the dais. They seemed focused on the coffin cart or Magistrate Anthony.

Katya caught Brutal's eye where he stood at the edge of the crowd. She flicked her eyes toward the moving figures, counting seven. He turned slowly. Tall enough to see over many of those behind him, he headed toward the nearest of the seven.

Starbride leaned up to her ear. "I see them."

Katya nearly chuckled. Of course she'd seen them. She didn't miss much.

The woman Brutal had been moving toward changed course and headed away from Magistrate Anthony. Brutal started toward the next closest suspect, never straying more than twenty feet from the coffin cart. If someone wanted to make the Umbriels' position more tenuous, they couldn't do better than murdering Magistrate Anthony and laying that crime at the Umbriels' door.

There was no way Brutal could stop all seven people, no way to tell who was really curious and who had darker thoughts on his or her mind. Da came to the end of his speech and announced that the Umbriels would donate gold to a cause both Magistrate Anthony and Appleton had championed: housing for the poor. As the crowd applauded politely, Katya touched the back of her father's arm and then walked down the steps. When she reached Magistrate Anthony, she patted him on the shoulder.

"Magistrate," Katya said loudly, "please accept my condolences on behalf of the crown."

Behind her, her father applauded; the nobles and courtiers behind him did the same, followed somewhat hesitantly by the crowd.

Magistrate Anthony frowned. They'd already done this. Still, he bowed. "Thank you, Crown Princess."

From the ground, Katya could see Brutal still on the move. She couldn't stand there and pat Anthony on the shoulder forever, though.

She turned to the crowd. "I hope you will all join me tonight in drinking a toast to Appleton's life. Let every barkeep know that each citizen of Marienne will receive one free beer this night, courtesy of their crown princess!"

The people paused, almost as if holding their breath before they roared in appreciation and clapped their fellows on the backs and shoulders as if she'd made them all rich.

"And the offer starts right now!"

They cried out again, and the front ranks bowed over and over. The crowd surged away and carried everyone with them. Brutal leapt to the front before the mob could catch him.

Magistrate Anthony's stunned stare turned suspicious. "They'd have mobbed you otherwise, Magistrate," Katya said. "You'd better go now, or you won't have any privacy."

Brutal breathed hard as if he'd just fought off a stampede of cattle as he moved to Katya's side.

"This is a friend of mine," Katya said. "He'll see that you and Mr. Appleton get to the cemetery in peace. You and those closest to you will have room to grieve."

"Thank you, Highness." He climbed up beside the driver on the coffin cart, and Brutal walked beside it as it drove away. Without the crowd to play on, Katya doubted any would-be assassins would be quick to attack.

She climbed up the dais and nodded at the nobles and courtiers who still applauded her. Her father bent down to her ear. "That'll put quite a dent in your coffers, my girl. Lucky for you, beer is cheap."

"It's a small price."

He smiled, and she wondered if he'd realized why she'd spent the money. She'd tell him later. He usually turned out to be wilier than she gave him credit for.

"Now we have a hunt to open, yes?" Starbride asked.

Katya nodded. The death of one commoner hadn't put the nobles or courtiers out of the festive spirit. She'd open an event for them, and by the time her family went out into the city later that day, hopefully, the crowd would be in a much better mood.

Chapter Sixteen: Starbride

At the opening of the hunt, Starbride watched Katya's brilliance; her voice rang out clear as a bell, her posture was the epitome of poise and grace, with just enough drollness mixed in to have the rich crowd eating out of her hand. The nobles and courtiers loved her, but most of them had done that before. The city would be the challenge.

The king and queen strolled through the grand marketplace of Marienne with Katya and Starbride half a step behind and Lord Vincent just beyond them with the youngest royals in tow. They sampled redberry cakes and pastries, all of which had been approved beforehand. Most people smiled at the royals, bowed and scraped and beamed under their praise. No doubt the free drinks helped.

Starbride kept an eye on the crowd. She didn't know if it was her imagination or not, but she thought she saw more furrowed brows, more frowns than before. Some clearly weren't won over by free beer. Starbride tried to shake the suspicious feeling off and told herself that these were just normal people with a range of expressions. Still, she stuck close to Katya, grateful that Hugo trailed them, along with a few privileged nobles. Behind them was an even smaller sampling of courtiers, including Starbride's mother.

In the back, Starbride reminded herself. Her mother was stuck at the back, out of earshot. The thought made her smile.

Starbride caught a flash of very pale hair out of the corner of her eye; Maia leapt to her foremost thoughts. She kept herself from whipping around and tried to maintain a pleasant expression as she looked for the hair again. There, between two stalls, hair nearly as pale as Lord Vincent's, and underneath that, a face Starbride knew well.

"Maia," she breathed. The crowd moved, and Starbride lost her.

"What?" Katya said through her smile.

"I saw Maia."

Katya stiffened. "Go. Take Hugo."

Starbride fell back to where he stood. He smiled genially and bowed. She threaded her arm through his. "I need an escort that way, quick as can be believable."

Smart boy, he paused for half a heartbeat then rallied. "Come, Princess Consort, you must taste these pastries." He hurried her along, his entire posture screaming boyish enthusiasm. The idea of adventure still excited him, and she had to admit, it thrilled her as well, though experience had taught her caution. She wouldn't be caught in a burning apartment, for a start.

While pretending to eat a pastry, Starbride turned full circle and caught that pale flash of hair again. "What about over there?" She practically dragged Hugo in Maia's direction.

The procession left them behind. The crowd eyed them curiously as they came near the edge of the marketplace, toward a decidedly dark alley. Starbride nearly swore. Why did it always have to be alleys?

"Are we chasing someone?" Hugo said. "We dare not go in there after them."

Starbride nearly stomped her foot. She agreed with him, but Darkstrong take her, Maia was getting away. And Hugo was armed. *And* it was at least open and not inside a building. "I saw your sister."

He leaned ahead as if his own desire to find Maia pulled him forward. Starbride looked over her shoulder and searched for Brutal, just one more ally to come with them.

"There she is!" Hugo lunged forward, but she wasn't about to let him go without her.

She grabbed his wrist and dipped into her dress pocket for a flash bomb. "This is undoubtedly a trap."

"I know." He drew his rapier.

"Be careful." Appleton's dead body flashed in her mind. "Accidents…happen."

She knew it sounded lame, but she had to say something, had to warn him from stabbing the first person who stumbled from a doorway. If Hugo killed a member of the populace so soon after Appleton, King Einrich would have to give them his head on a platter.

"Where in Darkstrong's name are you going?" a voice called from behind them.

Starbride whipped around, obeying that voice before she'd even registered who it was. Her mother stood behind them, fists on her hips.

"It's bad enough that our servants couldn't be part of this procession, and now you're leaving it, too?" Her mother glanced at Hugo and then at the point where Starbride touched his arm. "What are you doing? Who is this person?"

"Mother," Starbride said with forced cheerfulness, "this is Lord Hugo Sandy. Lord Hugo, my mother Brightstriving."

Even as Hugo bowed, her mother scowled further. "Only a lord," she muttered.

"We thought we saw someone we know."

"Someone you know? Going away from the procession? Down an alley?"

Starbride's smile turned to stone, but she kept it in place. "Yep." She tried a laugh, but it came out strangled. She could just start down the alley, but her mother would only follow, nagging all the while. "She's…a friend who's in a bit of trouble, so we thought we'd follow her to see if we might help." She gotten better at lying since being in Farraday, but this was her *mother*, who'd always been able to see through any lie she could conjure.

"She's carrying the illegitimate child of a married duke," Hugo said. "I'm sure we can depend on your mother's discretion, Miss Starbride."

"Of…of course," her mother said.

"The duke asked me to negotiate a price to keep the woman quiet," Hugo said. "And since the Umbriels need a representative…"

"Everyone would notice if one of *them* broke the procession, but my daughter…" She put on a smug, calculated smile. "I'll wait here, just in case someone tries to disturb you."

Hugo led the way down the alley. At least her mother hadn't wondered why he was armed. She probably assumed that was only natural, just in case the scheming pregnant woman became violent.

"How did you think of that so quickly?" Starbride asked.

"I've been working on it since we first left the procession. I want to help you and the crown princess, Miss Starbride. I always knew deception would play a part. When is it not a part of living at court?"

"True enough."

They turned a corner and pulled up short at the sight of the brick wall, a dead end. A green cloak lay in a heap off to the side, no sign of its wearer.

Hugo and Starbride spun around. No one stood behind them. Starbride stared at the surrounding walls. The palace was riddled with secret passageways. What if some of the buildings in Marienne were the same?

She ignored the cloak. If anything were trapped, it would be. She felt around the damp bricks and glanced up at three windows that looked down on the alley. She didn't know if even Pennynail could make the climb, certainly not before she and Hugo had rounded the corner.

"What are you looking for?" Hugo asked.

"A way out." She looked at the cobbles for flaked mortar or some other indication that a section of wall had moved.

Hugo bent toward the swath of fabric. Starbride grabbed his arm. "There are trap pyramids," she said.

"Can you disarm them?"

"I only have my flash bomb and a light pyramid."

He straightened slowly. Starbride followed him around the corner where he picked up a piece of broken brick and lobbed it at the cloak before she could stop him.

Starbride hauled backward on his coat. He stumbled into her, his wide eyes inches from hers before he staggered back, his cheeks blazing.

"Terribly sorry," he mumbled as if he'd made the choice to run into her. "Nothing happened." He gestured around the corner, but his face blazed as if he was speaking to someone who'd seen them so close together.

"If that cloak had been trapped, it could have blown your head off!"

"I'm…I'm sorry."

Starbride cast another glance at the high windows and wondered what it would take for someone to make that climb.

Before she could take a step into the dead end again, Pennynail dropped from one of the rooftops, caught a window to slow his fall, and then dropped noiselessly to the ground. Hugo stepped deftly around Starbride, his rapier on guard.

Starbride grabbed Hugo's arm. "We saw—"

Pennynail held up a hand and then pointed back the way they'd come. When they didn't move, Pennynail made a shooing motion. Starbride pressed her lips together, not liking being dismissed even before she was royalty.

"Perhaps he's right." Hugo slid his rapier home. "We're not dressed for a tour of the city's alleys."

Pennynail clapped him on the shoulder, but then stared at Starbride. She could almost see through the manic grin to Freddie's disapproval. "All right, but be careful."

He tugged at the buckles near his shoulders as if asking her who she thought she was talking to. "Let's get back," Starbride said. Hugo's pinched expression mirrored hers, but there was nothing else to do but collect her mother and rejoin the procession.

Chapter Seventeen: Katya

Katya took Starbride's report as they strolled. They had to speak in hurried, whispered voices when Katya wanted to pace and think and yell. She smiled at the populace and ate thrice-bedamned pie when she wanted to run after her cousin and comb the alleys until every square inch had been searched. Barring that, she wanted to tear her hair out and scream at Fah and Fey for cursing her luck at every turn.

A baker bowed to Katya. "Fresh just this instant, Highness."

Katya smiled and hoped to convey tolerant boredom. She gave half the cake to Starbride, took a bite, and nodded appreciatively. Her tongue was already coated with redberries, but even if she had been able to taste it, she wouldn't have paid much attention. How many times had she been forced to eat cake instead of doing her job? But, her inner voice reminded her, the crown princess would have to eat more cakes than the princess ever did. That meant sending Starbride on more missions, like exploring unknown, trap-filled alleys. Katya gritted her teeth, kept up her smile, and cursed Reinholt again.

Behind her and Starbride, young Vierdrin and Bastian squealed over their dessert. Their tutors taught them to school their expressions, but they slipped constantly. They called to Vincent more than their nannies or family.

"Lord Vincent, may I have a cake?"

"Lord Vincent, look at the banners!"

"A talking bird! May we see it, Lord Vincent, may we, please?"

Vierdrin did most of the talking, with Bastian echoing her like the parrot they were so fond of.

Lord Vincent knelt at their sides, his silver head bent over their blond ones as he explained about people, redberries, or decorations.

His expression stayed soft except when he had to rein them in; then he spoke to them evenly but sternly. Even though they were his betters, they were still children. Katya thanked every spirit that he knew the difference. She only wished he'd seen it in Reinholt.

To Katya's knowledge, neither child had asked about their father. There'd been some early crying for their mother, but that had mostly dried up. Now they clung to Lord Vincent's side.

"It's like Vincent's their father," Katya whispered in Starbride's ear.

"I noticed. It almost makes me like him a little, but I can still feel his disapproval."

"If you ordered him to flog himself, he would."

"An interesting idea." She glanced over her shoulder. "But the children would never forgive me."

Bastian caught her glance and held out one little arm. "Starbride!"

Vincent whispered in the child's ear. Bastian blinked for half a moment before he grinned again. "Crown Princess Consort Starbride," he said, stumbling over the words.

Starbride frowned, and Katya thought she might sigh at the protocol, but she managed not to. "I've been summoned." When she fell back to walk hand-in-hand with Bastian, Katya went with her. "Yes, young prince?"

Bastian giggled. When Vierdrin dashed to the side, Vincent stepped after her, pulling Bastian—and the rest of them—that way as well.

Vincent bowed as best he could while holding on to two children. "My apologies, Highnesses."

"Quite all right," Starbride said. "If you like, we could take charge of one, Lord Vincent."

His face tightened. He only left the children's sides when they were secure in the palace, but what Starbride had said was almost a request, and she outranked him. Katya could nearly see his mind racing.

"Oh," Katya said with a drawl, "we wouldn't want to deprive Lord Vincent of his duty."

"I thank your Highness."

Starbride gave Katya an impish look, and soon enough, Bastian lost interest in her. By the time the royal party circled back to the palace, Bastian had fallen asleep on Vincent's shoulder. He gave the boy to a nanny, and that was only so he could carry a tired Vierdrin. Still, he commanded the nanny to walk at his side, not to outpace him or fall behind.

As soon as she saw her family settled, Katya summoned the Order to her summer apartment, all except Pennynail, who still hadn't returned. They gathered around the table in Katya's summer sitting room, all of the other furniture still draped with white cloths for the winter. Averie must have been sneaking in there occasionally to dust.

"I've seen Maia," Starbride blurted when they were all seated.

"When?" Brutal asked.

"Where?" Crowe followed, nearly at the same moment.

Katya held her tongue as Starbride explained. Despite Starbride's certainty, Katya doubted if Maia had ever been there. It could have been a trick of the light or a disguise; Katya almost hoped it was. If it wasn't, if she really had seen Maia, that meant Maia had run away from her on purpose and didn't want to be found. It meant Katya had to consider that Maia was a willing part of the trap that had nearly burned Katya alive.

"Why did she run?" Brutal asked softly.

Katya shook her head. "Maybe we'll know more after Pennynail gets back."

"We have to consider that she's fallen under Roland's sway," Crowe said. "That he's either warped her mind by pyramid or found a way to release her Fiend without Waltzing."

"He never released Hugo's," Starbride said. "Perhaps that task is beyond even him."

"Why release it at all?" Katya rubbed her chin as she thought aloud. "Along with the power comes the ego, the evil ambition; that's what happened to Roland. Why would he risk Maia's Fiend rebelling against him?"

Crowe cleared his throat. When Katya glanced at him, he stared pointedly at Brutal. "The ritual that shares Yanchasa's essence between two people is easier if the person carrying the essence already has the Aspect."

Brutal snorted. "That's a very roundabout way of saying Roland would want her Fiend to be able to present before he forced her to have sex and pass the Fiend to her partner."

Starbride put a hand over her mouth, her eyes horrified.

"Enough," Katya said. "Brutal, did anything happen with Magistrate Anthony?"

"He didn't say a word the entire way to the cemetery, and no one tried anything."

Katya rubbed her temples and fought the urge to sink lower in her chair. "For now, we have to forget about Maia. We can't just follow her anymore. We need to focus on the populace of Marienne and anything Anthony gets up to."

Everyone nodded but stared at the table, lost in their own thoughts. "Check your contacts," Katya said. "And let me know what you find." As Crowe and Brutal shuffled out, Katya caught Starbride's arm.

The secret passage had just clicked shut when Starbride said, "After what happened in the Warrens, you are *not* going to lecture me about going down that alley."

Katya bit off those very words.

"I can't stand the thought that Roland might be using his own daughter in a ritual."

"What could you do against Roland if you found him?" Katya asked. "Hugo was completely under his sway once. Roland can mesmerize him with a pyramid."

Starbride tossed her hair over one shoulder. "He can't do that to me."

"He wouldn't have to. He could have Hugo stick his blade in your gullet."

"And what would you have done? You're the one that commanded me to go, remember?"

"Not into some alley."

"Oh yes, I remember that distinctly. 'Go,' you said, and then you added, 'unless it leads you somewhere dangerous.'"

"You know the rules. No unnecessary risks."

"No unnecessary risks for *you*."

"What does that mean? The rest of you aren't expendable. Or did you mean now that I'm the crown princess?"

Starbride took a deep breath and closed her eyes. Even angry, she was beautiful. Katya tried to banish the thought, to hold on to her own anger. She knew she didn't have the right to lecture after what she'd done in the Warrens, but she couldn't hold in her fear.

"I know you don't like to hear it," Starbride said, "but your life is more important than ours."

"And when I have to tell your mother that you died because of me, whose life do you think she'll find more important?" A vision rose in Katya's mind: Starbride dead in an alley, the cobblestones slick with blood. Katya's heart leapt into her mouth. She dropped to a crouch and buried her face in Starbride's knees. "You're every bit as important as I am, Star."

Starbride lifted Katya's chin until they could look eye-to-eye. "Horseshit."

Katya breathed a laugh. "I love you more than life."

"I love you too, but right now you're next in line for the throne of the most powerful kingdom in existence, however temporary the position would be. You have to hold it for your niece. I'm the one that has to go into dangerous alleys."

"Not without Brutal and Pennynail. I wouldn't mind having Averie with you as well."

"And Hugo? He knows all the secrets, Katya, and he's good with a blade."

Katya realized with a start that the idea of Hugo in the Order didn't make her wary anymore, not after the times he'd proven himself. "We'll have to ease him into it."

"We've already started."

Katya pulled Starbride up and into her arms. "I know."

"No more lectures?"

"But I'm so good at lectures."

"And I'm good at running off, it seems. I promised Crowe I would train with him this afternoon." Before Katya could argue, Starbride said, "The better I get at wielding pyramids, the more you'll know I'm safe."

Katya had to nod. "I just wish there weren't so many reasons for you to get better."

"Just think how boring life would be if court was all it was."

Even with all the danger, it was true. If all Katya had to do for Farraday was eat cake, she'd have flung herself from the highest tower ages ago.

Chapter Eighteen: Starbride

As Starbride trained in Crowe's office, she had to put anger *and* affection out of her mind. Either would impede her concentration. It was a shame Katya had to be so lovable and aggravating at the same time.

Starbride only wished some of the serenity she felt while practicing could carry into the rest of her day. Thankfully, when she and Crowe took a break, Pennynail walked in before Crowe could ask about her scowl.

He removed his mask, becoming Freddie again. "Well, I think you and Hugo were the target of a clever misdirection."

"But it was a dead end. Where could she have gone?"

"One the many doors leading off the alley before the dead end, or if she had a rope waiting, she could have climbed to one of the windows. The cloak was probably to distract you."

"My lack of experience with skulking rises again."

"Well," Freddie said, "tonight will give us another chance if you're interested."

"Fingers and toes?" Starbride shuddered. That had been what they called climbing work, scaling buildings to reach their destination.

Crowe chuckled. "I never cared for that either."

"No, tonight we hang around places rich boys and girls should never enter." Freddie leaned forward slightly. "Dare I say it?"

"You're talking of…dens of ill repute," Starbride said.

"Funny, they never think to call them that."

Starbride couldn't contain a clench of her fists at the idea of wantonly doing something her mother would disapprove of. Before she could respond, though, Crowe cleared his throat. "Katya won't like this."

A flash of irritation wandered through Starbride. If it had been Katya going, she was certain no one would have said, "Starbride won't like this."

"I can take care of myself, and I'm not going alone." She gestured at Freddie.

Freddie nodded. "Brutal's going to be out and about tonight, too, just not with us. If anything happens, we'll run right for him." He plucked the sleeve of Starbride's brocaded red shirt. "You'll have to wear something less noticeable, not this, and not that black leather suit."

"Black leather suit?" Crowe asked.

Starbride fought down a blush. "Since I can't completely disguise my heritage, how about I not disguise it at all?"

Freddie frowned, but Crowe chuckled. "A servant who slipped her mistress's grasp? An Allusian bond servant would never do that."

"Ah, but most Farradains don't know that. I can complain about my imaginary mistress to my heart's content."

Crowe nodded approvingly. "It just might work."

"There is one thing," Starbride said. "I promised Dawnmother that she could come with me if I'm sneaking around the city."

Freddie and Crowe glanced at each other.

"She'll be invaluable," Starbride said. "She knows about servants from the palace, what to say and do. You don't have to worry about her knowing who you are, Freddie. She knows even less about the history of crime in Farraday than I do. You can trust her."

"She wouldn't betray her bond," Crowe said. "It's not something Allusian servants are capable of."

After a long sigh, Freddie nodded. "Don't tell her why I should stay hidden, just that I should."

"If you wish," Starbride said.

As she left Crowe's office, Starbride's mind raced. She'd promised never to leave Katya in the dark, and they'd already had one conversation about dangerous missions that day. No one really wanted another.

There was one person whose advice she could ask. Dawnmother pursed her lips at the dilemma. "What does the princess do when she wants to avoid a fight with you?"

"I don't—"

Dawnmother held up a sheet of paper and a pencil, a slow smile on her face.

"I can't write Katya a note telling her I'm in the less savory parts of town checking to see how upset everyone is over Appleton's death."

"Keep it vague. That's what she does."

Would it be too wicked? Starbride grabbed the pencil and scrawled a few sentences about talking to the populace about what had happened, just like Katya had asked them all to do that afternoon. She noted that she was taking plenty of help. Hopefully, Katya would think she was frequenting a better class of tavern. Not an outright lie, but close enough. Starbride had seen the value of lies; she couldn't deny that.

"I never thought I'd be lying to her, though." The idea left her emptier than she thought. She scrawled a few more declarations of love and promises to avoid danger.

"It's a note, not a treaty," Dawnmother said.

Starbride glared, closed the note, and had Dawnmother send it to Averie. When Dawnmother returned, Starbride donned the simplest of her outfits and one of Dawnmother's cloaks.

Then they were out the door, no time for looking back.

"Shoulders down," Dawnmother whispered as they walked one of the seedier streets in Marienne. "Defeated, like your mistress beats you."

"How do you know so much about defeated looking servants?"

"They talk, I listen. How do you think your mother knows so much about court after such a short time? Rainhopeful has ears like a dog's and the eyes of a hawk."

Starbride blinked, lost in the idea that her mother's unobtrusive servant might be a master spy. "I'll keep that in mind."

"We're not going really low." Freddie had darkened his red hair and clothes with soot, a chimney sweep just off work. It brought out the green in his eyes. "It'll be servants and tradesman, the kind of people we're supposed to be. No thugs. Well, not many."

He led them up a set of rickety stairs connected to an equally rickety looking building, though it was a fortress compared to the structures in Dockland. Unlike most of the bars or taverns Starbride had seen, the front door was on the second floor. A handful of people lingered on the balcony near the door, watching the street.

Starbride nudged Freddie. "What are they doing?"

"They're watching for the money, employers coming to fetch people out of the bar. They give a signal, and everyone piles out the back while the money climbs up the front."

"The money," Dawnmother said. "That's what happens when you buy loyalty; you become *the money*, someone to be dodged."

"Don't tell me that un-bonded workers are so noble in Allusia," Freddie said.

Starbride shrugged. "Apparently, they're just more secretive about it."

Music poured out the door, beneath the sign of a horse and cart. Freddie passed a coin to the doorman, who let them straight in. Starbride had expected dark corners and lurking figures. This crowd was more raucous than those in the Gold Bar, but it looked livelier and friendlier. Most of the clothing was simple, though Starbride did spot some livery, unbuttoned at the collar, and the occupants were all drinking and laughing with friends. A small group played in the corner, two guitars, and two simple drums held between the knees. Near them, a small knot of people danced enthusiastically but without the polish seen in the palace.

The air of the place made Starbride relax a fraction. She bumped into a woman in a flour-stained blouse who smiled at her. "Long day, hon?"

Starbride nodded without hesitation. It had been a long day. It'd been a long couple of months.

The flour-stained woman pointed toward the bar in the back. "Get a few down ya, and whatever it is won't seem so bad."

Suddenly, the idea of a drink sounded like the most wonderful thing in the world. Starbride and Dawnmother followed Freddie to the bar, and soon, they all had a mug of beer to drink.

For the next few hours, they circulated, and Starbride heard about the worst masters and mistresses and bosses. She'd learn one story and then repeat it later when someone asked her about her job. Usually, she didn't have to claim the story as her own, simply deflecting the question of what she did all day. Dawnmother filled in the gaps with stories she'd heard from Averie or other palace servants. Whenever Starbride saw someone in actual palace livery, she turned the other way.

She soon discovered not to bother. With her simple hairstyle and outfit, no one saw the crown princess consort. The right clothing put people at ease. They knew where they were with an unadorned tunic and braid. They couldn't see a noblewoman in anything but silks and velvets. Starbride snorted to herself. Only a person who didn't *think* of herself as a noblewoman could pull off such a disguise. Katya knew how to think below her station. Starbride *was* lower than that station, at least by birth. She bet that if Hugo or Lord Vincent were put in homespun, they wouldn't look like farmers; they'd look like uncomfortable nobles in plain clothes.

When the bar crowd was well saturated with alcohol, Starbride found out what they really thought of the royals. To most, the Umbriels were creatures as far beyond normal people as the stars in the sky, but they didn't like Appleton's murder. More than once, she heard grumbling that it signaled a return to the old days when your boss was in charge of more than just your job; he had your life, too, could have you whipped instead of fired, or worse, didn't bother to fire you because he owned you.

Starbride, Freddie, and Dawnmother tried their best to put these notions off. They said that Prince Reinholt had been the problem, but he was gone now, thrown out by the king. Starbride had no problem putting the blame on Reinholt's shoulders, but the tactic didn't always help. Many muttered that all royals were the same. Katya's carefully established rake persona didn't help. Some wondered how she could be any better than Reinholt when all she cared about was wenching and hunting.

"But those days are over, surely," Starbride said. "Now that Princess Katyarianna has a consort."

The drunks she spoke to winked and leered at one another. "We'll see if the Allusian woman can keep the princess's trousers on," one said. He peered closely at her. "You're Allusian, too! What magic did the consort use to make Princess Katyarianna keep her hands to herself?"

"I would imagine," Dawnmother said sweetly, "that the consort simply warned the princess that should her eyes or hands roam, they would be cut off."

The drunks roared in laugher. Starbride managed a smile even as her stomach turned over.

Freddie sidled up to Starbride's side. He had to lean close before she could hear his raspy voice over the crowd and the band. "I think we've found out all we can, and the crowd's getting too drunk to really tell us anything."

"This is not a den of ill repute," Starbride said. "There's not any iniquity going on at all."

"Sorry, I get all those words mixed up. No formal education, don'tcha know."

"Don't give me that," Starbride said as he hustled her across the floor. "You gave me a soft job on purpose."

"Would you rather go down the street where good-looking young men and women take their clothes off for coin?"

"No!"

"Yes," Dawnmother said.

Starbride glanced over her shoulder. "You've had too much beer."

Freddie tightened his grasp on her arm. She tried to shake him off, feeling more than a little rebellious. Maybe she shouldn't have had that third beer either.

"Listen," Freddie said. "You..." He glanced over her shoulder. "Oh shit."

Brutal was walking down the stairs into the bar. His eyes fell on her as she stared at him. He frowned and took a few more steps down. When he glanced at where Freddie grabbed her arm, his brow darkened.

Freddie tried to fade into the crowd. Brutal's eyes followed him. "I'll get in front of him," Dawnmother said.

When Brutal reached them, he pointed in Freddie's direction. "What did he want? That man?"

"Who knows?" Dawnmother said. "He was drunk. I was just about to tell him to go away when you came in."

Starbride nodded. "You scared him off. I'm ready to leave anyway."

Brutal's glance flicked to her for a moment. "You looked angry, and so did he. If he's a possible anarchist, we have to investigate him."

"He was just mad because she wouldn't go to the back room with him," Dawnmother said smoothly.

But that was the wrong thing to say to Brutal. He cracked his knuckles. "I'll set him straight. The impassioned make the best fighters."

"He's gone, Brutal," Starbride said. "Leave him be."

"He just glanced this way." Brutal started in Freddie's direction. Freddie moved toward the back door, but there were too many people in the way. She didn't know how much Brutal knew of Freddie Ballantine, or what it would take for Brutal to recognize him.

Starbride turned to a man next to her. He held a mug of beer and had a dopey smile on his face as he swayed to the music. "I'm very, very sorry," she said. The drunken man managed to both smile and frown in happy confusion. "After the first hit," she added, "just stay down."

She grabbed his free hand and wadded her shirtfront in his fist. He hung on confusedly. She took his beer hand and moved it toward his shoulder, as if he were reaching back to hit her.

The drunken man's face screwed up farther, but he didn't resist, even when she shouted, "Brutal!" and clutched the mug as if holding the drunk at bay.

Dawnmother caught Starbride's shirt and made sure the drunk hung on. Starbride had just enough time to shout, "Brutal!" again before a slight vibration in the floorboards heralded his charge.

Brutal caught the drunken man's wrists. Starbride and Dawnmother let go and staggered back. The crowd gave way in a circle, probably as much for Brutal's red robe as for the fight. Brutal flung the drunk as if he were a doll and sent him crashing to the ground beside the bar. Someone shouted for the door guards, and several muscular people waded in from the balcony.

When the guards moved toward Brutal, a voice out of the crowd cried, "No, he was just defending that woman there."

"We'll leave," Starbride shouted. Adrenaline pounded through her, and she used it to summon tears to her eyes. "We never wanted trouble."

"Get going, then."

Starbride caught Brutal's arm in an unarguable grip and brought him with her. Dawnmother followed just behind, no doubt ready to push if she had to.

When they were out in the night air, Brutal asked, "Are you all right? Did he hurt you?"

"No."

He tilted her face up toward a nearby lamp. "Then why are there tears in your eyes?"

"It's the stress," Starbride said, hating the lie when he only wanted to be kind.

"And the beer." Dawnmother took Starbride's arm and got them going again.

Brutal fell in behind them. "Next time, I'll just come in with you. Pennynail was probably a heartbeat away from making an appearance."

Starbride felt like falling down laughing. It must have been later than she thought. Or Dawnmother was right; it was the beer.

Chapter Nineteen: Katya

Brom's father returned her without comment. The agreement to let her marry again seemed more than enough incentive. Katya could believe it. If Brom had to stay at her father's estate forever, people would know she was still out of favor, but the fact that she could marry again suggested that she and Reinholt had just proved incompatible. With all of Reinholt's dishonors, the public might begin to think that any problems between him and his wife had been his fault from the start.

Brom entered the royal apartments with a bowed head. She hadn't changed from the simple clothing she'd worn when she'd left Marienne. She looked even paler, and her cheeks and eyes had sunk. If she was eating, it wasn't much.

After seeing just how difficult Reinholt could be, Katya allowed herself to feel some pity. What did Brom think would happen if Roland won the day? Did she see herself fleeing with her children and returning home to her old life? Roland had probably promised her that, and like a fool, she had grabbed on to it. Katya felt her pity evaporating.

Starbride's touch on her arm calmed her, even though she was still upset by the note a few nights before that had told her Starbride was venturing out again. When Katya had found out Starbride had relied almost solely on Dawnmother for protection, Katya had wanted to yell until the top of her head blew off.

To her credit, Starbride had taken the display of temper in stride, even cringing a bit as if she knew she deserved it. Toward the end of the argument, she'd shot back a little, citing what she'd found out, that the Umbriels now knew the populace hadn't forgiven them despite the free drinks. She'd also added that Pennynail had been watching, ready to aid them. In the face of everything that hadn't happened, Katya had to admit that Starbride had done a good job. When she recalled that Katya often used notes to escape confrontation, Katya even felt a bit cowed.

"Brom," Ma said, breaking Katya's reverie. "Thank you for coming back."

"Please let me see my children." Her voice was so small, Katya had to lean forward. "I'll do whatever you want, go wherever you want, if you let me see them once."

Katya's parents glanced at each other. They'd expected this, and really, for what they were asking, it was a fair trade. Da nodded to Katya.

Katya knocked on the door to her parents' private sitting room. After a heartbeat, Lord Vincent stepped out with the two children. Tears sprang to Brom's eyes, and she dropped to her knees. Vierdrin and Bastian ran for her. She threw her arms around them, though none of them spoke. Vincent stayed on the children's heels, and when Brom glanced up, there was only gratitude in her eyes. So, she'd seen how Vincent was with them. Katya had to wonder if she knew of the affection he'd provided Reinholt as well.

After a few moments, Brom stood. Vincent pulled the children back to his side. "Thank you," Brom whispered.

He nodded and carried the crying children back into the private sitting room.

"Thank you for not making them Waltz," Brom said.

Katya mashed her lips together to keep in a snarl. They'd have to Waltz someday. All that had happened and Brom still didn't understand. The Umbriels bore Yanchasa's Aspect so the populace wouldn't suffer Yanchasa's wrath. Brom still thought everyone could go to hell as long as her children weren't marred by the Aspect, even though they still carried Fiends. She'd never understand that if Yanchasa got loose, everyone, including her children, would die a horrible death.

Katya didn't have the energy to remind her. "Is everyone ready?" She didn't include Brom in her look.

Ma and Da nodded. Everyone else was already down in the cavern. Katya saw no reason to waste time. The sooner Brom Waltzed, the sooner she could recover, meet her father at the front of the palace, and be on her way.

Katya and Starbride led the way through the secret passages and down to the cavern beneath the palace, where the pyramid that contained Yanchasa waited.

Katya had dreaded her first visit below the palace. The cavern had reminded her of a toothy maw, all jagged rocks except for the large pyramid in the center, itself merely a crystal capstone for a huge, underground pyramid. No matter how her family had tried to reassure her, it had taken everything she had to let Crowe fit the shackles around her ankles, to lean forward and touch the smooth pyramid's sides.

Crowe stood near it now, next to Hugo. He smiled nervously, and Katya spoke the words Crowe had comforted her with. "You'll do fine," she said. "You won't even remember."

"But then I'll have to wear the necklace so my Aspect can't emerge when I'm very angry. Mr. Crowe explained it."

Katya almost laughed. Mr. Crowe sounded like something a child would name a pet bird. "Don't take it off and you'll be fine."

"I've never seen you very angry, Hugo," Starbride said.

He rubbed the back of his neck. "I guess I'm lucky to be pretty cheerful."

"Are you up for this?" Katya asked Crowe. She gestured at the large pyramid he held, though it was dwarfed by the enormous capstone.

"Whether I'm up to it or not, it has to be done. The essence you… returned to Yanchasa must be distributed to the others." He hefted his pyramid. "This is the best way." When Katya frowned, Crowe frowned back at her. "Starbride will be assisting me. Not to worry. This old relic has some skill left."

"You're the most skilled relic I know."

Katya left him to his preparations. Brutal and Pennynail had done a sweep of the cavern and all the surrounding passages, even though Crowe had put up defensive pyramids to repel Roland or his henchman, Darren. Still, as Crowe readied everyone, Katya took a quick walk around, just to make sure no enemies lurked in the shadows.

Brom wandered toward the central pyramid and then stepped to the side as if she couldn't bear to come too close to it. She'd have to soon enough. But she began to back away, as if she'd changed her mind about the Waltz. Katya stepped between her and the exit.

With a frown, Crowe set his pyramid down and stalked toward Brom. She gasped and turned. The fear on her face made the hairs on Katya's neck stand up. Brom touched her chest as if there was something hidden under her dress, but that couldn't be. She'd been searched.

"Get back!" Katya shouted. She drew her rapier.

Crowe grabbed Brom's arm. "What are you—"

Brom punched herself in the stomach. A sphere as black as night blossomed around her and Crowe. It engulfed them in darkness and a deep, throbbing pulse. Katya's ears throbbed at the sound.

Her hand went numb, and her rapier clattered to the ground. The sphere winked out of existence. A perfectly round divot in the rock, like a bowl in the cavern floor, was all that was left.

"What the deuce was that?" Da shouted. "What—"

"It was a sphere," Starbride said, "a disintegrating sphere. He…he never taught me that pyramid."

Katya's mouth worked for a moment. All she could do was point at the divot. Finally, she shouted, "How did she sneak that in here? How in the spirits' names did she sneak that in here?"

"She must have swallowed it," Starbride said. "Oh, Katya." Her voice grew heavy with tears.

Katya whipped her head back and forth. "No."

"It…it just sent him somewhere, right?" Hugo asked. "And we can get him back?"

"No," Starbride said, and the word echoed around them. "They're both dead."

Katya's legs went watery, and she sank to the floor. Cimerion Crowe, her mentor, her confidante, blinked from existence as if he never lived.

Da's face was ashen as he approached the divot. "Stay back," Ma whispered. "Is it safe?"

Starbride knelt at Katya's side, weeping, but she choked out the words. "It…only has…one charge."

"He's dead." Katya suddenly remembered being awakened by sobbing the night Roland had died. When she'd gone to bed, she'd had an uncle, and in the morning, she didn't. Now here was Crowe, gone in the blink of an eye. No farewells, no apologies from her for any wrong words, no shouts of warning, just gone.

A pit opened up in Katya's chest, anger and hurt and so many things. It was the place the Fiend had once lived. Now all that looked back was her. She grabbed Starbride's arm; her throat tightened, and tears flowed down her cheeks as if summoned by that empty place.

"Crowe," she said, but that was all she could get out. She sucked in a deep draught of air, but instead of letting out a sob, she held it until it choked her.

She heard more weeping, and all the voices she knew. They were a ball of grief, but she sensed someone missing, someone who'd suffer for this more than she ever could.

Pennynail was on his knees near the bowl, and his shoulders shook as if he sobbed inside his mask. Crowe was the only one among them who knew Pennynail's identity, maybe the only one in the world. He was all alone inside that mask with no one to report to, to confide in, like an orphan, like Maia.

Katya shrugged off the embraces. She stepped past everyone to fall at Pennynail's side. His masked face swung toward her, and she threw her arms around him and pressed him close, feeling his long arms go around her, too. The buckles of his leather outfit dug into her body, but she didn't care. The side of his mask was cool against her face. Inside it, she knew his skin had to be as hot and tight as hers. He was the only one who understood how much Crowe meant to her, to the Order.

Katya's mind calculated without her. Brom must have thought Crowe had sensed the pyramid she'd smuggled in. Perhaps she'd wanted to destroy the family or maybe the grand capstone. But when she thought she'd been caught, she'd sprung her trap. If she'd hit the capstone, would Yanchasa have escaped?

As she wept on Pennynail's shoulder, Katya said, "She didn't understand what she was doing, but Roland would have."

Pennynail pushed her back to stare at her. The mask's manic grin suddenly seemed the most obscene thing in the world, and Katya couldn't look at it. "Where else could she have gotten a pyramid that powerful?" Katya asked.

"Roland," Starbride said from behind her.

Katya's mind raced, and she wiped her cheeks. Hatred for her uncle welled up in her, taking the place of tears. She helped Pennynail stand. "Now we know he's close. And if he's close, we can reach him."

As one, they looked at the central pyramid. They still had a job to do whether they had Brom or not.

"My mother will be here in a few days," Da said quietly.

Katya glanced at him. He wiped tears away, as upset as Katya had seen him since Roland had died. It seemed everyone was thinking the same thing and trying to pull themselves together. Only Hugo really stood apart. He held Starbride's elbow, but his face was dry, unlike hers. Starbride hadn't known Crowe as long as the rest of them, but she was attached to him as her teacher, as her mentor. She'd have to get help from the academy now. She couldn't stop her training just because…Katya took a deep breath. Crowe wouldn't want her to stop.

As they climbed back up into the palace, no one mentioned Reinholt or how he'd feel about his wife's death. Maybe if he'd elected to stay with them, he'd have been given some peace. As for the children, they'd be told their mother had left the palace again. Maybe when they grew up, they could know the truth.

Chapter Twenty: Starbride

There were so many people to comfort; Starbride couldn't think about herself. Maybe the comforting would keep the grief away.

She leaned on Hugo's supporting arm. His sympathetic face said she had a shoulder to cry on should she wish, but there were people who needed it more, people who'd known Crowe all their lives: Katya or her parents.

Or Pennynail. When he peeled off from the group inside the secret passageways, Starbride whispered in Brutal's ear, "Tell Katya I'll catch up with her."

"You're not going outside, are you?" Brutal asked.

Starbride shook her head. "Crowe…" She took a deep breath and tried to push down tears. "There are some things he'd want taken care of…by someone…" She fumbled for the words, not wanting to lie.

"By another pyradisté, you mean."

"I'll catch up with Katya as soon as I can." She wanted to throw her arms around Katya while they both wept, but Katya had her parents and Brutal to look after. When the group had gone ahead, Starbride hurried after Pennynail and followed him to his tower.

He waited at the entrance to his room and nearly shut the door in her face. Starbride pushed it open, and when they were alone, he tore the mask off his head, revealing his red, swollen eyes.

"Get out of here."

"You let Katya hug you but not me?" Maybe if she let him think he offended her, he'd calm a bit.

He sank onto a worn ottoman, his mask dangling between his knees. "She wasn't hugging me; she was hugging Pennynail, Crowe's contact, not his…" His mouth quivered, and he dropped the mask to cover his face.

Starbride sat next to him, her arm around his shoulders and her brain making connections almost before she was aware of them. "Not his…son?"

Freddie sobbed and leaned into her embrace. Why else would Crowe keep a criminal so close to him? Why let an accused murderer into a position where he could hurt the royal family? What other relationship would have such trust?

"I'm so sorry, Freddie," Starbride whispered. "I know you may not understand this as a compliment, but he carried the honor of his caste."

Freddie barked a laugh through his tears. "It always thrilled him to hear you say that." He closed his eyes and rested his chin on his palms, elbows on his knees. "He was training you to replace him, but you can't be king's pyradisté, not yet."

"I have to graduate from the academy." Training with Crowe would have amounted to the same thing, but now she would have to go the traditional route. The royal family couldn't take a rogue pyradisté to their bosom.

"You're the pyradisté for the Order." He opened one eye. "And for the dirty jobs. We're going to have to work on some persona, some reason Katya or the king would have to send you on various errands, like…he…did. Brutal or I could bring in prisoners, but Crowe had contacts and informants that are lost to us now, though I can handle some of them."

Starbride had to laugh. "I'm the crown princess consort and the royal watchdog?"

"Your mother is helping with all the nobles she's getting to know. You might have to be the palace rat, building a fear base. If you see courtiers getting into trouble, they're liable to disappear the next day, that sort of thing. Not many of them will clamor for your attention after that happens."

"Horsestrong be praised," Starbride said before she could stop herself.

Freddie chuckled slightly. "People knew he did the king's business, my father. That was one of the reasons people stayed away from him. If the palace knows you're taking his place, they'll stay out of your way, giving you a little room to maneuver, but they'll also be watching the rest of the Order less and won't question it if you're sometimes spotted in the seedier parts of town."

"I feel a headache coming on." Starbride switched to another chair, one she could lean back in. "Everything here is so complicated." She told him about Brutal's determination to skulk with her.

"Sounds like something he'd do. I'm very grateful about your ruse the other night. If Brutal ever got a hold of me, he could crack me like a nut."

"And he wouldn't even know what he'd done."

"You and I can meet in private if we have to sneak out."

Starbride couldn't hold in a grimace. "I'm going to have to lie more, aren't I?"

"Da said people have to be protected from the truth." He choked up again.

Starbride swallowed several times. "I remember him saying something like that once, hinting that Katya doesn't know half the events that make the Order function."

"King Einrich knows. He and Crowe were close; he knew what we had to do, if we ever had to quietly dispose of someone. Sometimes, King Einrich even ordered it done. Your relationship with your one-day father-in-law is about to change."

Starbride nodded, though she promised herself she wouldn't keep everything from Katya, that she'd let her into it gradually. After all, if something happened to King Einrich, Katya could find herself queen regent before her niece was old enough to take the throne. "I'm going to tell her that I know who you are, Freddie."

"You can't! She'll recognize my name. She won't…let me help her anymore."

Starbride peered at him, not missing the pause and guessing it covered the words, "won't respect me," or "won't like me." She didn't comment on that. "I'm not going to tell her your name," she said, "just that I know what you look like and that your face is recognizable."

"It'll eat at her until she gets it out of you." He still didn't sit.

"She never got it out of Crowe."

"She wasn't having sex with Crowe."

Starbride barked a laugh. "That would have to be some evening to get me to call out *your* name." The statement sounded wrong to her as soon as she said it, and she had to look away, hoping to hide her blush.

"True enough. And Katya knows you're my father's successor. She had to suspect he'd tell you who I am."

"Yes." That was one way to keep Katya from asking. She could say, "Crowe didn't want you to know." Not fair to use a dead man, but she was going to have to embrace whatever tactics worked. "I have to go to her."

Freddie gestured at the door and turned away. Starbride wanted to say more but had no clue what. "When you get a chance," Freddie said, "look in the bottom right drawer of his desk. There's something he wanted you to have."

Starbride only nodded and hurried to Katya's apartment.

Katya sat on her bed and stared at the wall, no one else with her. Starbride folded her into an embrace and stroked her hair. "Why did they leave you alone?"

After only a few moments in Starbride's arms, Katya sat up. "I'm sick of crying. Where did you go?"

"To see Pennynail."

"To…see him?"

"Without the mask."

Katya's sad face gave way to amazement. "What does he look like? Who is he? Is he even a he?"

Starbride took a deep breath.

"Spirits above," Katya whispered, "you're not going to tell me, are you?"

Starbride tried to force out the excuse about Crowe not wanting it, but the words wouldn't come. "I can't, and you know why."

Katya paced up and down the room, her face dark and angry. Starbride let her fume and waited. Finally, Katya took a deep breath of her own. "I know you're right, but…"

Starbride stood and kneaded her shoulders. Katya's head drooped as she leaned into the contact.

"Spirits above, Star," Katya whispered. "What am I going to do?"

"We're going to handle it together. All of it. We're all behind you, Katya, and some of us are even far out to the side of you."

Katya chuckled softly. "In the shadows, taking care of the things I can't. I miss just being the head of the Order."

"Oh, just being the head of the Order, secret protectors of the royal family, your family." She kissed the back of Katya's neck. "Poor, lazy, run-of-the-mill princess. What did anyone see in her?"

"Now that I'm the crown princess, are you saying I'm worthy of love?"

"I'm secretly holding out for queen, but sure."

Katya kissed her long and deep. "I love you, Crown Princess Consort Meringue."

"And I you, Crown Princess Steppingstone."

Katya hugged her hard, making the wind rush from her lungs. "Promise me you won't die."

"I promise." Starbride shut her eyes and just held on. "And I know you promise the same." She chuckled slightly, trying to get some air back into the room. "I might get to meet Crowe's seedy contacts. Do you pity me or are you jealous?"

"Both. If I'm out hunting traitors, I'll pity you. If I'm meeting with the nobles' council, I'll invoke the spirits with my raging jealousy."

Starbride waited until Katya was calmer before she went to Crowe's office. She'd done everything she could not to think of what Freddie had said, not to speculate on what Crowe might have left her.

In his desk, she found a small stack of notes, each with a different name on the front in Crowe's tidy handwriting. She opened hers with trembling fingers.

"If you're looking at this," it read, "I guess I died."

Starbride barked a half-laugh, half-sob. She could almost see his wry smile.

"Don't blubber," the note read as if it could hear her. "And tell the rest of them not to be foolish as well. If I died suddenly, the last thing you all need is to be carrying on like a bunch of children who've had your sweets stolen.

"Now, no doubt you'll have a new teacher from the academy, Starbride, but I want to give you a leg up and tell you which books from my study to focus on. I also want to give you a few more pointers."

He fell into a list of what to read and where she could find it in his office. He also named all the pyramids he kept in his cabinet. "Until you learn how to make the more powerful pyramids, use mine sparingly. And be careful with fire pyramids. They won't just burn your target." She paid special attention to any instruction he gave on how to subdue the Aspect and any advice he had on Fiends.

"Please, give the others my notes. And if you ever see Maia again, please tell her how sorry I am. If there's any of Roland left in that body, tell him I'm sorry, too. I'm proud of you, Starbride. I love how happy you've made Katya. I should have said it when I was alive. Maybe I got to at the end, but I'll say it again: Welcome to our family."

Starbride set the note to the side, laid her head on the desk, and wept.

Chapter Twenty-one: Katya

Katya stood with her parents when they broke the news to Duke Robert that his daughter was dead. They didn't mention Crowe, saying only that Brom had taken her own life. They'd told everyone else that Crowe had died from a heart attack that same evening.

Duke Robert stared without blinking. "And there's not even…a body?"

"No," Da said, and Katya was surprised at the grief in his voice. Maybe it was his feelings for Crowe coming through, or maybe the loss of his grandchildren's mother really moved him. It didn't move Katya an inch.

"Forgive me for…" Duke Robert shook his head, didn't seem to know whether he was coming or going. "Forgive me," he said again. "I can't believe it."

"Do you know who might have given her the pyramid?" Da asked.

"No."

Da put an arm around his shoulders. Katya might not have sympathy for Brom, but Duke Robert's grief moved her a little. Da guided him to a chair. "I hate to ask this so soon, Robert. I know how hurt you must feel, but we need to know how your daughter came by the pyramid she used. Would you submit to a mind probe?"

"Why?"

"Whoever gave Brom the pyramid might have tampered with your memory. The crown princess consort could check for you."

Duke Robert blinked at them, staring for so long that Katya wondered if he'd been hypnotized. "I will do this," he said slowly, "in order to find the person who helped my daughter…end her life. I must insist on a different pyradisté than the crown princess consort, one more advanced in learning."

"Of course," Ma said before Katya could argue. "I'll have someone sent to your apartment before you leave."

Duke Robert nodded and stood. He seemed shaky, but he made it through the door unaided.

Da turned to Katya. "Tell Starbride not to be offended, my girl. He's of the old guard and wants someone more his age, that's all."

"She won't be offended," Katya said. Well, she might be a little, but Katya would tell her to ignore grief-stricken Duke Robert. Or maybe they should focus on him. Maybe it would give them something else to think about besides the empty office down the hall.

Katya had to catch herself as she walked toward Crowe's office or reminded herself to tell him something or ask his advice. Starbride had told her that she and Pennynail would take care of Crowe's property, his personal effects. Katya could almost picture them doing it together, though with the laughing Jack mask always covering Pennynail's face.

How long had Starbride known who he was? Since Crowe took her as his protégé? Or more recently? After a few deep breaths, Katya told herself not to worry. That was Crowe's line, his area. He'd had his reasons for keeping Katya in the dark. Now, Starbride had adopted those reasons. Katya tried to tell herself not to be bitter, but bitter felt so much more comfortable than grieving.

With no body, they couldn't even lay Crowe to rest, not that many of the people would have come to his funeral. The king's pyradisté hadn't been nobility. He'd had no real money to attract hangers-on, and his reputation as the king's sneak—as he'd always called himself—guaranteed that many were wary if not outright afraid of him. When Da held a candlelight vigil for Crowe outside of Marienne's largest knowledge chapterhouse, only the family and the Order attended. His notes brought them all some measure of comfort.

If all had gone as planned, the fall festival would have marked the end of Reinholt's visit to Marienne. He would have taken a long, winding route to his holding while stopping at the country houses of various nobles, and spreading goodwill through the villages. Katya couldn't do the same in his place. With Roland lurking about, she had to stay close to Marienne, and there was no way her father was letting Vierdrin and Bastian out of the city.

Life in the palace gave Katya a chance to get back to normal, lazing through the hallways like she used to, gathering information, sometimes with Hugo pretending to be a languorous noble at her side. She was glad of his company. Starbride spent most of her time practicing pyramid magic.

Katya had only taken one step toward the crown, but the effect was immediate; nobles and courtiers clamored for her attention like never before. With the children under the strict gaze of Lord Vincent, she was one of the few royals they could get to. The fact that she might one day be in charge of the kingdom, if only for a short while, made them far more desperate to speak to her than before. When she tired of them, she could usually slip away with Hugo covering her. She knew the palace better than any of them.

When she ducked away one afternoon, Lady Hilda waited for her around a corner. Katya pulled up short, nearly gaping at the display of stealth.

"Bored already with your new admirers, Highness?" Lady Hilda slinked forward, as provocative as ever, but Katya spotted a new wariness in her stance.

"Court can be tedious at times, Lady Hilda. One must be very careful with the company one keeps."

"I was just thinking that." She glided closer and toyed with the clinging bodice of her dress, as if she might pull the plunging neckline down farther. Katya had to resist taking a step back. She didn't need Lady Hilda for her court persona anymore so saw no reason to spend time with her.

Before Katya could think of a reason to leave, a voice hailed her. Castelle strode toward them at a fast clip. "I see you still prefer dark corners, Lady Hilda," Castelle said as she reached them. She offered Katya a deep bow. "Highness."

Lady Hilda curtsied. "Baroness Castelle. I haven't had the pleasure since you've been back."

Castelle gave her a lecherous wink. "Oh, believe me, the pleasure's all mine."

Lady Hilda smiled slightly, clearly appreciating the compliment.

"What can I do for you, Baroness?" Katya asked.

"No offense, Highness, but I was actually looking for the lady. There's a picnic I've been bribed into attending this afternoon, and I'd be blessed beyond belief to have the lovely Lady Hilda on my arm."

Lady Hilda blinked a few times. "It would be my honor, Baroness."

Castelle held out an arm. "With your permission, Highness?"

Katya waved them away, so grateful she could have thrown her arms around Castelle's neck. Before Castelle turned away, she winked as if to acknowledge the great favor she'd just done the crown.

The sight of Queen Mother Meredin sitting in her parents' sitting room stopped Katya cold. Her petite grandmother smiled and opened her arms. "Granddaughter."

Katya had such a clear memory of hurling herself into those arms as a child that she had to pause. Now she'd probably knock her grandmother over. She walked forward calmly and folded her in a hug. She felt fragile in Katya's arms, and her head fit under Katya's chin. Her voluminous gown probably weighed more than she did.

"No fanfare for your arrival?" Katya asked.

Her grandmother sank back onto the settee across from Ma. "I'm too old for fanfare. I came in an unmarked coach, as befits the queen mother." She patted the seat next to her. "I want you to know how proud I am of you, Katyarianna. You've followed beautifully in the footsteps of my son. I only wish I could say the same for your brother."

At the mention of Reinholt, Ma's face didn't show any slip of its serene mask, but Katya knew she had to be awash in feelings.

"I wish I could say the same for my youngest, too," her grandmother said.

Katya sucked in a breath, surprised by her sudden urge to defend her uncle. She'd convinced herself that the Fiend had taken control of him, that so little of Roland remained that he could be absolved from any blame.

Instead of responding, Katya blurted, "I'm sorry you had to come here like this, Grandmother." Not Grandma, not out loud anyway; that was reserved for Ma's less strict parents.

"The kingdom's needs, dear heart. I know you understand."

A moment later, Starbride came in, probably looking for Katya, or maybe Averie had told her the queen mother had arrived. She bowed deeply, and Katya's grandmother gave Starbride a gracious nod, clearly pleased with the level of respect. When Da entered, his mother embraced him with a happy smile. When asked if she wanted to see her great-grandchildren, though, she waved the idea away.

"Perhaps after the Waltz," she said.

"Don't you want to rest, Mother?" Da asked. "You must be tired."

"I'd rather get the unpleasantness out of the way."

Katya narrowed her eyes. She didn't doubt her grandmother, but she felt there was an undercurrent in the room that she wasn't quite picking up. A pall settled over her shoulders, both at her grandmother's haste and at the thought of going back into the cavern so soon.

But the Waltz had to be done, and her grandmother would suffer no delays. They sent for Hugo and trooped again to the cavern beneath the palace.

On the walk, Katya leaned close to Starbride's ear. "Crowe taught you what you need to know to do this?"

"We came up with it together, and I've got his large pyramid waiting by the central capstone. There isn't much for me to do, to tell the truth. The great pyramid does the work." She gripped Katya's hand. "Pennynail won't be joining us. Are you all right coming down here again?"

Katya gave her a tired smile. With all that had been happening, she hadn't allowed herself to think of returning to the site where Crowe had died. She braced herself for the bowl-shaped depression.

No one really spoke on the trek through the passageways. Any attempts at conversation died before they began. The Waltz had always been matter-of-fact to Katya; she'd known about it for as long as she could remember. It was just something that happened every five years, whether she was directly involved or not. Since Roland, it had taken on a sinister edge that she supposed she should have associated it with from the beginning. Starbride surely did. When Katya stepped into the toothy cavern, her heart quickened.

She looked for the bowl in the earth, the place where Crowe had died. She wanted to get her sorrow over and done with. Someone had laid flowers in the bottom of the bowl.

Katya stared at the blossoms, so bright against the browns and grays of the stone. "I thought Pennynail didn't want to come back here."

Starbride shrugged. "Maybe he just didn't want witnesses."

Katya faced the great capstone and squared her shoulders. The shackles coiled on the floor like snakes. Starbride approached them with measured steps, lending the Waltz more of a sense of ritual than Crowe ever bothered with. Slowly, she snapped the shackles around the ankles of Ma, Da, Katya's grandmother, and Hugo.

"Help me, Katya," Ma said. Katya nearly jumped. The silence had grown so heavy she feared she was deaf.

Katya helped her remove her bodice and pull down the back of her chemise, leaving her chest covered, but making room for her wings.

"It seems an almost silly consideration," Ma whispered.

Katya gripped her mother's arm, suddenly so nervous she couldn't speak.

"Dear heart, let me go, and stand back now."

Katya obeyed without question, feeling very young suddenly. When her grandmother held out a hand, Katya moved toward her, and her grandmother kissed her cheek before shooing her away.

Why did it feel like they were saying good-bye?

Starbride collected the pyramid necklaces. Katya's parents and grandmother leaned forward to touch the pyramid, and their human faces fell away.

Da's two horns curled back over his head. His eyes turned all blue, and a spike jutted from his chin. The wings of a crow sprouted from Ma's back in four places. Her eyes shone light blue, and fangs pressed down from her upper jaw against her lower lip.

Four horns sprouted from Katya's grandmother's head, two over the back, and two across the sides. Her face elongated, and fangs curled from her top and bottom lips. Her skin appeared smoother, younger, and Katya wondered if all Fiends were ageless, deathless. If they didn't manage to kill Roland for good, would he plague them forever?

Hugo blanched as Starbride approached him. Katya moved to stand at his back, her courage growing when someone needed her. "You might want to take off your shirt and coat," she said in his ear. He nodded and obeyed, his eyes fixed on the Aspects of the other three.

Starbride patted Hugo's bare shoulder and whispered something to him. He smiled, but the look didn't erase the pinched worry from his face. He rubbed his hands together once before he leaned forward and touched the great capstone's side.

His eyes were the first to turn, becoming wholly light blue without white, or pupil. A spike jutted from his chin and two crow's wings sprouted from his back. Fangs from his upper jaw plunged down well past his chin, forcing his lips into a snarl. Katya tried to combine all the traits of each Aspect, trying to comprehend what Yanchasa actually looked like, but she knew her former Fiendish face had sported different traits than these, and Roland and Reinholt had still more.

Katya took a deep breath and tried to banish the feeling that she was the reason her grandmother had to come, the reason Brom had murdered Crowe. If she'd held on to her Fiend, she could have prevented both incidents.

Crowe would have told her that was nonsense. She stood to the side and watched both the pyramid and the entrance to the cavern.

Starbride stood back from the four Fiends and picked up Crowe's large pyramid. Her eyes went half-lidded as she focused. The capstone began to glow, and each of the Fiends groaned, a noise that made Katya's stomach churn, as if she might void her breakfast. The glow from the capstone spread to each Fiend like creeping fungus until it engulfed them. Katya couldn't remember anything from her own Waltz except the exhaustion.

When the glow began to recede, Katya squinted into it. Something was wrong. Only three forms still stood. She stepped closer, but paused, not wanting to get drawn into the magic, especially now that she had no Aspect to protect her. When she saw her grandmother sagging toward the ground, held up only by contact with the pyramid, she rushed forward. The glow subsided, and the Fiends collapsed onto their backs, slipping away from the pyramid's sides. Her grandmother slid forward, threatening to smack face-first into the ground.

Katya grabbed her and turned her over. "Star! Brutal!" Her Aspect had withdrawn, and like the other unconscious royals, she had bloody streaks across her face, but her chest didn't rise and fall as theirs did.

Starbride unfastened her shackles while Brutal laid her flat on the floor. He peered under her eyelids and put his ear to her mouth. "She isn't breathing."

Katya's heart leapt into her throat. "Make her!"

Brutal opened her grandmother's mouth and peered inside. "She hasn't swallowed her tongue." He leaned her forward and smacked her on the back. When that didn't work, he pushed on her abdomen as if working her lungs.

"Grandmother!" Katya shouted in her ear. She turned to Starbride. "Can you use a pyramid on her?"

"To help her breathe?" Starbride shook her head.

Brutal laid his ear on Katya's grandmother's chest. "Her heart isn't beating." He tried pushing on her abdomen again, but nothing happened. "She's dead, Katya."

Katya tried to shove him out of the way, but it was like trying to move a tree. "Get out of the way." She knelt beside her grandmother's head. "Grandmother." She stroked her grandmother's cheeks. She seemed even smaller and older than in the sitting room, but more serene, almost peaceful. "Please, Grandma. Brutal, you have to—"

"Katya, there's nothing to do."

"Oh, Katya," Starbride said, tears in her voice.

Katya whirled on her. "Get some more of Yanchasa's essence from the capstone and put it in her!"

"I won't do that!"

"You have to!"

Starbride's mouth set in a firm line. "Do you want her to be like Roland, Katya?"

The breath caught in Katya's throat. "No...but..." But everyone was leaving her, one after another. She fell forward into Starbride's arms.

Everything after that was a blur: Brutal fetching Dawnmother and Averie, and toward the end, Pennynail, all of them carrying unconscious members of her family. Just as they had done after she'd first defeated Roland, they were all bundled into the same room. Brutal laid her parents in their bed, leaving them to Averie. Out in the king's sitting room, Pennynail put Hugo on a couch, and Dawnmother covered him with a blanket. Starbride's arms never strayed from Katya. Out of the corner of her eye, she saw Brutal leave the sitting room with a blanket. When he returned, his arms were full, and the blanket covered what could only be her grandmother's body.

Katya's tears started again at the sight of the blanket-wrapped bundle. Averie came out of the bedroom, and she and Dawnmother made plans with the efficiency of lifelong servants.

"How long will they sleep?" Dawnmother asked.

"Not more than an hour," Averie said.

"We should stay in here until then," Starbride said, her voice coming from above Katya's head, her arms still cradling Katya close. "When the king and queen wake, they can decide what we should tell everyone about the queen mother. Until then, no one should see our faces, not until the king is ready."

Katya nearly sat up and stared at her. Such authority in her voice, and a course that Crowe himself would have ordered. She also showed reverence for Katya's father, for his position, his decision. It was like she'd been born in their circle.

"That's good thinking." Brutal had placed the body on another settee, at the far side of the room.

"What about Yanchasa?" Katya said. Shame prickled her that she should fall apart when her team needed her to be strong. She cleared her throat and said the words again in a clearer voice. "Did the Waltz work? Is he pacified for now?"

Starbride wiped Katya's cheeks with her thumbs, a sweet gesture that almost made her pull away. She needed strength, not softness.

"From what I could sense, it worked. I should check, though, just to make sure."

"Pennynail, go with her." Katya wiped her cheeks herself and stood. With a nod, Pennynail walked toward the secret passageway again before Katya had a chance to remember why he might not want to go. Her shame deepened. It seemed everyone but her could cast off emotion and get the job done. "Wait, I didn't mean…"

Pennynail saluted her and continued toward the passageway. Starbride followed him into the darkness again.

Chapter Twenty-two: Starbride

Starbride lifted her pyramid from the cavern floor. She had funneled some of Yanchasa's extra essence into each Umbriel to make up for what Katya had given back. Sharing it between them had, she hoped, guaranteed that it wouldn't make any of them more of a Fiend. She couldn't get the idea out of her head, though, that the extra essence was what had killed the queen mother.

"Stop that," Freddie said. He had the mask sitting on top of his head, ready to pull down at a moment's notice.

"Stop what?"

"Feeling guilty. We do what has to be done. The old lady knew that."

Starbride supposed it was true, but she'd hold on to her guilt for a while longer. It had so much grief to keep it company. Starbride hugged the large pyramid to her chest as though she wanted to hug Katya again. Their promises to keep from dying echoed in her head.

As she'd done during the Waltz, Starbride fell into the pyramid in her arms, and used it to touch the capstone's magic. She didn't go deep, didn't want to encounter Yanchasa any more than she had to. Before the Waltz, the capstone had roiled with the great Fiend's energy, barely containing it. Now the energy felt subdued, almost placid. Starbride eased her focus. "Yanchasa is asleep."

Freddie only nodded. He was too busy staring at the divot in the floor.

Starbride pulled his mask down for him. "Let's get back."

When they returned to the royal apartment, Hugo was awake and trying to sit up with Dawnmother's help. "What happened?"

Dawnmother patted him on the back. "Just rest."

Starbride nodded at Dawnmother to keep tending him and followed Katya into her parents' bedroom. They were sitting up in bed.

"Da," Katya said. "I'm sorry, but Grandmother is…"

Starbride took her hand. "She passed away, King Einrich. I'm so sorry."

To her surprise, King Einrich didn't cry like he'd done for Crowe. He simply sat on the edge of the bed and rubbed his temples. "She knew," he said. "It's why she didn't want to see the grandchildren. She didn't want them to ask where she'd gone."

"I thought so, too," Queen Catirin said.

Katya took several deep breaths. "I should have seen it."

"Katya," Queen Catirin said, "don't blame yourself."

"Maybe she didn't want you to worry," Starbride said.

"That's why she said she was proud of me," Katya said, "because she knew it would be the last time she could say it."

"She said that because it's true," Queen Catirin said.

Katya shook her head. "I should have seen it."

"We've had too much loss," King Einrich said, "more than our share, but…" Tears threatened his voice, but he swallowed them down.

"I know, Da. Duty."

King Einrich kissed her on the top of the head. "You do know, don't you, my girl."

"What are we going to tell people?" Katya asked.

"That age took her. She's had her state funeral planned for years."

"That was her to the hilt," Katya said.

Starbride suddenly wished she'd known the old lady better. "Well, no one will question why the crown princess is staying in Marienne now, with all the funerals." As soon as the words left her, she thought of how callous they were. "I'm sorry."

"No, my dear, no apology necessary," King Einrich said. "My mother would have said the same thing."

They spread the news through different channels; it couldn't be doubted when it came from so many quarters. The queen mother had collapsed while taking tea in the king and queen's apartment. She'd come to support the crown in its time of transition, but the trip to Marienne had been too hard on her. Many of the older nobles praised her as they had during the reign of her husband. In death, she was still the epitome of nobility.

Queen Mother Meredin was laid to state the next afternoon with all the pomp the kingdom could muster, almost as much as Queen Catirin would get if she died while King Einrich still ruled. They used a glass carriage, a contraption that cost a fortune, so very Farradain. When the gilded, inlaid coffin was placed inside, it was covered with so many flowers that Starbride could barely see through it. It reminded Starbride of Appleton's funeral, though he hadn't rated the glass carriage, and the royals gathered on the dais again; the black bunting and armbands were back.

As Starbride watched the carriage roll by, she remembered the first time she'd seen the Umbriels gather in front of the palace. They'd waited for Reinholt's entrance into Marienne, just before Roland attacked them beneath the castle. How the crowds had cheered the crown prince then. Now, scant months later, those same crowds were eerily silent as the glass carriage rolled by. Many wept, caught up in the pall of sadness that always surrounded a funeral.

"As a kingdom," King Einrich said to the crowd, "we've suffered much tragedy recently. My mother, my pyradisté, and of course, our own Mr. Georgie Appleton, three persons who lived for the good they could do Marienne."

"Appleton lived for the people, not you, Umbriel!"

Everywhere, heads turned, and people babbled confusedly. Katya stepped up beside her father and scanned the crowd for the speaker. Starbride dipped into the concealed pocket of her dress.

"Parliament!" someone else shouted, as lost among the faces as the first speaker, though it sounded like a woman's voice. "We need a parliament!"

Heads nodded now, though most still seemed curious rather than angry. "Did the queen mother suggest it, too?" a third voice yelled. "Is that why she died?"

King Einrich's brow darkened. Behind them, the gathering of nobles and courtiers gasped. The crowd rumbled now. Starbride could almost see the idea of King Einrich killing his own mother spreading through the crowd like wildfire, as absurd as it seemed.

"Please," King Einrich said. "Ladies and gentleman—"

"Monster!" the female voice shouted.

"Murderer!" another said.

Starbride fought to keep from gaping. Where had this come from? Had this dissent been gathering all the while, only the Umbriels hadn't seen it?

The king's Guard spread into the crowd, some of whom tried to push them back. Several officers of the Watch were coming at the crowd from the city side, catching the people in a dangerous vise.

Katya pulled on Starbride's sleeve. "We need a distraction, now."

Starbride turned as King Einrich called for order. His voice was lost in the angry shouts below them.

Starbride scanned the nobles and courtiers. Among them stood the masters of the city's chapterhouses and academies. She hurried for Master Bernard of the Pyradisté Academy.

"Master Bernard!"

"Whatever's going—"

"You're lighting the academy earlier than expected."

His response was cut off by gasps from those around them. From out of the crowd, something flew at the dais in a high arc. Katya leapt in front of her father and bashed a piece of fruit out of the way with her rapier guard.

"Now!" Starbride said. "Master Bernard, please!"

The Guards at the side of the dais surrounded the royals. Starbride spotted Lord Vincent carrying Vierdrin and Bastian toward the palace doors.

Master Bernard lifted one hand. On the roof of a building across the square, a woman turned toward the pyramid rising from the streets of Marienne and waved a red flag.

Katya yelled at the Guard to pull back from the crowd, but there was no way to tell the city Watch to do the same. Every second felt like hours until the central pyramid of the Pyradisté Academy glowed like fire.

Heads turned. Starbride glanced that way herself as the capstone of the pyramid shone bright white, the light so powerful that it bounced along the clouds like a living thing. The crowd fell silent as quickly as if they'd been shut off by a switch.

"We are all Farradains!" King Einrich boomed. "There is no strife that we cannot handle together. No problem which cannot be overcome through discussion."

"He's right!" someone called from the crowd. Starbride recognized Captain Ursula as she was hoisted up on the shoulders of her fellows. She raised her arms as if directing a choir. "We meet and we talk. That's how we get things done. If we resort to violence, we're no better than the worst wharf rat in Dockland."

That got them thinking. Some resident of Marienne might have less than his neighbors, but he always had more than the people in Dockland. If Captain Ursula had been in arm's reach, Starbride would have been tempted to kiss her.

The crowd muttered, but no one threw anything. The Guard and the Watch waved them to disperse. They went, leaving nothing but the glass coach with its flowers and coffin. When the path was clear, the black-clad driver rushed the coffin toward the stables. All that was left was to get the royal family back inside the palace. They walked, all of them acting as if what had happened outside was of no consequence. The nobles and courtiers crowded around them and spoke of the stinking rabble and how it didn't know its place.

As Starbride rejoined the Umbriels, she tried to deter such words. It was just what the "stinking rabble" would be most upset about.

King Einrich waved such comments away. "I thought it rather thoughtful that the crowd offered me something to eat." He had them laughing soon enough, but the older nobles still seemed scandalized and stared into the city as if they'd never seen it before. Some appeared frightened, but most were angry, even offering to teach a few lessons if that was what it took.

"Three voices from out in the crowd," Katya said in Starbride's ear, "two male, one female, both impossible to spot and yet still loud. Augmented by a pyramid?"

"I don't know enough to say. But this…" She gestured at the scandalized nobles around them. "Turning the nobility against the peasantry is just the thing Roland would want."

When they slipped back into the king and queen's apartment, Katya sank into a chair. "Did anyone actually see any of the instigators?"

Starbride shook her head. "I went straight for Master Bernard."

"Well done," Queen Catirin said.

Starbride breathed a nervous laugh. "We were lucky Captain Ursula was there."

"The Watch captain who spoke to the crowd?" King Einrich asked. "Might be time to promote her."

"Any higher and she'd be unreachable by the populace," Starbride said. When everyone glanced at her, she shrugged. "I mean, well, that's what I think anyway."

"Upon reflection," King Einrich said, "you're quite right."

"We have to find these instigators, no matter who they are, and shut them up," Queen Catirin said.

"We'll need to do more than that," Katya added. "If they've got people believing in them, we'll have to make deals. If they disappear or turn up dead, they'll become martyrs."

"Unless they're controlling people with pyramid magic," Queen Catirin said.

"Then we need to find the pyramid users," Starbride said. "Brom's father doesn't remember meeting any pyradistés who could have given Brom a pyramid, and we know she didn't have it when she left here. And since Duke Robert had his mind examined for tampering, we know he hasn't been influenced by a mind pyramid. So who gave Brom the pyramid she used to murder Crowe and how? The same person who did that might be the same one stirring up the town."

"Duke Robert would have remembered meeting Roland or Maia," Katya said. "He's met them both before."

"And he wouldn't have let an unknown like Darren get near his coach," King Einrich said.

"What if Roland has allies we haven't considered?" Katya asked. "Duke Robert wouldn't have thought twice about letting another noble's caravan join his own."

Queen Catirin shook her head. "My mother always told me that living in the palace would be like living in a nest of vipers."

"I can think of a few vipers in particular," Starbride said. "And I know a guide that can help me sort them."

Katya laughed. "Two guides, yes? Since your mother's already been doing just that?"

Starbride beamed at her. "She does love to be helpful. Let me see what I can learn." She only hoped she didn't uncover that trouble had been brewing in Marienne for some time, but the Umbriels didn't want to see it.

Her mother met Starbride an hour after the funeral. With Rainhopeful behind her, she rushed inside Starbride's sitting room in a swirl of skirts.

"I saw what happened, Star," her mother said. "Are you all right?"

Starbride nodded as they embraced. "I wasn't the target."

"Nonsense. You're every bit as much a target as the Umbriels."

"I…I suppose. Well, I'm free to act where they might not be, so that's what we have to do."

"You're not going to break off the consortship, are you?"

"What? Why would you think—"

Her mother clucked her tongue. "People would be more willing to talk to you if they think the princess has thrown you over. Isn't that how the Umbriels think?"

Starbride held her breath. That was not only genius, it was far more devious than she'd come to expect from her mother. She knew she should suggest it to Katya, but the thought left her empty, almost hollow, as if the lie would be a precursor to a real event. Her fingers began to ache, and she glanced down to see she was clutching the consort's bracelet.

"Come," her mother said, "sit with me."

Starbride shook her head to clear it. "Katya wants me to talk to the nobles. She thinks the people who tried to start a riot today might have noble backing."

"Oh, of course." Her mother rolled of her eyes. "Because the common people couldn't *possibly* be upset without someone to *think* for them."

"Mother, the Umbriels don't think that way!"

"Don't give me that. If more common people were allowed to attain the lofty rank of nobles through intelligence and drive, the established nobles would be besieged by new neighbors." She tossed her head and sniffed. "Like me."

Starbride had to smile. "Well, Katya thinks that *incredibly smart* commoners like you are being bankrolled by nobles, and I agree."

"Well, money and brains make a good partnership. But the people wouldn't be easy to rile unless they were upset in the first place."

Starbride ducked her head. "I've been thinking the same thing, but now that all this has happened there's no way to know for sure."

"And now the princess wants you and me to find her deep-pursed noble, yes?" her mother said. "Should I be slightly disapproving of how the Umbriels treat you and see if I can catch any sympathizers in my net?"

Starbride didn't know whether to laugh or be appalled. Katya should have recruited Starbride's mother right away. "Get Countess Nadia to help you. Or rather, I should do that. She's particular about how she spends her time."

"She's probably already begun a search on her own. She's very loyal to the Umbriels, by all accounts."

"Yes, she was kind to me even before I became princess consort."

"She smells the right course on the wind." Her mother rose and retrieved Starbride's hand-embossed paper from a desk in the corner. "Invite the countess to tea."

Countess Nadia arrived promptly at teatime. Her graying blond hair had been swept upward in a sensible twist, and she wore a riding dress of deep gold. Evidently, she had plans to go out later in the day, uprising or no.

She pulled off her gloves and sat while Dawnmother poured tea for her and Starbride. "I saw the debacle on the steps of the palace. I knew you'd be calling on me." She winked. "Always glad to be of service."

Starbride took a page from Katya's book and dove right in. "Are there any members of the nobility that want the people of Marienne disturbed?"

"Well, some of the nobles are quite close to the throne. They can trace their ancestry back to ancient Umbriels."

Starbride nearly choked on her tea. There were people who had Fiends in their ancestry and didn't even know it? Luckily, they couldn't really have Fiends unless both their parents carried the taint. Just carrying it wouldn't make them aware of the responsibility that came with ruling Marienne. They'd capture the throne only to have it taken away from them by Roland, or if not him, Yanchasa itself.

"Anyone spring to mind?" Starbride asked.

Countess Nadia clucked her tongue. "They all merit suspicion, but the question is, how many have the ambition? That weeds them slightly. Those you have to find will be suspicious, ambitious, and *brave*. Now we have a much smaller pool to fish from."

Starbride toyed with the hem of her shirt and thought on her next words so she wouldn't give away too much. She couldn't mention that the noble in question might have so few scruples as to work with the Fiendish Roland. Of course, if Roland was pulling the strings of these nobles, they might not realize he was there at all.

"I can think of a few nobles who employ pyradistés," Countess Nadia said as if reading Starbride's mind.

"How did you know I was going to ask that?"

"It makes sense. A noble who's thinking of overthrowing the throne wouldn't have any qualms about using mind pyramids in a pinch."

Starbride nodded slowly. One name sprang right to the top of her mind, Lady Hilda, who employed a pyradisté and who'd had far too little to do in court lately.

Chapter Twenty-three: Katya

When Starbride walked into Katya's sitting room, she had a knowing smile on her face. Katya stood to greet her. "Did things go well with Nadia?"

"I've got a prime suspect."

"Dare I ask?"

"Lady Hilda."

Katya was tempted to smirk. "Still suspecting her, are you?"

"And why not? Now that you're the crown princess, she'll be even more interested in you." She tapped a finger against her lips, drawing Katya's attention to her beautiful mouth. Katya shook her head to banish the feelings. She couldn't embrace romance again so soon after Crowe and her grandmother's death. Instead, she took a seat opposite Starbride.

"You know," Starbride said, "the pyradisté who works for Lady Hilda looks remarkably like your uncle, if I remember correctly."

"What of it?"

"Well, Darren and Cassius Sleeting claimed to be your cousins, descended from your grandfather in the same way that you are. And they were reported to have another brother, an older one that we weren't able to locate."

Katya felt her face grow hot. "Are you suggesting they were telling the truth about being Umbriels? Crowe proved that their mother's schemes were all lies; her 'love letters' were faked."

Starbride gave Katya a sympathetic look. "That doesn't mean there was nothing to the claims at all."

"Well, my grandmother's dead now, so there's no one to ask." She hated her own bitterness but didn't have enough energy to take it back.

Luckily, Starbride shifted to Katya's settee. "I know she is, and I'm sorry to be bringing this up, but there are just too many maybes surrounding Lady Hilda." She laid a finger across Katya's lips. "I know what you're going to say. It's not jealousy. If it was, I'd be plotting against Castelle."

Katya felt the heat come into her cheeks. She ducked her head and hoped Starbride wouldn't see it.

"Are you blushing?"

"Just about the past. It embarrasses me to think I was so close to her, of all the time and energy I wasted before I found you."

Starbride pressed her lips against Katya's, a delighted little smile curving her lips through the contact.

"I love you, too," Starbride said. "But I still want to investigate Lady Hilda further. For a while there, she was conspicuously absent from court."

"So?"

"She could have been spending that time meeting Brom outside of Marienne. Duke Robert wouldn't have thought anything of a noble lady traveling alone wanting to join his caravan. Lady Hilda could have batted her eyes and appealed to the duke's old-fashioned sensibilities."

Cold settled in Katya's gut as she thought about it. Even if the connection to the Sleetings didn't work, there were too many other "maybes," just like Starbride said. Any gaps in the royal family would leave Lady Hilda a way in, especially if that gap happened to be Starbride's position…or Katya's mother. And they'd already proven that Lady Hilda had a powerful pyradisté working for her.

"You think it could be that easy?" Katya asked. "That Crowe's murder could have no connection to Roland whatsoever? That we have two separate enemies, Lady Hilda who murdered Crowe for her own ends and Roland stirring up the populace?"

Starbride tilted her head back and forth. "Lady Hilda and her pyradisté could still be pawns of Roland, even without a Sleeting connection. Lady Hilda wants power; she doesn't care how she gets it. If Roland promised her something…"

"He could have told her that he was exiled or stripped of title seven years ago, that his death was faked."

"It would blend well with the recent events surrounding Reinholt. Roland could have told Lady Hilda that the Umbriels' black sheep are sometimes ousted, but now one of them has returned. Oh, I can see him doing that all right. And I bet he's scouring the countryside for your brother."

"I can't believe that Reinholt would side with Roland."

"Katya—"

"No!" Katya stood and paced around the low table between the two settees. "Reinholt's angry, but Roland tried to kill his family. Roland turned Brom against us."

"Your brother is one to hold a grudge, that's true."

"Thank the spirits we can count on that."

"We still haven't figured out how to get Lady Hilda."

"Get her?"

"How do we catch her in a trap?"

That was the question of the moment. Katya tried to think logically, tried to block out all the death and pain that surrounded them. "Crowe couldn't have been Lady Hilda's target, and since everyone else is still alive, Lady Hilda knows she failed. Question is, will she try again?"

"I don't doubt it. If Roland has convinced Lady Hilda that she can be his queen, she could be trying to kill all of us."

Katya shuddered as she thought of the woman who'd sought her bed for so long trying to murder her. She'd always known Lady Hilda's admirations were as fake as they were fleeting, but the thought of Lady Hilda's lust turning to malice so casually was unnerving.

"Maybe I can get Lady Hilda to make a move," Starbride said. "Before she's ready."

"How?"

"Well, I'll invite her to a party, for a start." She narrowed her eyes. "I can question her off-handedly, make her squirm."

"Star, Countess Nadia explained this to you. Lady Hilda is dangerous."

"Don't worry. I won't let her near my food or drink. And I'll have Nadia to watch her." She smirked. "And my mother."

"My dearest love, there's no need to be cruel."

"I can't wait."

Katya knelt and kissed her but broke contact quickly. She shouldn't be having fun, shouldn't be enjoying love when two people she cared about were gone. Before Starbride could ask if she was all right, Katya tried to laugh her feelings away. "I was just thinking…you'll, um, you'll have to venture to the academy for your pyramid instruction."

"To secure a teacher? You're right. And I should go sooner rather than later. Will you come with me?"

Katya cupped Starbride's cheeks. "For you, anything." When Starbride didn't brighten, Katya stroked her chin with thumb and forefinger. "What else is worrying you?"

"After what happened during the queen mother's funeral, how long will we be able to go out in public, to the academy or anywhere else?"

Anger welled up in Katya as she saw the angry crowd in her mind again. "No more pleasure trips, not for the foreseeable future. For the simple tasks…" She grinned as one face popped into mind. "There's always Hugo."

"We can't send him alone."

That was true enough, but Katya didn't want to send the king's Guard into the city as Hugo's escort, not with the climate the way it was. Any show of force was bound to be answered. The tenuousness of the royal position settled around Katya's shoulders. If the Umbriels closed the gates of the palace, they could hold it forever against a mob, but as elite as the king's Guard was, they were outnumbered by the populace itself, especially if the townsfolk got the city Watch on their side. The Umbriels might be forced to rely on the private guards of the nobles, but without knowing who to trust…

Katya rubbed her forehead. "What a pretty mess. But private guards…I wonder…"

"You think we should hire guards?"

"No, some of the nobles keep private guards, people who are loyal to them but who could pass without notice in the town." She grinned as ideas raced through her mind. "And I have the perfect group in mind."

"Countess Nadia's guards?"

"Castelle's. She's a thief catcher now. She'd never operate without a team, plus she's no small fighter herself." And it would give Castelle something to do besides waiting in the halls to run into Katya. If Katya could shift her from whatever she now was to comrade-in-arms, it would make life much easier.

Starbride crossed her arms. "You sound almost admiring."

"Jealous?"

Starbride rose and walked around the small table. "You'll have to start asking yourself that question."

"Why?"

"If I'm going to be going back and forth to the academy, I'll need an escort, too."

Katya laughed but had to admit the thought of Castelle having the time to flirt with Starbride under the guise of escorting didn't sit well. "But can we trust her?"

"You'd know better than I."

"She may be callous, but she's never been disloyal to the crown."

"Just to you."

Katya followed Starbride far enough to kiss her on the cheek. "Then I'll have to make sure she knows it's the crown asking as well as me."

"Going alone?"

"If you think that's the best way."

"Whatever gets her to agree is the best way. Just know, if either of you gets any romantic ideas, you'll never see Dawnmother coming."

Katya didn't want to ask the courtiers in the halls to point her toward Castelle; that would set too many tongues flying. Luckily for her, the courtiers were more than happy to speak of Castelle at every opportunity. Katya quickly grew tired of having to head in the opposite direction of wherever Castelle was rumored to be and then get back on track via secret passageways or quick sprints down deserted hallways.

When she approached the kitchens, Katya didn't need directions. She simply followed the singing. Castelle and a few leather-clad men and women were in one of the small servants' dining rooms. Even though it was only early evening, they lifted beers and sang their lungs out with a few liveried servants. Katya waited for a break in their melody and then cleared her throat as loudly as she could.

They turned to stare, some eyes more half-lidded than others. A heartbeat passed, then two, and then they all surged to their feet and bowed enough to knock into one another. Castelle laughed as she separated from the bulk and executed her own graceful bow.

Katya leaned against the doorjamb. The servants made a hasty exit through the rear door. "If I can have a word with you, Baroness?" Katya asked.

Castelle followed her into the hall. "I'm sorry you had to hear such bawdiness, Highness."

"I've heard worse."

"I know."

A tingle passed down Katya's back. She willed it away and resisted the temptation to shiver. "Let's talk about your team."

"My team?"

Katya nodded past her toward the people still in the room.

"They're my friends, not my *team*."

"Splitting hairs."

"Some would say, Highness, that your confusion about the two words is an example of how you see duty everywhere you look."

Katya almost took a step back. "What?"

"Nothing."

"That didn't sound like nothing. If I recall, it's you that has a problem with words like 'duty,' not to mention 'commitment.'"

"I didn't have a problem committing to you, Katya. My problem was your commitment to everything else."

Katya opened and closed her mouth and tried to think of an argument about how duty wasn't something one decided to commit to and then break, but another thought struck her. "That was the first time you called me Katya since you got back."

"It is? Ha! I've been trying very hard to think of you as 'Highness.' It must be the beer talking."

"What happens if I'm Katya?"

Castelle's lips parted, and she gave Katya a look filled with such heat that it almost pushed Katya back. She'd forgotten what effect Castelle's gaze could have on her.

Katya resisted the urge to fidget but took a small step away. "As I was saying, I need to talk to you about your…friends. I don't know if you noticed before the beer, but the city's become a dangerous place. I don't want to send the Guard out—they're too noticeable—but I might have jobs for you from time to time."

"And you're ordering me and my friends to help you?"

"I'm asking."

Castelle's brow furrowed, and she nearly glared. Katya had forgotten how drink brought all of Castelle's emotions out in the open, including her lust. One lingering, passionate encounter in a large cupboard sprang to mind.

"Come find me when you're sober."

"Katya, wait. I'm sorry, Highness. My friends and I are at your service. We'll be happy to carry out your wishes." She smiled softly. "Am I to be escorting the crown princess consort?"

"And if you are?"

"If we could all be friends, what better?"

Jealousy tried to rear within Katya again, and she shook her head to banish it. "When I have a task, I'll send for you."

Castelle looked back into the room at where her friends had continued drinking. "Might want to give us an hour or so."

When Katya returned to her apartment, Starbride was back again, this time with a letter.

"As promised," Starbride said, "Countess Nadia's list of nobles that merit significant suspicion. And Lady Hilda is at the top."

Katya grinned as she sat next to Starbride and draped an arm around her shoulders. "Did she really name her list 'Nobles That Merit Significant Suspicion'?"

"Oh, that's not bold enough for Countess Nadia." Starbride cleared her throat and read, "'My dear, your vipers. Regards, Nadia.'"

Katya leaned in for a long kiss and let her arms hang loosely around Starbride's waist. The images of the recently lost rose again in her mind, but before she could pull back, Starbride held her close. Desire stirred inside Katya at being so captured, pushing the dark feelings back.

"What now, my scoundrel?" Starbride said. "Do you no longer desire me?"

"Of course. But…right now?"

"We should be happy while we can. Everyone we'd lost would want that." Her lips pressed to Katya's with gentle pressure that increased slowly until her tongue flicked into Katya's mouth. Katya drew her closer, letting passion guide her.

The settee was comfortable enough; they never seemed to find the time anymore to walk all the way to bed. Katya let her thoughts go and focused solely on Starbride in her arms.

When they'd stilled and were staring at the ceiling and smiling, Starbride laughed into Katya's neck.

"Stop that," Katya said, "unless you have more plans for me."

"I was just thinking of how Averie hasn't offered us tea in a long time. How does she always know what we're getting up to?"

"Probably the same way Dawnmother does."

"I think Dawn just doesn't come in the room when you're there. But Averie always brings refreshment."

"Maybe she listens at the door. Maybe she's out there listening right now."

Starbride turned her face into Katya's neck again. "Now I'm embarrassed that she knows how loud we can be."

Katya dipped her chin low enough to give a quick kiss. "You should be proud."

Chapter Twenty-four: Starbride

Brutal escorted Katya and Starbride to the academy the next morning. Starbride knew Pennynail was also watching. She only hoped they wouldn't need him.

They hurried through streets they would have previously lingered to enjoy. Would the city become so unstable that the royals couldn't venture from the palace at all? Escorts like Castelle's guards might become necessary for everyone if that happened. Starbride only hoped she and Katya wouldn't regret not bringing Castelle along to the academy.

Starbride's spirits lifted as they approached the massive pyramid rising from the city—its shining walls were like a doorway in the skyline—topped with a crystal capstone that sparkled in the sun. She'd never been inside. There had never seemed enough time, even though she'd met the academy's master on a number of occasions. Her joy at finally seeing inside the great structure almost pushed her worry away.

They hurried past the Halls of Law, the school that shared a courtyard with the Pyradisté Academy, and then past the dormitories where students of both schools lived. Starbride's friends from Allusia would be coming soon to take their place at the Halls for the winter term, Katya had seen to that. The idea used to fill Starbride with pride. Now she wondered if she should write and tell them to wait for next spring. She doubted they'd obey. They were as anxious to learn Farradain law as she had been when she'd first come to Marienne. The problems with Farradain traders in Newhope wouldn't wait until spring.

Once inside the academy, Starbride's jaw dropped. Rooms lined the pyramid walls, but the middle had been left hollow in a shaft that ran from the capstone to the floor. Light filtering down the shaft caught the sides of other pyramids as it descended, sending light blazing throughout the entire first floor. Beneath the shaft, a columned area sported an indoor garden. A water-filled basin sat in the center, and a crystal pyramid as large as a pony rotated above it. It sparkled and shone in the light from above, almost too brilliantly to look at.

Master Bernard met them just inside the doors. He spread his arms as if taking in the entire ground floor. "Your Highness," he said to Katya, "so nice to see you again. And I've anticipated your visit, Crown Princess Consort," he said to Starbride. "Tell me, what do you think?"

Starbride couldn't find the words. "It's…"

Master Bernard smiled and stroked his full beard. "That's the reaction we're always looking for. Please, follow me to my office."

They followed him up the stairways while he told the history of the academy and paused every so often so they could admire the view.

Once they were seated in his small, simple office near the top of the pyramid, he poured them all a cup of tea. "After the untimely death of Cimerion Crowe," he said, "I knew you'd need a teacher. I thought it only fitting that you be taught by the heads of department, given your station. We haven't had such an esteemed student since Prince Roland ages ago, before my time as master."

Starbride almost felt the blood drain from her face. Katya's hand tightened in hers.

Master Bernard leaned forward. "Forgive me for mentioning Crowe so casually. I see you're both still in mourning."

"He was a good man," Starbride said, and her chest ached at the loss, but it was thoughts of Roland that took her color.

"And quite young to have heart trouble," Master Bernard said. "He'll be greatly missed. If you'll oblige me, Highness, what disciplines had Crowe instructed you in?"

Starbride thought that an odd question for Katya. She frowned until Katya nudged her. "He isn't talking to me," Katya muttered.

"Oh! I'm sorry, Master Bernard. Nobody's called me that before."

He smiled indulgently, but it didn't quite reach his eyes. He was a busy man, after all. Quickly, she went through what she'd learned from Crowe, leaving out any practice she'd had with Fiend magic.

"Here is a list of the heads' schedules," Master Bernard said. "Would you rather be instructed at the academy or have private tutoring at the palace?"

"The palace," Katya said before Starbride had a chance. She used her bored court drawl, but Starbride knew she had real concerns.

Master Bernard nodded. With promises to send someone as soon as possible, he escorted them to the doors of the academy and bid them farewell.

When they reached Brutal in the courtyard, Katya said, "Sounds like fun."

"I liked the way you jumped on private tutoring. Was that just so I wouldn't be escorted by Castelle?"

"I will never admit to that, even if it's true."

They collected Brutal and headed home, trying to avoid crowded areas like the central market, but staying away from alleys.

When they reached a short, residential street, lined with small staircases and porticos, four figures ducked into their path. The figures bent close to the ground and moved their heads to and fro like hunting dogs.

Brutal pulled on Starbride's shoulder. Katya had already slowed. The only other people on the street turned the corner far ahead, past the hunting four who tilted their faces up.

Wrongness radiated from them, a malevolent energy that almost bent the eye, causing Starbride to doubt what she was seeing. Their skin was grayish, matching their white eyes, and reminded Starbride of poor Layra, Hugo's dead mother who'd been reanimated by Roland. She'd had a glazed, vacant look about her, though, and these four seemed intelligent and wary. Their white eyes glittered. Their mouths eased open in feral snarls.

Brutal moved to stand shoulder to shoulder with Katya. Starbride glanced back the way they'd come, but no more of the creatures appeared, and no one from the market ventured down the street.

"I've got the man and woman on the left," Katya said.

"Right." Brutal hoisted his big mace.

Starbride peered at the four figures, at their emaciated frames and drawn faces. Their clothing hung from them like sacks on pegs. "How can you tell which is which?"

Katya paused. "What?"

"A man from a woman?"

The four creatures advanced; each of them sported long knives. Wide hats covered their heads, and Starbride bet the brims concealed pyramids in their foreheads, just like Layra's had.

"It's plain as day," Brutal said. "The redhead on the end is clearly a woman."

To Starbride, the "redhead" appeared as colorless as the rest of them. She drew a pyramid from her satchel, one which let her detect pyramid magic, and focused.

"Starbride?" Katya asked.

"One moment." The four figures stalked closer, and Starbride could "see" the pyramids planted in their foreheads. The light from them shone to her enhanced eyes, but it didn't just shine outward. She looked closer.

"Starbride!"

"Not yet!" The pyramids weren't just controlling the bodies; they were holding something inside. Every one of those poor dead people seemed to hold a living flame, only this wasn't fire, though it did burn with the harsh sear of bitterest cold.

"We have to move," Brutal said.

"They're Fiends," Starbride said.

"What?" Katya asked.

"Fiends trapped inside dead bodies."

"I don't see—"

"Trust me, Brutal." Still gripping her pyramid, Starbride tried to pull Katya backward. "What you're seeing is some kind of illusion. Those are dead bodies occupied by Fiends."

The four creatures smiled, so close now that Starbride could see their blackened gums. A wave of fear tingled through her innards, and she could tell by the shudder that passed through Katya that she wasn't the only one affected. Still, it didn't cripple her as it had in the presence of the Umbriels' Fiends. These were lesser, somehow, only distorting the bodies of their hosts enough to give them that aura of menace and cold.

Starbride dipped into her satchel again, but before she could draw another pyramid, the Fiends leapt.

Brutal and Katya sprang back. Starbride stumbled and banged off a nearby staircase. Katya ducked out of the way of a Fiend's slash and came up hard against the stair's railing. She blocked the thrust of the creature farthest to her side—the "redhead"—dashed past it, and then ran her rapier through its heart.

The Fiend only smiled and stepped so that the blade left its chest. The wound didn't even bleed. And now Katya was on one side of the creatures, with Starbride and Brutal on the other.

A knife flew from a nearby rooftop and punched into the back of the creature that faced Katya. It didn't even turn its head; the knife stuck out of it like an ornament.

Brutal pushed his two opponents away, though their strength had nearly forced him to the ground. He held his mace in front of him lengthwise and set himself to block. Starbride pulled a pyramid from her bag, but she knew as soon as she gripped it that it was only a light pyramid. Before she had a chance to curse her luck and try again, the creature that had failed to connect with Katya darted after her.

Faster than a normal human, it still didn't compare to the speed of a royal Fiend. Starbride shoved off the railing. The Fiend's long knife sliced through her cloak and shirt and drew a searing line across her upper arm. She threw the light pyramid in its face.

The pyramid shattered; the creature paused, unharmed. Brutal spun while it was distracted and bashed it with his heavy mace. It careened into the wall, its head pulverized like a ripe melon.

His two opponents sprang for him. Starbride called a warning, but one of them sank its long knife into his back. He grunted, kept spinning, and forced the armed one to back off a step.

Pennynail's leather clad form dropped from a windowsill, and he shoved the unarmed Fiend into a staircase.

The creature with the crushed head didn't move, but Starbride guessed that had less to do with the head and more to do with the pyramid.

"Aim for their foreheads!" she cried.

Katya dueled with hers and scored shallow cuts all over its body, to no avail. She had a cut upon her cheek, and lines along her sleeves oozed blood. Starbride rushed the creature's back. The unarmed Fiend sprang at her from the staircase, but she twisted out of the way. They were fast, but they didn't seem smart. Starbride called for Katya's attacker to turn, and it spun around. Starbride pulled up short to avoid impaling herself on the Fiend's long knife. Katya's rapier burst through its skull, skewered its hat, and shattered the pyramid.

Starbride dodged past it and scooped up the long knife that clattered from its fingers. She didn't stop until she stood by Katya's side, and they had the remaining two attackers surrounded.

Brutal's movements were slowing. The unarmed Fiend tried to claw him while its companion attacked. Pennynail kicked at the unarmed creature, backing it into Katya. She stabbed for its head, but it ducked out of the way. Starbride threw her long knife at the Fiend still attacking Brutal. The butt of the knife struck instead of the blade, but it served her purpose. The creature divided its attention, and Brutal caved in its skull.

The remaining Fiend twisted out of the way of Katya's blade again and leapt for Brutal. It landed atop his shoulders and reached for the knife buried in his back. Brutal grabbed hold of one of its legs and hauled, but it buried its fingers in his hair. Pennynail stabbed its other leg over and over, but it ignored him.

"Kneel!" Katya cried.

Brutal dropped to his knees. Katya swung her rapier as the creature turned to face her; the point sheered across its forehead and shattered the pyramid. It dropped from Brutal's shoulders, and the malevolent light faded from its eyes.

Chapter Twenty-five: Katya

Katya stared down at the four corpses that had been vibrant people a moment before. Now it looked as if they'd been dead for days, like someone had pulled a colorful cloth from her eyes. "What in the spirits' names?"

Brutal sagged against the wall. Pennynail tried to hold him upright. Katya reached for the knife in his back, but then hesitated. "What do I do, Brutal?"

"Don't pull it out. We need bandages first."

Katya glanced toward the sounds of the marketplace and wondered where they could go for help. "Can you make it to your chapterhouse?"

"Better that than all the way to the palace."

Katya nodded at Starbride's arm, where the fabric of her shirt had been torn. "How bad?"

"Shallow." Starbride tore off the end of her sleeve and wrapped it around her arm. "I'll try and hide it in my cloak. You look cut all over."

"Scratches." Katya licked her thumb and wiped the blood from her cheek. There was nothing she could do about the numerous stings on her arms until they reached safety. She nodded to Pennynail. "Can you clean this mess up on your own? We're taking Brutal to the chapterhouse."

Pennynail saluted and bent over the bodies.

Katya took one of Brutal's arms and laid it across her shoulders. Starbride mirrored her on his other side; Brutal towered between them.

He wheezed a laugh. "Just what will the two of you do if I collapse?"

"Cushion your fall?" Starbride said.

"You'll be unconscious," Katya said, "but you'll be comfortable." They staggered down the street together, Brutal setting the pace. Katya tried her best not to grunt, but she couldn't help feeling that she was trying to lug a horse down the street.

"I can run ahead and bring someone," Starbride said.

Katya considered. "No, we need to stay together."

"They were Fiends," Starbride said. "Fiends inside the pyramids on their foreheads."

"How? Like my…family's?"

If Starbride noticed the pause, she gave no indication. "No, not as strong. Not as smart either, or so it seemed."

"Plenty clever enough," Brutal rumbled.

"But animal clever," Katya said. "I felt a chill, but I thought…" She didn't know what she'd thought, maybe that it had been a breeze.

"Fiendish energy put into corpses." Disgust threaded Starbride's voice. "Roland's messed about with corpses before. But is he using his own Fiend or pulling the essence from somewhere else?"

Brutal sighed against Katya's shoulder. "Like Maia."

They limped down the alley and then turned down another street. Anyone they passed gave them curious looks. Before they'd gone far, a Watch patrol called out from up the lane. No doubt one of the pedestrians had felt alarmed enough to report them.

Katya breathed a sigh of relief at the sight of Captain Ursula. She also recognized the sergeant with her as Rhys, the man who'd examined Appleton's body.

"Your Highness?" Ursula asked. "What happened?"

"My friend was stabbed by a mugger," Katya said.

"Several muggers," Brutal said. "I have my pride."

Ursula eyed the mace hanging from his belt. The corpses they'd fought might not have had much blood, but they'd probably left something behind. "Did you get a piece of them?"

"One or two," he said.

"Got a knife in his back, Cap," Sergeant Rhys said as he walked around them.

Ursula pointed at Brutal's red robe. "Headed for the chapterhouse?"

"That's right," Starbride said.

Ursula sent Sergeant Rhys ahead while she helped support Brutal on Starbride's side. "This related to what happened at the funeral?"

"We were just at the Pyradisté Academy," Starbride said.

"And your friend got mugged?"

"In a side street near the market," Katya said.

"They took off after I connected with two of them." Brutal's face had slowly drained of color as they walked. "Helped each other away before the ladies arrived."

"And they cut your cheek on their way, Crown Princess?" Ursula asked.

Katya fought the urge to swear. She wondered how visible the cuts on her arms were, or the slash to Starbride's forearm. "A separate incident."

"Cut herself shaving," Brutal muttered.

Katya and Starbride snorted laughs, but Ursula wasn't put off. "How many muggers were there? And what were they after? I'm given to understand monks don't carry much money."

"Enough," Katya said.

"I have to investigate crimes, Highness."

"He's weak. Investigate after we get him seen to."

"As you wish. You should know, though, that the people's anger from the funeral isn't isolated. We've heard grumbling all over the city, and Magistrate Anthony is fanning the flames."

"Appleton's boss?" Starbride asked.

"Seems the state funeral didn't impress him too much, especially given the more lavish nature of the queen mother's," Ursula said.

Katya nearly grumbled that her grandmother had been royalty, but she kept that to herself. Brutal stumbled, and they all grunted as they held him up enough to keep going. "Should we stop, Brutal?" Katya asked.

"No," he said between clenched teeth.

"That's a yes." Katya led the way over to the wall and made him lean against it. The rest of them leaned forward on their knees and breathed hard. Katya touched Brutal's pale cheek. "I'm not losing you, too."

He grinned lopsidedly. "Best and Berth aren't done with me yet. Think of how many people there are left to fight."

"Yes, think of them."

"Captain Ursula," Starbride asked, "do you think Magistrate Anthony was behind the near riot at the queen mother's funeral?"

"We haven't determined the ringleaders, yet, Crown Princess Consort." She stared hard at Starbride for a few moments. "If you have any new information—"

"We don't," Katya said.

Ursula turned that hard gaze on Katya. She bowed, unpracticed and shallow, but respectful and conveying complete disbelief. "As you wish, Crown Princess."

Katya didn't have time for a retort. Sergeant Rhys came up the lane, a pack of brothers and sisters of strength with him who pushed a flat cart with a single wheel on one end. The monks examined Brutal's wound before announcing they could better treat it at the chapterhouse. They loaded him on his side on the cart.

Brutal grabbed Katya's arm. "Don't wait for them to heal me. Go back to the palace."

Katya clamped her lips together but nodded. "I'll see you to the chapterhouse."

"I can escort you to the palace," Ursula offered.

"Completely unnecessary," Katya said. The last thing she wanted was to be hounded with questions for the entire trip.

"Are you certain? After everything that's happened…"

"I think it's a fine idea," Starbride said. When Katya glanced at her, she shrugged. "The captain is right. The city's too volatile." Her eyes widened, as if she was trying to will Katya to see her point.

Katya tried to see the benefit, but then she got it in a flash. If Ursula was with them and Roland tried something, they had a witness. "Fine."

They walked with Brutal to the gates of the chapterhouse, just two more blocks away. The huge stone archway was held up by statues of the twin spirits Best and Berth, their well-muscled backs the supports of the arches. Still, the male and female faces were serene for all the weight, as if the feat of strength came naturally to them and the fortitude to withstand it came from their bones.

Katya clenched Brutal's hand before they wheeled him inside. Even if she wanted to go with him, she could only go as far as the chapel. Crown princess or not, only brothers, sisters, or initiates could pass into the chapterhouse itself.

Brutal gave her a wan smile, but it made her feel better. The walk back to the palace held fewer pitfalls than she thought. Captain Ursula didn't ask a single question. Rather, she spoke mostly to Starbride, and her conversation leaned toward the everyday. By the end, though, Katya began to get the feeling that Ursula was trying to get a feel for their lives, for why someone might be targeting them and why they wouldn't want help dealing with it.

At the entrance to the palace, Katya caught Ursula's arm, ready to give her a small test to see how far she could be trusted. "Do you believe I would turn against my own subjects, Captain? That any of my family would?"

Ursula stared into Katya's eyes for a moment. "I believe your brother would, Highness."

Katya heard Starbride's sharp intake of breath. A few weeks ago, she would have had her own surprised reaction. Now, she just nodded. "Thank you for your honesty."

"But I've seen your Highness work for the good of the people on more than one occasion, and you made sure your brother was taken care of the night Mr. Appleton was killed before you guarded yourself. I believe you are an honorable woman."

"Thank you." Katya took a deep breath before plunging on. "I think we were deliberately attacked today for who we are."

"I see. Not muggers, then."

"Someone either means to undermine us or kill us."

"And by us you mean?"

"The Umbriels," Starbride said.

"And by undermine, you think this mysterious someone seeks to turn the townspeople against you?"

"Exactly," Starbride said. "We're in it up to our ears, Captain."

Ursula smiled slightly before she swallowed the look. "It's not surprising really, that someone would be stirring such a pot. You're not thinking the man killed by your brother was part of this conspiracy?"

"No," Katya said. "That was my brother's own stupidity."

"And the people who attacked you today? Did they really flee?"

"They are gone," Katya said.

"Very inconvenient." The words could have been mocking, but Ursula stared at the cobblestones and stroked her chin. "Could these 'muggers' have been under the influence of a pyramid?"

Katya couldn't help a glance at Starbride "Why?"

"Well, you were at the academy."

Katya smiled her droll, courtly smile. "To secure a teacher for my consort."

"Of course. I'll investigate everything you've said." It sounded both a promise and a threat, but it was exactly what Katya wanted.

"I know you will."

After another bow, deeper this time, Ursula headed into the city.

Chapter Twenty-six: Starbride

Starbride and Katya had to split up again after only a quick good-bye. Both had work to do, and Starbride couldn't get the faces of the Fiendish corpses out of her mind. She promised Katya she'd go through Crowe's books to look for more information, but that would have to give way at the moment for another investigation.

She and her mother had invited a snake to tea. Luckily, they'd invited many people to cover their true purpose.

Starbride returned to her apartment shortly before her guests, leaving Dawnmother only a few moments to bind the wound on her arm and hide it behind fresh clothes. Starbride quickly told her what had happened.

"I should have been there," Dawnmother said. "Better there than laying out teacups and fetching cake."

"There was nothing you could have done. We have work to do, and tea and cake are our weapons."

Her mother's entrance saved them from an argument. "They're right behind me. Places."

Unlike the first time she and Lady Hilda had dined together, Starbride was armed with allies well versed in Lady Hilda's tricks. When Starbride told her mother that Lady Hilda might also be a traitor, she'd gotten a gleam in her eye. Even if they didn't uncover evidence at their tea party, she might find some eventually.

Lady Hilda entered Starbride's sitting room in a gown that plunged straight to her impressive cleavage and kept going.

As Starbride stared at the obviousness, her mother whispered in her ear, "Be smarter than to fall for that. You're not a man."

"I'm not leering, Mother! I'm…amazed."

Her mother gave her a look. Starbride almost asked her if she desired every *man* she saw, but the thought of her outlining her sexual appetites quashed that notion. Starbride moved away instead and nodded as Countess Nadia entered along with the other guests.

As everyone began to mingle in babbling little groups, Starbride worked her way over to her prey. “Lady Hilda, always a pleasure.”

Lady Hilda bowed the appropriate number of inches and not a hair more. “Princess Consort. Or do you prefer Crown Princess Consort? Is there really such a position? I didn’t think consorts ever got to put the crown before their titles.”

Starbride’s back teeth ached; she relaxed her jaw and held up the wrist with the consort’s cuff as she stroked her chin. “Let me think. You may use crown if it pleases you. What does it really matter? The position is the same.”

“It matters a great deal. Why, if the unthinkable happened, you stand to be queen.”

“Yes, that is unthinkable.”

“Positively tragic.” Lady Hilda flashed a beautiful smile.

Starbride sought to change the subject before her spleen curdled. “We’ve had a lot of tragedy lately. What with the death of Appleton, then the king’s pyradisté, and of course, the queen mother.”

Lady Hilda’s frown increased as if unsure where Starbride was going. “Quite.”

“Then again, weren’t you gone from court for the first funeral?”

“Yes, Hilda.” Countess Nadia moved to Starbride’s side. “Where did you run off to? You missed Lord Ferguson’s fall party, and that’s not like you at all.”

Lady Hilda dipped her head as she bowed. “Countess. I do love a party, but I had some unfortunate estate business to take care of.”

“Now that is odd,” Countess Nadia said, “because my late husband’s relatives didn’t mention that you’d returned to your estate, and an appearance by the local nobility is always such an affair in the townships.”

Lady Hilda’s eye twitched. “I came in very discreetly, didn’t need the invitations pouring in for a lot of provincial parties and fetes, not when I wanted to finish my business and get back to court.”

“Well, that’s it, then. They will be sorry they missed you.”

Before Lady Hilda could finish her bow, Countess Nadia said, “Still, I do wonder how you went home under cover of darkness, as it were. No matter how ‘discreet’ I try to be when traveling to my own estate, someone always spots me. A carriage train is hard to conceal when traveling past lonely farms or, spirits above, through a township.”

Starbride chuckled with her. Lady Hilda had lost her smile and whisked a glance toward the door. "I went home on horseback."

Countess Nadia's face was the perfect mix of innocent confusion. "Without your clothes, your jewels, your servants? I would be lost without all my pretty baubles."

"Are you not lost without your baubles, Lady Hilda?" Starbride asked.

"I've learned to do without."

"The servants you leave at your estate must have been working nonstop to replace what you had to leave behind," Countess Nadia said. "I'll tell my husband's relatives to send them some help, maybe some extra food to make up for what they used while you were there." She looked skyward. "In fact, I believe that some of my relatives' servants are related to those in your township. It's a simple thing to figure out how you stayed out of their sight so well. I really must learn your tricks so I won't be bothered the next time I'm home."

"You needn't bother, Countess, with the food or the help. We managed quite well. As for my secrets, they're nothing of consequence. Just a few sharp orders, not to mention a whip for those who disobeyed."

"Tsk, so heavy-handed, Lady Hilda," Countess Nadia said. "Whipping the servants went out before my day."

Lady Hilda cast a glance in Starbride's direction. "Maybe some traditions should come back, such as…" She gestured around. "Well, such as nobility mingling strictly with nobility."

Starbride smiled. "Or such as a noblewoman traveling alone seeking solace with a traveling noble*man*."

Lady Hilda's nostrils flared.

"Too true, my dear," Countess Nadia said, "though that one was going out of vogue when I was young as well. Still, I used it now and again just after my husband died if there was a handsome nobleman passing my estate." She winked. "I'm sure you must have used that one once or twice, Hilda."

"I can take care of myself, Countess, begging your pardon."

"Well, that's not really the point, is it? You're just making them *think* you need their protection." She snapped her fingers. "Now I know how you did it."

Lady Hilda froze. Starbride wondered if she even breathed. "Did it, Countess?"

"Sneaked away from your estate! Duke Robert was traveling to court at exactly the same time to return his daughter. You could have easily blended with his caravan."

Lady Hilda's smile had an edge of panic. She could deny it, leading the conversation back to how she'd sneaked into and away from her estate. She could say yes, ending the conversation, but connecting herself to Duke Robert's caravan, somewhere she wouldn't want Katya to place her after what had happened to Crowe.

"Yes, that's where I was." She sipped her drink, covering her expression and clearly hoping Starbride and Countess Nadia didn't know enough to connect her to Brom and the pyramid.

"That poor man," Countess Nadia said. "First his daughter is disgraced, and then she takes her own life just as the king allows her marry again. They say she was just so brokenhearted about what she'd done, what she'd lost." Countess Nadia's face took on hardness. "It really is something the way someone on top of the world can be brought low just by the company they keep."

Lady Hilda met that unblinking stare with one of her own. "Yes, that is something."

"Did you talk to her?" Starbride asked.

Lady Hilda blinked as if she'd forgotten Starbride was there. "Did I…What? Who?"

"The former crown princess. When you were part of the duke's caravan, did you speak to Brom?"

"Briefly."

"I was just wondering what would prompt someone to take her own life. We don't have many suicides in Allusia. It's considered bad luck for the rest of your family. I wondered if she gave any indication of…what she meant to do."

"Yes," Countess Nadia said, "and such a shame that the strain caused poor Cimerion Crowe's heart to give out." She turned to Starbride. "Why, just like you said, my dear. Poor Brom's suicide caused bad luck for those left behind."

Starbride didn't stop staring at Lady Hilda. "Almost as if one caused the other."

Lady Hilda snorted a laugh. "I suppose it would seem that way if you believed in superstition."

"I wasn't talking about superstition."

"Seems you're at the crux of more than one mystery, my dear Hilda." Countess Nadia patted Lady Hilda's wrist. "We'll find out your secrets one day, though never all of them, I'm sure."

Lady Hilda bowed again, but she couldn't leave, not while Countess Nadia and Starbride were taking an interest in her, not until relieved by a bigger fish. Starbride almost laughed at the thought that it would take Katya—at least—to rescue her.

"Well, let's not keep her ladyship tied up when she has circulating to make," Countess Nadia said. "Come, if you please, Crown Princess Consort, and hear what Duchess Skelda has to say about this year's fashion."

Starbride let herself be pulled away.

"Don't look back," Countess Nadia said. "She's slipping out."

"I didn't expect her to leave so soon. I have to ask Dawnmother—"

"Don't worry, my dear. Your mother has already thought of it. Dawnmother is following Lady Viper as we speak."

"Remind me never to try and hide something from you, Countess."

Countess Nadia chuckled. "Oh, my sweet, you can try all you like."

As soon as she could, Starbride ducked out of the party and left it in her mother's capable hands. She hurried to Katya's apartment where Dawnmother would meet her. She only had a few moments of pacing before Dawnmother came in.

"She went directly to her townhouse," Dawnmother said. "I wasn't able to follow her inside, but I bribed the potboy to tell me what she was doing. I was quite clever, telling him that my mistress had to know what Lady Hilda planned to wear to the next—"

"I'm sure you were as clever as Horsestrong and Birdfaithful combined, Dawn, but please tell me what happened."

"She summoned her pyradisté immediately. The potboy couldn't catch everything they said, but Lady Hilda was yelling about needing another plan. If she isn't the assassin, then she's plotting something else. Whatever it is, we can finally be rid of her."

Starbride grinned. "You want that more than me."

"A woman who threatened you deserves no less." Dawnmother bustled around the room, straightening it, even though Averie kept it tidy. It was her nervous habit. When Katya came in, Dawnmother retired to the formal sitting room.

Katya had changed her clothes and bandaged her scratches, though Starbride could still see the weal on her cheek. Starbride told all that she knew of Lady Hilda.

Katya rubbed her chin as she paced. "Now all we have to do is dangle a fish so big she can't resist. She has to be confident you know she's guilty, Star. She won't walk easily into a trap."

"You're right."

"We need to spread a rumor of something she can sabotage." Katya grinned. "Did I tell you how happy I am that you and your maid are so devious?"

"Devious? Us? We're models of lawful decorum."

Katya sank to her knee and took Starbride's hand. "Oh, the very model!"

Before Katya could rise up for a kiss, Starbride planted her palm against Katya's forehead. "Stop! We've spent enough time on this settee lately."

"We're heading to the bedroom, then?"

Starbride gave her a black look, but then thought about it. "Well, we do seem to come up with our best ideas just after." While Katya was still blinking in shock, Starbride ran for the bedroom door.

"How do you do that to me?" Katya lay on her side, her breath coming as hard as Starbride's, and her flesh shining amidst the wine-colored sheets.

"Would you like me to show you again?"

With a tired smile, Katya kissed her cheek. "Though your skills are a miracle, I meant your ability to make me forget all my cares, all my responsibilities. You're quite addictive."

"I think we clear each other's minds, and then we can think."

Katya kissed her deeply, stealing her thoughts again for a few moments. "You drive all sorrow away, that's what it is."

Starbride captured Katya's face before she could get away and returned the deep kiss. "As long as we have each other, what sorrow can truly capture us?"

"Is that Horsestrong's wisdom?"

"Spoken to his love." Starbride didn't mention that in the tales, Horsestrong's love usually met a tragic end, all so Horsestrong could continue to mature and grow. As a girl, she'd always thought the lovers had gotten a bad deal, and she wouldn't have been one for all the world.

"And how will we catch Lady Viper?" Katya asked.

"With me as bait."

Katya drew back quickly.

"It's the only practical solution," Starbride said. "I'm an irresistible target whether she's still after you or not. If she still wants to be your consort, she needs to kill me. That would give her two avenues to power, a chance at you and whatever Roland's offered her, if he's working with her."

"And if she doesn't still want me?"

"How could she not? But even if she has gone insane and no longer wants you, she'll want to kill me anyway. I've thwarted her too many times."

"She won't risk her safety on a poorly planned attempt to kill you."

"Ah, that's where the irresistible part comes in. The rest of the family will be safe and secure, and I'll be on my own."

Katya shook her head. "She wouldn't fall for that."

"You sound as if you know her very well."

"Star—"

"I know, I know. It's my jealous heart speaking. We have to make her believe the trap. While you and your father remain here in Marienne, I will tour the countryside in your place, just as your brother would be doing if he were here."

"Tour?" A grin started over Katya's face. "Outside the palace visiting the homes of nobles. Lady Hilda will think she'll find only you, but the Order will be waiting for her whether she takes the bait or whether she waits in Marienne."

"Brutal's feeling better, then?"

"Yes, I had word from the chapterhouse while you were at your party. He thinks he may be back to fighting shape in a day or two. The monks are plying him with herbs and good food and making him rest. In the past, Star, this plan would be perfect, but now…" She shook her head. "If we leave the safety of the palace for the countryside, we could run into Roland and more of those things we met in the street, and we don't know how many guards Lady Hilda has."

Starbride sighed, hating what she'd have to say next. "The hunting princess isn't going to work anymore. As crown princess, you're not that free."

"I never thought I'd be sad to drop the hunting stories."

"I am sorry so much has changed for you, dear heart, but I have faith in how adaptable you are." She lifted an eyebrow. "And how flexible."

Katya snorted a laugh. "Then we'll truly have to sneak out of the palace, but with Roland creeping around…"

"That's the genius part. We're not going anywhere. A carriage train will leave Marienne, supposedly carrying me. Imagine Lady Hilda's surprise as she attacks and finds it filled with members of the city Watch."

"You mean the king's Guard."

"No, Captain Ursula wanted a catch for all her trouble. We'll give her one."

Katya nodded slowly. "We lay the blame for unrest at Lady Hilda's feet since we can't mention Roland."

"And an unprovoked attack on me will prove it."

"You're getting very good at this, Star."

Starbride kissed her softly, glad she didn't have to push for her plan. "I've learned from the best."

CHAPTER TWENTY-SEVEN: KATYA

For three days, they could only wait, tell Ursula of their plan, and finalize arrangements. When she wasn't wandering the palace halls and being seen, Katya stuck as close as she could to Starbride's side, even through her first encounter with a head of the Pyradisté Academy.

They practiced in Crowe's office, though Katya guessed it would be Starbride's now. It hurt to think about. She sat on a leather couch, surrounded by the smell of ink and paper, while Starbride met with the head of mind magic. He was a fussy little man who perched with her at the practice table and drilled her on the subject of mind pyramids.

He seemed more patient than Crowe, if less open to questions. To most, he simply answered, "In time."

Katya watched Starbride's pinched look of frustration. She always burned with curiosity. Someone who dodged a question was almost as bad as a liar in her book, especially when he wouldn't tell her *why* she couldn't know.

After they were finished and saw the little man on his way out, Katya gestured after him. "Well?"

"What he wouldn't tell me I'll look up in Crowe's books."

Katya's heart ached again, but she smiled, too. Crowe would have been proud of her tenacity. "Do you have your schedule set up now?"

"Every waking moment I'm not spending working with the Order or smoothing out the nobles, I'll be learning."

Katya draped an arm around her shoulders. "You're fantastic."

Starbride beamed, and Katya suddenly wished they had longer just to learn and wander around court. Even a week before, she would have kicked herself for such a thought.

❖

On the day of their trap, Katya fidgeted, even though she had Starbride with her. The only people who'd be in danger were Captain Ursula and her people. The city Watch employed one or two pyradistés, though they couldn't use mind magic without a magistrate's permission. They were only present to combat criminal pyradistés, like the one Lady Hilda might be using to attack the fake Starbride.

Secretly, Katya hoped they'd catch Roland in their net and not Lady Hilda. She was willing to forgive Lady Hilda all her machinations if the matter with Roland could be put to bed. Of course, if Roland were with the attackers, Ursula and all her party might be as good as dead.

Dawnmother's servant spies informed them that Lady Hilda didn't leave the palace, but that her townhouse in Marienne emptied of guards. The princess consort *was* too big a fish to resist, that or Roland had commanded Lady Hilda to go after Starbride. Whatever the cause, Katya waited with Starbride in her apartment, both of them pacing a hole in the carpet.

When a light scratch came from the secret passage entrance, Katya nearly jumped out of her skin. "Come!"

Pennynail stepped out and pointed to the ceiling, telling them he'd received the signal from his post atop a tower. "How many lights?"

He held up three fingers. The trap had been sprung, and the pyradistés had signaled a catch. Katya slapped a fist into her other palm. "Finally, some good news. Now all that's left is Lady Hilda herself. Are you ready?" He nodded. When Katya looked to Starbride, she nodded, too. "Good. We'll collect Hugo on our way. Let's catch her before she escapes the palace."

Starbride grabbed her arm. "Brutal wants to come, too. He sent a note."

"Is he well enough?"

"He claimed to be."

Katya chewed her lip for a moment. "He knows his limits. We'll gather him on our way."

If Katya was waiting for a signal, no doubt Lady Hilda waited for one, too. Katya hurried for the stables where Lady Hilda kept her carriage and her fastest horse. That last bit of information had come from Castelle, of all sources. She'd been getting to know the servants and grooms like she always had, and her team had found out a great deal of information about Lady Hilda's movements.

With her usual alacrity, Castelle had known Katya would be looking for the source of the recent troubles in Marienne. Katya had always thought she'd concealed her involvement with the Order, but Castelle was more observant than Katya had given her credit for. Castelle didn't know about the Order itself, but she knew Katya had a greater role in security than what was widely known. That was surely what all her talk about duty had been about.

Katya needed all the help she could get. Castelle's team waited in Marienne just in case Lady Hilda got away. She'd already cleared the front stable not only of grooms, but horses as well.

Just after the Order hid, Lady Hilda hurried into the empty stable, two servants with a lot of baggage in tow. Katya leaned against a post as if simply lingering there.

Lady Hilda pulled up short. "Hi…Highness." She and her two servants bowed.

"It doesn't surprise me that he'd sacrifice you as a pawn."

"I…don't know what you mean."

Katya leaned forward and relished the anger that pounded in her, for once enjoying that she didn't have to worry about the Fiend. "Roland."

Lady Hilda sucked in a breath, but she didn't look confused or blink or ask who Katya meant.

"I had rather hoped you wouldn't know who I was talking about. I can't save you if you've gotten in bed with him."

Lady Hilda dropped her bag. Her servants followed suit. She put on a languid smile and threw the cloak from her shoulders. No low-cut gowns today, only sensible leather trousers and a plain white shirt. Her long red hair had been braided behind her. "Wanted to save me, did you? Then you should join us. All he wants is his rightful place. There's nothing to say you couldn't still be the heir."

"Ah, so that's the song he sang you." As Lady Hilda's hand inched toward her pocket, Katya held up a finger. "No, no, no."

From the corner of the stable, light blazed, and Starbride held up a pyramid. "I've neutralized the fire pyramid you're concealing and the two flash bombs carried by your ladies." She put on a smug smile.

"My, my, haven't we been learning. And here I thought you were just a pretty face, but it seems you bring more to the table than just the stink of horses."

Starbride stepped forward and held the pyramid high, revealing Brutal and Hugo standing in the corner behind Lady Hilda's servants, their weapons already drawn. "I suppose I should tell you to surrender," Starbride said, "but I'm so hoping you won't."

"Politics isn't the only thing I've learned under your uncle's tutelage." Lady Hilda's smile stretched far to the sides as her eyes went all green. "You missed one." Little horns erupted from her forehead, curving slightly over her hairline.

Katya drew her rapier even as she gaped. Roland had given Lady Hilda a Fiend. More than that, he'd somehow taught her how to control it. Lady Hilda leapt at Katya as her two servants drew weapons and rushed Hugo and Brutal. Lady Hilda didn't move as quickly as one of the Umbriel Fiends, but she was faster than the dead creatures from Marienne. Katya tried to dart out of the way, but Lady Hilda's claws grazed her arm and shredded both her coat and the shirt underneath.

Katya tried to return the strike, but Lady Hilda dodged, her pointed teeth snarling. A knife sank into Lady Hilda's side before she could attack again. She shrieked, and the sound brought the metallic tang of blood to Katya's mouth.

Katya darted in for another attack. Lady Hilda slapped the rapier away and dashed into the shadows of the stables. A moment later, Pennynail flew by as if thrown by a catapult. He slammed into a wall and thudded to the ground.

"Temperance!" Starbride cried.

Katya shielded her eyes. Lady Hilda loosed that horrible screech again. Starbride ran toward her, another pyramid raised. Katya followed and aimed for the Fiend's heart.

Lady Hilda knocked Starbride to the side. The sudden movement sent Katya's rapier into her shoulder instead of her chest. Lady Hilda shoved Katya, pulling the rapier free, and then knocked Katya to the floor, making her teeth rattle in her skull as she hit.

Katya tried to scramble up, but the wind had fled from her lungs. Brutal's mace flew over her head and slammed into Lady Hilda's midsection. Roland should have left her mindless; she didn't know how to use her speed.

Lady Hilda staggered. Her hideous face swung to and fro as if seeking a way out. Katya scrambled up, still gasping, and put herself in the stable doorway. Hugo raced to stand beside her. He had a line of blood across one cheek, but seemed otherwise unhurt. From the corner of her eye, Katya saw Pennynail and Starbride standing up. Brutal stalked toward the Fiend, his opponent on the ground behind him.

Lady Hilda screeched again. Hugo grabbed his left ear, but she didn't try to rush them. She ran for the wall and slammed into the wood, breaking through. Sunlight streamed in through the hole and a scream came from the courtyard. When Katya ran into the light, she saw a groom on the ground, clutching his bleeding face. If Lady Hilda had passed him, she'd gone around the corner, into the street, into the city.

Katya started to run but skidded to a halt. Several servants were hurrying toward the downed groom from the street, but they didn't seem alarmed, as if they *hadn't* seen the Fiend.

Katya glanced up. Several roof tiles for a neighboring building hung askew. "She went up there."

Even clutching his ribs, Pennynail dragged himself to a windowsill and then to the roof.

Starbride pointed at Katya's shredded clothing. "Are you hurt?"

Katya shook her head. "You?"

"I'll have quite the bruise, but that's all."

Katya looked to where Brutal and Hugo bent over the injured groom. Damn the man, why had he come back just then?

"Princess Katyarianna," one of the servants said, "what did this to poor Gregory?" She seemed to realize who she was talking to as the words left her mouth. She bowed deeply.

"Some fool noble brought a hillcat to court as a pet, and the damn thing escaped," Katya said. "I'll have someone's head for this."

The servants tried to back away. Katya sheathed her rapier and gestured to Lady Hilda's downed maids. "The hillcat attacked the groom and the ladies over there. It would have killed more if we hadn't showed up. See to it that Gregory is tended by my personal physician."

"Your Highness," the grooms and servants muttered. The bowed again.

Brutal and Hugo stood with her as she walked to the palace doors. "The groom will be fine," Brutal said, "though he'll have several scars."

"And the ladies?"

"Dead," Brutal said. He looked sharply at Hugo. "Well, mine is."

Hugo's eyes flashed. "I saw no reason to kill her."

"And that's why you've got that scratch." Brutal nodded at Hugo's face.

"Peace." Katya hurried toward the lady in question, happy to have a captive. One lady was crumpled near the stable wall, part of her face gone from Brutal's mace. The other lay curled in a ball, unmoving. She had a dagger sticking out of her abdomen.

"Spirits above!" Hugo cried. "I left her alive, I swear!"

"Evidently, she preferred this to capture," Katya said.

A scuff near the door made them turn. Pennynail stood there, still cradling his ribs. He shook his head.

Katya bit her lip. She hadn't really expected him to catch Lady Hilda, but it would have been nice. "Take these bodies away before someone follows us over here. They won't believe an escaped hillcat stabbed one and bashed the other's head in."

Brutal and Pennynail wrapped the bodies in their cloaks and carried them outside. The groom had gathered quite a crowd, including the royal physician.

"Your Highness?" the royal physician asked. He inclined his head at the two cloak-shrouded bodies.

Katya shook her head. "The cat was on them before we could do anything."

"Who did it? Who brought the animal?" someone called.

Katya hesitated, but Starbride said, "Lady Hilda Montenegro. She's always desperate to impress everyone."

Katya nearly glanced at her in surprise. "Yes, she is that." She gestured for the two dead bodies to be loaded on a cart. "These were her servants. Spirits knows where the lady herself is now." She turned to another servant, glad there were so many about. "Find my lady-in-waiting and tell her to make inquiries as to who the maids' families are."

The onlookers seemed impressed. Lady Hilda might have gotten away, but she'd given the Umbriels an opportunity to foster some goodwill with the common people.

Pennynail and Brutal drove the cart into the city, presumably to the mortuary, but Katya didn't know where the two ladies would really end up, if they'd find a new home with Pennynail's infamous pig farmer.

Lady Hilda had vanished. Dawnmother's spying said that she hadn't returned to her townhouse, and news of her "hillcat" had everyone in the palace keeping an eye out for her. She couldn't stay in the city and not be called to task.

"Someone has to be sheltering her," Katya said to the Order that evening. Hugo attended as well as Averie. She hadn't found any family to receive the bodies of the maids. Katya tried not to think about where they'd have to end up now.

"She has to have a bolt-hole," Brutal said. He leaned forward from time to time and massaged his back. "Somewhere she can go to ground. All of the nobles do."

Katya nodded. "Who did Captain Ursula bring in from the countryside?"

"Mostly guards working for Lady Hilda," Starbride said. "The Watch is holding them in the city jail. Ursula's agreed to let me use a pyramid on them without a magistrate's permission, on one condition."

"Let me guess, she wants to know what we find out."

"You've got it."

"Lady Hilda wouldn't have told her guards anything, would she?" Hugo asked. "She wouldn't share her mind with hired thugs. Do we really need to break the law to interrogate them?"

"There's more than ethics at stake here, Lord Hugo," Brutal said. "If the Umbriels fall, it's likely Yanchasa could escape and destroy Marienne or even all of Farraday."

"I know that." He frowned and looked away, reminding Katya of Maia's occasional pouts.

Brutal must have seen the same thing. "You need to get a little hard, friend. If you can't kill a minor enemy, how are you going to face Darren or your father?" He didn't mention that they might also be facing Maia as well.

"I had that maid beaten. Why kill her?"

Brutal clucked his tongue. "What if she'd felt well enough to come to the door of the stable and throw that knife of hers? Or sneak up on us while we were preoccupied with Lady Hilda?"

Hugo stared at the table and didn't say anything.

"I felt the same way as you when I first came here," Starbride said. "I didn't think I could really be hurt, that anyone could. I thought the danger was exaggerated, but then Lady Hilda almost attacked me in her room. You're fighting someone who wants to kill you, Hugo. They won't hesitate, and you have to learn to do the same."

Katya didn't mention that she doubted if Starbride could kill yet without a second thought, but she let the words sink in.

"I'll…yes, I'll keep that in mind," Hugo said. "Still, can you see Lady Hilda sharing information with her guards?"

"Maybe, maybe not." Katya turned to Starbride. "If you see something about the Fiends, about Roland, in the guards' thoughts, can you lie to Captain Ursula?"

Starbride blinked, but then she nodded.

"I guess there's no way Ursula will bring the captives here?" Brutal asked.

"I doubt it," Katya said. "She's desperate to know what's going on. I imagine she'll do whatever it takes to hold on to her leverage."

"Do we know if she had her pyradistés read the captives already?" Hugo asked.

"They're taught to wait for a magistrate. But whatever the protocol, we'd better get there soon." Katya crossed her arms and looked to Starbride again. "I don't like sending you into the city, not with Lady Hilda on the loose and those Fiend corpses running around."

"Never fear," Starbride said. "I shall go in secret."

"I can go with you," Hugo said.

Katya resisted the urge to chuckle at his enthusiasm. "Your kind of escort would make her a little too obvious, Hugo."

"But thank you for the offer," Starbride added.

"If we want to go in secret," Katya said, "Castelle's out, too." She pointed at Pennynail. "We need your particular talents."

He saluted, but Starbride sighed. "Fingers and toes again, isn't it?" she asked.

He saluted her, too, and when she sighed again, he put his masked face in his palms as if weeping. Starbride wadded a stray piece of paper and threw it at him.

Katya scrubbed her face, dreading what she had to say now, but seeing the sense in it. "Now that the sun is down, it's the best time to go."

"Understood."

Katya caught her elbow as she stood. "Be careful." She tried to put all her feelings into the words, tried to make them as powerful as a guarding pyramid.

"Promise me the same," Starbride said, "and I'll be as careful as you like."

"I promise."

Pennynail put his hands on his stomach as if about to be ill. Katya glared at him. "I don't have any stray paper, so whatever I choose to throw, you'll definitely feel."

Starbride kissed her quickly. Katya couldn't watch as they walked out the door.

Chapter Twenty-eight: Starbride

Starbride braved the chill in her black leather outfit. No matter what Pennynail said, it was the best she had for sneaking through a dark city. Dawnmother had pinned her hair in a tight bun, making her even colder. Maybe some activity would warm her up.

In his room, Freddie grinned at her outfit, and she gave him a look. "Don't poke fun."

"Wouldn't dream of it."

"Maybe someday I'll have a grotesque leather mask of my own."

"It's good to have ambition."

He led her down into the palace, so far that she expected to emerge into the cavern that held the huge capstone. Instead, he stopped at a blank wall that sported a single pyramid and lifted his mask onto his head. "My father never tuned this to you, so stay behind me. You can retune it later." He blew out their lamp, and only the glow of the pyramid filled the space.

Freddie stripped off a glove and pressed the pyramid. A section of bricks swung inward, and Freddie had to bend double to get through. Starbride ducked and followed him. She smelled the faint scent of horses, but they weren't in the stables. She could stretch her arms to both sides and feel walls, though the way in front of her was clear. It was a narrow corridor, almost completely black under the night sky.

Starbride felt Freddie's grip on her arm and his lips near her ear. "Let your eyes adjust."

Soon, she could make out dim shapes from the light beyond the walls. When she could see Freddie's white mask, she nodded, and they moved quickly. The narrow space ended in another blank wall. Starbride hoped for a door, but Pennynail wedged his feet into cracks in the brick and scampered up.

"All right," Starbride muttered. She put her foot in the first crack and bounced, getting a feel for how well it would support her. Pennynail sat atop the wall and reached down. Starbride pushed off the ground and grabbed his hand before she could sink. Her foot slipped, and she clamped her teeth on a yelp, certain she was about to fall. She steadied after a moment and felt along the wall until she located another hold. With help, she was up and over faster than when she'd climbed Lady Hilda's garden wall. That seemed an eternity ago. It was a good thing her pyramid satchel fit snugly to her body.

The next hours in the city were a whirlwind of stops and starts, turning away from light and noise and diving through alleys or scaling walls and fences. Starbride discovered such a variety of smells as she never hoped to experience. At one point, Pennynail helped her up the front of a small townhouse, one among an entire row of them. When she reached the roof, her muscles gone to liquid, she collapsed in a heap and just breathed for a few moments.

After too short a time, she felt a touch on her arm. In the weak light coming from the street below and the stars and moon above, she saw Pennynail kneeling over her. He gave her another pat as if to ask if she was all right. She nodded. They hadn't spoken aloud since his words near the palace. She had to trust he knew what he was doing, where he was going. He led her to the side of the house, near where a dark dovecote waited, and pulled her into a crouch. Starbride looked past the roof to the back of the well-lit Watch house below, a destination that seemed miles away. Pennynail seemed determined to sneak up on it completely, not taking the chance of coming within the reach of its brightly lit white walls until they were on top of it.

Starbride scanned the houses abutting the townhouse, all of them with no access between. If they wanted to come at the Watch house from behind, the only way seemed up and over. But the back of their townhouse didn't sport as many climbing holds as the front had. She held her arms out as if to say, "What now?"

Pennynail laid a finger beside the mask's long nose and walked to a short doorway, more a raised hatch that rose from the house's roof. He took a length of rolled-up leather from his belt and pulled out several long, slender pieces of metal. Well, he'd been a thief, by his own admission. Only natural he'd have a set of lock-picks. Starbride wished the light was better so she could see what he did with them. She'd only ever read about housebreaking. As the chill wind touched the sweat on her face and neck, she couldn't contain a shiver.

After several soft sounds from the door, Pennynail had it open. Starbride held in the urge to leap forward, the cold flooding through her. Pennynail pointed ahead. She squinted in the gloom. A slight glint betrayed the presence of more metal. Pennynail lit a match, and Starbride's eyes widened. A bear trap rested just beyond the hatch. Evidently, the occupants of the house had tired of nighttime visitors. Starbride let her mouth hang open, shocked that someone would set such a trap for a human being, and wondered at the same time if they'd ever caught anyone.

Carefully, she and Pennynail stepped over the bear trap, and he shut and locked the hatch as soundlessly as he'd opened it. He extinguished his match, and Starbride commanded her light pyramid to glow very softly.

As she glanced down a long wooden hallway, the realization of what they were doing hit her. They were in someone's house! She mashed her lips together to prevent an outcry, a demand that they leave. The invasion of privacy had her stomach flip-flopping. Fear prickled over her scalp, but other emotions bubbled to the surface. Exhilaration crawled through her body as she followed in Pennynail's footsteps.

She fought the urge to hold her breath and moved as silently as she could. Through an open doorway, a bed sat on one side of a narrow room, its occupant not more than a lump. Starbride had the grace to be appalled at her grin. She was a prowler but nonetheless thrilled; her mother would have been horrified, but the owners were *unaware*. She could rearrange their house, and in the morning, it would be as if they'd been visited by a ghost.

When Pennynail finally unlocked the back door and let them out, Starbride's legs almost gave out. She gripped his arm as hard as she dared, and when he turned to her, the manic grin on his mask made sense. She echoed it with her own.

Pennynail relocked the door, and Starbride turned to find a small yard, one side occupied by a huddled gaggle of geese. She put out her light, and Pennynail gave the birds a wide berth as he led her to the shed. One quick climb and they were over, right into the yard of the Watch house.

A shadow separated from the others at the back of the building. "I should arrest you for trespassing," Captain Ursula said. She lit a lantern. "Don't tell me you went through that house or I'll make you turn out your pockets."

Pennynail had frozen into a statue.

Starbride took the lead. "Okay, I won't tell you that."

Ursula gestured with her chin at Pennynail. "Your masked friend doesn't talk?"

"He can't say anything at all," Starbride said. She tried to think like Katya. "His face was burned by acid, and it robbed him of his voice."

"Oh. I see." She retreated to her all-business stance. "My captives are this way."

Pennynail tapped Starbride's shoulder and pointed to the ground. He'd stay put. Starbride nodded. That was probably best. He attracted too much attention. She supposed she'd be safe enough in a Watch house.

She followed Ursula through a space teeming with officers. As before, they seemed far too busy to speak with her, all except Sergeant Rhys, Captain Ursula's right hand, who leaned against the doorway they approached. Starbride wondered how he always managed to look so languid, as if he had all the time in the world. Or maybe nothing upset him. Pennynail managed that very same posture. Maybe before he'd been a thief, he'd tried being a member of the Watch.

Sergeant Rhys led them into a hallway lined on one side with a row of cells, reminding Starbride of the dungeon, but there were no glittering pyramids here, no pall of underground depths. These cells had bars fronting them and moonlight leaking through the small barred windows at their rear.

Torches burned at intervals along the other wall, a holdover from before the Watch house had gotten lamps. It said something that Ursula hadn't bothered to replace them, probably that she didn't have the funds to do so.

Sergeant Rhys approached the bars of the first cell and opened the door. "You." He pointed at one of the men inside, the closest to the bars.

The man looked to the others before stepping into the light. One of his cellmates laughed at him, drink tanging the sound. The other just turned away. They were both dressed in homespun, but the man Sergeant Rhys singled out wore well-worn leather.

He rubbed the blond stubble on his cheeks. "What do you want with me?"

"Step out," Ursula said.

"Can't have no tribunal in the middle of the night."

"We want to give you a chance to tell your side of the story." She gestured to a closed door at the end of the hallway.

As they led him past the other cells, three men and one woman dispersed among the other captives came to the bars to watch him go. The one on the end tried to grab the blond prisoner's arm, but he ducked out of the way.

"Keep your mouth shut!" the man at the end of the cells commanded. The blond prisoner just stared at him and then continued on his way. Everyone who'd watched his progress wore the same kind of well-worn leather. Starbride wondered if splitting them up into different cells really did that much good.

Behind closed doors, Sergeant Rhys guided the prisoner to a chair on one side of a small table.

Ursula leaned to Starbride's ear. "The only reason I'm allowing this is because they attacked us like you said they would and because they know about the unrest in my town."

Starbride smiled at "my town." "It's good that you care."

Ursula frowned and then gestured at the prisoner. Sergeant Rhys stooped with surprising speed and wrapped one arm around the blond prisoner's neck, getting him in a chokehold. The prisoner tried to kick up from the chair, but Sergeant Rhys held him in place.

Starbride darted forward, drew her mind pyramid from her satchel, and pressed it to the prisoner's forehead before Sergeant Rhys made him black out.

She fell into the pyramid immediately, but instead of occupying the small crystalline space, she fell through it, into the mind beneath. The prisoner's thoughts and murmurs of memory engulfed her like warm water. Starbride fought panic and focused, settling the memories into their threads, one leading to another, all the way back to the beginning of his life. She looked at the whole of the threads and knew him as Christopher Allen.

Starbride focused on Lady Hilda, and the threads reformed, each memory connected with her becoming one long line. Starbride spun the memories and looked for one in particular, letting the images play in her own mind's eye.

Lady Hilda had hired Christopher and his fellows to take her to and from her country estate. The pay was good, the food outstanding, and the actual combat minimal. It was a dream, much better than anyone in Christopher's family had been able to get. Starbride sped forward, fighting against getting caught in memories not hers.

She saw Duke Robert's caravan, the one that carried Brom, and felt Christopher's anger at joining it. He'd been protecting Lady Hilda for a long time. He and his fellows were more than capable of keeping her safe on a jaunt across the countryside.

Lady Hilda had fawned over old Duke Robert, flashed those fabulous breasts and that winsome smile, and the old codger almost fell on his ass to welcome her. She couldn't want to marry such an old coot. What kind of bedmate would he make? If Lady Hilda had an itch to scratch, she had many willing, young volunteers. Christopher had thought on more than one occasion about how he'd like to peel her out of those clingy dresses, and—Starbride yanked herself from that memory. Her own body responded as Christopher's had, and she shook the feeling away. The last thing she needed was lust for Lady Hilda. Still, she'd confirmed that Lady Hilda had joined Duke Robert's caravan.

Dimly, she heard Sergeant Rhys ask, "How long is this going to take?"

"It'll be finished when it's finished," Starbride mumbled, her best Crowe impression before she dove back in.

After a long period of inactivity, Christopher was ready for some action. Lady Hilda had called him and his fellows to her townhouse, plied them with drink and good food, and then ordered them to kill someone. Christopher had recoiled. He didn't mind dispatching the odd bandit, but Lady Hilda wanted them to waylay someone, a woman. She'd added that she didn't mind if the guards wanted to "play" with this woman before they killed her. A few of the guards had sniggered, but Christopher and the others shared a look between them. That wasn't how civilized people acted.

He'd thought to quit, to walk out on his dream job, but Lady Hilda would hardly give him a reference. She'd probably tell all her fat cat friends to stay ten feet away, and he'd wind up guarding some caravan out of Dockland for pennies.

Reluctantly, Christopher had agreed to the job, hoping that the woman they were supposed to kill would run away and get lost in the woods forever. Even if they did catch her, Christopher told himself he'd put a knife through her heart before the perverts got a crack at her.

That was his last memory of Lady Hilda. Starbride searched for Roland, Maia, or Darren, but Christopher hadn't had contact with them, and there were no gaps to indicate tampering.

Starbride pulled out of Christopher's memories, back through the pyramid and into herself. Christopher slumped, unconscious. Starbride stared at him as his emotions leaked away now that she wasn't inside his mind. She felt a little sorry for him until she remembered that he'd been planning to kill her. At least he would have made it quick, unlike some of his friends.

"Well?" Ursula asked.

After a sigh, Starbride told her all. There were no Fiends or Order to keep silent about. Lady Hilda was what she was, a lowlife out to move up the social ladder via murder.

"Does this cook her goose enough for you?" Starbride asked, remembering that phrase from Maia.

"If I can take your word for it." She stared at the man now slumped over in the chair. "Can he lie to you like this?"

"Hiding one's memories takes a disciplined mind and special training. Another pyradisté could cover them up, but that hasn't happened." She grimaced at the thought of pyramiding the rest of the captives, including those who'd been imagining doing terrible things to her before they killed her.

Crowe wouldn't have stopped. Starbride straightened. "Can I have the next one, please?"

Ursula narrowed her eyes. "Didn't you say you had enough for me to arrest Lady Hilda?"

"The others may have been privy to more information, like where she's hiding." And whether she knew Roland. It was worth the risk, worth any ugly feelings.

"All right." Ursula gestured at Sergeant Rhys, and he dragged the unconscious Christopher into a corner before going toward the door.

"No need to panic them until we get them in the room." He flashed a crooked grin.

Starbride tried to smile back, but it was too much for her to manage.

Only two of the remaining prisoners had indulged in nasty thoughts about Starbride, and those seemed to have dissipated now that they were in prison.

Their captain was dead, so any secrets he'd known were gone. Starbride struck gold in a treasured memory of the handsomest guard, Timat. Lady Hilda wasn't above getting her feet wet in her own household, it seemed. She'd taken the young man somewhere special for their dalliance, a two-storied house in the forest. They'd shared a few nights of passion and then returned to the city, the young guard under orders not to tell anyone what had happened. He'd kept the secret, but he'd overheard Lady Hilda instructing her pyradisté to blank his memory.

Timat had paid the pyradisté ten gold crowns to leave his memory alone. With a laugh, the man had done so. Starbride lingered on the pyradisté's face, one she remembered. The more she stared, the more he looked like Darren and Cassius. And Roland. The pyradisté in the memory had to be Roland's nephew, Katya's cousin. But if they wouldn't see that, well, Starbride supposed it didn't matter in the end.

When she opened her eyes, she realized she was sweating, both from the strain and the very vivid memories of Timat's time with Lady Hilda. They weren't far off calling her a snake; she was so flexible.

"Is that the last one?" Starbride asked.

"Yes," Ursula said. "Did he give you anything more? You seem… flustered."

Starbride turned to find Ursula giving her a wry look. "It's the strain."

"Of course."

Starbride related the tale of the house in the woods and tried to ignore the way her memory flashed with images of Lady Hilda's naked body.

Ursula tapped her lips. "My jurisdiction's not good outside the city, not unless I'm operating on a joint venture with the palace, like this afternoon."

"I think that can be arranged."

"Do you want to be there when we search the house?"

The question stumped Starbride. Ursula didn't even ask if Katya wanted to be there. She still hadn't caught on to the idea that Katya was a force to be reckoned with. Or perhaps she thought Katya would have the common sense to protect herself now that she was the crown princess. Well, maybe Ursula knew her and didn't, all at the same time.

"If not me," Starbride said, "then a representative."

"The big guy or the masked man?"

Starbride rolled her head, trying to stretch the tired muscles. "I'll have to get back to you. We have more friends." Hugo sprang to mind or Castelle. Katya seemed to be willing to trust her to a point. The idea rankled faintly. On the one hand, Starbride was happy if the two could be friends. On the other, she didn't really want them to be, not if there was any chance of rekindling sparks.

Instead of making them sneak back the way they'd come, Ursula put Starbride and Pennynail in the back of a cart and covered them with a canvas tarp for a bumpy, if less strenuous, ride to the palace. Easier on the muscles, yes, but Starbride's belly tingled at the thought of being in someone else's house again.

When they were safe in Freddie's room, Starbride sagged onto his battered ottoman.

"The sneaking…" She shook her head and laughed. "I can see why you like it, Freddie, though I could never be a thief."

"Sneaking was the reason I did it. The thieving was just to survive. Would it help if I said I tried to steal from evil people?"

"If you were trying to survive, would it matter what kind of people you stole from?"

"Even in Dockland, there were rich and poor, though the rich that live there wouldn't be accepted in the polite society of Marienne."

"You stole from thieves."

"Never steal from someone who identifies himself as a criminal. I stole from those who called themselves businessmen, but it was the same thing."

She had to laugh, but without adrenaline to go on, she started to sag. "Why did you freeze when we saw Captain Ursula?"

He didn't answer, and when she glanced over, his thumbs traced the scar around his throat. "She's the one who hanged me."

"But then she knows you got away! Is she still after you?"

"That's a long story, Starbride, but the short version is, she thinks I'm dead now."

"Does she know you're innocent of the crime she tried to hang you for?"

He nodded, his gaze still far away. "She wouldn't be happy to find out I'm alive. Before I 'died' a second time, she'd decided to banish me from Dockland and Marienne. She was just a sergeant then. It's good to see she's moved up in the world."

Starbride shut her teeth on other questions, though they burned in her. She couldn't help but wonder if there'd been something more between them.

Before Starbride could think of how to broach the subject, Freddie said, "Don't you have a report to make to Katya?"

Starbride nodded and stood. "As soon as I know what she wants to do, I'll let you know."

He went back to staring into space. In the past, he could have gone to his father with his troubles, but he was all alone now. Starbride didn't know him well, but if she was all he had…

"Freddie?"

He glanced at her again.

"If you ever…want to talk. That sounds like something out of a soppy novel, I know, but…"

"You'll want to have a soak before you go to bed or your muscles will stiffen up."

She smiled once more before she went through the secret passageway to Katya's apartment. Luckily, Katya was waiting for her. Starbride hugged her close and held on for a long time.

"I was worried for you," Katya said into her hair.

"I'm so happy I have you."

When Katya smiled, Timat's memories of Lady Hilda rushed into Starbride's mind. She kissed Katya softly, and then deepened it, letting the heat of a moment if not the memories take over. Katya gasped. Starbride reached to the small of her back and mashed them closer.

"My, my," Katya said. "Are you trying to show me just how happy you are?"

Starbride leaned forward until she could trace Katya's ear with her tongue. "I've been advised that a nice hot bath is the only cure for sore muscles."

"I know a maid that can summon one in record time." Katya's voice was shaky, and Starbride had to admit that throwing her off balance never failed to appeal.

Katya wouldn't be overthrown for long, though. Already one of her hands had found its way to the front of Starbride's tight leather outfit, and clever fingers worked their way inside.

"Call Averie," Starbride said. She relished the shakiness in her own voice and loved it, loved the feel of Katya's touch, the way it made her skin fire. "She can help Dawnmother set up a bath in my room."

"Not here?"

"We'll be busy here."

The tub was narrow, with just enough room to sit one in front of the other. Starbride sat against the hard wooden end, Katya's back against her chest, long hair trailing over Starbride's shoulder. As she craned her neck, Starbride grinned to see that Katya's eyes were closed. Starbride tightened her thighs so she wouldn't slip under the water.

"I'm fine, nursemaid," Katya said.

"It's not a crime to care."

"I could live in here."

Starbride had already told her about Lady Hilda's house in the woods, just vaguely mentioning Timat's memories. She didn't want any teasing about lusting after Lady Hilda. What had happened before the bath was all Starbride's lust for Katya, and she didn't want Katya thinking anything different.

Starbride trailed her fingers down Katya's shoulder, along her arm, and slowly over the curve of her breast. Katya gave a very contented sigh.

Starbride chuckled. "If we live in here, meetings with the Order and the nobles' council might be awkward, not to mention dinner with your parents."

"We'll have baths drawn for them, too, then we'll all be on equal footing. I love you, Star. Have I ever mentioned that?"

"It's a complete surprise."

Katya turned, lifting up out of the water just enough to brace her arms on the sides of the tub. "I can't let that pass."

One kiss and then Starbride said, "Who is going with Captain Ursula to Lady Hilda's secret house?"

Katya sagged against Starbride's shoulder. "Do we have to go back to the real world now?"

"I told Ursula I would get word to her tonight so she can plan. She's probably wondering what happened to me."

"She knows you're my consort. She's not wondering too hard."

"Oh, ho! Does everyone in the palace think I'm in your bed day and night because of your appetite?"

"Probably."

"I should get out on my own more. People will worry I'll die from exhaustion." Starbride sighed and took a leap. "I could *start* by trapping that snake in her own nest."

"What did we say when we planned to trap her guards in the first place? You and I are both targets."

"I'll go in secret. I'll be hidden amongst the Watch, and Roland will steer clear of them, never knowing I'm there."

"What's to say I can't be hidden among them, too?"

Starbride opened her mouth, hoping a reason would come to her before she had to actually speak, but it wouldn't.

Katya nodded, a very satisfied look on her face. Starbride crossed her arms, making the water splash over the sides of the tub.

"You know I don't see your life as less important than mine, Star, so don't give me that. The Umbriel line will remain unbroken as long as my niece and nephew are alive. Do you have another reason you don't want me to come besides my safety?"

"I'd love to have you. It's just that, since I've taken over for Crowe, I've adopted his logical arguments for why you shouldn't take unnecessary risks."

"Those arguments could equally apply to you." She moved Starbride's wet hair back over her shoulders. "Let's both ignore them when we catch Lady Hilda tomorrow."

Chapter Twenty-nine: Katya

Captain Ursula raised an eyebrow when Katya climbed out of a covered cart beside Starbride, Pennynail, Brutal, Averie, and Hugo.

From her perch on the driver's seat, Castelle grinned at Ursula's expression. "I've learned it pays to expect the unexpected when dealing with the royal family, Captain."

Katya gave her a dour look and adjusted her chain shirt over her plain hunting gear.

"This is no ordinary hunt, Highness," Ursula said.

"You're right. I'm not used to hunting hillcats."

Everyone else chuckled, but Ursula didn't lose her frown. Katya hated that she had to keep the court persona up even as she was undertaking an adventure for the Order, but she couldn't have the Watch thinking she hunted fugitives all the time.

"Lady Hilda wanted to kill my consort," Katya said. "The fact that Starbride was nowhere near her trap makes no difference."

Ursula sighed and turned away. However she chose to deal with Katya's presence was her own business, as long as she dealt with it.

"We're all accomplished fighters," Starbride said. "We can take care of ourselves. We won't treat this like a picnic."

"Eloquently put, Crown Princess Consort," Hugo said, making their journey to catch a murderer sound more like a nobles' outing.

"I do believe your word, Highness," Ursula said, "and it's always lucky to have more capable allies, but…"

Castelle jumped down from the cart. "If anyone gets hurt through her or his own stupidity, no one will blame the brave Watch captain." She winked as she said it, ever the flirt.

"That's one thing to say, Baroness, and quite another to have happen. I hope you'll all forgive me if some in my company keep an extra eye on you. I understand why you feel the need to be there, Highness. As an actual traitor to the crown, the lady's more under your jurisdiction than mine. You'll no doubt want to hold her in the palace."

She took a deep breath.

"But?" Katya prompted her.

"*But* I wish we were taking the king's Guard instead of you."

"It would alarm the populace to see them march," Katya said. "Plus, we need them at the palace while there's still unrest. I understand your frustration, and I share it. I hope that by bringing in Lady Hilda, we'll quash other would-be rebels."

Reluctantly, Katya climbed back into the cart. Castelle's friends had horses waiting in the forest, and Katya's cart along with Ursula's troops would meet them there. While still in Marienne, though, they had to hide under a stiflingly heavy tarp, even with the chill breezes outside.

Katya lay between Starbride and Brutal, with Hugo on the other side of Starbride, Averie between Brutal and the driver's seat, and Pennynail by their legs. Castelle laid straw on top of the tarp to disguise the shape of their bodies, and it clogged their noses with the smell of hay as well as raised the temperature even more.

"Cobblestones never bothered me until now," Brutal said.

"Your back?" Katya asked.

"Among other things."

"Like my bottom," Averie said.

Katya snickered along with all of the others, and for a moment, it felt like the way it used to be, before Roland, before Crowe's death and Maia's disappearance, before Katya lost her Fiend. Of course, that was also before Starbride. Katya linked her fingers in Starbride's and squeezed. Meeting her, falling in love, Katya wouldn't give that up for the world.

The cart hit a particularly nasty bump, and Katya clamped her teeth on a cry. She heard a *whuff* of breath as the others tried to do the same. The occasional soft laugh was one thing, but they couldn't have a cart full of hay crying out at every lump in the street.

"Cheer up, Hugo," Starbride said. "This is the glamorous side of being a noble."

"Indeed, this is exactly how I pictured court."

"Well," Brutal said, "better this than a ball or a fete any day."

"Fetes have pretty dresses," Averie said.

Starbride chuckled. "And jewelry."

"Sorry," Katya said, "I'm with Brutal."

"Then it's down to Pennynail to either tie the vote or cast his for the hay cart," Starbride said. "Pennynail, if you agree with Averie and me, say absolutely nothing."

That got a soft chuckle from everyone again. They hit another bump, there was another collective huff, and Hugo said, "I'd like to vote for the party now."

"Ha, Hugo's with us," Starbride said softly. "Fete it is."

"Pennynail's fine for a fete if he still has your old dress," Katya said.

A finger poked her in the leg, and she grinned.

The road from Marienne to the forest had no cobblestones, but it bore a number of potholes, and the slight hill had Katya and her friends bunched against the front and the back of the cart. Brutal murmured sorry over and over as he squashed them, particularly Averie against the driver's seat. She told him it was all right, but Katya could hear the strain in her voice.

When the cart finally stopped, Katya felt both Brutal and Starbride tense, all of them ready to be out in the fresh air. When Castelle rolled back the tarp, they all sighed at once.

Castelle grinned. "Good ride?"

Katya glared at her and knew she wasn't the only one. They filed out and finally got a look at Captain Ursula's troops and the horses that would be theirs for the day.

Ursula had brought fifteen officers of the Watch including herself. In Castelle's band, there were six besides her. They sat in the cart as Katya and the Order took their horses. Katya had never been so glad that her position allowed her to commandeer what she wanted.

The twenty-eight of them started into the woods. It would take most of the day to reach Lady Hilda's secret hideout. They set off at a steady clip but not so fast that they'd wear their horses out before they reached their destination.

It was late afternoon when they skirted the small village closest to where Lady Hilda's house rested. Harvest season was almost over, and the fields farthest from the town had already been stripped, so Katya's party could travel on the edges without being seen. The locals probably didn't even know who owned the small house near their town. Unlike Lady Hilda's estate, no one here would pay her taxes, so they probably thought it was any old noble staying there. That was good. No one would notice that she'd gone.

The road was no more than a grassy track with two dirt ruts, but anyone coming down it would be visible from the house, and Katya wanted all the surprise she could get.

They picketed the horses where they could graze, and Ursula chose one of her party to guard them. The young man looked distinctly unhappy, but he couldn't argue. If they caught Lady Hilda, Katya promised herself she'd give him a gold crown for his trouble.

Under the forest's canopy was a maze of shadows. Katya and her team walked almost silently, even Hugo and Starbride, who'd spent a little time among trees. Castelle's friends seemed equally noiseless.

Ursula's Watch officers sounded like a troop of three-legged bears; they managed to find every pile of dead leaves, every half-rotted branch, and every snagging bramble. Katya had to watch them to make sure they weren't actually rolling through the underbrush to make as much noise as possible.

Katya crept to Ursula's side. "We'll circle around the back. You keep coming from this side." She glanced at the officers again. "Slowly."

Ursula nodded. She had to know how noisy they were.

Katya inclined her head toward her people. Castelle tiptoed over and whispered in her ear, "We'll sneak clear around to the other side of the house."

Katya nodded and gestured for her team to follow her. Brutal grimaced every time he had to bend low. Katya considered telling him he could hang back, but he knew his limits. He wouldn't want to miss a chance at combat, nor would he want his friends to go into danger without him. Even injured, he hit like a horse and cart. After all the guards she'd committed to ambushing the decoy Starbride in the woods, Lady Hilda couldn't have many left. But they hadn't caught her pyradisté. They needed everyone.

The house seemed small for a noblewoman, only five or six bedrooms. The exterior was stone, covered in ivy, probably very old. The windows held bubbles of imperfection. The shutters were closed on the second story, a sign that the servants had already started closing part of the house for the winter and that they weren't expecting guests.

Some of the shutters on the first floor had been reopened hastily, not fully secured against the house. Someone was in there, and she'd come unexpectedly. There was no one in the small garden, though, no one under the iron gazebo that had already had its awning packed away. No candles or lamplight shone from the windows.

From the side of the house, a bird called, a starling that had no business being out at that time of year. Katya nodded to Averie, and she repeated the whistle, signaling their readiness. After a few moments in which Katya could actually *hear* Ursula's officers getting into place, a poor starling call came from that side, too.

"Someone doesn't get out of the city much," Brutal muttered.

Katya only had time to grin. Pennynail sprinted toward the house, and the others ran in a line behind him. They pressed their backs against the stones, in between the windows. Two faces peeked around from both sides of the house, telling Katya they were all in place.

Starbride slipped a pyramid from her satchel. She gripped it and closed her eyes. After a moment, she leaned to Katya's ear. "There are pyramids active on all the windows and doors."

"Damn!" Katya had been hoping the second floor windows would be guarded only by shutters. "Can you disable them?"

Starbride frowned and closed her eyes again. "He's very powerful."

"He's no match for you."

Starbride smiled slightly but didn't open her eyes. "I disabled the first floor windows closest to us and the back door."

Katya leaned back on her heels. That was fast, far faster than Crowe and more than he'd ever done at one time. Either his age had been affecting his skills ever since Katya had known him, or Starbride was just more powerful.

Katya held up a hand, fingers flat, signaling the watching faces to wait. Pennynail took a quick look into a window and then slipped a long metal rod between the window and the jamb. With a flick of his wrist, he had the window open, the entire thing rotating in place so that it blocked the middle of the window but let air in on either side. He peeked inside again before he slipped over the sill, his lean body easily fitting through the gap. Starbride slid through after him, though she had to wriggle a little.

Katya leaned to Brutal's ear. "Keep Averie and Hugo and meet us at the door."

When he nodded, Katya followed Pennynail and Starbride into the house.

Her feet came to rest in a flour-spattered kitchen. The cupboards were open, hastily unpacked, utensils and globs of ingredients everywhere, as if someone with no skill in the kitchen had tried it out. Pennynail peeked into the hallway beyond. Starbride gripped her detection pyramid again and then shook her head.

They proceeded into the narrow hallway that extended in both directions. Pennynail crept to the back door while Katya and Starbride stayed in the hall. Katya heard the quick snick of the lock, and then felt the draft as the door opened. Now Brutal, Averie, and Hugo could come inside, but if the inhabitants of the house were unaware of the intruders' presence before, the draft surely told them now. Katya peeked around the corner, toward the front of the house. She and Starbride crept that way. After a moment of concentration, Starbride nodded. She'd disabled the pyramids on the front door. Katya unlocked it, and Castelle's troops plus Ursula's made their way inside.

One of Castelle's men looked deliberately up the staircase and shook his head. No one there, either. It seemed strange for such a suddenly crowded house to be so quiet.

They might have been bears in the forest, but Ursula's men were silent as thieves in the huge house. They made a quick search of the downstairs rooms. Light flooded through the open shutters of the bedrooms, but Katya thought it unlikely that anyone had slept on the bare mattresses. In the downstairs sitting room, papers lay everywhere, and cabinets had their doors thrown open. If she'd found what she'd been looking for, Lady Hilda might already have flown.

That left the upstairs. What better place to sleep, with not only pyramids but shutters to protect you? Katya would have done the same. Live on the first floor during the day and the second at night. But it was already far into the day and no one seemed afoot. Unless they were upstairs, waiting for the first intruder to crest the staircase.

Whoever set that first foot on the stairs would be vulnerable, and a person tumbling down might knock over anyone coming up.

Katya nodded to Starbride. After a few moments of concentration, Starbride said in her ear, "The pyramids on the windows above are still active, and I sense several others inside the house. I can't disable them unless I get closer."

"Are there any on the stairs?"

"Let me see if I can reach anything." She closed her eyes again while their troops took cover under the staircase or in the back door entryway. "There's something just above us, like…like it's in the floor." Her eyes crept open. "Why would you put a pyramid in the floor?"

"A trap?" Brutal asked.

Starbride shook her head. "You put a trap in the wall. A pyramid in the floor could get damaged by normal foot traffic." Her eyes widened. "We need to get out."

Katya's stomach roiled even though she didn't know the cause. "Out!" she hissed. "Doors and windows, get out now!"

As everyone hurried to obey, a boom sounded over their heads, making the floor rock beneath Katya's feet. Wood and plaster rained down amid screams and cries of pain.

Katya dove down the hallway and pulled Starbride with her. A beam from overhead slammed down on one of Ursula's men, pulping him on its splintered end. Katya fought to wipe the stinging plaster out of her eyes and tried to get her disorganized thoughts together. An arm pulled her to the side, and she looked up at Averie. She'd lost her bow and was pale with plaster dust, but she appeared unharmed.

"Where are the others?" Starbride shouted.

"Brutal and Hugo were on the other side of the hall," Averie said. "I don't know about Pennynail."

"He'll be fine," Katya said. She coughed and fought to wipe the dust from her face. If she knew him at all, he was finding a way to creep upstairs.

Katya stepped over some debris and searched the floor. She scanned the wounded and the dead, hoping that she wouldn't see a mass of curly dark hair.

"Katya!" someone shouted from the front, and then Katya heard the clash of steel on steel.

Leaving the wounded until after the fight was done, Katya leapt over the remaining debris. "Averie, get people out!"

Castelle and one of her friends fought three assailants in the front foyer. Castelle had one arm tucked into her jacket as if it was useless. She fought well with her off-hand, but she only parried and tried to stay ahead of one opponent as her friend tried to take on two.

Katya struck at the back of Castelle's opponent. He cried out as she scored a cut through his leather armor. When he tried to turn, Castelle slashed him across the throat. One of the other two men turned to face Katya. He swung his sword in a wide arc, driving her back. A shadow loomed over his shoulder. Katya kept her eyes on her opponent's face.

Brutal's mace smashed down on the swordsman's head. Katya turned away as his face crumpled downward, his skull crushed.

Castelle and her friend made short work of the remaining man. Katya turned to the stairs. Ursula and one of her men were trying to get to them over the debris. As they stepped beneath the gaping hole in the ceiling, a hand shot out.

"Down!" Katya shouted.

Ursula dropped, but her fellow officer was too slow. Quick as a blink, the hand grabbed him by the hair and hauled his screaming, kicking form out of sight.

"Back, back," Ursula shouted at those trying to follow her. She launched herself over the debris to land near Katya's feet.

"What is it?" Ursula said. "What in the name of the spirits—"

A strangled cry from upstairs cut her off, and the body of her officer dropped through the hole, minus his head. The laugh that echoed from upstairs had the cold tang of the Fiend in it, making Katya's mouth fill with the taste of blood.

Ursula wiped her lips. "Everyone stay away from that hole."

Katya glanced to her side. Starbride hadn't followed her into the foyer…had she? But maybe she had, right under that hole, that grasping hand. Katya knelt and tried to peer through the dust into the cluster of people at the back of the house. "Star?" she whispered. No one answered. "Averie? Hugo?" She glanced to Brutal, but he shrugged. "Starbride? Has anyone seen her?"

She heard only confused mutterings or cries from the wounded. Fear clenched Katya's gut as the laugh came from upstairs again.

Chapter Thirty: Starbride

Starbride helped Averie pull the wounded down the hall. One young woman cried out as they tugged on her arms, but they couldn't do anything for her while she was half buried in rubble. Just outside the kitchen, they stopped, and Averie knelt beside the downed woman.

"I don't know how much I can do for her," Averie said. "I'll look for something to use as a bandage."

"Right." Starbride started back toward Katya, toward where a scream had come only moments earlier.

Pennynail stepped toward her out of the gloom and pointed upstairs and then at one of the open windows.

"You want to go in an upstairs window?"

He nodded.

Starbride shook her head. "I'll need to be close to disable the pyramids."

He raised his arms above his head, palms flat, as if he would lift her, and then patted his shoulders, saying she could stand there.

"Well, if I lose my balance at least I'll fall in the bushes." She followed him toward the window just as Hugo caught up to them.

"Someone's pulling people up through the hole in the floor," he whispered. "Katya is looking for you." A scream sounded down the hall again. "Sounds like it got another one."

Starbride bit her lip. "I'd be of better use upstairs. Can you tell Katya?"

He shook his head. "I'm coming with you."

Starbride let out a breath, annoyed at his insistence yet glad to have him along. She knelt next to a female officer slumped against the wall and holding a bloody elbow. "Can you move?"

The woman nodded.

"Go back down the hall, stay away from that hole, and see if you can get a quiet word to the princess. Tell her Starbride is all right and trying to get upstairs." She left without waiting for an answer.

The three of them climbed out a window, and then Pennynail and Hugo boosted Starbride up on their shoulders. She wobbled, and her stomach turned over, but she leaned her knees against the stones and gripped her pyramid, fighting to concentrate.

She disabled the pyramid guarding the window, picturing it as a soap bubble she could pop. She tried to search farther inside the house and spotted an active pyramid, there and then gone. Someone was on the move. Starbride focused harder and tried to determine the type of pyramid, maybe even disable it, when pain stabbed through her skull. Her pyramid went dark, and she lost her balance. She tumbled onto the two beneath her.

"Starbride?" Hugo asked. He gently untangled himself from her. "Are you all right?"

"He…he disabled my pyramid." She stared at the dark, useless thing, all of its magic stripped away, turning it into so much junk. "He disabled the damned pyramid that I worked so damned hard to make!"

Hugo actually took a step back. Pennynail's mask was as cheerful as ever. Starbride glared into it. "The window is safe. Can you get us inside?"

He hesitated but then nodded. Starbride took a deep breath, glad he hadn't gestured for her to stay put. He scampered up the wall, balanced in cracks in the stone and the window lintel, and jammed his dagger into an upstairs shutter.

After it swung open, he dropped straight down. A burst of flame shot from where he'd been, catching his long red ponytail. When he hit the ground, he rolled, and tried to smother the flames. Starbride tackled him just as Hugo threw a cloak over his head. They stifled the flames, and when they uncovered him, he tugged them flat against the house before fingering the remaining inches of his mask's hair.

"Are you burnt?" Hugo said.

Pennynail shook his head. They all stared upward.

"He found the window I disabled," Starbride said, "the clever bastard, and waited for you there. Two can play that." She fished around in her satchel and found a flash bomb. "Temperance." She lobbed her pyramid through the upstairs window.

When the flash went off, they were rewarded with a little cry. Pennynail was up the wall and through the singed remains of the window in a heartbeat. He appeared a moment later and dangled both arms down, gesturing for them to hurry up.

Hugo boosted Starbride into the air. She heard him grunt and felt him shake under her weight; she fought the urge to stand on his face. She grasped Pennynail and pushed off the wall as he pulled.

The room was bare of furniture, and black scorch marks dominated the walls. A man in a chain shirt lay in the corner, a neat wound in his neck. His dead eyes still bore the red rims that came from looking at a flash bomb. Starbride searched him, grimacing at the dead flesh, but she didn't find a pyramid. She went through her satchel again; she'd only brought one disabler. Crowe would have called her shortsighted. She readied another flash bomb instead, the one pyramid she'd gotten really good at creating.

A thud came from behind her as Pennynail pulled Hugo inside. When Hugo caught his breath, he nodded at the hallway. Starbride didn't want to take any chances peeking around corners, but she didn't have enough flash bombs to chuck them around. She took a piece of crumbled plaster from the floor and tossed it into the hallway. A gout of flame answered her actions, just as she suspected.

Starbride didn't wait for the heat to fade before she pitched her flash bomb. Another wounded cry came from the hallway. Pennynail leapt over the few tongues of flame that clung to the floor. Starbride ran after him and dug another pyramid out of her satchel.

A bearded man sagged in a doorway off the hall and grasped his face. He fumbled inside a satchel and clung to the doorjamb. Pennynail rammed the pommel of a dagger against the man's forehead, and he slumped like a wet sack.

"Starbride!" Hugo cried.

The air rushed from her lungs as she pitched forward under his weight. Her knee slammed into the floor, and she threw her arms forward to catch herself. Behind her, she caught the ring of swordplay. Starbride scrambled forward, and turned to see Hugo on one knee, parrying the furious blows of a lithe, leather-clad woman. He'd knocked Starbride out of the way, and now he couldn't get back up again.

Leather Woman ducked to the side as a throwing knife sailed over Hugo's head. It missed her by inches and stuck in the wall, but it gave Hugo time to stand. Pennynail stepped past Starbride and moved to flank Leather Woman. She dodged to the side and kept them both in front of her, rapier snaking back and forth, and her dark eyes shifting to each target.

Starbride scooted to the downed pyradisté and tugged the satchel free of his body. She slung it around her own torso and then went through his clothes. When she found one more pyramid, she stashed it in the enemy satchel.

Leather Woman parried a strike from Hugo and gave ground as Pennynail came in for a jab. They backed her into the room they'd come from. Starbride stood to join them when she heard a crash and scream from farther down the hall. She scurried past the fight and peeked around the corner. Fiendish Lady Hilda had blown another hole in the floor, above the intruders, and as Starbride watched, she pulled a screaming man through the small space. She widened the hole with his body and turned his screams into half-conscious moans.

Lady Hilda's head snapped up. She stared at Starbride, her too-wide mouth smiling with sharp teeth. Starbride dipped into her satchel and curled around the first pyramid she found. Before she could throw it, Lady Hilda flung the man's body. Starbride ducked out of the way as the living missile streaked by and smacked into the wall. The body flopped down and lay at an odd angle, unmoving.

Starbride resisted the urge to run. Instead, she shouted, "Look out!" knowing Lady Hilda couldn't be far behind the flying body. Pennynail sprinted to her side while the sharp clash of steel said that Hugo still dueled with Leather Woman. Starbride pressed herself close to the wall, out of Lady Hilda's line of sight.

"We've found Lady Hilda!" Starbride yelled. She hoped the rest of the house could hear her. A clawed hand broke clear through the corner of the wall. It shredded the leather on Pennynail's sleeve and drew lines of blood across his arm, the droplets spattering the floor. Starbride flung her pyramid around the corner, and flame blossomed.

Lady Hilda screeched and drew back. Pennynail left off clutching his arm long enough to throw a knife as she stepped around the corner. Not even singed, Lady Hilda caught the knife in mid-air, clearly more at ease with her speed than she'd been the day before. Maybe she'd never put her Fiendish Aspect away.

A yelp from behind made Starbride turn. Hugo held one leg off the ground, but he'd scored a hit. Leather Woman clutched his rapier where it entered her chest, her eyes wide as she sagged and took his weapon with her.

"Hugo!" Starbride cried.

His eyes snapped to her at once, and he reclaimed his rapier before he crossed to stand beside her. Lady Hilda hesitated before three people instead of two. From below, Starbride heard Katya bellow, "Starbride!"

"Up here! We've found Lady Hilda!"

She had just enough time to stumble backward as Lady Hilda rushed them.

Chapter Thirty-one: Katya

Katya started toward the stairs, but Captain Ursula pulled on her arm. "Wait!"

"Get off of me!" All that mattered was reaching Starbride, but Ursula's grip was like steel.

Brutal grabbed a huge piece of debris and chucked it up the stairs. He grunted, bent double, and grabbed his back. The debris hit the top of the staircase and rolled down, rattling all the way across the steps.

Halfway up, the middle of the staircase exploded. Katya raised an arm to protect her head as debris pattered over them. She looked in awe at Ursula. "How did you know?"

"Seemed safe to assume."

"Katya!" Starbride screamed from upstairs.

"I'm coming!" Katya darted up the stairs, not caring if even the spirits got in her way. Brutal stayed at her side, and the others clattered behind her. They leapt or edged around the hole in the center.

On the second floor, Katya rounded a corner just in time to see Lady Hilda rake her claws across Pennynail's chest and send him crashing into Starbride and Hugo.

The surprised cries of those who'd never seen a Fiend echoed around her, along with footfalls as several people retreated down the stairs. Castelle and Ursula stood fast, each of them murmuring, "Spirits above!"

Lady Hilda crouched as if to spring up and run away again.

"Not this time!" Katya lunged just as Lady Hilda jumped through the ceiling. Her rapier pierced Lady Hilda's thigh and continued clean through, sticking in a wooden beam. Lady Hilda shrieked. Stuck halfway through the wood and plaster, she yanked on the rapier but couldn't pull it free. Katya tried to push farther into the wood, though Lady Hilda's thrashing threatened to shake her arms loose from their sockets.

Brutal grabbed Lady Hilda's uninjured leg and yanked, trying to wedge her into the hole she'd created. She shrieked again and kicked, but Ursula helped him pull. Castelle stabbed Lady Hilda in the stomach and gut, over and over, with her off-hand.

Someone behind them fired a crossbow bolt into Lady Hilda's chest, and with one final pull from Brutal and Ursula, she fell from the ceiling in a rain of plaster dust and wooden shards.

From where she'd collapsed, she swept out with her claws, and everyone jumped back. Castelle pulled on Katya's shoulders, making her lose her rapier in Lady Hilda's thigh but keeping the claws from opening her up.

Starbride yelled, "Shield your eyes!"

A glittering pyramid arced through the air and landed squarely atop Lady Hilda's head. Katya closed her eyes just in time to miss the flash. She hoped everyone else had the sense to do the same. Lady Hilda shrieked again, but it had a ragged edge, as if her strength was fading. While Castelle still blinked, Katya grabbed her sword and aimed to slice Lady Hilda's head clean off her neck.

"Princess Katyarianna, stop!"

At the top of the ruined staircase stood Duke Robert with several of his guard.

Katya blinked at them. "What in the spirits' names are you doing here?"

Breathing hard, his hunched form even lower, he pulled a scroll from out of his coat. "By order of the noble's council, I am taking Lady Hilda Montenegro into custody."

Katya turned back to Lady Hilda. She'd pulled the bolt from her chest and the rapier from her thigh and appeared human again, though bloody, disheveled, and dirty. She smiled, almost reclining in the debris in the tattered remains of her clothing.

"I see you got my note," she said.

Duke Robert nodded "Lady Hilda has asked to be tried by the noble's council as is her right."

Katya shook her head. "She's guilty of treason. She belongs to the crown."

"She has the right to be tried by the council of her choice," Duke Robert said. "You do not have carte blanche to execute people, Highness. No Umbriel does."

Katya almost winced at the reminder of what Reinholt had done, and what Duke Robert probably suspected the Umbriels had done to Brom. But by the spirits, she was so close! "You don't understand what she's become."

"I think, Highness, it's you who don't understand. I'll take her now. I have my own pyradisté to guarantee she won't escape."

Katya tightened her grip on the borrowed sword. She glanced at Brutal. He narrowed his eyes; he was with her. If he could stand, Pennynail was with her. Starbride would always be by her side, and Hugo would follow her lead.

Castelle tapped her shoulder. "Prudence."

Katya almost replied that she was one to talk.

Ursula cleared her throat. "Well, the nobles may get custody of Lady Hilda, but I'm in charge of keeping order in Marienne. My remaining officers and I will accompany you, your Grace, in order to guarantee that Lady Hilda remains in custody." She knelt and hauled Lady Hilda to her feet.

"Let go of me, peasant," Lady Hilda said, "before I stain my hands with your gutter blood."

Ursula drew her face close. "I'll give you the same choice I give any lowlife. We can do this the easy way or the very easy way." She aimed the pommel of her sword at Lady Hilda's chin.

Lady Hilda sneered, but Duke Robert stepped up before she could respond. "Accompany us if you wish, Captain, but we're leaving now." He took Lady Hilda's other arm, and one of his guards fitted her with arm and leg irons. Katya almost rolled her eyes. The Fiend could break those in a heartbeat. A cassock-clad man came forward and before Lady Hilda could protest, lifted a pyramid to her face.

She slumped in the arms of the guards.

"Starbride," Katya said, "is she really out?"

Starbride rustled in an unknown satchel for a moment before she produced a pyramid. "It seems so, but I can check further if—"

"You cannot pyramid a noble without their express permission or the permission of the nobles' council," Duke Robert said. He waved at his men, and they hauled Lady Hilda down the stairs.

"Form up!" Ursula called. She looked Katya in the eye. "I won't let her out of my sight. You could come with us…"

"Thank you," Katya said, "but I'm not joining the duke's party without a few more friends to watch my back. I'll take care of your wounded. Just leave us the cart."

Ursula nodded, gratitude in her eyes, and then she was away after the duke.

"Did the nobles just declare their defiance?" Hugo asked quietly.

"Certainly seems that way," Katya said. "How is everyone?"

"Pennynail is hurt the worst." Starbride helped to support him while he tried to stem his wound.

Brutal knelt in front of them. "Let me take a look."

"Has anyone seen Averie?" Katya asked.

"Seeing to the wounded." Starbride held a handkerchief to a gash on her forehead. "We sent someone to tell you where we'd gone."

Katya shook her head, feeling her own injuries at least. Even Hugo was favoring a knee. "I didn't get it." She couldn't let all the worry out right then. She'd collapse.

They climbed down the ruined stairway and carried the bodies of the dead Leather Woman, the living enemy pyradisté, and the barely living Watch officer. Maybe Lady Hilda thought her pyradisté already dead; more likely, she didn't think of him at all. Pennynail had trussed him with his arms behind his back.

Castelle gathered her own fighters. She'd lost one, and another was badly injured. She helped Katya gather the dead and then stood outside and stared at the house.

Katya followed her. "How's your arm?"

Castelle just shook her head. "I don't like this, Katya."

"I know. I'm sorry you lost a friend."

"He went the way he wanted to go, in combat. No, I don't like that Lady Hilda is going to get away with this."

"I'm on the nobles' council and so is my father. And we have allies besides."

"Count me as one of them, but the look in old Robert's eye makes me think that some of the old school will use Lady Hilda to defy your family. Unrest in the capital smacks of weakness to them."

Katya moved a few steps farther from the house. "It's not weakness. What Reinholt did might have blown over if not for…" She shook her head.

"If not for what?" Castelle stepped closer. "What the hell is going on? I don't know if you noticed, but Lady Hilda wasn't exactly human during our little confrontation."

"I know."

"If I didn't know better, I'd say she was a Fiend."

Katya took a deep breath. "She was."

"What?" Castelle rubbed her tattooed temple. Her hat had fallen off at some point, and she hadn't bothered to retrieve it. "If you want my help, tell me what's happening. I'm no good to you if I don't know what I'm up against."

In all their time together, as close as they'd gotten, Katya hadn't shared the Fiend or the Order. Castelle had never pried, unlike Starbride. Castelle hadn't cared enough to follow, to stumble onto the truth.

But here, now, was a different Castelle, more mature, a woman ready to help, to be involved. She'd already committed to helping Katya's cause, and she didn't even know what that cause was. *That* was the same old reckless Castelle, but this new one wanted to know what her friends were dying for.

Katya told her part of it, that the Umbriels were part Fiend, that they had to be in order to pacify the great Fiend Yanchasa, who rested under the palace at Marienne. "That's what it means when the kings and queens of Farraday call themselves the 'foes of Yanchasa the Mighty.'"

"So when you and I were a couple, you were a Fiend?"

"Not anymore. That's a long story, but when we were together, yes."

"I would have noticed. All the time we spent together…"

Katya shook her head. "It only came out when I was enraged or during the Waltz."

"I made you plenty angry."

"Not just angry. When someone threatened to hurt Starbride, I broke through the enchantment and became the Fiend. That's how she knows."

"To save her. How romantic."

Katya rolled her eyes. "And dangerous."

"That's when you knew you loved her, wasn't it? When you broke a powerful enchantment by will alone?"

Katya swallowed, thinking of that day and of the tenderness that came after. "Yes."

Castelle looked away. "Well, we, uh, we won't have to worry about that anymore. So does this mean that Lady Hilda is an Umbriel?"

"No." Katya told her as little as she could manage about Roland, about him merging with the Fiend, about it taking over upon his "death" and how he was determined to take the throne even if it meant tearing Marienne apart.

Castelle nodded along with the tale. "He's given this Fiendish essence to Lady Hilda."

"That's what I'm guessing."

"So the younger brother of the king whom everyone thought was dead became a Fiend and now wants to destroy you."

"You've got it," Katya said.

"How exactly is the Fiend transferred?"

"Well, one can be born with it, like I was, if both their parents have it."

"But you said it could be passed from person to person through a ritual."

Katya's cheeks burned hotter, and she cursed them. Why did only Castelle have such an effect on her?

"You're blushing. It must be what I think it is."

Katya turned away.

"So, ex-Prince Roland and Lady Hilda…Ah well, it doesn't matter. The important bit is that he's collecting allies. You're sure the civil unrest is his fault? From what I've seen, Magistrate Anthony is the one kicking up all the fuss."

"Roland has to be at the center. There have been too many pyramids floating around."

Castelle jerked her thumb to where Lady Hilda's pyradisté lay bound in the cart. "There's the pyradisté that could have provided them."

"It has to be someone of Roland's skill."

"Well, since I know little to nothing of pyramid magic, I'll have to take your word for it."

Katya smiled softly. "I have an inside source."

"She's very beautiful." Castelle gazed at the house as if she could see Starbride through its walls.

"And she's already given her heart away."

"Am I making you worry? You know what I always used to say."

"'If you know you've got her heart, you never worry'? Yes. That's why I always worried with you." Katya didn't wait for a reply. She moved into the house instead, suddenly needing to be near Starbride as if the mere thought of her conjured great power.

Starbride knelt in a sitting room and helped Averie and Brutal dress the wounded. As Katya came in, Hugo shuffled in from the kitchen with a large cauldron of water. "I don't know how you carried two of these, Brother Brutal."

"Training, Lord Hugo, that's all."

"I think you started with more muscle than I'll ever have."

Brutal chuckled, but his attention remained on those around him.

Katya knelt by Starbride's side. "How are they?"

"Besides one of Castelle's men, we lost five Watch officers. We're trying to get the rest ready to move. It's going to be crowded in that cart."

"We'll have to head for the Watch house as quickly as possible and hope Roland doesn't see an opportunity. How is Pennynail?"

"Stitched and resting."

Katya grimaced. She'd been stitched in the field a few times. Averie and Pennynail had to sit on her once after a brigand cut the back of her thigh wide open.

Soon, they had everyone patched and wrapped for travel. There were plenty of free horses. Katya wondered if Duke Robert had wanted to confiscate them to slow Katya down, but Captain Ursula wouldn't let him.

They traveled as quickly as they could. Duke Robert couldn't hold a council without someone from the royal family in attendance, usually the king, and Da would try and slow things down, as would Countess Nadia and her friends. Katya tried to tell herself that she was far from alone in her troubles, but she couldn't shake her unease. Nobles and courtiers were scheming, but she'd never expected rebellion inside the palace itself. All the givens she'd taken for granted were abandoning her one by one: the love of the populace, the love of her brother, the cohesion of her family, the support of the nobles. Even the strength of her Fiend.

With her Fiend, Katya could have torn Lady Hilda apart in the stable and prevented this mess. Afterward, Starbride could have returned her to normal.

Or she would have turned on her friends, hurt them, run amok through the stables, and into the streets. And with two Fiends present, Hugo might have broken his necklace, and then they would have had three rampaging Fiends. There were too many ifs. Katya tried to tell herself she was better off Fiend-less. Or so she hoped.

After a rattling ride through the forest and then Marienne, they paused by the Watch house and unloaded the officers. One of the sergeants informed them that Ursula had continued to the palace with the captive.

Katya and her friends rocketed through the streets, not wanting to give Roland time to put an ambush together. Katya kept her cloak close around her and ducked her chin into the mantle. They'd braced Castelle's wounded and Pennynail in their saddles, but it couldn't have been a comfortable ride. When Katya skidded to a halt in the royal stables, she nearly ran down one of the grooms.

"Star," Katya said, "can you see to the wounded?"

"Yes, go!"

Katya ran into the palace, Castelle right behind her.

To her surprise, Hugo followed them, too. He limped but managed to keep up. "I've never attended the council, but I have my title."

"Glad to have you," Katya said.

They went straight for the council rooms, no cleaning up, and no stopping for breath or food. The guards bowed before Katya, though their eyes narrowed at Castelle and Hugo.

Katya pushed past and left the guard to find Castelle and Hugo in the nobles' book. She burst into a room filled with angry voices. Da stood at the head of the table, and by the red tint of his neck, he was on his way to losing his temper.

"At last!" Da shouted, and the room went momentarily quiet.

Duke Robert was on his feet like many others. He stood near the end of the table closest to the doors, and by the faces around him, Katya could tell lines were being drawn, allegiances clear by what end of the table one chose. Countess Nadia and Viscount Lenvis were near her father's side as well as old Earl Lamont and several others.

Lady Hilda was nowhere in sight, nor was Captain Ursula.

Katya moved to stand with her father, Castelle and Hugo behind her. She bowed to Da, and he inclined his head. As if introduced to civility by this exchange, the rest of the nobles bowed to Katya.

"We are debating whether to have a trial for the traitorous lady," Da said.

"I beg your pardon, Majesty, but treason has yet to be determined," Duke Robert said. "We must have a trial to even put that label upon her."

"I see you've got the argument well and circular," Katya said in her court drawl. Several people laughed, including some at the other end of the table. Even though they'd chosen sides, some clearly weren't happy with arguing.

"A traitor to the crown falls under the jurisdiction of the crown," Duke Robert said, slowly and carefully. "No one disputes this, but the lady has asked the noble's council to decide whether or not she is a traitor."

Katya fought to keep her own temper in check. Before she could even begin to try a reasoned argument, Hugo blurted, "She tried to kill the princess consort!"

Katya grabbed his arm. When he looked at her, she stared pointedly at his chest where his pyramid necklace hid under his clothes. He swallowed so forcefully she saw it in his neck. The nobles murmured amongst themselves.

"I saw no such a thing," Duke Robert said. "I saw the lady attacked in her own home. I understand there is evidence of a crime, but that evidence should be laid before this council. Otherwise, it seems as if the Umbriels are taking whatever course they choose, whenever they choose, and to *whomever* they choose."

"All for no cause," another of the nobles said, and others echoed the sentiment.

There was greed and lust for power on some faces, but on more, there was simply anger, as if they were appalled at the royal family's actions. Katya couldn't help but wonder if some of them were influenced by Roland.

"We have not had a trial by nobles' council in many years," Da said.

That was because traitors to the crown were taken out by the Order, but Katya didn't mention that.

"There are more nobles now than in the past," Da said. "This room is so full that not every noble can have a seat at the table. And if we are obliged to invite every noble from the countryside to a trial, how will we fit them all?"

Heads nodded along the room.

"And how, Your Grace," Da said, "will we deal with so many tongues wanting their say? A trial could take years."

"Fair point," Countess Nadia said.

Earl Lamont knocked on the wooden table. "We must consult the records. Our forebears laid out rules for just such occasions."

Everyone was forced to agree, and page boys were sent to fetch the fat old volumes from the library, rules of order and guidelines for how a trial would be set forth. They spent the next hours poring over them, sifting through old-fashioned terms and outdated courtesies.

Nobles' trials were meant to have selections of nobles from every tier, with the greatest landowners holding the most seats. The king or queen and the heir would attend, so would every duke or duchess. Below that, it became a bit hazy, the lesser nobles being divided by acreage. The whole enterprise made Katya's head spin. They finally settled on every earl—there were three left—four counts, three viscounts, three barons, and two lords, each to be chosen by seniority and regardless of gender.

The lords and ladies grumbled, but since most of their tier rarely came to court, the rest of the party shouted them down. Some of the nobles would have to be called in from the countryside and given the option to decline being on the council at all.

Earl Lamont thumbed through another old document. "Our forebears wrote of a gallery as well, holding some nobles who may not speak but shall bear witness." He made a note on a piece of parchment. "There's another list to argue over. As well as…" He peered at the yellowed pages. "It says, 'various leaders of great standing and appreciation in the city of Marienne and those courtiers who have proven themselves of honorable fashion and unstained character.'"

"That rules them all out," Castelle said. Only a few people snickered.

One lord sneered. "Leaders of the city? Some of us will be excluded to make room for commoners?"

Katya fought not to roll her eyes.

Earl Lamont looked over his spectacles. "The law is the law."

"A captain of the Watch," Castelle added smoothly, "is a leader in great standing and appreciation of the city."

"So are the masters of the Pyradisté Academy and the Halls of Law," Da supplied.

"The champion of Farraday," Countess Nadia said.

Duke Robert frowned. "He's a lord."

Earl Lamont scanned the book again. "This calls for the champion, though not as a speaker on the council."

"Well," Duke Robert said slowly, "a city magistrate has as great a standing and appreciation of the city as a Watch captain."

Katya's gut froze. She knew he was speaking of Magistrate Anthony. She was about to protest when her father touched her shoulder. Anthony wouldn't be able to speak, after all. He would only be a witness.

"It seems we have another list to make after our arguing nobles, Lamont," Da said.

They debated again for hours and finally decided on the gallery, including a great many nobles and courtiers, the masters of the Pyradisté Academy and the Halls of Law, a commander of the Watch instead of a captain, a magistrate of the people and his assistant, and the supreme heads of all the various chapterhouses in Marienne.

As each was decided, Katya tried to list in her head who would stand with them and who against them but found the task almost impossible.

CHAPTER THIRTY-TWO: STARBRIDE

As soon as Starbride saw the enemy pyradisté locked in the dungeons, she retreated to her apartment to clean up and change. Everyone else was tending to their wounds; Starbride had something more important to tend to.

Her mother fussed over the cut on her forehead and her dirty, disheveled outfit full of tears and snags. The leather had probably saved her life, but all her mother could see was the mess.

"You should go home," Starbride said, interrupting her mother's rant about nobles and their parties.

"What did you say?"

"There won't be any more outings or picnics or parties. The nobles are gathering, Mother. It may be that…it won't be safe here."

"If it's not safe enough for me…"

"I can't go. Katya needs me."

"And you need me."

Starbride shook her head slowly. "Only pyramids and weapons can help me now."

Her mother stared at her. As silly as she seemed at times, she wasn't stupid, far from it. "They could use me against you."

Starbride closed her eyes, terrified by the thought, and yet so relieved she hadn't been the one to say it. Her mother's touch on her chin made her open her eyes again.

"How can I leave my extraordinary daughter in danger? My one child?"

"If it becomes too dangerous, I'll gather the lot of them, and we'll all vacation in Allusia."

Her mother breathed a laugh. "I'll have the spare room made up. I hope they don't mind squashing together."

Dawnmother and Rainhopeful said their own good-byes. Starbride's mother never lost the pinched look between her brows, even when Starbride saw her packed and stocked with provisions. They'd have to stop for the night not far out of Marienne, but Starbride thought that better than staying another night in the palace. Her mother gave her one last hug, and then they were gone into the dusk, Starbride marveling at the idea that she could feel heavier and lighter at the same time but for far different reasons.

Hours later, Starbride waited, and at last the dirty, bedraggled Katya wandered into her apartment. She sent Dawnmother for hot water. After the exhausting day, Dawnmother had ordered Averie to bed hours before. Katya smiled when she heard it. "I bet her face was something to behold."

"She barely argued," Dawnmother said, "just made some feeble protests until her head hit the pillow. I had to cover her with a blanket." After the hot water and a small basin arrived, Dawnmother left them alone.

"I'm too tired for a bath," Katya said.

"Then we'll do what we can with a washcloth and soap."

Katya grinned and eased into a chair. "Can't sleep with stinky royalty?"

"You'll feel better once you're clean." She helped Katya strip off her clothes and then sit in a robe with her feet in the washbasin.

Katya raised an eyebrow. "I didn't know you were going to bathe me."

"*Bathe* being the word. Don't expect anything more."

Katya groaned in disappointment, but it was a feeble protest. Even as Starbride scrubbed up her legs, her eyes were going half-lidded. They popped open briefly as Starbride ventured higher, but she didn't linger on any specific area.

After Katya was clean and her wounds tended, Starbride leaned her back in a chair, over the basin. "Now, let's see what we can do about that hair."

Katya hummed in pleasure as Starbride massaged her scalp. "We have our council, finally. It took some doing to get everyone to agree."

"I was wondering if you were going to tell me now or wait until morning."

"My father and I are included. The rest was a struggle down to the last courtier. Every noble got to choose an assistant to take notes for them. I chose you, since consorts can't be present in their own right."

"Should I love you or hit you?"

"I doubt my father will choose anyone. He won't need notes; he'll crib from Earl Lamont."

"And what of the other nobles?"

Katya went through a long, exhaustive list, most of whom Starbride didn't know. She picked out Countess Nadia, Earl Lamont, and Duke Robert.

"It *would* be Duke Robert," Starbride said.

"All of the dukes and duchesses who don't decline to come will have a seat."

"No Viscount Lenvis, Baroness Castelle, or Lord Hugo?"

"Far too young to make the cut."

"Do we know anything about the rest?"

Katya shrugged, and as she spoke, her voice lost momentum. "Not as much as we'd like. Master Bernard from the Pyradisté Academy will be there as a witness."

"Moral support, then."

"Lady Hilda wouldn't ask for a council trial unless she had something up her sleeve."

Starbride finished rinsing Katya's hair and wrapped it up in a towel. "I sent my mother home."

Katya opened one eye. "Is that good or bad? I can't recall."

"Both. I pronounce you clean."

"I pronounce me tired."

"This way then, Crown Princess Tired. The royal bedchamber awaits."

Katya's lips were warm against her cheek. "Why were you ever a courtier when you could have been a lady's maid?"

"I wouldn't bathe anyone but you."

"For that I am very grateful."

The next morning they prepared for the trial. The servants cleared one of the ballrooms of frippery; it was the only space large enough to accommodate the council. They left the dais where it sat. As the king and crown princess, Katya and King Einrich had the right to sit above the others. They thought it best to remind everyone of that fact.

Starbride tended to agree. Katya's family were not only the rulers, they were the injured party. Everyone needed to be reminded of both those facts. The servants brought in long tables and laid them out in a square, with one end open so witnesses and the accused could pass in and out, and so the Umbriels, separate on their dais, would be sitting at the figurative head.

As the debate began about who would sit where, Starbride tried her best not to sigh. The nobles would sit in order of title, starting from the empty middle where the king would be and leading around both sides, leaving the lords to sit at the opposite end. Chairs were then put in rows behind the square for the gallery, nobles up front, everyone else behind to bicker amongst themselves as to who would sit where.

Starbride watched the arrivals from the curtained area behind the dais, the royal waiting room. The commoners who filled most of the gallery seats didn't seem to care where they sat as long as they were in the room.

The Umbriels would enter the ballroom last, not for another hour, but the commoners seemed so excited that most had already arrived, all except Magistrate Anthony and his new assistant. Most of the nobles relegated to watching were there as well; they scooted away from the common people with looks of distaste. Luckily, the courtiers served as a nice buffer between the two groups.

The curtain moved slightly, disturbed by someone entering the small room by the door at Starbride's back. She turned, expecting to see Katya, maybe King Einrich.

Roland stood there, bold as brass, and smiling as if they were old friends. Starbride forgot to breathe, too stunned to even fall backward through the curtain.

Roland put one finger to his lips. "Cry out and you force me to activate every pyramid on my person. I'd survive. Would you?"

Starbride's breath came in shallow gasps. She wanted to run, but his words seeped into her thoughts.

"You look like a gasping fish." He stepped closer, fingers splayed on the breast of his simple coat. "I'm only here today in an advisory capacity, but I knew you'd see through my disguise, so I thought I'd say hello."

He looked different from when she'd seen him, it was true. He'd dyed his hair redder, and his beard wasn't so neatly trimmed. It made the lower half of his face far heavier, but he was still plainly the dead Prince Roland. "Your own family will know you," she whispered.

"You and Master Bernard will be the only ones to see through my disguise."

Starbride squinted at him, fascinated in spite of herself. "You're using a pyramid?"

"Master Bernard and I have never actually met, so no trouble there."

"You're betting a lot."

He actually laughed. "You're so bright, perfect for my niece. Are you sure you won't join the winning team? Won't convince Little K to join me?"

"You're a murderer!" She cast a glance at the curtain again. "You tried to kill us."

"I wouldn't have killed you. Lady Hilda acted on her own. It just happened to fit very neatly with what I have in mind for Farraday. Nothing I've done could have been accomplished if people were perfectly happy under Einrich's rule."

"No one is ever perfectly happy."

He didn't lose his smile, but it gained a sinister edge, and his features seemed to ripple before settling. "They will be during my reign."

Starbride backed away and tried to edge around him. She couldn't lead him out among the crowded ballroom.

Roland stepped aside and gestured toward the door. "Go ahead. I won't stop you."

"I'll tell Katya."

"Do so. If she chooses to draw on Magistrate Anthony's assistant, how will that look? Ah, did you suspect that? In his grief, the dear magistrate needed a firm hand holding him up. I've done what I can."

Starbride licked her lips and tried to think. No wonder the magistrate had turned against them so completely.

Roland shrugged. "I've already told you what will happen if the, uh, fur begins to fly. Do you really think I'm above killing everyone in that room?" His eyes flicked toward the council chamber. "Einrich and Katya might survive it with their Fiends, maybe, but everyone else?"

After a wink, Roland strode through the door, leaving it open. Starbride waited a few heartbeats. If she told King Einrich and Katya, they would insist on acting, but that might play right into Roland's plans. Disguised as Anthony's assistant, he would plead ignorance and look like a victim, more than that, a victim under the supposed protection of the Umbriels' most-outspoken opponent.

But Anthony himself might be under pyramid influence. An idea flashed into Starbride's head. If she could break Roland's disguise pyramid, then everyone would know he was a pyradisté. They might not recognize the man, but he would be exposed as a pyramid user.

What might exposure get them? If King Einrich recognized him and convinced the others that he was the dead prince, Roland would lay waste with his pyramids. Starbride couldn't neutralize them all, not before he detonated them. How many people would die in those first few seconds?

Katya could be among them. She no longer carried a Fiend.

Starbride ran from the room. She needed advice quickly, and she couldn't get it from Katya. She raced to Freddie's tower. He was stepping into his underwear as she burst through the door. He hopped back, grabbed a dagger from a nearby table, and cocked to throw before he seemed to recognize her.

"Starbride! What in the spirits' names—"

"No time!" She rattled off the story, watching his face grow horrified. Only halfway through did she realize he was naked, but there was no time to blush. All she could do was finish.

"He's in the council ballroom right now?" Freddie asked.

"But if we warn the others—"

"Everyone could die."

"Yes!" She paced, grabbed up a pillow, and twisted it. "What should we do?"

When she turned back around, he had a towel draped around his waist. She couldn't remember when he'd put it on, but she was so relieved to be part of a "we" in her situation, that she didn't feel anything but nervous, terrified energy.

"Don't tell the council," Freddie said. "It can't make anything better. If you do, and Roland manages to kill the council while sparing the royals, what does it look like?"

"Like the king's supporters killed the council and its witnesses."

Freddie nodded. "Including a reformation-preaching magistrate and his assistant. Who would believe the dead prince came back to life as a Fiend in order to take the kingdom through non-violent reform?"

Starbride bit her lip. "He's a genius."

"You should have known him when he was alive. I heard he was beyond compare."

"When do I tell them? When do I tell Katya?"

"Afterward."

"She'll be so angry. Her father will be furious!"

"You'll have to weather it, just like Crowe did when he kept things from them for their own good. You won't have to tell them alone."

Starbride nearly sagged in gratitude. "But you won't be able to speak."

He grinned, but it had a sad edge. "Moral support."

She hugged him then. She had no choice. His arms went around her hesitantly, and she remembered with a start his state of undress. She nearly jumped back, shaking as the adrenaline left her.

"Are you all right?" he asked.

"I better get back to the council room."

"I'll come through the passageways and be behind the curtain in the waiting room."

Starbride hesitated, unable to believe they were just going to sit in a room with Roland and not say anything. "I thought about using a pyramid to expose his disguise."

"He'll have something else in place. He's a genius, remember?"

"The best way to act is not to act? I'm terrible at that."

"You'll learn."

Starbride waited outside his room while he dressed and then she hurried to the small waiting room, Pennynail with her. Katya and her father were waiting. They stared at Pennynail in surprise.

Starbride nodded at him. "In case of surprises."

Katya nodded slowly, but suspicion didn't leave her eyes. "I guess it would be foolish to ask if we were expecting any surprises."

Starbride only laughed, but she heard the nervousness in it. She didn't know how she would go beyond the curtain and not call Roland out, how she could possibly sit through a trial and listen to evidence.

And Roland would be waiting for her to act. Starbride kept telling herself that, kept picturing the broken, scorched bodies of the council members, the divot in the floor that would be all that remained of Katya, her body engulfed in nothingness.

The herald announced them. Starbride forgot to breathe as she walked past the curtain. Her eyes raked over the council members and audience until she found him. He watched her, a little smile on his face.

"Star," Katya whispered in her ear.

Starbride whipped her head around so fast that Katya leaned back. "They can't sit until we do," Katya said.

Starbride looked down to see that she was standing in front of her chair on the dais. She sat without a word, but when she looked back, Roland was still watching her. When the herald listed the reasons they were there, Roland finally looked away, and Starbride could breathe again. After the herald finished, the Guard escorted Lady Hilda inside.

She had cleaned herself up and chosen a simple, demure dress in a light mint color. She looked calm, not at all haughty, as if being escorted to a garden party. She sat in a chair at the center of the square of tables and tucked her legs discreetly to the side.

The herald read off the charges against her. Lady Hilda dabbed at her eyes with a handkerchief. The herald then called for evidence. King Einrich motioned toward the doors, and Captain Ursula strode into the room. She told them of Lady Hilda's men attacking the caravan containing the fake Starbride, of the evidence gleaned from the men's memories, evidence that had been confirmed by a pyradisté working for the city Watch.

Duke Robert stood. "Captain Ursula, was Lady Hilda present at this attack?"

"No, Your Grace."

"And you know she was involved in this scheme only from the memories extracted first by the crown princess consort."

Ursula nodded. "And then confirmed by one of my pyradistés."

"Could those memories have been planted by the crown princess consort?"

Starbride bristled. Katya patted her arm as if telling her to take it easy.

"I don't have the expertise to answer that question, Your Grace," Ursula said.

"Luckily," Countess Nadia said, "we have someone who does, if Master Bernard is allowed to speak."

The nobles conferred with one another briefly before they agreed.

Master Bernard walked to the front of the room. "Any implanted memories would have been detected as such."

The supreme head of the intelligence and wisdom chapterhouses raised a hand from the gallery. Duke Robert's assistant courtier rushed back, collected a note, and hurried it forward.

"Is that really the case, Master Bernard?" Duke Robert said after he read the note. "What if the pyradisté who inserted the memories is stronger than the person reading them? Research indicates that the superior pyradisté could hide his work from the lesser."

Starbride narrowed her eyes. Well, they knew whose side the knowledge chapterhouse was on.

"No student, no matter how prestigious her title, could have magic strong enough to hide from a graduate of the academy, Your Grace," Master Bernard said. "Some of our best pyradistés work for the Watch."

Duke Robert smiled. "What if such a student had the power of a Fiend on her side?"

As the ballroom erupted in mutterings, Starbride's belly turned cold. She avoided looking at Katya, barely, and looked to Roland instead. He had his head bent over a sheaf of papers, as any good assistant would.

Lady Hilda burst into tears before the babble of the council could get any higher.

Duke Robert patted her shoulder. "What is it, my dear?"

"I didn't know what it would mean!"

"What are you speaking of?"

Lady Hilda took a few deep, shuddering breaths. "I only wanted to please her. I didn't know what a night of passion with her could bring!"

Duke Robert glanced at the dais. "Who?"

Lady Hilda pointed a shaky finger at Katya. "The crown princess. Making love to her did this to me!" Her features blurred into the cold eyes and horns of a Fiend.

Everyone in the room leapt to their feet. Even though he wasn't armed, Lord Vincent stepped in front of the dais. Chairs toppled as people sought to back away. Even Duke Robert seemed discomfited, and he knew what was coming or Starbride was a horse's uncle.

Roland acted as afraid as the rest, but he must have been grinning inside. Lady Hilda simply sat in her chair, sobbing quietly. Cold came from her in waves.

"Can you…control yourself, my dear?" Duke Robert asked, but he didn't dare touch her.

Lady Hilda took a deep breath and then blurred again, as human as the rest of them after a heartbeat. "If one night of love could do this to me, what must it have done to her?" Lady Hilda pointed again, this time at Starbride, and her face was the picture of sympathy. "You poor thing, what did she do to you?"

Everyone's heads swung toward Starbride. She shook her head, letting all her confusion show. "She did nothing to me."

"Perhaps," one of the other nobles said, "it's you who did something to her."

Duke Robert nodded as if a sudden idea occurred to him. "Yes, if the princess's…affection could always turn her lovers into Fiends, who knows how many monsters we'd have running around? When you had your affair, Lady Hilda, was it after Starbride became the consort?"

Lady Hilda nodded and sobbed.

"And then you became part…Fiend."

Lady Hilda wept through another nod. Starbride almost bit through her lip. She felt Katya's grip upon her arm.

"What are you saying?" Starbride asked.

"Master Bernard?" Duke Robert asked. "How much do you know of Allusian pyradistés?"

"I…I…" Mater Bernard looked from Lady Hilda to Starbride. "I don't know…"

The supreme head of the knowledge chapterhouse lifted another note, as quickly retrieved as the other. He stared at Lady Hilda with fascination.

"It seems little to nothing is known about them," Duke Robert said. "So you see, Lords and Ladies, ladies and gentlemen, there are two sides to this story. True, Lady Hilda acted unconscionably, but how could she do otherwise under the influence of this evil creature living inside her, a Fiend like Yanchasa the Mighty, the very creature the Umbriels are supposed to oppose."

The council mumbled. Countess Nadia rapped her knuckles on the table. "What proof against the Umbriels, Robert? Any at all?"

Duke Robert walked slowly toward the dais. "Against the Umbriels? None. After their family summoned Yanchasa centuries ago and then had to defeat him, they would not willingly embrace such a creature again."

He pinned Starbride with his eyes, and his deep voice seemed to echo in her stomach. "If I recall, Crown Princess Katyarianna changed once you arrived, Starbride. On the night of your first public appearance as princess consort, a violent earthquake killed many people inside the palace. Several partygoers spotted you running deep into the palace, into lost corridors. Do you deny that you were communing with Yanchasa, bargaining with the creature?"

"That I was…what?" Starbride couldn't help a nervous laugh. "That's absurd!" She glanced to the side, but Katya hadn't moved. King Einrich also sat completely still. Like a bolt of lightning, Starbride realized they were hypnotized. She dipped into her pocket and pulled out a pyramid that would break Roland's hold.

The room erupted in cries. Master Bernard pulled a pyramid of his own, and Lord Vincent leapt onto the dais to stand between Starbride and the Umbriels. Starbride stumbled away from his intense stare.

"Put it down," Master Bernard said.

"She's done something to the king!" someone in the room cried.

"And the princess," someone else shouted. "They're both so still!"

"No!" Starbride pointed at Roland. "It's him!"

Roland's mouth dropped open. He clutched his sheaf of papers to his chest and stood on shaky legs. "Me?"

"My assistant?" Magistrate Anthony asked. "He's just been sitting here this entire time."

Starbride's heart pounded. She couldn't think. All she could see was a room that had been friendly one moment and hostile the next. She pleaded with herself to think of something, but the pleading got in the way of thought. In the center of the room, unobserved by anyone else, Lady Hilda smirked.

A knife flew out of the curtain behind Starbride. It streaked through the room to strike Roland in the leg. With a curse, he sagged and hung on Anthony's arm. Starbride focused and put all her heart into what she was doing. Her eyes fell into the dark haze of pyramid sight, and she saw a golden bubble surrounding Katya and King Einrich. A tendril from that sphere flowed from Roland and led to a pyramid hidden in his clothing.

Starbride attacked that golden tendril with sheer panic, making her head pound and stealing her breath, but desperation served her well. Roland's pyramid went dark. King Einrich and Katya gasped, but something struck Starbride from the side. She staggered on the steps of the dais. Lord Vincent had pushed her and knocked the pyramid from her grip, but she kept her feet. Master Bernard stomped toward her, pyramid held high; several council members howled for her blood. Any cries begging for everyone to keep their reason became lost in the flood of voices.

Starbride ran. Pennynail's leather-clad arm shot from the curtain and pulled her inside, but her pursuers followed her. She grabbed one of the stiff, high-backed chairs just inside the curtain and threw it, tangling the steps of those following her. The door to the secret passageway stood open, and Pennynail waved her inside. She ran through, and he shut it behind them. Starbride lit the lamp just in time to see Pennynail plunge a dagger into the mechanism that opened the door, locking it from their side.

Starbride wanted to collapse against the wall, wanted to weep, wanted to make sure Katya was safe, but there wasn't time. Pennynail hauled her to her feet, and she ran with him through the passageways, not heeding where they were going.

Chapter Thirty-three: Katya

Katya took a deep breath. For the last several minutes, she had struggled, mentally shrieking, but unable to move as the council fell to chaos.

Starbride had fled. Several people chased her while Lord Vincent stood just in front of the thrones. Katya shoved out her chair and tried to escape the strangling feeling that had overtaken her.

"Enough!" she shouted.

The room stuttered to silence. Katya cast a quick glance at her father. He coughed and waved for her to proceed.

"Everyone, get back in here!" Katya yelled. "This council isn't dismissed."

Word passed, and those who'd ran into the waiting room trickled back inside. Their faces ran the gamut from confused and angry, to stunned and frightened.

"Take your seats." Katya wanted to race after Starbride, but she had to see if the disastrous council could be reassembled. They couldn't lose the chance to prove Lady Hilda's guilt.

Several people from the gallery clustered around Magistrate Anthony's assistant. He seemed young, no more than nineteen or twenty, and he held a bandage to his leg. What had Pennynail been thinking?

"Is he all right?" Katya called.

The supreme head of the strength chapterhouse stood from where she investigated the wound. "Should be, Crown Princess. The wound wasn't so deep."

"Lords and Ladies," Katya said, "ladies and gentlemen, hear me. I am not now, nor ever was, under any malicious influence by Princess Consort Starbride. She did *not* make me a Fiend."

As people shuffled back to their seats, they looked to Lady Hilda, who kept up her hiccupping, miserable façade.

Duke Robert stepped forward. Color had bloomed in his cheeks, pushing back his pallor. "Then you would not object, Highness, if we tested you for the same Fiendish essence that Lady Hilda possesses?"

Katya smiled slowly. Roland, wherever he was hiding, had given this man some bad advice. "Of course not."

Duke Robert's face twitched. Katya looked to Master Bernard. He put a pyramid back in his cassock pocket, a very sheepish look on his face.

"Can you do it, Master Bernard?" Katya asked. "Is there a test for Fiends?"

"I…I suppose it might work like any other mind pyramid. If I could locate the part of the mind that houses the…creature, I could search for it in anyone except a fellow pyradisté."

"Seems a simple answer then," Da said. "If Master Bernard can locate this part of the mind in Lady Hilda, he will know what to look for in my daughter, though I am certain he will not find it." He gave Lady Hilda a cold glance. "I don't know what you have been cavorting with, madam, to give you such an affliction, but it did not come from the crown princess."

No, Katya thought, but it came from a prince.

Lady Hilda shook her head wildly. "I will not submit to this."

"Quite right," Da said. "The council must first agree to proceed. What objection might anyone have?" He glanced around the room. The occupants looked to each other and shrugged.

"You brought this to our attention, your grace," Countess Nadia said to Duke Robert. "Shall we vote? Unless you object to Master Bernard conducting the test?"

Duke Robert shook his head slowly. "We all trust the master, of course."

Lady Hilda stared daggers at Katya. "Why are you so calm?"

Katya blinked, feigning ignorance. "Because your lies are about to be exposed for what they are."

"Let us vote," Da said. "Master Bernard will use a pyramid on Lady Hilda to determine the part of her mind that gives her the appearance of a Fiend, yea or nay?"

"Yea," the party said.

"Master Bernard, proceed."

"No!" Lady Hilda shrieked, and her Fiendish aspect blurred over her features again. She leapt from her chair.

Master Bernard dug for his pyramid. Lady Hilda slammed into him and knocked him sideways. Lord Vincent and Captain Ursula streaked forward, but Lady Hilda flung both of them away.

The supreme head of the strength chapterhouse tossed her red robe aside, revealing her heavily muscled body clad only in a breechclout and leather halter. She rushed from the gallery, leapt over the table, and knocked Lady Hilda over. Lady Hilda grabbed the woman's muscled arms and pitched her, trailing blood as she flew, through the air and into the wall. Guards clattered in the hallway outside. Lady Hilda hurled herself toward Katya.

Katya rolled to the side, narrowly dodging the claws over her head. "Protect the king!"

Lady Hilda pounced and knocked the breath from Katya's lungs. She grabbed Lady Hilda's wrists, but they pushed steadily for her face, like she'd grabbed hold of a horse. Katya kicked, and Lady Hilda grunted, but it didn't stop the slow descent of her claws.

A chair crashed across Lady Hilda's shoulders. Countess Nadia let go of it and then sprang away with more spryness than Katya would have given her credit for. Just as Lady Hilda glanced up, she caught Ursula's boot full in the face. She rocked backward, her arms going slack.

Katya wriggled free. She resisted the urge to punch Lady Hilda in the face, knowing the Fiendish visage might break her fist. With a pyramid raised, Master Bernard crept up on them. Lady Hilda whirled around, caught hold of his arm, and twisted it until Katya heard a horrid snap. Master Bernard paled, made a strangled gurgle, and stared at his arm as if just noticing it had been attached upside down. Only when Lady Hilda shoved him away did he scream.

The Guard charged, weapons ready. Lady Hilda screeched, eyes fixed on Katya, and crouched as if ready to leap again. Before she could move, her eyes flew wide, mouth working, and her shoulders slumped. Her features bled to normal as she swayed back and forth, and then fell, giving Katya a view of the knife sticking out of the back of her neck.

Magistrate Anthony's assistant stood close behind her, his fist clenched as if the knife was still in his grasp. He must have had the speed and silence of a serpent. He glanced at Katya, and for a moment, she thought she saw something in his eyes, something she recognized. Before she could study him further, he limped back to Magistrate Anthony's side.

Lady Hilda was an unmoving lump, though human again. Katya looked for her father. Vincent and the Guard had backed Da into a corner, clearly trying to avoid everyone and get to the exit. Vincent had appropriated a sword and held it ready.

Katya stalked toward him. Vincent lowered his sword and bowed. "Crown—"

She slammed her fist into his nose and felt it squelch under her fingers. Blood sprayed before he clapped one hand over his face.

"Katya!" Da said.

"If you lay a finger on Starbride again, I'll have your head." Katya turned to the room at large. "How many of you helped that thing malign an innocent woman?" She turned to Duke Robert, who'd gone white as a sheet. "Your Grace, out of all the tales you've ever heard of Fiends, you've never heard of their power to manipulate?"

His mouth worked for a moment. "It all made sense."

"The princess consort did flee," Magistrate Anthony said.

Katya snorted. "From a band of people calling for her hide? I would have fled, too."

"But…" Duke Robert wiped his lips and swallowed. "If not from Allusian magic, then how did Lady Hilda come to possess the attributes of a Fiend?"

Katya gestured at the head of the knowledge chapterhouse. "Why don't you ask our learned friend here who knows so much?" She would have glared daggers at the head, but he crept toward Lady Hilda's corpse as if sneaking up on a treasure trove.

"Utterly fascinating," he said. "Can I take the body?"

"No. We'll keep it here for you to examine." Like hell, she thought, but it bought them time to figure out what to do. She gestured two of the Guard forward. "Take it to Crowe's old study."

"I'm sorry, Crown Princess," Vincent said, the words made ridiculous through his clogged nose. "If the princess consort is innocent, I wholeheartedly apologize and submit myself for punishment."

Katya ignored him.

"You did appear transfixed," Countess Nadia said. "You stared straight ahead and didn't move."

"It must have been Fiendish power," one of the barons said.

"Oh!" a courtier exclaimed. "The princess consort was trying to free you! How romantic!"

"Go and find her," Da said in Katya's ear. "I'll be fine here with the Guard."

Katya scanned the council one last time and left before anyone could object.

Chapter Thirty-four: Starbride

Starbride ran for her apartment but paused just outside the door in the secret passageway. "If they're looking for me, this will be one of the first places they check."

Freddie lifted his mask and listened at the door. "Stand clear. I might be coming back in a hurry." After he pulled his mask down, he toggled the switch and leapt through.

Starbride heard a scream from the other side: Dawnmother. Her voice asked an urgent question, but Starbride couldn't make out the words. When Freddie didn't come dashing back, Starbride followed him.

"Star!" Dawnmother cried. She stared at Freddie as if he were a mad strangler.

"Dawn, we have to go. No time to explain."

Dawnmother followed them without question. Freddie disabled the mechanism for this door, too, leaving it only accessible from inside the secret passageway.

"What's going on?" Dawnmother asked.

As they walked, Starbride told her what had happened in the council chamber. Dawnmother cursed those who'd attacked Starbride with the worst swears in the Allusian language. Freddie took them to his hidden room in the tower.

"Should we get out of the city?" Dawnmother asked.

"If I didn't free Katya and King Einrich, we can't. If Roland can keep them hypnotized…I have to try again."

"Star, they'll kill you, especially that awful Lord Vincent."

Freddie lifted his mask again. "That bastard. If he hadn't been so quick with his blade, we wouldn't be in this situation."

Dawnmother shrugged. "Every 'if' is a hole in the road."

Starbride had to grin. "You're right. Horsestrong wouldn't be sitting here moaning. He'd have a plan."

"Let me talk to the servants and find out what's happening."

"Dawn, they'll grab you, too."

"If I'm careful, they'll never know I'm there." She turned to Freddie. "Can you get me to the secret passages by the servant quarters? Somewhere the nobles won't think to go?"

"I can get you close enough."

"I can't just sit here and wait for you!" Starbride said.

"I'd never dream of it," Freddie said. "You shouldn't stay anywhere for long."

Starbride let out a relieved breath. "When Katya is free, I'll tell her you saved me from insanity."

After grabbing some candles, they hurried to the servants' quarters, and Starbride and Freddie stayed in the passages while Dawnmother ventured into the palace.

Starbride rubbed her arms and paced as far as she could in the small space. After what seemed like hours but couldn't have been more than twenty minutes, Dawnmother slipped back inside.

"There are too many rumors to sort," Dawnmother said. "The entire palace is abuzz."

"What rumors?" Starbride asked.

"Rumors of Fiends, including that one is holding court, having eaten the king. I've heard that Yanchasa has risen and is sitting on the throne. No one can agree on who is dead, but the servants are having a fine time arguing about it. No one knows anything specific, let alone true."

Starbride sighed. At least no one had put forth the idea that Allusians were evil.

"We need Averie or Brutal or Hugo, even Castelle," Starbride said. "Someone Farradain who can show their face."

"If you were hidden," Freddie said, "could you disable Roland's pyramids? Then we can expose him, and he couldn't blow up."

"He'd just transform into a Fiend and kill everyone," Dawnmother said.

Starbride shook her head. "I don't know about that, Dawn. Lady Hilda seemed weak. Maybe Roland had to weaken his own Fiendish essence to give some to her."

"So, how about his pyramids?" Freddie asked.

Starbride thought of the strength of Roland's pyramids. She wasn't even sure how many he had. Only desperation had let her disable the one she did, and she wasn't sure that had worked.

"I don't think I could get them all," she said. "Crowe wasn't lying when he spoke of Roland's skill."

They headed for Katya's summer apartments, the abandoned rooms that the Order of Vestra used for meetings.

"If Katya were free, wouldn't she be looking for you?" Dawnmother asked when they found no one in the Order's rooms. "Should we pick a place and stay?"

"Unless she's hurt," Starbride said.

Dawnmother put an arm around her. "Someone friendly will be looking for you. They'll know you didn't hurt her, Star."

"Wait. Dawn, the queen should be on her own, waiting for the results from the council."

They stared at one another for a moment. "If Roland slipped away from the council, he could get to her," Freddie said.

"Or the children," Dawnmother added.

As one, they turned for the passageway again. "Wait." Starbride pulled out the scroll and pencil she always kept with her and scrawled a quick note to the Order that they were all right but on the move.

At the door that led to the royal sitting room, they paused again, and Freddie listened. After a moment, he waved them forward but didn't open the passage.

Starbride put her ear to the door. She could hear voices but couldn't make out what they were saying, though she thought one a man's and the other a woman's. When Freddie pulled his mask down, Starbride scratched on the door, hoping to sound like a rodent. If either of the voices wasn't in Katya's circle of allies, they might mistake the noise.

The woman's voice paused, and the man spoke, a question by the inflection. The woman spoke again, and then they heard a soft thump like the closing of a door.

A moment later, the door to the royal sitting room swung open. Queen Catirin stood back and peered into the gloom. "Everyone's looking for you three." She gestured for them to come out.

"Your Majesty," Starbride said, "I did nothing to—"

"I know. Luckily, those fool councilors figured out the truth. Katya's looking for you. Einrich just sent a bloody-nosed Lord Vincent to tell me so."

"Lord Vincent was hurt?" Part of her found the idea extremely satisfying.

"Apparently, Katya punched him in the nose."

"I knew I liked her," Dawnmother mumbled.

Starbride fought the urge to put on a very satisfied grin. "Did he say what happened after we left the ballroom?"

"Duke Robert knew about our Fiends," Queen Catirin said, "but he didn't know Katya has lost hers. Lady Hilda attacked as soon as Katya agreed to a Fiend test. Magistrate Anthony's assistant killed her."

Roland had killed one of his most powerful allies? But of course he had. Her usefulness had ended. Once Katya had been willing to go along with the test, Roland had figured out that she could somehow pass. If Lady Hilda was proven a liar, she'd move from asset to liability. She would lose Roland and Magistrate Anthony the approval of the nobles, if they hadn't lost it already.

"Starbride?" Queen Catirin asked.

"I'm sorry, Majesty. It's just that...things suddenly fell into place for me."

"Would you care to explain?"

"I should wait for Katya. Or maybe we should find her?"

Queen Catirin crossed to a desk and wrote a hasty note. "Best to send a servant. I want you both together before we figure out what to do."

And then there was only the cursed waiting to be done. Pennynail hovered in the corner. Queen Catirin hadn't spoken to him, hadn't really looked at him. Katya had said once that the queen didn't care for him, that she wouldn't trust anyone who didn't show his face. Starbride had almost laughed. The Umbriels were forced to put on false faces all the time. Pennynail just took the same idea to the extreme, and he was upfront about it.

Eventually, Katya burst into the room, not even bothering to knock. "The secret passageway from Starbride's room has—"

Katya caught sight of Starbride mid-sentence, and then rushed in her direction, each of them opening their arms and then swallowing the other in an embrace.

"I thought you'd been hurt," Katya said. "That they'd—"

"You always wanted me to run from danger, didn't you?"

When Katya pulled back, her expression was so relieved that Starbride wanted to kiss her senseless, but Queen Catirin cleared her throat.

"Did you tell them what happened, Mother?" Katya asked. "Did someone tell you?"

"You should reverse those questions, but yes and yes."

"I can hardly believe it," Katya said. "The council's in a tizzy. Father is handling them, but I should get back soon. Anthony's assistant dealt the death blow. I thought he'd prefer me dead, for sure."

Starbride glanced at Pennynail. He stepped around a chaise until he stood just behind her shoulder.

Katya glanced at him. "What is it?"

It was best to just blurt it out, Starbride told herself. That's the way Katya did things, the way she seemed to prefer they be done. "Anthony's assistant is Roland."

Katya smiled for a moment, either confused or maybe thinking Starbride made a perverse joke. "He's..."

"Roland."

While both Katya and her mother were speechless, Starbride told them all. Katya paced up and down the carpet, her scowl deepening when Starbride told her of the ultimatum Roland had given, either Starbride keep still about his identity, or he would kill everyone in the room.

"Even then," Starbride said, "when the council accused me of hypnotizing you and the king, I pointed to him, but he did exactly as he said, feigned total ignorance. And no one believed me. I suppose that with all the hullabaloo, everyone's forgotten I ever accused him."

"I certainly forgot it," Katya mumbled. "You should have told me."

Pennynail stepped to Starbride's side and shook his head.

Katya switched her glare to him. "And why not?"

Pennynail drew a triangle in the air.

"How do you know he would have actually risked killing me and my father, two people he wants alive? It was a bluff!"

"I couldn't risk that," Starbride said. "He said he would live because of the Fiend. That might have saved your father, too, but you? Even if you reached him before he could attack—and you would have tried, Katya, I know you—he might have let you stab him. How would that look for our cause? You stabbing Anthony's assistant?"

"She's right," Queen Catirin said. "It's the kind of frustrating thing Crowe would have done, for our own good."

Katya pointed at the door. "My father is sitting at a table with his murderous brother right under his nose, and you're telling me that's right?"

Queen Catirin shook her head. "I'll have this same fight later with your father, but you have to let Roland get away, Katya."

"Spirits above! We can't let him run loose in the palace."

Queen Catirin turned to Pennynail at last. "Can you follow him?"

He nodded.

"Mother..." Katya pulled her hair back from her face until tears formed in her eyes.

"Katyarianna, you mustn't."

"Please, Katya," Starbride said. "This is a wonderful opportunity. Pennynail can find out where he's hiding. If he thinks I'm still running for my life with Pennynail helping me, he won't expect to be followed."

Katya nodded, but a vein stood out at her temple. Queen Catirin made a shooing gesture. Starbride heard the gentle click of the secret passageway as Pennynail left them.

"So what now?" Katya asked. "I sit and let someone else do my job again?"

"Sulk on your own time," Queen Catirin said. "You have a task. Go to the ballroom and look worried. You haven't found Starbride yet, but you've decided that the best place is by the king's side, doing your duty."

"Everyone will expect me to be hunting Starbride."

Starbride chuckled. "But duty comes first to you, always has. Everyone knows that since you agreed to become crown princess."

"And I can keep an eye on Roland until Pennynail takes over."

"You cannot do anything to him Katya, cannot approach him, or speak to him," Queen Catirin said. "You must be every inch the haughty princess and not stoop to speaking to someone's assistant."

"You're not supposed to know who he is," Starbride added, "because you haven't found me yet."

"It will be very difficult," Katya said.

Starbride kissed her cheek. "I have every faith."

"As do I," Queen Catirin added. "Go, before the council ends. When we finally catch Roland in one of his own traps, I promise, you won't have to stay your sword."

Chapter Thirty-five: Katya

The council chamber was far more orderly when Katya returned. Lord Vincent had cleaned up his face, but his nose was beginning to swell. He'd have one hell of a bruise.

He deserved much more. She stalked past where he stood next to her father on the dais and resumed her seat. Da held up a hand to stop one of the nobles from speaking. "Did you find her?"

Katya shook her head and put on her best pained expression. "Lords and Ladies, ladies and gentleman, the princess consort is still missing. I would appreciate it if when our business is concluded, you would do me the honor of sending your households to look for her, as I have sent mine. Since I cannot find her, I have decided to rejoin you with the hope that I might help put an end to this unpleasant business."

Countess Nadia thumped the table, a noble's applause. The others followed suit while the commoners clapped for her.

Duke Robert stood. "I must apologize for my zeal in this matter. I thought Lady Hilda a maligned woman."

"No need, old fellow," Da said. "Yours is a family recently beset by tragedy, as is mine. After my son's unfortunate actions, I can see how one might begin to lose faith."

Duke Robert bowed deeply and sat. Magistrate Anthony cleared his throat from the gallery. "Majesty, may I speak?"

Murmurs echoed through the ballroom. With Lady Hilda dead, they no doubt hoped that the council would be dismissed. The nobles looked scandalized, but Da waved him forward.

Katya kept her eyes glued to Anthony as he stood, not daring to look to his side, to his "assistant."

"By your son's unfortunate actions, Majesty," Magistrate Anthony said, "I assume you mean the murder of my former assistant, my dearest Georgie Appleton."

"I am as sorry for your loss, Magistrate," Da said, "as I am of Duke Robert's daughter, my old friend pyradisté Cimerion Crowe, and of course, my mother."

Katya almost smirked. So the magistrate wanted to play a game of hurts, did he? Let him challenge those.

Magistrate Anthony simply bowed. "If you will, Majesty, I have a solution as to how you might win the faith of the people as completely as you have won that of the nobles."

Da inclined his head and gestured for Anthony to continue.

"Let us have a government where we have a voice, Majesty. Let us have a parliament." He waved at the assembled party. "An august council such as this one, to have a voice in the ruling of this kingdom."

The council erupted into impassioned voices. The nobles, even Duke Robert, shook their heads. Some of the commoners nodded, most at least appeared thoughtful. One of the baronesses stood. "Do you really think that would be a good idea, Magistrate? Most of the common people don't even know how to read."

Magistrate Anthony gestured to those gathered around him. "I challenge you to find a man or woman here among us, Baroness, who does not know."

The baroness blinked for a moment, her mouth working. "Well, of course yourselves, but…"

"Even a man or woman who cannot read should have a say in the course his or her life takes. Such people could elect someone to represent them, just as the people have elected me to judge them in matters of law. These representatives would form the parliament."

With a shake of his head, a viscount rapped on the table and gave Magistrate Anthony a pitying look. "You may have learned the law, Magistrate, but how could you know anything of politics, of war, of how to shape a kingdom?"

"Forgive me, Viscount, but did you know such things when you inherited your title at birth? A person may learn."

The nobles fell to angry murmuring again. Da raised his hands. "Peace, fellow councilors, please." After a moment, they all fell silent. "Do I take it, Magistrate Anthony, that you have a particular problem with how our kingdom is ruled?"

Anthony bowed again, the slippery eel. Katya saw right through his fawning. "I believe all men and women should be subject to the same law, Majesty. That cannot happen unless we all have a say in how we are governed."

"You would have had my son arrested and tried."

"No, Majesty. I do not believe one man is wholly under the control of another. I would have the champion arrested and tried."

Lord Vincent didn't bat an eyelash, though the rest of the room murmured. Da gave Magistrate Anthony a friendly smile. "I will take your words under advisement, Magistrate."

Most of the nobles seemed aghast that Da hadn't shut the man down completely. They were probably aghast that Da didn't order Vincent to chop off Magistrate Anthony's head. But Da never shut anyone down. He had no wish to be a tyrant and, "take your words under advisement," never closed a door. It never made people unhappy.

Even Magistrate Anthony smiled. "Thank you, Majesty."

"Shall we declare this council closed?" Da asked. "Unless there is any other strange business this day?"

Heads shook, and people stood and bowed as Da prepared to exit. Katya stayed on his heels and finally did what she'd been avoiding, what she'd been desperate to do: she let her eyes rest on Roland. His eyes met Katya's, and for a moment, they locked. He bowed, his face surprised, almost in awe. Katya barely avoided a snarl and looked away.

She didn't say a word to her father on the way back to the royal apartment, but he whispered in her ear, "If you want to duck away and go look for her…"

Katya shook her head, not trusting her voice. When they entered his apartment and Starbride was waiting, Da stopped in surprise.

He glanced at Katya. "Would have thought this was one of the first places you'd look, my girl."

Katya let the story tumble out of her. When he'd been informed of everything, Da turned nearly as red as she felt.

"And you didn't tell me?"

Katya nodded. "That was almost exactly what I said."

"The swine was in the same room with me, under my very nose!"

"And that."

"It isn't funny!" He nearly roared, and Katya took a step away. She looked to her mother who stared at her father as if she'd never met him. Starbride faded to the back of the room. Ma made a shooing motion, and Katya started for Starbride while nodding at the door to the secret passageway.

"Where are you going? Where is she going?" Da shouted.

"I can fill in the gaps for you," Ma said. "I've heard all sides of the story, now." Ma touched Da's chest over his pyramid necklace. Katya opened the door to the secret passageway, waved Starbride in, and then turned to stare again at her mother.

"Einrich," Ma said, "you must calm down. Your daughter is waiting to see if your head bursts open."

Da stared at Katya for a moment before he rubbed a hand through his beard and closed his eyes. "Go, my girl. But come back in an hour to check on me."

Katya smiled and left, giving Ma room to work her magic.

As soon as the door to the secret passageway was closed, Katya wrapped her arms around Starbride, not caring that they were still feet away from her parents. "I was so worried for you, Star."

"Does this mean you aren't angry with me anymore?"

"I'll likely be angry for a long time, but not at you. Even when I'm angry, I love you."

"I heard you punched Lord Vincent."

"He laid his hands on you."

"My savior." Their kiss lasted only a moment. "Roland seemed very confident his plan would work. Makes me wonder if he has a backup plan up his sleeve."

Katya led the way down the secret passage. "Where has Dawnmother gone?"

"To warn Averie that we're coming."

"I wish I could just not think for a few moments."

"No time, I'm afraid."

"What now?"

"Ursula and Castelle. They're in the thick of this, Katya. We have to decide how much to tell them or if we should warn them off."

"I, um, I already told Castelle some of it. She knows about the Fiends and about Roland."

Starbride's eyebrows shot up. "You told her without me?"

"We needed the help, and I didn't know what else to do. She wanted answers, especially after one of her friends had just died. And she saw Lady Hilda as a Fiend."

"So did Captain Ursula, but you didn't rush away to tell her."

Katya took a deep breath. "There wasn't time."

By the twist of Starbride's mouth, Katya could tell she wasn't happy, but she nodded.

Katya wrapped an arm around her shoulders, hoping to turn anger into humor. "Should I take it personally that you're not jealous enough to forbid me from working with my old flame?"

"Tsk, I trust you, and if I can't trust her, I can always have her killed." Starbride paused for a moment before she said, "Why didn't you ever tell her about the Fiend or the Order before now? If I hadn't stumbled onto them, would you have told me?"

"Or course," Katya said, and even though the words came easily, part of her doubted them. "I love you."

"You loved her, too. Don't deny it."

"Ah, but she didn't love me like you do. Castelle has always been more worried about herself than she could ever be about someone else."

"And yet, she's gone to great lengths to help you recently, including putting herself in danger."

"But was that for me or for the adventure?"

"Can't it be both? I'm not saying I know her better than you, Katya, but time changes people. Maybe you couldn't share your secrets when you were lovers. If she hadn't been able to join your life as I have, it would have hurt you. But now, as an adventurer, she's ready for the responsibility that comes with being your friend."

Katya mulled that over for a moment. "You are the spirit of wisdom. And you are an absolute *ferret* when it comes to hunting secrets."

"Isn't that a rat?"

"No! It's more like a…" Katya couldn't think of the word.

Starbride slapped her lightly on the shoulder. "It *is* a rat!" She laughed, but when she tried to slap at Katya again, Katya ducked, and then wrapped Starbride in her arms.

"If I'm a rat," Starbride said, "that makes you a pervert rodent fancier."

"So that was what I saw in Castelle."

"Ha! So now we just have to tell Castelle about the council? What about Captain Ursula? How much do we tell her?"

"I don't know her well enough, and she puts the city first. If she discovered that the Umbriels carry part of Yanchasa, she might decide it would be better for the city if we weren't on the throne."

"Then we don't tell that part. We simply say our opponent is a… friend of Yanchasa's, a half-Fiend that wants to let Yanchasa loose." Starbride shrugged. "It's partly true."

Katya kissed her long and soft. "I don't know why we need two spirits of wisdom and intellect when we have you."

They met with Captain Ursula and told her what she needed to know about Roland, leaving out the history of the Order and the Umbriel Fiends, as well as Roland's true identity. Shocked though she was, Ursula concluded in the end that everything Katya and Starbride said made sense. The only thing she wanted to know was why Katya had bothered to keep an opponent like Roland a secret.

"Though 'Foe of Yanchasa' has always been a title of the ruler of Farraday," Katya said, "it's mostly symbolic. Occasionally, we have to face allies of the great Fiend. It's traditional that the royal family takes on this task themselves, along with a few trusted friends. However, a few of my trusted friends are no longer with us." Maia's face flashed in front of her mind's eye, but she shook her head to clear the image.

Ursula nodded slowly. "And now you're looking for more *trusted* friends?" Her brows were down, skeptical, as if she didn't want a special relationship with the crown.

"Allies, with the city's best interest at heart, would be nice."

Ursula smiled at that and promised she would make inquiries into Magistrate Anthony and his assistant, especially after Katya and Starbride told her that Fiends might be manipulating the magistrate for their own ends. She still seemed suspicious, but that might come in handy.

The tale for Castelle took less time. Since she already knew about Roland and the Fiends, all they had to tell her about was the council.

Castelle rubbed her chin. "So Roland's plan to get the nobles on his side has failed, and now we have to try and guess his next move. Do we know his location?"

"Pennynail is looking for him. As Anthony's assistant, he can't hide," Starbride said. "We need your thief catcher skills."

"I've learned a lot in my years away from the palace. Sounds like we'll need your pyradisté skills, too. So what do you need from me right now?"

"At the moment..." Katya's words tapered off as she heard a slight scratching from her private sitting room door. Someone had arrived through the secret passage. "Nothing. But I have a feeling we'll have news soon."

Castelle nodded slowly. She'd heard the slip.

"I'll see you out," Katya said. When Castelle stood, Starbride stood also, nodding at the two as Katya walked Castelle into the hall.

Chapter Thirty-six: Starbride

Starbride waited for the door to the hall to close before she rushed to the other. There was only one person who'd wait at the door instead of coming through the regular halls. Pennynail bowed when he saw her.

"Katya will be right back, so don't take anything off."

He pressed the mask's cheeks as if hiding a blush. Starbride laughed. Why was it so much easier to relax around him when he had the mask on?

Katya slipped inside a moment later. "Is there news?"

Pennynail nodded, but then plucked Starbride's sleeve.

"Who could you possibly be that you can show her and not me?" Katya asked.

He fidgeted. Starbride shook her head. "Please don't force this. Let some secrets lie."

Katya gave her a wry look. "Who are you again?"

Starbride turned to the private sitting room door. "Promise you won't peek?"

"I'll be awaiting your news."

Once inside the sitting room, Starbride leaned against the door. She didn't want to lock Katya out of her own room, but she had to prevent any surprise inspections.

Freddie pushed his mask on top of his head. "I guess I'm lucky I don't have to keep my voice down."

"What news?"

"Roland isn't hiding at Magistrate Anthony's house. They've rented a warehouse at the edge of Marienne, near the road to Dockland. I watched it overnight, saw quite a few people coming and going. I think we may have our first dissident hideout."

Starbride clenched a fist. Just like the attack on Lady Hilda, they had an opportunity to get ahead of their enemies, maybe even surprise them. Pennynail gave her as many details as he could, and then they let Katya into the room.

Her dark looks vanished when Starbride filled her in. "Finally! We'll get Captain Ursula to clean out the warehouse while we wait for Roland to show himself."

"Katya..."

"I'm going, Star."

"This isn't some jaunt outside the city; this is going after Roland himself—"

"Jaunt? You're calling hunting Lady Hilda a jaunt now?"

Pennynail saluted them before hurrying toward the secret passages again. Starbride waited for the door to close before she rounded on Katya.

"Is this what you felt like all the times I insisted you be protected?" Katya asked. "It's hard to breathe."

"Thank you for understanding that."

"Good, since I understand, it's settled. I'll take care of any courtly duties before we go. I'll send Castelle to collect Ursula. Get all you can from Pennynail, then we'll all meet here with Brutal and Hugo. We can fill Averie and Dawnmother in later."

Starbride closed her mouth on her argument. The comment about knowing how she felt did her in. Protection could be suffocating, especially when she could take care of herself. She supposed Katya could do the same, but she had to try one more tactic.

"What would your father say?"

"Are you going to tattle on me, Star?"

"Crowe said I would have to develop a closer relationship with Einrich, reporting to him and so on. Would he have you locked away?"

Katya's face tensed for a moment before she seemed to see the teasing in Starbride's face. "I didn't know you wanted to bring chains into our relationship. If I die, my family won't have you thrown into the dungeon." She put a finger to Starbride's lips, sealing in a protest. "I know that's not what you're really worried about, but you do realize that you'd be safe, don't you?"

Starbride nodded, swallowing her vehement denial that she was worried for her own skin. "As long as you trust me to guard your back, I won't go tattling to your father. But I will insist on disguises for all of us, convincing ones."

"I don't do them any other way."

❖

Starbride had been researching everything about how to contain a Fiend. She didn't want to be surprised by Roland again. The next time she encountered him, if he let her get close, she was going to hit him with the kind of pyramid Crowe had been using for years, the kind that siphoned off a Fiend's energy, that turned the Umbriels back into their human selves. The kind that had let Starbride drain Katya's Fiend in the first place.

She made several. One for Roland, her most powerful, but another for Maia if Roland unleashed her Fiend. After what had happened with Lady Hilda, Starbride had little doubt that he'd already done that. She hesitated to bring it up to Katya, but suspected Katya knew already. The only reason Maia hadn't come back to them was because her Fiend didn't want her to.

That led her to how Roland was unlocking Fiends in the first place without the owners performing the Waltz. Not only unlocking, she reminded herself; he'd taught Lady Hilda how to control it. Lady Hilda's pyradisté might not choose to answer, and she couldn't use a mind pyramid on him. She left him in Freddie's capable hands. Crowe hadn't been fond of torture, but Freddie would know whatever tactics he'd used to get information out of an uncooperative pyradisté.

Lady Hilda's body was another story. Freddie helped her bring it to the dungeon where they laid it on a slab of stone that seemed made for holding bodies. Starbride didn't want to ask.

"What are you looking for?" Freddie said. "You can't use a mind pyramid on a dead person."

"When we first ambushed her at the stable, she said that I'd missed one. I have to assume she meant one pyramid since I disabled the active pyramids she and her maids were carrying." She picked up a pair of scissors and cut Lady Hilda's dress up the middle. "Roland couldn't have just taught her how to bring her Fiend out and control it. Crowe trained me in how to sense an active pyramid, but maybe Roland used something very subtle, very small."

When Lady Hilda's naked body was exposed, Starbride had to breathe deep as Timat's memories tried to resurface.

Freddie looked over her shoulder, his expression flat. "I don't see anything, and there's all there is."

"He hid something inside of me once. We need to look for scars." As they examined the body, Starbride tried to tell herself it was anything but a dead person. Maybe a dead animal, or a bundle of wood, or a painting, something she could just look at without having to think about.

They found only old scars and the wound in her neck. Freddie peered at that. "Can you bring a light pyramid over here?"

Starbride knelt beside him and brought the light closer. Her bile rose at the sight of the bloody hole, but Freddie bent closer and tugged at the skin. Starbride clamped her teeth together harder.

"Do you see it?" Freddie asked.

She couldn't come closer, she couldn't. But Crowe would have done it immediately. Starbride forced herself to have tunnel vision and edged closer. All at once, she saw it, tiny sparkles within the wound. Disgust blew away before curiosity. "Glass?"

Freddie stuck one of his slender knives into the wound and pulled out a shiny fragment. "Crystal. Here's your pyramid."

"Roland killed her right where he'd put the pyramid that controlled her Fiend. He knew we'd be looking." She grinned at Freddie. "But he underestimated you."

"Leaves us nothing to study, though," Freddie said.

"But now we know where to look. If I get a hold of someone else who can control their Fiend, I need to aim for the back of their neck."

"I'll clean all the crystal out and then hand her over to the knowledge chapterhouse. There's nothing for them to find anymore, but it might make them happy."

"If that's what Katya and her father want, sure. What are you going to do with her pyradisté?"

He gave her a wry look. "Do you really want to know? My father used to tell me that Prince Roland advocated a firmer hand with prisoners. My father disagreed, and King Einrich felt as he did, so they didn't use torture. Now, though, I think Roland had a better idea."

Starbride shuddered. "You think the man that's trying to kill us all had the better idea?"

"Well, then, not now. Now he's a monster. But he might never have 'died' if he'd been let off the chain a little."

"Are you saying this is my decision?"

He shrugged.

Starbride bit her lip and turned away. "Do as you will." She hurried out of the room, not ready to face the consequences of what'd she just done.

After all, she had a page to take from Roland's book as well.

Starbride dug through Crowe's notes and books, stayed up half the night, and figured out how to devise a pyramid that would bend the eye of the viewer, ensuring a disguise. Crowe had never attempted it, mind magic not being his forte, but Starbride wrestled with the problem.

Through a good deal of trial and error, she projected her thoughts into a pyramid and then focused them outward, so that anyone not a pyradisté would see what she wanted them to see. The trick was to make the false features in her head match Katya's and hers. So a woman of Katya's height and build, but slightly different features, different hair and eyes, a broader nose, fuller lips. Starbride added a scar for good measure.

She made herself Farradain, blond like so many of them, with thinner, sharper features, remembering Katya's rodent reference. By the time Katya had worked out a plan with Captain Ursula and Castelle, Starbride was ready to try her pyramids out.

Katya had darkened her hair, completely concealing the new gray at her temples, and instead of wearing it in her customary bun, she had a long braid that went down her back. She wore the simple clothes of a laborer, as well as the heavy leather smock that let her conceal a chainmail shirt under her clothes. When Starbride arrived, Katya was practicing drawing her rapier and scowling at the smock as she did so.

"I can't move my arm properly," Katya said. "I think the smock will have to go. But laborers don't often go around in chainmail."

"I have the answer. With my help, the only people who'll be able to see the chainmail are pyradistés. And we'll never fool Roland into thinking you're not you." She activated her disguise pyramid and left it on.

Katya took a step away. "Star? What did you do?"

Starbride turned the pyramid off. "I learn fast."

"And how do I know that's really you now and not a disguise for that other woman?"

"You're welcome to search me."

Katya grinned. "And my disguise?"

"It won't fit me as well as it'll fit you, but..." She activated Katya's disguise pyramid.

"You're right. It's...hazy, as if it's a bit too tall, but still, it's brilliant, Star."

The others would have to rely on traditional disguise. Starbride had only had time to make two, and she knew they weren't perfect. She and Katya would both have to wear cloaks. Brutal traded his red robe for homespun. All of them dressed down, including Hugo and Castelle. Pennynail would insist upon his mask, but he would stay hidden for the journey.

They lurked outside the designated warehouse and watched people go in and out. The Watch had it surrounded, and they'd take care of the crowd within. Starbride and Katya were only there to catch any large prey that might fly out.

They split the Order into two groups to watch the front and back of the warehouse at the same time. Starbride, Hugo, Dawnmother, and Pennynail watched the front, behind Ursula's main pack of Watch officers. As the only non-fighter, Dawnmother was there to run to Ursula if Starbride's group needed help.

Katya snuck around the back with Castelle, Brutal, and Averie. They'd split according to specialty, though Katya had frowned at not being in Starbride's group. It was just easier that way.

The Watch stormed the building and called for everyone to stand where they were. Shouts and cries of pain erupted from the warehouse. Starbride's eyes darted over the building as she watched for any escaping figures. Pennynail grasped her arm and pointed. On the sloping roof of the warehouse, a skylight banged open, and five figures crawled out. Katya wouldn't see it from the other side.

"Let's move," Starbride said. Her group dashed for the adjacent building. Unless the escaping group sprouted wings, they'd have to use the other building to get to the ground.

If Roland was among this group...Starbride pursed her lips. They'd hit him with everything they had and send Dawnmother for reinforcements. Of course, everything they had might not be enough. Starbride cast a glance at Hugo. If Roland was among them, maybe she could rip the necklace from his throat and let his Fiend out. It might keep Roland occupied long enough for Starbride to drain his Fiendish essence. She didn't know if he was also vulnerable on the back of his neck, but it was worth a shot.

If she could get close enough without being killed.

The group of five climbed down a long ladder and had nearly reached the street. Pennynail yanked the first man from the ladder before he'd set foot on the cobblestones and slammed him against the ground.

The next in line shouted, "Go back up!" and tried to scramble over his fellows.

"Temperance!" Starbride lobbed a flash bomb at the ladder, near the topmost climber. She shut her eyes and waited for the flash to fade, so she only heard the cry as the climber fell to the pavement. He rolled there, clutched his knee, and wailed.

"Search him." Starbride pointed to the downed man. Dawnmother hurried to obey.

The last three had frozen on the ladder, having been shielded from the flash and terrified into remaining still. Pennynail tied his opponent on the ground and left him.

"Come down slowly," Starbride said. "One at a time."

They inched down. Pennynail and Hugo grabbed them as they left the ladder. Dawnmother searched them, and Pennynail tied their wrists with leather cord. Three men and two women, no Roland, Darren, or Maia. No pyramids and hardly a weapon to speak of. They didn't look rich nor very poor, somewhere in between, and they watched Starbride with a mix of fright and anger.

"You're not in the Watch," one man sneered, the one that Pennynail had yanked off the ladder. Blood trickled from his nose.

She didn't answer him. "Dawn, go fetch one of Captain Ursula's men to take these five."

Dawnmother hurried away. The man with the nosebleed called out again. "I'm talking to you! On whose authority are you arresting us?"

"We didn't do anything wrong," one of the women said.

"I told you we shouldn't have come." The other woman crowded against those next to her and sobbed. On the end, the man with the broken knee wailed as they jostled him.

Starbride fidgeted. She didn't have permission to do anything with these people. She'd been looking for Roland, and she'd only gotten those smart enough to be near the skylight when the raid began. She could pyramid them and hope to catch a glimpse of her true quarry, but that would take too long and leave her exposed. She didn't have time to search their memories and then cover her tracks. The last thing the Umbriels needed was a group of revolutionaries crying that they'd been pyramided without a magistrate's approval.

"Dawnmother can catch up with us. Let's see how Katya is faring around the back."

Chapter Thirty-seven: Katya

Katya eyed the warehouse and wished Roland was a little stupider. The Watch seemed to have netted everyone; Katya and her team would look them over, but she doubted her prey would be among them. And now the raid drew crowds of gawkers from nearby, people on their way home or starting the night shift in the warehouse district.

Starbride approached, still looking like a blond Farradain girl. Katya had to smile at the disguise but frowned when Starbride told her they'd only caught a few people, none of whom seemed important.

"Don't worry," Starbride said. "We'll go through them at the Watch house. Maybe we'll find Magistrate Anthony."

Katya nodded, but inside she seethed. What good was the puppet without the master? Roland would only find someone else. Ah well, she supposed that would buy them some time.

After they collected Dawnmother, they headed away and left the bulk of the crowd behind. With their pyramid disguises, no one spared them much of a glance, especially with Brutal walking several steps away from them, and Pennynail doing his usual hide and watch from the rooftops. They crossed a courtyard, mostly deserted except for one man in the simple brown mantle of a law student who sat under a street lamp with a book and shivered.

"I wonder why he doesn't study inside," Starbride muttered. "It's pretty chilly, especially now that it's getting dark."

"You're right."

The student shivered too violently, even for the chill. He looked up, and his eyes were red and swollen, his face scared.

"What's going on?" Hugo asked.

Castelle stepped between Katya and Starbride and the young student. “Everyone stay close.”

Starbride took a pyramid from her satchel and stared into it. Dawnmother stayed at her elbow. Everyone readied their weapons. The student stretched toward them as if pleading. One hand was concealed beneath his mantle.

“He has a pyramid,” Starbride said.

“Everyone back up,” Katya said. “Can you tell what kind?”

“It’s like…a coil of flame wrapped around his arm, almost dancing in his palm.”

Katya lifted a finger over her head.

A knife punched into the student’s chest, and he staggered. Averie fired at nearly the same time and hit the student in the gut. He kept up his shamble and made it into the light. His pained, fearful expression stayed the same.

“He should be bleeding,” Katya said.

“Scatter,” Brutal said. “He can’t hit all of us.”

Starbride shook her head “The fire pyramid is big…and it’s not his only one.”

“Run!” Brutal charged the student.

Katya gripped Starbride’s arm. “Damn it, Brutal!” But she ran all the same and took Starbride along with her. Katya cast a look over her shoulder just as the student lurched into a run, *away* from Brutal. He threw the pyramid, not at any of them, but off to the side, where a gaggle of townspeople stood, backs turned and watching the warehouse.

“Look out!” Katya cried.

The flames engulfed them, and the courtyard erupted in screams. Katya and Starbride pulled up short. The group of townspeople flailed, screaming.

Starbride turned to the side and vomited over the ground. Katya clutched her stomach, trying to control it, but the scent of burning flesh flooded her nostrils and her mouth every time she tried to take a breath. Dawnmother bent to help Starbride, and Averie ran to them at full speed.

“What in the spirits’ names?” Castelle said. Hugo stood with her, one hand plastered over his mouth.

Someone tugged Katya to the side. Pennynail gestured wildly that they should get the hell away from whatever was happening. Brutal had caught the student, but before Katya could speak, she glanced at Starbride’s face, her real face, the disguise broken.

“What happened to our disguises?” Katya asked.

Someone shouted, “She killed them!”

Katya spun around. In Brutal's arms, the student had plucked the dagger and arrow from his body and shouted at the top of his voice. "She killed them!"

Running footfalls clattered around them. Some people hung out of nearby windows. Others ran into the courtyard from all directions, and the student's voice seemed louder as he called again, "The princess and her consort killed them all!"

For a moment, silence reigned. Then the crowd focused on Katya and her party, standing alone, in a huddle. With a cry, the crowd moved as one, a living, breathing mob.

Katya ran, her friends beside her. The faces of the mob were twisted, bestial, unblinking. They wouldn't listen to any arguments, probably *couldn't* listen. Even if they were being helped to rage by a pyradisté, it didn't matter. Katya's heart was in her ears, her brain screaming with the knowledge that if they stayed, they would be torn apart.

Brutal caught up with them swiftly. They headed for the only clear street.

"Can't let them herd us!" Brutal cried.

Katya would have agreed, but what else could they do? Starbride dipped into her satchel again. A group of people gathered at the end of the alley, blocking their path.

"Temperance!" Starbride lobbed the pyramid ahead of them.

The glow lit up the insides of Katya's eyelids, and she opened them as soon as it faded. The people at the end of the alley were down on the ground or sagged against the walls. They rubbed their eyes and clutched their heads.

Katya's party raced past the fallen mob and out into a connecting street. People glanced at them now, but confused and curious, no longer angry. "Slow down," Katya commanded.

Little purple spots had begun to dance in front of her eyes, and she tried to take deep breaths instead of gasps. They fanned out. Pennynail hid between Katya and Brutal, a surprise weapon for anyone who got too close.

"A setup, a spirits' bedamned setup!" Katya said through gritted teeth. "Did he know we'd come or was he always just prepared?"

No one had any answers.

Behind them, angry voices echoed up the street. The mob had reached their exit route. Starbride tensed. Katya gripped her arm.

"Don't run."

It was so hard not to. Everything primal in Katya's brain wanted to take off again, to not risk getting caught by the mob. She waited and tried to breathe quietly so she could hear any cries over the bustle of the city streets. They steered deeper into the crowd, toward the market.

Starbride tensed again. "Shouldn't we stay away from people?"

Katya shook her head. She understood that fear. It was hard to see large groups as anything but a vicious pack that could turn murderous in an instant. "More people will help us hide."

Starbride drew her cloak around her. Katya tried to walk just in front of her and help to hide her heritage. Roland had to have broken their disguises, but how? When? They were lucky it was already dark, though the market still bustled.

"They're on our left," Brutal's voice rumbled above her head.

The mob hunted them like dogs. Katya frowned. That wasn't like any mob she'd ever heard of. If they couldn't get their quarry, they turned their violence on anything handy.

"They should have stayed back in the square." She kept her rapier drawn but hidden in the folds of her cloak. She squeezed Starbride's arm and nodded toward the men Brutal had seen. They wore leather, some of it studded. "Those aren't townspeople. They're hired thugs."

"To attack the Umbriels on the streets of their own city? Without the mob to back them up? Has it gotten that bad?"

"Ah, but you don't look much like royalty right now, do you?" Castelle said over her shoulder.

Katya had to nod. They were sweaty, disheveled, and disguised. If they declared who they were, would anyone believe them? Would it hurt or help? So much of Katya's royal life was spent hiding her identity. Maybe she'd done too good a job. Maybe those who didn't know her personally wouldn't recognize her at all, despite how many portraits they'd seen.

"They won't see a princess," Starbride mumbled, "because they don't expect to see one."

"Don't despair. We're far from helpless."

They reached the edge of the market. A few twists and turns would bring them to the palace, but they'd have to leave the safety of the crowd to get there. Of course, if someone was using pyramid magic, safety could become danger in an instant.

"Spread out a bit," Katya said.

"Do we run?" Starbride asked as the amount of people began to thin.

"No. Can you see them, Brutal?"

"Yep. We need to pause here just a minute and then quick step around the corner. Wait."

Starbride was still shaking. Katya leaned close to her. "Breathe. We'll come through this together."

"I just keep seeing those faces…"

"Go," Brutal said.

They hurried around the corner.

"Risk straight on or a few more turns to throw them off?" Brutal asked.

"The shorter route," Katya said. "We'll fight through a couple of them if we have to."

As if summoned by her words, two thugs stepped into the street, their leather-studded armor giving them away. Castelle launched herself forward and stabbed one just as he pointed at them. The other raised a whistle to his lips. Katya felt the movement of air behind her and then the whistle man had a knife in his throat.

"Leave them," Katya said. She couldn't afford to break their party up, not knowing if she'd ever see anyone she left behind again.

They reached the safety of the palace, and once Katya had informed her father of what had happened, he had no choice but to lock the palace down.

Da paced up and down the sitting room rug while he read from a paper one of his clerks had given him. "There are fires breaking out all over the city."

It had only been hours since the incident, and already the city was ablaze. Katya shook her head. Roland lost no time. She and her companions had barely moved from the royal sitting room since the trouble had started.

"How can they think we'd do something like that, kill that many people?" Katya said.

"Some of it has to be pyramid influence, doesn't it?" Starbride asked.

Castelle shrugged from where she leaned against the wall. "Mobs take on lives of their own, and the people involved start to enjoy it."

"You've seen a lot of them?" Starbride asked.

"A few and we've all seen people give in to their animalistic natures more than once."

Katya turned back to the room at large. "So what should we do? Is there any calming the people down?"

"Have you spoken to your captain friend, my girl?" Da asked.

"She hasn't sent word. And we could really use her right now."

Castelle pushed off from the wall. "I could go find her."

"No noble will be looked on with a friendly eye out there," Katya said.

"I can be discreet when I want to." Castelle cast a glance to where Hugo sat next to Brutal. His eyes had roamed from face to face, but he'd offered nothing to the discussion.

When he caught Castelle looking at him, he straightened. "You want me to come with you? I'll do it."

"Good man," Brutal said.

Starbride cleared her throat. "I should go, too."

"Star…" Katya searched for the words to express how idiotic she thought that idea was. "They're looking for you more than they are for me. They think you killed those people."

"Do we have another pyradisté to send? Do you know someone else who can counter a pyramid?"

Katya tried to squelch her anger, but it seemed determined to come out, even if it was just through her ears. "You cannot do this."

"Oh?" Starbride said. "I *cannot*?"

Castelle cleared her throat. "She does have a point, Katya." Everyone else was studying the walls.

"You stay out of this," Katya snapped.

"I'll go in secret," Starbride said, "and no one will ever know that it's me. Katya, think."

Katya felt like tearing her hair and settled for rubbing her temples.

Ma crossed to the door to her private sitting room. "In here, I think."

Katya strode through the door without looking back. She heard it shut quietly, Starbride's doing. Her eyes were steadfast, but also a little pleading, as if asking Katya again to let her go.

"I know you're capable, Star, but…"

"You have to stay here; you have to protect your family."

"You're my family." All their recent troubles seemed to settle on her shoulders, and she was ashamed to feel tears in her eyes.

Starbride's arms were around her in a moment. "I'll come back in a few hours. It'll go so smoothly that I'll be able to pick up some of those sweets you like."

Katya laughed a breathless laugh as she held her tightly. It was the only sensible course. They needed information they could trust, and Starbride had proven she could take care of herself. "I'm sorry I'm always asking you to stay behind. It's just…"

"I know what it is. You're a lovesick fool."

Katya kissed her deeply. "Only for you." She glanced at the door and thought briefly of Castelle. Anything she'd felt then paled to how Starbride consumed her. "I love you, Star. Get Captain Ursula and as many of the Watch as you can grab. They can be stationed outside the palace, and the king's Guard can help them keep order. If we start here, we can spread order through the city."

"I love you, too. I'll be back before you can miss me."

"Too late." Katya had to shut her eyes as Starbride left. She wondered when she could stop doing that, when her worry would be less. Never, she decided. Parting would always be like a knife in the chest. The day she didn't feel it would be the day she died.

Chapter Thirty-eight: Starbride

Castelle, Pennynail, Hugo, Dawnmother, and Starbride crept through Marienne. They kept to the shadows and tried to stay out of the lamplight. Castelle's friends crept with them but didn't stay by their side; that would have been too many people trying to walk together.

They'd already dodged several mobs, though Starbride couldn't be sure of their intentions. Her party went armed and cloaked. It was all about a show of force, or so Castelle said. She had forsaken her big hat for a cloak with a hood. Pennynail had a hood pulled over his mask and walked with them instead of skirting the rooftops. Starbride didn't try the disguise pyramid again. She feared it had only made her a target before.

They passed a few groups like theirs, smaller knots of hooded people trying to get their business done quickly. They passed the occasional fire but kept well away from the flames. Smoke drifted through the city in eddies and currents; it swirled around the streetlamps like ghosts. Now and again, they heard the clanging bells of the fire brigade, but could they move fast enough to get every fire?

When they got near the Watch house, they stopped at an alley. Starbride asked Pennynail why they didn't take the rooftop approach again, and he pulled her to the side and whispered that the thieves were out in droves during the chaos, and they had less of a chance of trouble on the streets.

A mob had gathered around the Watch house. So far, they just yelled and threw the occasional bottle, but some drank and staggered about, growing louder by the second. Watch officers hovered in the doorways of their house. One or two told the mob to shove off. Some did, but others only walked a few feet away and then returned.

"Captain Ursula must not have enough officers to disperse the crowd," Starbride said.

Hugo shrugged. "Or maybe she's hoping that if she abstains from violence, the crowd will follow suit."

"We could try rushing through," Castelle said. "We form a wedge with Starbride and Dawnmother in the middle and push through before anyone realizes what we're doing."

"If they grab at us," Hugo said, "it could get ugly."

"What if we act like part of the mob?" Dawnmother asked. "We mingle with them until we get close enough to the gate and then run for it."

"Then we might have the Watch tackle us," Castelle said. "And if it looks like we're townsfolk getting in a scuffle with the Watch, that could ignite the crowd, too."

Starbride nodded. "Then we need to move the mob, at least enough for us to get through. We need a distraction."

Castelle smirked suddenly. "I've got just the thing." She crossed to the other side of the street to where her friends waited. Starbride heard some abbreviated laughter, and then the friends were off around the corner.

Castelle crossed back over. "Get ready to run."

Starbride looked to the Watch house, hoping like hell there wasn't about to be a rain of arrows or a charge from Castelle's friends. In a few moments, she heard shouting and laughter. The mob around the Watch house heard it, too. They turned to look, especially as one male voice shouted, "Naked parade!"

The mob glanced at one another and repeated the phrase in confusion. They crept away from the door of the Watch house, clearing a path.

"Not yet," Castelle said.

A group of men and women jogged across the street a few streets down, completely naked and laughing, swinging one another around and shouting, "Come join the naked parade!"

The mob moved that way, jollity or shocked laughter lighting their faces. One or two even pulled off their shirts.

Starbride had to admit, it was hard not to stare. When Castelle said, "Now," she had to pull her eyes away and sprint across the street with the others.

A few lingering drunks turned to stare at Starbride's party; one shouted something, but the others couldn't tear their eyes off the naked parade. The Watch seemed a little alarmed by the charge, but Castelle brought them up short just inside the gate, before the Watch house door.

"We need to see Captain Ursula," Castelle said.

The officer frowned and opened his mouth. Starbride stepped forward and tilted her face up to the light so the man could see her Allusian features.

"Can we see her now?" Starbride asked.

The man swallowed whatever he'd been about to say and waved them inside. Pennynail stayed inside the doorway while Starbride led the way to Ursula's office. She stared at a map of the city and glanced up with irritation as they entered.

"I was just about to head out again," she said when Starbride lowered her hood. Soot darkened Ursula's face, but not as much as the circles under her eyes.

Starbride started with, "I didn't kill anyone," and went on with all that had happened in the streets.

Ursula waited until the end of the tale to respond. "I knew you hadn't killed those people. Doing so would net you nothing but trouble. So this adversary you told me about, this pyradisté enemy of the crown started all this strife. To what end?"

"Probably to propel Magistrate Anthony to a position of power," Starbride said.

Hugo snorted. "He'd have to kill every noble in order to get it."

"No, just those we care about." Starbride rubbed her temples since Katya seemed to do it so often, but it didn't help with the stress at all. "Without the Umbriels to rally around, I expect many of the nobles would fold." She glanced at Castelle and Hugo. "Present company excluded, of course."

"Of course," Castelle said with a small smile. "But you're right. Those that didn't cave to pressure would run to their holdings and move the country toward a civil war with at least eight or nine sides."

"Are you telling me to arrest a magistrate?" Ursula said. "Because if he's obeying this pyradisté willingly, that's a crime. If not, I can only arrest the pyradisté."

Starbride thought back to her meeting with Roland before the council and shuddered. "He's made it clear that if we try to expose him, he'll attack."

Ursula shrugged. "If he does, we've got all the proof we need."

"You don't understand," Starbride said, "all the trouble with Lady Hilda will be nothing compared to the grief this man will give us. Innocent people will be killed."

"That might be preferable to sitting back and watching him tear this town apart," Hugo said. "Innocent people are getting hurt right now."

Ursula planted her fists on her hips. "Some of the fish we caught know of another rebel bolt-hole. Your pyradisté and the magistrate are probably hiding there. I'll get some officers together. Gather the people you left outside, and we can a put a stop to this right now. If this man is manipulating Magistrate Anthony, we can break his hold, and the magistrate can help us bring order to this chaos."

Starbride looked to Castelle, who shrugged. "If we have a chance to strike…"

"Katya's going to kill me," Starbride said.

Hugo nodded. "She's going to kill all of us, but at least the city will be safe. We can take that to our graves."

"We're in for a big fight," Starbride reminded them all. And they wouldn't have a greater Fiend to help them. Starbride clutched her satchel closer and wished Katya were there, both for the support and also for another ready blade.

Ursula sent messengers to her other captains, telling them about her decision to move, that she'd heard of another mob uprising and hoped to nip it in the bud. She didn't report to the watch commander. "He'll have his hands full," she said with a sly smile.

Starbride didn't question it. It would take too long to explain to the commander anyway. Surrounded by officers of the Watch and Castelle's now-clothed people, Starbride and her friends made their way into the poorest district of Marienne.

"It's an apartment building," Starbride said when she saw it. The narrow building reminded her of a similar one in Dockland, but this one was much better maintained, even though most of the shutters were sealed. "How many people are in there?"

"My friends and I could go in first," Castelle said, "and see if we could evacuate quietly."

"You wouldn't get anyone to do anything without an officer with you," Ursula said. "Even then, with the current climate, you might get a brick in the face for your trouble."

They glanced at Starbride, and with a start, she realized she was the highest ranking person there, the one who might be a queen if the right series of unfortunate incidents happened.

Still, there was a time for rank, and a time to depend on expertise. "Did your captives tell you where in the building they met?"

Captain Ursula shook her head.

"If we go inside for anything other than a fight," Starbride said, "we lose the element of surprise. Let's make them come to us. What's the quickest way to empty a building?"

Ursula's face turned to stone. "If you're suggesting we light that building on fire, you're under arrest."

"I'm delighted that you feel that way," Starbride said. "But I was thinking we make the occupants think it's on fire rather than light it up."

Castelle and Hugo both grinned.

"The Watch goes door to door, floor to floor," Dawnmother said, "claiming the building is burning but making sure the people don't stampede. Enough buildings are on fire that they might believe it."

"Even the magistrate and his assistant will have to believe it," Hugo said. "He couldn't risk staying inside."

Ursula turned to two of her men. "Get some straw and some water. We'll need smoke to make it convincing." She nearly grinned. "We may get the better end of this yet."

They brought bundles of straw and set them alight at the corners of the building, well away from the walls but concealed by alleys. Each bundle was attended by several officers with buckets of water.

As the smoke rose, Ursula sent her officers into the building. It wasn't long before people streamed out. Officers on the street ushered everyone down the block and told them to find somewhere to take shelter.

Luckily, the building was far from full. Most of the people who emerged were dirty and clad in raggedy homespun, seeming more like homeless people who'd broken into the building to seek shelter. Most of them would be at home in Dockland, but even Marienne had its share of poor.

They saw neither Anthony nor Roland, and soon, the officers of the Watch called that the building was clear.

Starbride and her party came out from hiding. "Where could they have gone?" Starbride asked.

Ursula pointed into the smoke near the doorway. "Sergeant Rhys, that building is not clear! Someone's coming out."

Two figures walked out of the heavy smoke, but they didn't cough, run, or duck from the imaginary fire. Starbride grabbed Hugo's arm as Maia and Darren stepped into the glow of the streetlights and Watch lanterns. Hugo sucked in a deep breath at the sight of his sister and the man who'd been his ally, the supposed illegitimate grandson of old King Bastian.

Maia's eyes were wide, terrified. Darren's fingers closed around her upper arm. Even amid all the Watch officers, Castelle's group, and Starbride's friends, Darren wore a smirk. When Hugo took a step forward, Darren whipped out a dagger and pressed it to Maia's throat.

"Now," he said, "isn't this a surprise worth waiting for?"

Chapter Thirty-nine: Katya

Katya paced up and down her sitting room rug. Averie sat near the door to the bedroom and Brutal at the door leading to the hall, as if they'd leap on her if she tried to leave.

"She should have been back by now," Katya said.

"It's only been a couple of hours," Brutal said.

"That's all it should have taken to get there, talk to Ursula, and come back."

"Being slow and cautious is a good thing," Averie said. "How about a cup of—"

"No tea, no sandwiches, no thrice-bedamned banquets!" Katya stopped and forced herself to calm down after several deep breaths. "I'm sorry, Averie."

"You're worried," Brutal said.

"Yes."

"Only natural."

"Thank you."

"Still doesn't give you leave to act like an ass."

Katya barked a laugh. "I thought being royalty gave me leave to act like an ass whenever I want." The words made her think of Reinholt, and she wanted to retract them immediately. "I want to go looking for her."

"And you know why you can't," Brutal said. "If you want me to go, I'll go, but there's more of a chance that she and I will miss each other than that I'll actually find her."

"What I really want is for the spirits to whisk her here."

"Ah, the whisking twins," Averie said.

Katya glared at both of them. "What else can I do? If I wander the halls, I'll be crowded by scared courtiers. I don't have it in me to reassure them right now." She sighed. "I suppose I'll have to *find* it in me. I can assure the people in the palace that the royals haven't abandoned them. My father is too busy taking reports."

Brutal nodded. "We'll trail behind you at a discreet distance."

"Damn the discreet distance," Averie said. "I'm tempted to bring my bow."

Katya belted on her rapier. "It would be prudent to go armed. No one would think twice."

Averie grabbed her bow and arrows and belted a long knife on her hip.

Brutal had his huge mace on his belt already. "Being a brother of strength always lets me get away with carrying weapons. People just expect it."

Katya had to agree. And they weren't the only ones sporting weapons in the hallway. Most of the courtiers didn't have them, but the nobles and their servants did, those who still wandered the halls at least. Katya was right about the courtiers. They flocked around her like geese. She had to keep guaranteeing them that there was no safer place than the palace, that anyone coming in or out was carefully screened. She urged them to keep to their rooms.

Most of the nobles did just that, though some walked the halls boldly, either making a silent show of confidence or fluttering around and speaking of picnics and games they were planning. They dealt with the fact that the city was burning by not acknowledging it.

Katya felt drawn toward the back stables, the place where Starbride would make her way inside the palace. Brutal caught her arm before she could go down the long hallway.

"They've closed all the doors," he said. "The guards know what she looks like; they know to let her in."

"I'm aware of all of that, thank you, Brutal."

"Then don't go down there," he said. "I know you. You'll keep saying, 'Just a little farther,' and soon you'll be out of the stables and down the block."

Katya turned the other direction when a far-off boom made her stop. The deep sound reverberated in her stomach, and the floor seemed to shake beneath her. Distant screams came from her right, toward the front of the palace.

"What in the spirits' names?" Katya braced herself to run in that direction, but then changed her mind. She had to protect her family.

A short scream made her spin around in time to see Roland drop the body of a guard onto the carpet. "Hello, niece," he said. A group of townsfolk stood behind him, their faces contorted by unnatural hatred.

"You really should have put more guards on all the doors. We walked right in the back!"

Katya drew her rapier, but Brutal grabbed her arm. "There are too many!"

If he said that about a fight, it must be true. They ran. Katya hated herself with every step, but that anger flew away before the cries of the townspeople as they gave chase.

"Left!" Averie cried.

Katya obeyed, but she wanted to turn to the right, to resume her course to the royal wing. Averie seemed to be leading them down a dead-end.

To Katya's shock, Averie toggled a switch on the wall that opened up into a secret passageway. Once they were through, she broke the latch.

"Where in the hell is this?" Katya yelled.

Averie led the way down the corridor. "The Umbriels have their passages and the Umbriels' servants have theirs."

All Katya could do was follow her through the twisting maze and try to ignore the occasional scream that filtered through the stone. They had to run through the hallways at one point, to go from one maze of passageways to the other. The palace was filled with screams and the clash of metal against metal.

Katya shut it out, plunged through the next secret passageway, and didn't stop until they'd reached her parents' sitting room.

As they burst through the secret door, Lord Vincent rounded on them, sword drawn. As soon as he saw Katya, he lowered his blade.

Ma was on the far side of the room with Bastian and Vierdrin. Two of the nannies crouched near them. "We heard screams," Ma said.

"We have to run," Katya said. "The palace is breached."

Ma dashed to the corner, to a heap of bags. The nannies shouldered the bags while Ma lifted Vierdrin. One of the nannies lifted little Bastian. Both children cried quietly, and the nanny tried to stifle them.

"Should I?" Vincent held out his arms.

Ma shook her head. "You four need your arms free in case we run into trouble." She nodded at Katya. "Your father is in the council room."

"Let's go through the passages."

The nannies were pale with fright, but they stepped inside the walls without argument and stayed close to Katya's mother.

Close to the council room, Katya peeked into the hallway. There wasn't a secret door into the actual room itself. Two guards outside the council chamber slumped in heaps, and the doors were wide open.

"If he's in there…" Vincent said from where he crowded behind her. He didn't finish the thought.

Katya swallowed hard. If Da was in that open room, he was probably dead.

"Katya," Ma said, "there's something on the wall here."

Katya stepped back inside the passage and shut the door. An arrow had been drawn on the wall with chalk, pointing toward the ballroom where the special council had been held. "Why didn't he go to your room?"

Ma sucked in a breath. "We're not the only ones who know these passages. If he was being followed…"

"He would lead his pursuers away from us." Katya bit her lip. Did she go after her father, the rightful ruler of Farraday, or did she leave the castle by the quickest route and save the future ruler? Katya looked to her young niece and nephew. She had a responsibility to them, but she also had one to her father.

"Go after him," Brutal said. "I'll keep them safe."

Ma sucked in a breath, but Katya gave him a grateful smile. "I'll catch you as soon as I can."

"We'll take horses from the cache behind the palace and meet you at the old place in the forest."

Katya nodded. Ma pressed in close and surprised Katya with a kiss on the cheek. She hushed Vierdrin's little whine at being pressed between them. "Be safe. Bring him back."

Katya cast one glance at Lord Vincent.

He bowed low, and she knew her family would only be hurt over his dead body. For once, his stodgy adherence to tradition warmed her. She waved them away, and then they were disappearing through the gloom. Averie didn't move. When Brutal turned back for her, she motioned him on without her.

"Averie," Katya said. "Go."

Averie shook her head. "My place is by your side. They'll be fine with Lord Vincent and Brutal. Besides, you'll need me to find them. You don't know the forest for shit."

Katya had to smile, had to admit she was relieved at the company. "All right. Let's go get my father."

Chapter Forty: Starbride

"Take your hands off my sister!" Hugo yelled, a roar that nearly made Starbride let him go.

Darren smirked and held his blade steady on Maia's neck.

Everyone had their blades or bows drawn. Castelle sidled close to Hugo. "If you screw this up by rushing him, I'm tripping you," she said.

Starbride had to agree. She eased into her satchel and let Castelle serve as cover. "She's right, Hugo. Wait."

Captain Ursula stepped toward Darren. "Best you let that woman go, son. There's no way out."

"Who's this, now?" Darren asked, still with his sneer. "Are you so desperate for allies that you've taken the Watch to your bosom, Starbride?" He leered. "Though I don't blame them for wanting to be there."

"So let Maia go," Starbride called. "She'll only slow you down."

"As your new friend said, there's no way out. I don't see why I shouldn't take her with me into the spirit world."

Hugo tensed. "Stop, stop," Starbride whispered as loudly as she dared. "Think!"

She had to do the same and quickly. If she lobbed a flash bomb, she was likely to catch her allies in the blast. Darren would also suspect such an attack after spending so much time with Roland. She couldn't throw anything deadly with Maia in the way.

But she could try to hypnotize him. She'd never tried before, but with all her studying, she'd learned how to use the right pyramid. She'd have to get him quickly. If he had time to react…

"When I say, Castelle," Starbride said. "Step to the side."

Starbride fell into the pyramid. A thousand facets waited in her mind, ready to splinter Darren's thoughts so that he couldn't control his body while still retaining the ability to see, and hear, and feel.

"Now."

Castelle stepped to the side. Darren looked to the movement, and Starbride held the pyramid aloft. She felt his gaze on it and pounced, drew his thoughts in, captured his mind, but he bucked against her. Starbride tried not to fight directly, to let the pyramid do the work instead of making it a battle of wills. Within seconds, he was hers, lost in the pyramid.

"Take him!" Starbride cried.

She felt rather than heard the rush. It wasn't a perfect pyramid, and she had to maintain eye contact to hold him. Someone screamed, and Starbride glanced that way. She gasped to see Maia holding a Watch officer aloft, her face stretched and terrifying, fangs and horns and all blue eyes.

As she threw the officer to the side and laughed, Starbride knew Roland had implanted the pyramid in her neck, letting her summon her Fiend and control it. And she was an Umbriel, born with a Fiend, as strong as Katya had been.

With a start, Starbride realized that her concentration had slipped, and Darren was free.

As his features melted into those of a Fiend as well, Starbride's stomach dropped to her feet. Dawnmother pulled her to the side, shaking her into wakefulness. Her arm slipped free from Hugo's coat.

Maia and Darren moved as blurs. They cut down those closest to them before the others could blink. With screams, most of the Watch officers broke and ran.

Who could blame them? Starbride's thoughts took a moment to orient themselves before she hurled a flash bomb at Darren where he was busy cutting a Watch officer in half with his claws.

Darren shrieked, a harsh sound like a rusty saw on metal. Castelle ran him through with her sword. His flailing arms knocked her out of the way. Two knives thudded into his chest before Pennynail aimed a kick at his head. It glanced off Darren's temple, and Darren slammed him to the ground.

Hugo dove at Maia. Starbride screamed for him to stop, but Maia's arms shot out, and he bounced off her as if he'd run into a brick wall.

Maia stared at him, her inhuman face alight with glee. "Is this the baby brother I've heard so much about?" she asked, her voice deep and cold.

Hugo could only gasp. Starbride started toward him, but not before Maia reached into the collar of his coat.

"Join the fun." She ripped his pyramid necklace from around his neck.

"Maia, don't!" Darren yelled.

Maia stared at Darren until Ursula stabbed her from behind. Maia whirled, but Ursula sprang out of the way.

Starbride reached Hugo's side. "Control yourself." She dug in her satchel for the pyramid that would suppress a Fiend. If Hugo could maintain control, Starbride could leap on Maia and press the pyramid to her neck.

"Anger is the last thing on my mind," Hugo said between clenched teeth as he clutched his shoulder.

Out of the corner of her eye, Starbride saw Pennynail scuttle out of the way of Darren's stomping feet. Someone yelled from the edge of the courtyard, catching Pennynail's attention, and he passed out of view.

Starbride tried to help Hugo to the edge of the fight, but he couldn't seem to get his feet under him. Dawnmother tugged on his side, favoring his shoulder. Her head jerked up, she looked past Starbride's shoulder, and screeched.

A grip like steel grabbed Starbride's arm, nearly dragging it out of the socket as it spun her around, face-to-face with Darren.

His Fiendish breath chilled her as she stared into his all-brown eyes. "I was hoping I'd be the one to catch you."

Darren's free arm was a streak across her vision as it slammed into something she couldn't see. She heard a grunt: Dawnmother. And Hugo was down but not out. Starbride tried to bring her Fiend-suppression pyramid to bear, aiming for Darren's neck. She only had a moment before—

Hugo's Fiendish form barreled into Darren, tearing him away from Starbride so forcefully it sent a shockwave through her shoulders. The two forms writhed in the dirt, one blur atop another, only distinguishable by the wings sprouting from Hugo's back.

For a moment, Starbride could only stare. How in Darkstrong's name was she ever going to tear them apart? When Ursula's voice yelled, "Starbride!" she whirled around.

Maia's claws streaked for her face. Starbride dropped. She tried to scurry backward, but Maia was on her before she could move. Searing heat rolled up Starbride's arms as Maia's claws dug in just below her shoulders. Starbride cried out and kicked, connecting with Maia's legs, but her ankle shuddered under the impact, as if she'd kicked a side of frozen meat.

Maia lifted her, claws digging in harder, and Starbride's mind screamed that it couldn't hold, that either her skin would tear free, or her arms would come loose from their sockets.

Starbride couldn't feel her hands, but she raised them as Maia laughed in her face. She needed to stab Maia's neck with the suppression pyramid and focus. She struggled, straining against the agony.

Her hands were empty.

Forcing herself to look down, Starbride saw her pyramid lying in the dirt between Maia's feet.

Chapter Forty-one: Katya

As Katya hurried to find her father, she couldn't help thinking of Starbride. From the outside, she'd be able to see that the palace had been breached. She wouldn't walk into that mess, would she?

But of course she would, if she thought Katya was trapped inside. Katya would do the same in her place. Pennynail could guide her to the meeting spot in the forest. But would she go?

Maybe if Castelle, Hugo, and Dawnmother made her. Castelle and Pennynail would probably sneak through the chaos to find Katya and her family. Maybe they could help Starbride do the same.

The time to think about it was over, though. She and Averie reached the secret doorway into the waiting room behind the ballroom. It stood open a crack. Katya crept close and strained to hear.

Someone was speaking, pontificating, by the sound.

"You have no choice but to acquiesce to our demands for a parliament," Magistrate Anthony said.

"Oh, yes," Da replied. He sounded tired, maybe a little injured. "Parliament at sword point. Is this how you plan to run your new government? It *will* be you in charge, I'm guessing, as the man who clearly knows and understands best how things should be done."

Anthony chuckled. "Only if the people vote me as their leader."

"I'm sure a pyramid will garner you lots of votes."

There were murmurs, enough for a room full of people. Katya looked to both sides of the doorway, but no one stood in the waiting room. The curtain had been pushed aside, but there was still enough to hide behind. Katya saw the back of her father's head. He sat on his throne on the dais. An armed man stood beside him, but Katya couldn't count the number of people on the floor of the ballroom. She took a careful step out of the doorway and tiptoed to the curtain, not wanting to move the fabric in the wake of a dash. She stepped to the edge, just to the side of her father and waited. When no one seemed to notice, she waved Averie forward.

"I knew you would claim the people were under pyradisté influence," Magistrate Anthony said. "Richard guessed as much."

"Richard your assistant?" Da said, and there was sadness and anger in his voice.

"Yes, the only good thing to come from Georgie Appleton's murder."

"Lucky he was there for you," Da said, "ready to step in at the last, a brilliant man you'd heretofore overlooked, the perfect man for the job. I bet everything he said was like gold."

"This stalling is pointless. No one is coming to vanquish us at the last minute."

Katya pressed her lips together. Her father wasn't waiting for rescuing; he was stalling Magistrate Anthony so his family could escape. She tightened her grip on her rapier and waited for any distraction.

"You poor, misguided young fool," Da said. "I was considering your parliament idea, I really was—crown and commoner working together for a brighter future—but this violence won't serve that cause."

"Then what cause does it serve?"

"That of a tyrant."

"I told you, only if elected will I—"

"He doesn't mean you," a new voice said.

Katya peeked under the curtain rather than around it. Magistrate Anthony's young assistant, Roland in disguise, had walked into the room.

"I prefer to think of myself as a visionary." Roland smiled. "Hello, brother. Believe it or not, I am finally glad to be rid of this façade." His features blurred until he became Roland again, only his beard was longer, the color slightly altered, but the face she would never forget.

The room erupted in a tizzy of voices. The man who'd been guarding Da let his sword dangle between his knees. Katya sprang forward and knocked the guard off the dais. She skidded to a halt, grabbed her father off the throne, and yanked him toward the curtain. He made a strangled yelp and clutched his side.

Katya ignored his pain. Averie was beside her, bow trained on the crowd that now divided its attention between Roland and Katya.

Roland lifted a pyramid. "Now, now, niece, no running off until the party's over."

Katya froze. If that was a flame pyramid, he could kill them all. She'd have to wait until he was distracted.

"What is this?" Magistrate Anthony bellowed.

Katya nearly sang his praises and prayed that Roland would focus on him.

"Richard," Magistrate Anthony said, "what are you—"

"Come, fool, you've had your moment in the sun." Roland chuckled. "Parliament indeed."

Magistrate Anthony's supporters didn't know who to target. Everyone muttered and gestured, growing louder by the second. Averie trained her bow on anyone close, and Katya kept in front of her father, rapier at the ready. Roland's gaze was still on her. She couldn't even sidle for the passageway door.

Magistrate Anthony and the others advanced on Roland, shouting now. He raised an eyebrow. The doors behind him banged open, and in walked a host of gray-skinned people. No disguises this time, the Fiend-filled corpses marched with purpose. Pyramids glinted from their foreheads, and cold poured from them in waves. They leapt upon the crowd.

Katya pushed her father toward the exit. Before she could take two steps, the waiting room curtain burst into flames. Katya staggered back; her father grunted again. Roland, Fiendish face on, leapt onto the dais.

"I told you," he said, and his voice brought the tang of blood to Katya's mouth. "Once the party starts, you stay for the duration."

Katya stabbed for Roland's heart. He shoved the blade wide. A shudder rolled up Katya's arm, as if he'd parried her with a steel bar. She swung again, but he knocked the blade away with the same lack of effect. He smiled as the room erupted in screams. Out of the corner of her eye, Katya glimpsed the townsfolk trying to fight the lesser Fiends, but they weren't having as much success as they'd had with her unarmed father.

"Roland," Da said, "if there is any of my brother left within you—"

"Oh, there is." Roland blinked back to his human form for half a moment. Katya struck, but he ducked to the side. When he straightened, he wore the Fiend's face again. "See?" With his arms out to the side, he advanced.

Katya gave ground, but they were running out of dais with the fire on one side and the lesser Fiends on the other. Averie guarded Da's back, shooting at any of the Fiends that came too close. Sweat rolled down Katya's face, and she blinked it out of her eyes.

Roland laughed. "The Fiend knows more about ruling than we ever will, brother. They once held this entire land under their sway. I want my family to embrace their nature, to rule as they should have done from the beginning, without bowing to any constraints." He sneered at Katya. "Well, not you, not anymore. That Allusian tick sucked the Fiend out of you, didn't she? You're not even one of us."

To her horror, the words stung, but Katya lifted her chin. "The Allusian tick and I look forward to thoroughly killing you."

He smiled, seeing right through her bluff, but it was the best she had. Maybe she could clear a path through the lesser Fiends and get Da into the hall, but they'd have to get away from Roland first.

Magistrate Anthony tottered up the steps. He bent over his stomach, as if nursing a stab wound. "This isn't what I wanted!"

Who he was speaking to, Katya never knew. Roland ripped his head from his shoulders with one clawed strike. He didn't even have the courtesy to look while he did it, smiling all the while.

A flash of blinding light from the door caught everyone's attention.

A squad of armed guards, led by Earl Lamont, ran through the doorway, several cassock-clad pyradistés among them. While Roland looked at them, Katya grabbed her father's arm and ran into the press, Averie right behind her.

One of the Fiends slaughtered a man in Katya's path. She swung for its forehead, and cut through the pyramid, but she didn't stop to watch. Da tugged on her arm. Katya spun, thinking he might be in danger, but he picked up a short sword.

She'd never seen her father armed before. He swung at a nearby Fiend as it reached for him. The swing was unpracticed, as if he'd learned at one time and then forgotten. Katya yanked him off balance and pushed past him.

"Stay clear, Da!" She lopped the Fiend's arm off. Averie shot it in the head, and it crumpled.

"I'm not helpless," Da yelled.

"Pretend you are!"

Earl Lamont appeared through a break in the fighting. He held an ancient looking broadsword, but swung it with more practice than her father had. Dimly, Katya recalled that he'd been the champion during her grandfather's reign. Now, the younger men and women around him did most of the damage. They encircled Katya, her father, and Averie.

"This way, Majesty!" Earl Lamont said.

A clawed hand shot out of the crowd and took the old man through the neck, fingers bursting through his skin. His mouth was open as he half-turned, eyes wide, but they dimmed as he fell.

Roland stepped into the gap, squarely in front of the door, his confident smile in place.

Chapter Forty-two: Starbride

Captain Ursula tried to stab Maia from behind. Maia kicked back, perfectly balanced on one leg and still holding Starbride aloft.

Trying to block out the pain in her shoulders, Starbride lifted her legs and pushed against the Fiend's chest. Maia tried to pull her in closer. The claws dug through Starbride's skin and stuck along the way as if hitting bone. Starbride kept repeating to herself that it wasn't bone, that couldn't be true, and that no matter how much crippling ache rolled up her arms, she needed to get free.

With one last shove, she went weightless, and flew from Maia's grasp. The ground hitting her back was almost enough to drive the agony of her shoulders out of her mind. Together, though, the pain coupled with the breath driven from her lungs crippled her.

She chanted at herself to get up, get up. She had to move. She saw her pyramid lying in the dirt and pushed toward it; her torn skin cried out for her to stop. She could almost feel the blood pooling beneath her.

Someone plucked up the pyramid and then grabbed around her waist and pulled her up.

Starbride looked into Dawnmother's face, but Dawnmother watched the battlefield. She heaved Starbride to the side. Starbride tried to hold on, but her arms wouldn't obey her.

Maia grabbed Dawnmother's legs and yanked them out from under her.

"No!" Starbride crashed to the ground, but forced herself to hang on to Dawnmother. She fumbled into her satchel and threw the first thing she found, her mind falling into it without thinking.

Maia burst into flames. She danced away, howling, before she rolled in the dirt. As she fell, Ursula and Pennynail ducked in and stabbed her over and over.

Dawnmother shouted, "Down!"

Starbride tried to obey, but something hit her from behind, and she toppled at Dawnmother's side. A painful shudder ran up her spine again, along with a sharper, warning pain. Dawnmother grabbed Starbride's hands and pressed the Fiend-suppression pyramid into them before she rolled Starbride over.

Hugo stood over them, his features twisted in Fiendish malice, his all blue eyes without recognition. A line of claw marks across his face slowly oozed blood, but as Starbride watched, those wounds closed. His coat and shirt had been torn away, and his skinny boy's chest was pale, as if carved from marble. His black crow's wings fluttered lightly, and his fangs already forced his lips open, but they grimaced farther, as if he was trying to smile. He reached for Starbride, impossibly fast, but Dawnmother shoved against Starbride's back, forcing her past Hugo's arms to smack into his chest.

Starbride grunted as her nose connected, and she felt blood trickle down her face. Hugo's arms closed around her. Starbride lifted her arm with every ounce of will she possessed and got it between them. Hugo's neck didn't hold the key. She could get him anywhere. She pressed the smooth side of the pyramid against Hugo's chest, felt the point just prick his skin.

Inside the pyramid, Starbride could see the two sides of Hugo, the Fiend and the human, the one asleep under the influence of the other. She focused hard, but it felt like trying to turn a rusted handle; the Fiend bucked, fighting her. As Hugo shrieked above her head, Starbride pushed harder and flipped that handle, pushing the Fiend down and bringing out the human.

Hugo slumped over her, bearing her to the ground, unconscious in the Fiend's absence.

Starbride tried to push him off of her, but her entire body ached. Ursula and Pennynail lifted him and dumped him to the side. Bloody tracks ran from his eyes, mouth, and back, but he was alive.

Starbride tried to struggle to her feet, tried to find Maia and Darren in the streetlights. "Where are they?"

Ursula held her sword up in her left hand, her right just hanging at her side. "The male picked up the burnt one and left."

"The burnt one." Now that she recalled it, the scent of flesh still hung in the air. "Horsestrong forgive me. Was she alive?"

"I hope not."

"Star?" Dawnmother said as she inched over. "Are you all right?"

The answer was most definitely no. Her arms were on fire. Her back felt awful and twisted. Dawnmother used her knife to tear long strips from the end of her shirt and wind them about Starbride's arms. Starbride couldn't look; she only hoped the leather had helped her a little.

"Where is Castelle?" Starbride asked.

Ursula nodded over her shoulder. "When the Fiends attacked, several gangs of people rushed us from the alley. She and her people held them back."

Castelle jogged over. Lines of blood dotted her, as if she'd been nicked over and over, the red stripes spoiling her blue clothing. "We've got other problems. A stream of liveried servants just ran by. The palace has been overrun."

Starbride's stomach dropped. Katya, the Umbriels… "By the mob."

Castelle nodded. "Though some of them said something about monsters."

"We have to get there."

"Agreed," Castelle said. She glanced at Starbride's arms and grimaced. "Do you think you can?"

"I can make it, but start without me. Save…who you can. I'll catch up."

"If she's stuck in there, I'll get her out." Castelle gathered her friends and took off down the street.

Pennynail crooked a finger as if she should follow him. "I'll be right back," Starbride said.

Ursula nodded. "I'll see to my men, and we'll try to fix this miserable failure as best we can."

Dawnmother and Starbride leaned on each other as they followed Pennynail into an alley. He shoved his mask on top of his head. "There's a place the Order always meets, in the forest. If they got away, they'll be there."

"We won't know if they got away until we go to the palace," Starbride said.

"Star," Dawnmother said, "maybe we should see if they're at this meeting place first."

"Every moment I'm not headed toward the palace is a moment Katya could be dying."

"She knows what she's doing," Pennynail said. "She's been at this game a long time."

"Really? Because I thought a Fiendish uncle who was plotting to overthrow the government was a rather new development."

Pennynail shut his mouth and nodded. "All right. Let's do it."

They bandaged one another. Ursula left the least wounded in charge of the most wounded, and then they headed out. No matter who won, Starbride wanted to be near the palace. Ursula's mouth set in a firm line. Starbride knew she cared about Marienne, not necessarily the Umbriels, but Magistrate Anthony and his band had caused the damage racing through the city. If keeping the Umbriels on the throne was the cure to this madness, Ursula would do it; that much was clear. Starbride had to wonder, though. If putting Magistrate Anthony on the throne led to a cessation of violence, would Ursula help with that, too?

Either way, Starbride was certain Ursula wouldn't stand by while the royals were killed. Maybe her influence could get them exiled, anything that would save their lives, Katya's in particular.

CHAPTER FORTY-THREE: KATYA

Katya stepped back beside her father. He'd torn open the neck of his coat, and she knew by the way his eyes slid to hers what he had in mind. If he took his pyramid necklace off, if he got angry enough, his Fiend would emerge and attack Roland.

But he could also attack everyone else. "No, Da."

A few of the Guards moved to engage Roland, but they wouldn't distract him for long. Katya led her father into the press again, looking for a way out. A man staggered close, slashing at everything in terror. Katya ducked his swing and then bashed him in the face with her guard. He crumpled, probably to be trampled, but she couldn't care about him.

Roland appeared in front of them again and laughed. "Perseverance can be tiresome. You don't want that."

That sounds of combat were dying, left to Earl Lamont's guards and the remaining lesser Fiends. The men and women who'd been with Magistrate Anthony were either scattered around the walls, clutching their wounds, or heaped around the room, a grisly glimpse of Roland's sovereignty to come.

Averie shot an arrow into Roland's chest. He glanced down at it as if it were annoying fly and pulled it out, dripping with blood, before tossing it away.

Another arrow replaced it. Roland sidestepped the next shot, but now he frowned at Averie, clearly annoyed. And she knew Fiends, knew how anger moved them. She dashed away from Katya, spun, and shot again, over and over. Roland moved through the crowd and headed for her as a blur.

"The fire has died down!" Da said.

The fire had consumed the curtain but had no other fuel. The open secret passageway beckoned.

"Averie!" Katya cried, but she only had time to look back. She had to get her father to safety.

Averie didn't acknowledge the cry, but her eyes flicked to Katya's, and she seemed to mouth the word, "Go, go, go," over and over. Or was it "No, no, no," that she whispered? She raced along the ballroom, still firing at Roland. Face pinched with fright, she locked her eyes on him, even though she couldn't really hurt him. He gained on her, almost catching her before Katya followed her father into the passageway. With a half-sob, Katya shut the door and braced it, but she didn't know how long that would hold Roland. She grabbed her father and ran.

"They're in the forest," Katya said. All she could see in her mind was Averie's terrified face chanting as death came for her. And all she could feel was fear for Starbride, for what Roland would do to both of them if he could. Katya prayed that Starbride had seen the palace and high-tailed it for the forest, that Pennynail had taken her there.

Katya shook the thoughts away and focused on how to get out. She ducked down an intersecting hallway.

"Where…going?" Da asked.

Katya slowed. Not only had he been knocked about, but he wasn't used to running. "Do we stay in here and risk Roland finding us or go into the halls and risk everyone else?"

"Better the hallways. We know he'll come after us this way."

Katya led her father toward the royal summer apartments, near where the Order met. Just as they opened the door into the hallway, a boom sounded from down the passageway, and the rushing air snuffed their lamp. Roland had entered the tunnels behind them.

"Averie," Katya said softly. "Oh, spirits, no."

Da took a deep breath and wiped his pale, sweating face. "What's your plan, my girl?"

Katya's mind raced. That was the question for the day. Around her, pyramids glinted in the hallway walls. "Those will keep us safe from the townsfolk and the lesser Fiends."

"They won't stop Roland."

Katya heard a scuff from down the hallway and glanced in that direction.

A mud-caked woman peered back at her. So, people had wandered this far into the palace. "Here's more!" the woman cried, a cackle of glee in her voice. "I found some more fat cats to string up, boys!"

A group of young men hurtled around the corner behind her. "Here, kitty, kitty!" several cried.

The man in the lead burst into flame that consumed him completely and then winked out just as suddenly, leaving the carpet only mildly singed.

The others skidded to a stop, but not before two more met a similar fate.

"They're Fiends! Fiends!" the mud-caked woman cried. They turned and fled. Well, they'd be seeing Fiends soon enough. Still, their reaction gave Katya an idea. She didn't want to kill commoners if she could avoid it, but she had to protect her father. She pried several of the guardian pyramids off the walls.

"If we use those, won't we get caught in the blast?" Da asked.

"We'll have to be quick and throw them before anyone comes near us."

He frowned but dug another of the pyramids out of the wall and fashioned the remains of his purple mantle into a sack. "You keep your rapier out, my girl. I'll handle these."

Katya nodded, and they were off again. They worked their way toward the servant stairs, the last place anyone would be with the rest of the palace wide open. They met several courtiers huddled in their rooms or nobles held captive. Each time, Katya chased the commoners away, with pyramids if she had to. By the time she and her father reached the back stables, there were twenty people with them, though they had to keep their distance from Da and his pyramids.

The eastern sky had begun to lighten. Katya kept her lantern lit. In the darkness of the rear stables, a group of people approached the flickering glow.

Katya raised her sword, but the figures kept coming. One of them called, "Katya?"

"Step into the light," Katya said. Castelle appeared out of the gloom.

Katya breathed a sigh of relief, but then stiffened as she lifted her lantern. Castelle had only her own friends with her. "Where's Starbride?"

"Right behind us, making her way toward the palace. Come on, we've got horses. We should be able to pick her up on our way out."

Da had to leave the pyramids behind. With so many non-royals among them, there was too great a risk of them going off. Katya looked over her shoulder at the palace that had been her home, now in the grip of a monster and the tomb of so many friends. Still, sadness couldn't defeat her. Her family had escaped, and soon, Starbride would be in her arms again.

Averie would want that.

CHAPTER FORTY-FOUR: STARBRIDE

Starbride could see the palace down the street, and it broke her heart. Almost all of the first floor windows had been smashed. Several statues in the front walk lay broken on the ground, and one of the ancient oak doors was pitted and scarred as if someone had tried to light it on fire and failed. One of the Umbriel banners was missing and the other had been torn in half.

"Castelle said to go to the servants' stables in the back," she whispered. "We have to keep going." She and Dawnmother had Hugo dangling between them. The Umbriels usually took an hour to wake, but they didn't have Dawnmother splashing them with water and slapping them. Still, he was only half-conscious, and he stumbled as if drunk, but he became more awake with each footfall.

She only wished he didn't put such terrible pressure on her wounds. Several times, an evil little voice originating from her torn shoulders and aching back suggested she dump him in an alley and be done with him.

Pennynail led the way around the palace. Starbride craned her neck and hoped to see Castelle leading Katya around the corner, safe and sound.

A cry sounded behind them, a wordless shout that was taken up by many voices. Starbride turned just as Dawnmother shouted, "Run!"

A group of torch-bearing people charged up the street, setting fires as they came. Many waved sticks or blades or iron bars. They struck at their surroundings indiscriminately, as if they didn't care what they destroyed as long as they hit something. In front of them, shouting them on, ran Maia and Darren, both fully healed. Their eyes seemed to glitter in the rising light.

Captain Ursula didn't even try to stand up to the crowd. They had her remaining officers outnumbered three or four to one. They all lifted Hugo and took off down a side street, running like mad.

The cries of the mob changed to words, nonsense mostly, but Starbride could pick out something about "fat cats," whatever they were. What she understood most clearly was, "Kill them!" Her injuries screamed, her back burned, and her very lungs ached. They were all wounded, struggling and pulling on one another in their haste. Even Hugo seemed to awaken more and tried to run under his own power.

They zigzagged down alleys and hoped their pursuers would give up, but the shouts seemed always at their backs. They came out of the city beside the palace, opposite the royal stables.

A mounted party stood in the small courtyard. As one more of their member swung onto a horse, a voice called, "Starbride?"

Starbride rushed toward anyone who knew her name and wasn't yelling to kill her. In the dim light of dawn, she spied Countess Nadia and Viscount Lenvis.

"My child," Countess Nadia said, "they attacked you!"

Starbride waved toward the sounds of the mob. "They'll kill us."

Shouts echoed behind them. They were almost caught.

"Hide!" Countess Nadia said.

Pennynail dragged Starbride to the side, and she and her friends climbed into a shallow ditch behind a stack of crates. Even Ursula let herself be pulled by Sergeant Rhys.

"Come now, you sons of whores!" Countess Nadia called. "You want some fat cats?" To Starbride's surprise, she drew a sword from her belt. "Come catch your death!" Contrary to her bravado, she sped away into the early light, her friends with her. "Ride, Princess Consort!" she called to one of her hooded companions. "Ride! We go to fetch the king!"

The mob screamed and gave chase. Up the street, Countess Nadia and Viscount Lenvis slowed their horses enough for the mob to almost reach them and then sped up again. Maia and Darren went with them, but a few hung back, too tired to keep up, or maybe their energy deserted them. Either way, Starbride knew she was stuck in her hiding place for some time.

She closed her eyes and hoped that Katya had gotten out of the palace and away, that Countess Nadia got away, too, and that the Umbriels were safe. Even if they were stuck inside the palace, Starbride wouldn't stop until she found them, until she found Katya.

"I'll find you," she whispered.

Chapter Forty-five: Katya

Katya heard a roar that sounded nearly on the other side of the palace. She rose up in her stirrups and tried to peer into the dim light; she wished she could see through stone.

"Katya," Castelle said. "Careful."

"You said she'd be on our way."

"Something must have turned her path."

"Like that bloody great roar." A thousand nasty images came to Katya's mind. "I've got to find her."

"All suicide is stupid," Castelle said, "but unintentional suicide is the stupidest."

Katya rounded on her. "I love her."

In the almost dim light, she couldn't make out Castelle's face. "I know you do."

Da sighed. The three of them were the only ones in their party who weren't sitting two to a saddle. If it came to a chase, they had no chance. "I'm tempted to tell you to ride off and find her, no matter what," Da said. "It's the kind of thing I've always wished I could do."

"But?"

"But you're my daughter, and I don't want you torn apart."

Katya tried to shake the image of Starbride's blood-soaked body from her mind. She wouldn't even let Averie come near her thoughts.

"Starbride is resourceful," Castelle said. "I don't say this about many people, but she can take care of herself. And she doesn't even have to. She has your sneaky man, the young lord, her wise maid, and a contingent of the Watch headed by a level-headed and very attractive captain."

Katya almost barked a laugh, but the situation wouldn't let her. "I can't leave her here, not while I run away." She'd already left one dear friend behind that day.

"Can't leave her while you protect your family, you mean?" Da asked.

"Not while you do your duty?" Castelle added.

Katya ground her teeth. "Damn you, Castelle." She took a deep breath. "I'll see you to the rendezvous, Da, but then I'm coming back for her."

He was silent for a moment. "As you wish."

Katya tried to force down the nagging thought that she was abandoning her duty if she left her family in the forest. At least she was seeing them there. Reinholt hadn't even bothered to stay, to help them with the mess he'd started.

Katya didn't want to lose herself in anger, but it helped her focus. The tightening in her gut lessened when they escaped the city and entered the forest to find her family safe and sound. Her parents wrapped each other and their grandchildren in an embrace.

Brutal patted Katya's shoulder. "Where's everyone else?"

"I'm going back for them." Katya dismounted and headed for the fresher horses.

Castelle stepped behind her. "Katya—"

Katya shook her head. She knew Castelle was going to offer to go with her, and she didn't know whether to accept or not. "Brutal, can you help Vincent guard my family?"

"I'd rather come with you, but of course I'll do it." He gave her a grim smile. "Bring them back safely."

Katya nodded and sent a prayer to the spirits to let Starbride know she was coming. "Da, please." She needed to hear again that she could slip her duty just this once.

Da nodded and turned his face away. Katya had half a second to wonder if that was disappointment in his eyes before something cracked into the back of her skull, and she pitched forward into darkness.

Katya heard voices echoing around her. She had a sudden thought that she was lying down, but that was all that would come to her. Again, she was waking up not knowing where she was or how she'd gotten there. She hated the feeling.

"We're still too close," Da said by her side. "And we can't go hitting her over the head for the entire journey."

A cool hand touched Katya's forehead. She tried to keep her eyes open and focus. "Star?"

"Do it," Ma said.

A pudgy man bent into Katya's vision. He lifted something that sparkled toward her forehead. Katya tried to struggle, but someone held her arms.

"Katya, please don't fight." That was a woman's voice, but it couldn't be Starbride. Starbride wouldn't let them do this to her.

"Castelle?" Katya slurred. The cool pyramid settled on her forehead, and all was darkness again.

The wind blew across Katya's face. Strands of hair tickled her cheeks. She'd fallen asleep outside. Had they been on a picnic, she and Starbride, and fallen asleep in each other's arms?

"Star?" she whispered. Her throat ached at trying to speak. She swallowed, but that hardly helped at all.

A water skin entered her vision. "Drink." Brutal's voice. He sat beside her in a wagon.

She frowned at him. "What?" He lifted her head and helped her drink a little. "What?" she said again when the ache in her throat eased. "What happened, Brutal?"

"Give it a minute."

Memory hit her like a brick. She raised up as quickly as she could muster. Grassland surrounded them. In the distance, buildings clustered before the great, sparkling expanse of the ocean. Katya breathed deep of the salt air and heard the far off screams of gulls. "Where?"

"Your parents had us stop at a duchess's estate in the country," he said. "The one we visited on our hunt for the bearded man." He looked at the distant sea and not at her. "They didn't want to keep knocking you over the head, you see, so they needed her pyradisté to keep you out. They half woke you up several times to eat."

Katya stared at him, dimly recalling someone pouring broth down her throat, but it had the haze of a dream. The road was off on her other side, and a man stood several feet away from them, watching the road.

"The others went to town," Brutal said. "That's your father there. Lord Vincent's hiding nearby. They said that they had to keep you out so you wouldn't go running back to look for her, and they told me I could either guard you or go back." Brutal looked at her then, and she almost gaped at the tears standing in his eyes. "I chose you, Katya. Can you forgive me?"

"To look for her?" Katya whispered. Cold settled in her gut, but her throat tightened. "Where are we, Brutal?"

"Almost to Lucienne-by-the-Sea." He shut his eyes. "Where we'll set sail and get as far from Marienne as we can."

Katya curled her hands into her fists and fought the urge to scream. "You left her…" Starbride was many miles away, maybe hurt, maybe dead. "How long?"

"Too long for you to—"

"How fucking long!" Her father turned to look at her.

"A week," Brutal said.

A week, but that was pulling a cart and with who knew how many people. If she had a fast horse, she could cover the same distance in half the time. Katya struggled out of the wagon. Brutal didn't try to stop her. When she gained her feet, though, her father approached her.

"Da," Katya said, and she didn't know whether she wanted to scream at him or be comforted by him.

"If you're going to yell, yell at me," Da said.

Katya shook her head and tried to fight the frustrated tears in her eyes.

"I won't give you speeches about duty because you know them already." He wore plain brown clothes and looked more like a normal man than a king. "You've lived your whole life doing your duty, and now I'm asking you to give up the one person you've ever really wanted, at least for the moment. It was too much for your brother. And I'll tell you now, my girl, that even if it's too much for you, I will always be your father. I will always love you."

Katya's lip quivered. Even though his face held nothing but honesty, she had to wonder if his words were a ploy. Such suspicion had always been part of her duty.

"Roland is scouring the countryside for us," Da said. "And the few rumors we encountered before we got this far didn't mention Starbride at all. If he'd caught such a big fish, he would have bragged about it, would have tried to draw us in with her as bait."

"Da, I can't just…"

"I know, my girl, I know. But for a little longer, you'll have to. We need to stay together, regain our strength, and take the city back." He sighed deeply. "I need you, Katya. I know she no doubt needs you, too."

Her choice, then. She could almost hear Brutal in her head, telling her not to be stupid. What would she do when she got back to Marienne? Stop outside the gates and demand Starbride be released? Sneak into a city that was probably overrun by undead Fiends and whisk Starbride away? If it were that simple, Starbride would have already escaped. She might be on the same track as Katya and her parents.

Or she might be cold in the ground.

Katya fell into her father's arms and sobbed. He held her tightly. After a few shuddering breaths, Katya straightened. "I'll tear Roland apart with you, Da."

He kissed her forehead. "And I'll help you find her myself."

About the Author

Barbara Ann Wright writes fantasy and science fiction novels in between blogging and caring for her army of pets. She is married, lives in Texas, and is a member of Broad Universe and the Outer Alliance and helped create Writer's Ink in Houston. Since moving to Austin, she's also joined too many writing meet-ups to count.

Her writing career can be boiled down to two points: when her mother bought her a typewriter in the sixth grade and when she took second place in the Isaac Asimov Award for Undergraduate Excellence in Science Fiction and Fantasy Writing in 2004. One gave her the means to write and the other gave her the confidence to keep going. Believing in oneself, in her opinion, is the most important thing a person can do.

Books Available from Bold Strokes Books

Battle Axe by Carsen Taite. How close is too close? Bounty hunter Luca Bennett will soon find out. (978-1-60282-871-1)

Improvisation by Karis Walsh. High school geometry teacher Jan Carroll thinks she's figured out the shape of her life and her future, until graphic artist and fiddle player Tina Nelson comes along and teaches her to improvise. (978-1-60282-872-8)

For Want of a Fiend by Barbara Ann Wright. Without her Fiendish power, can Princess Katya and her consort Starbride stop a magic-wielding madman from sparking an uprising in the kingdom of Farraday? (978-1-60282-873-5)

Broken in Soft Places by Fiona Zedde. The instant Sara Chambers meets the seductive and sinful Merille Thompson, she falls hard, but knowing the difference between love and a dangerous, all-consuming desire is just one of the lessons Sara must learn before it's too late. (978-1-60282-876-6)

Healing Hearts by Donna K. Ford. Running from tragedy, the women of Willow Springs find that with friendship, there is hope, and with love, there is everything. (978-1-60282-877-3)

Desolation Point by Cari Hunter. When a storm strands Sarah Kent in the North Cascades, Alex Pascal is determined to find her. Neither imagines the dangers they will face when a ruthless criminal begins to hunt them down. (978-1-60282-865-0)

I Remember by Julie Cannon. What happens when you can never forget the first kiss, the first touch, the first taste of lips on skin? What happens when you know you will remember every single detail of a mysterious woman? (978-1-60282-866-7)

The Gemini Deception by Kim Baldwin and Xenia Alexiou. The truth, the whole truth, and nothing but lies. Book six in the Elite Operatives series. (978-1-60282-867-4)

Scarlet Revenge by Sheri Lewis Wohl. When faith alone isn't enough, will the love of one woman be strong enough to save a vampire from damnation? (978-1-60282-868-1)

Ghost Trio by Lillian Q. Irwin. When Lee Howe hears the voice of her dead lover singing to her, is it a hallucination, a ghost, or something more sinister? (978-1-60282-869-8)

The Princess Affair by Nell Stark. Rhodes Scholar Kerry Donovan arrives at Oxford ready to focus on her studies, but her life and her priorities are thrown into chaos when she catches the eye of Her Royal Highness Princess Sasha. (978-1-60282-858-2)

The Chase by Jesse J. Thoma. When Isabelle Rochat's life is threatened, she receives the unwelcome protection and attention of bounty hunter Holt Lasher who vows to keep Isabelle safe at all costs. (978-1-60282-859-9)

The Lone Hunt by L.L. Raand. In a world where humans and praeterns conspire for the ultimate power, violence is a way of life…and death. A Midnight Hunters novel. (978-1-60282-860-5)

The Supernatural Detective by Crin Claxton. Tony Carson sees dead people. With a drag queen for a spirit guide and a devastatingly attractive herbalist for a client, she's about to discover the spirit world can be a very dangerous world indeed. (978-1-60282-861-2)

Beloved Gomorrah by Justine Saracen. Undersea artists creating their own City on the Plain uncover the truth about Sodom and Gomorrah, whose "one righteous man" is a murderer, rapist, and conspirator in genocide. (978-1-60282-862-9)

Cut to the Chase by Lisa Girolami. Careful and methodical author Paige Cornish falls for brash and wild Hollywood actress Avalon Randolph, but can these opposites find a happy middle ground in a town that never lives in the middle? (978-1-60282-783-7)

More Than Friends by Erin Dutton. Evelyn Fisher thinks she has the perfect role model for a long-term relationship, until her best friends, Kendall and Melanie, split up and all three women must reevaluate their lives and their relationships. (978-1-60282-784-4)

Every Second Counts by D. Jackson Leigh. Every second counts in Bridgette LeRoy's desperate mission to protect her heart and stop Marc Ryder's suicidal return to riding rodeo bulls. (978-1-60282-785-1)

Dirty Money by Ashley Bartlett. Vivian Cooper and Reese DiGiovanni just found out that falling in love is hard. It's even harder when you're running for your life. (978-1-60282-786-8)

Sea Glass Inn by Karis Walsh. When Melinda Andrews commissions a series of mosaics by Pamela Whitford for her new inn, she doesn't expect to be more captivated by the artist than by the paintings. (978-1-60282-771-4)

The Awakening: A Sisters of Spirits novel by Yvonne Heidt. Sunny Skye has interacted with spirits her entire life, but when she runs into Officer Jordan Lawson during a ghost investigation, she discovers more than just facts in a missing girl's cold case file. (978-1-60282-772-1)

Murphy's Law by Yolanda Wallace. No matter how high you climb, you can't escape your past. (978-1-60282-773-8)

Blacker Than Blue by Rebekah Weatherspoon. Threatened with losing her first love to a powerful demon, vampire Cleo Jones is willing to break the ultimate law of the undead to rebuild the family she has lost. (978-1-60282-774-5)

Silver Collar by Gill McKnight. Werewolf Luc Garoul is outlawed and out of control, but can her family track her down before a sinister predator gets there first? Fourth in the Garoul series. (978-1-60282-764-6)

The Dragon Tree Legacy by Ali Vali. For Aubrey Tarver time hasn't dulled the pain of losing her first love Wiley Gremillion, but she has to set that aside when her choices put her life and her family's lives in real danger. (978-1-60282-765-3)

The Midnight Room by Ronica Black. After a chance encounter with the mysterious and brooding Lillian Gray in the "midnight room" of The Griffin, a local lesbian bar, confident and gorgeous Audrey McCarthy learns that her bad-girl behavior isn't bulletproof. (978-1-60282-766-0)

Dirty Sex by Ashley Bartlett. Vivian Cooper and twins Reese and Ryan DiGiovanni stole a lot of money and the guy they took it from wants it back. Like now. (978-1-60282-767-7)

The Storm by Shelley Thrasher. Rural East Texas. 1918. War-weary Jaq Bergeron and marriage-scarred musician Molly Russell try to salvage love from the devastation of the war abroad and natural disasters at home. (978-1-60282-780-6)

Crossroads by Radclyffe. Dr. Hollis Monroe specializes in short-term relationships but when she meets pregnant mother-to-be Annie Colfax, fate brings them together at a crossroads that will change their lives forever. (978-1-60282-756-1)

Beyond Innocence by Carsen Taite. When a life is on the line, love has to wait. Doesn't it? (978-1-60282-757-8)

Heart Block by Melissa Brayden. Socialite Emory Owen and struggling single mom Sarah Matamoros are perfectly suited for each other but face a difficult time when trying to merge their contrasting worlds and the people in them. If love truly exists, can it find a way? (978-1-60282-758-5)

Pride and Joy by M.L. Rice. Perfect Bryce Montgomery is her parents' pride and joy, but when they discover that their daughter is a lesbian, her world changes forever. (978-1-60282-759-2)

Ladyfish by Andrea Bramhall. Finn's escape to the Florida Keys leads her straight into the arms of scuba diving instructor Oz as she fights for her freedom, their blossoming love…and her life! (978-1-60282-747-9)

Spanish Heart by Rachel Spangler. While on a mission to find herself in Spain, Ren Molson runs the risk of losing her heart to her tour guide, Lina Montero. (978-1-60282-748-6)